JULIE BENSON

An avid daydreamer since childhood, Julie Benson always loved creating stories. After graduating from the University of Texas at Dallas with a degree in sociology, she worked as a case manager before having her children: three boys. Many years later she started pursuing a writing career to challenge her mind and save her sanity. Now she writes full-time in Dallas, where she lives with her husband, their sons, two lovable black dogs, two guinea pigs, a turtle and a fish. When she finds a little quiet time, which isn't often, she enjoys making jewelry and reading a good book.

Julie Benson
and
C.C. Coburn

HOME ON THE RANCH: COLORADO

⟨H⟩HARLEQUIN® THE COWBOY COLLECTION

Recycling programs
for this product may
not exist in your area.

ISBN-13: 978-0-373-60134-9

Home on the Ranch: Colorado

Copyright © 2015 by Harlequin Books S.A.

The publisher acknowledges the copyright holders
of the individual works as follows:

Big City Cowboy
Copyright © 2011 by Julie Benson

Colorado Cowboy
Copyright © 2011 by Catherine Cockburn

HARLEQUIN®
www.Harlequin.com

Printed in U.S.A.

CONTENTS

BIG CITY COWBOY

Julie Benson

To Kevin. Thanks for sticking with me through the ups and downs of life, and for believing in me and this dream. You're definitely a keeper.

To Dr. Angela Krause and David Goddard. Thanks for the wedding invitation and for introducing me to Estes Park. This story never would have happened without you two.

CHAPTER ONE

Estes Park, Colorado

"THERE IS NO WAY I'm getting on a horse."

Elizabeth Harrington-Smyth pulled into the Twin Creeks Ranch parking lot, vowing she'd never attend another wedding, not even her own should she ever make time to date. So far, being her cousin Janice's bridesmaid hadn't been the greatest experience. And don't get her started on the problems with the whole destination wedding idea that was the trend now.

"Estes Park is so beautiful, and what better way to see the scenery than going horseback riding?" Since moving to Denver three years ago, Janice had gone all outdoorswoman. Today she really fit the part, wearing jeans, a denim shirt and a red bandanna tied around her ebony ponytail.

Elizabeth shuddered. "Looking at the mountains as I sat in the hotel bar was good enough for me."

"I think this will be a great bridesmaid outing," chirped Laura, obedient bridesmaid number one. Her Katie Couric perkiness had overwhelmed Elizabeth within five minutes of meeting Janice's coworker.

"I was hoping we'd get time to go riding. It's something I've always wanted to try," chimed in Claire, perfect bridesmaid number two, as they spilled out of

Janice's Camry. In addition to being a morning person, Claire had the irritating characteristics of being tall, slender and possessing a disgustingly high metabolism.

"I let you out of the hike yesterday because you were queasy and tired from the altitude, but I want us to have a good time together," Janice insisted. "It's girl bonding."

"The wedding party activities are half the fun of being a bridesmaid," Claire said.

According to whom? Clearly, Elizabeth and the rest of the bridal party had different definitions of fun.

Dust swirled around her, making her sneeze. It seemed as if they were surrounded by bales of hay. At least she'd taken a Claritin this morning, so she wouldn't look like a red-eyed monster due to raging allergies.

"My idea of a good time is having a massage, facial and pedicure at the hotel, not riding on a smelly horse." Elizabeth waved a fly away from her face. "The outdoors is pretty to look at, but I'm not keen on actually being *in* it. I'll wait here by this fence—"

"It's a corral, Elizabeth," Janice corrected.

"Then I'll wait here by the corral. The rest of you go ahead and enjoy."

"I've never ridden a horse, but I'm willing to be adventurous, Elizabeth," Laura coaxed.

"You're here, so you might as well come with us," Claire added.

"I'm afraid my Jimmy Choos aren't meant for horseback riding." Now that was an excuse any woman could understand and respect.

"Didn't I tell you to wear sensible shoes that you didn't mind getting dirty?" Janice asked.

Elizabeth stared at her cute leopard-print flats and

her blood pressure rose. "All you said was wear sensible shoes, which I am. These *are* flats. I'd never have worn Jimmy Choos if you'd mentioned getting dirty."

"Sorry. I guess I must've forgotten the getting dirty part." Janice flashed her an I'm-the-bride-forgive-me smile. "There are so many details to planning a large destination wedding. I'm surprised I haven't forgotten more things. You'll have to make the best of the situation now."

The cool March breeze blew a strong odor of horse manure Elizabeth's way. "Too late. It smells terrible out here. Flies are everywhere, and the quiet is driving me crazy. Everyone moves too slowly! I almost mowed over two people when I walked down to the hotel lobby to get coffee this morning."

"Exactly why you should join us," Claire insisted. "You need to slow down and learn to appreciate nature's gifts."

"I'm in advertising. *I* determine what people appreciate, not the other way around. And who says I don't appreciate nature?"

"You have to go, Elizabeth," her cousin whined. "I want *all* of us to go. This means so much to me."

Elizabeth bristled. "Isn't it enough that I took off work for your wedding when I've got a major ad campaign due? Between all the activities, the spotty internet service and a slight case of altitude sickness, I haven't gotten half the work done here that I need to."

Her job was hanging by a thread. Devlin Designs wanted to launch a new jeans campaign and she had the perfect one all mapped out, but couldn't find the right spokesman. On top of that, the contract for the remainder of Devlin's business was up for renewal soon. No spokesman, no new campaign, no contract renewals—and then she'd be out of a job.

"What an honor, you taking off work to come to my wedding," Janice snapped.

Laura and Claire slid a few feet away, obviously wanting to avoid the awkward conversation.

In addition to the wedding, Elizabeth had hoped to spend a little time with her parents, who were flying in, as well. But when she'd checked her voice mail after arriving in Denver she'd learned they weren't coming.

"I'm sorry, Janice, really. I'm out of sorts. Did Mom and Dad tell you they've headed off to some mountain in Germany on an archeological dig? I haven't seen them in forever, and though I shouldn't be, I'm pretty disappointed."

"No. How could they do that at the last minute? Don't they know we'll have to pay for their dinners whether they're here or not?"

Elizabeth shrugged. "They said a bone flute and an erotic figurine had been discovered there. If these pieces are authentic, it'll be the best example Upper Paleo-lithic art ever. They insisted they absolutely couldn't pass this up."

"They say that about every dig."

"You think I'd be used to their last-minute cancel-lations by now." Elizabeth smiled weakly. This kind of parental disinterest and disappointment had filled her life for as long as she could remember. "Then there's work. My job's on the line with this campaign."

"Come on, Elizabeth. You're not going to lose your job. They'd have to hire three people to replace you," Janice said.

"We're on the verge of losing a client that represents

over half of our business." Her cousin didn't realize how precarious the advertising business was.

Elizabeth was good at what she did. She knew this crazy ad world well. No one had given her the management supervisor job; she'd earned it. She'd started at the bottom and from there studied the market, worked hard, learned from her superiors and was the ultimate team player. She gave two hundred percent without being asked, and had eventually secured her current position. Unfortunately, sometimes hard work counted for squat.

"If we lose this account the company will have no choice but to lay off a lot of people, including me, since it was my account."

"Work is all that matters to you." Janice crossed her arms over her chest. "You're a workaholic. You always have been. You're just like your parents."

Ouch. "I am not, and that's a low blow."

"You need to get some balance in your life," Janice continued, shifting into sympathetic mode. "You're all work and no play. You need to date. Have fun."

Elizabeth winced, knowing where the conversation was headed. Why did every married or engaged person feel they possessed a sacred duty to impart relationship advice to single relatives and friends? "Work is so crazy right now I don't have much time for anything, especially dating."

"Is it a time issue, or is it because no guy meets enough requirements on your ridiculous checklist?"

"It's not silly. I have to know what qualities I want in a partner, and what things are deal breakers."

"You'll be surprised how fast you'll throw out that list when you find the right guy."

Elizabeth had begun to think the right guy for her

didn't exist. Or if he did, she worried she wouldn't find him without a map and a guide.

She grabbed a deep, calming breath. "Can we start over? I know I haven't been the most fun lately. We've had one round of layoffs already at work, and with this client halfway out the door, I'm way past stressed out."

"It's really that bad?" Janice asked, genuinely concerned.

She nodded.

"I'm sorry my wedding turned out to be poor timing for you." Janice reached out and clasped her hand. "I appreciate you being here, considering what's going on with you. Is the altitude sickness getting any better?"

Biting her lip to hold back her emotions over her cousin's unexpected empathy, Elizabeth nodded. "I'm tired and a bit queasy, but I can handle it, as long as it doesn't get worse."

"Look at that gorgeous cowboy walking our way," Claire said, popping up beside them. "Not that your wedding isn't reason enough, but this guy makes the entire trip worthwhile."

Janice squeezed Elizabeth's hand and let go. "Yum-oh." Her face lit up like Times Square after dark. "Elizabeth, you've got to see this guy. He's behind you a few feet. Turn, but don't be obvious that you're looking."

Behind her in the corral stood an attractive cowboy. His dark brown hat cast a shadow over his face, but didn't conceal his strong jaw or classic cheekbones. Dressed in a simple navy button-down shirt, jeans, chaps complete with leather fringe and dusty cowboy boots, he was the real deal.

"I'd be willing to risk getting hay in all sorts of awkward places for a little time alone in the barn with him," Claire said.

"Close your mouth, Janice, or you'll start catching flies," Elizabeth teased. "Plus you're getting married tomorrow."

"That doesn't mean I'm dead. I can still appreciate the exceptional scenery."

Elizabeth shook her head. "Sure he's good-looking, but what's so fantastic about a cowboy? I don't get it. They smell like horses. They spend a good part of their days cleaning manure out of barn stalls. What about that inspires romance?"

Claire looked ready to tackle the cowboy. "They're so rugged. So strong."

"Janice Rogers and party," cowboy hottie called out in a lazy drawl.

"That's me, or us, rather." Janice waved her hand and gave him a big smile.

"Let's see about getting you ladies on some horses." He pointed to Claire. "Come with me."

Claire beamed and practically ran over Laura to get to the cowboy. Then she introduced herself, giggled and tossed her hair.

Elizabeth laughed. Watching this show unfold might be fun, after all.

The ranch hand tilted his hat and nodded. "Rory."

"Even his name's gorgeous," Laura crooned dreamily to no one in particular.

"Clem, help this lady with Biscuit."

Claire slowly started moving toward an older cowboy, but kept glancing over her shoulder at Rory all doe-eyed.

Then he motioned to Janice, who stepped on Elizabeth's foot in her haste to reach him.

"Watch it," Elizabeth snapped.

"Sorry," her cousin said, but her gaze remained locked on the cowboy. If he offered to sell her the Rocky Mountains right now, she'd be whipping out her Master-Card.

Wait a minute. Elizabeth smiled. That's exactly what she wanted people to do—open their wallets. *Thank you, Lord, for sending the answer to my prayers.* She just might be able to pull this campaign out of the fire.

When she'd proposed that Devlin Designs center its men's jeans campaign on a cowboy, she'd had this type of female reaction in mind. Micah Devlin liked the idea, but not the models she'd suggested. Now she understood what he'd meant about something being missing in all the models dressed like cowboys. They weren't *authentic.*

Bingo. Yes, sir. Rory could be the answer to all her problems.

By the time he motioned her forward, she had a tentative pitch mentally mapped out.

"I hope the horse knows what he's doing, because I don't have a clue," she joked as an icebreaker. Starting her conversation with, "Come to New York to model designer jeans," seemed a little abrupt. She needed to loosen the guy up first. Appear to be interested in his life here in the great outdoors.

"As long as you hold on to the reins and sit up straight, you'll be okay. We haven't lost anyone yet."

"Elizabeth might be the first." Janice laughed. "She's not exactly athletic."

Rory looked her up and down with eyes that were

liquid gold. She could feel herself blush, something she hadn't done in years.

"She looks like she can handle herself well enough."

Apparently chivalry wasn't as dead as everyone believed.

"Put your left foot in the stirrup," Rory said as he pointed toward the saddle. "Then grab hold of the saddle horn with your right hand and pull up while you swing your leg over."

She glanced at the horse, an amazingly large one, and then back at Rory. The man had to be kidding. "Have you noticed how big the horse is, and how short I am? There's no way I can get up there."

"You are a little thing," he said, smiling.

Again, she blushed. This blushing was getting a little out of control.

"I'll help you."

How, exactly? She pictured this gorgeous man pushing her butt to shove her into the saddle. Could this experience get more humiliating?

She'd get on the horse on her own if it killed her. After placing her foot in the stirrup, she grabbed the saddle horn. Then she pushed off with her right foot and pulled as hard as she could. She was about to swing her leg over the saddle when she started slipping back down. Then she felt Rory's firm hands on her rear end, and next thing she knew, she was sitting on the horse.

Now she wished she hadn't skipped so many Pilates classes lately.

A minute later they headed off down a path into the great outdoors. The trees formed a canopy around them as they rode. The mountains loomed, harsh and demanding, making her feel incredibly insignificant.

Birds chirped. Wind rustled through the leaves. A stream babbled past. How did people stand the quiet?

Flies swarmed around her and the horse. She wanted to swat at them, but feared she'd fall off if she took one hand from the reins. To keep her mind off the insects and her already screaming thigh muscles, she focused on Rory at the front of their little caravan. The set of his shoulders spoke of his confidence. He moved in the saddle with a casual grace. Everything about him said how comfortable he was in his own skin. Then there was his voice as he tossed out tidbits about the area and its history. Slow, melodic and deep, it wrapped around her like a warm hug.

Rory pointed to the towering oak to his left. "That's our wishing tree. If you make a wish and circle the tree three times, your wish will come true. Feel free to hop down and make a wish while we're here."

Laura and Claire immediately vaulted off their horses, dashed to the tree and circled it three times. "What did you wish for?" Janice called out as she joined her friends.

"I wished to find someone as wonderful as David," Laura chirped, referring to Janice's fiancé.

Claire giggled. "I wished Michael would propose."

Janice dashed around the tree. "I wish that I'll always be as happy as I am right now."

Why did people wish for things like that? Only the foolish wished for something impossible.

"What about you?" Rory asked. He'd dismounted, and now stood beside Elizabeth.

Even if she were willing to get off her horse and risk needing Rory to give her another boost into the saddle, the only thing she'd wish for was landing him as a spokesman for the jeans campaign. Wishing wouldn't make that happen. She'd rely on her business skills to accomplish it.

"I think I'll pass."

"Come on, Elizabeth, make a wish," Janice coaxed. "What could it hurt?"

If only her cousin knew.

The remainder of the ride passed in a blur of trees, rocks and mountains. Three hours later, when they returned to the corral, Elizabeth didn't like the outdoors any better, but she knew her instincts about Rory had been dead on. He'd make the perfect spokesperson for Devlin Designs men's jeans. He spun a good tale, which would work well in TV commercials, and then there were his looks and the way he moved. A guy either had a presence or he didn't, and Rory had it in spades.

"I'm a management supervisor at Rayzor Sharp Media. It's an advertising agency," she said, ignoring her protesting muscles when he helped her off the horse. "You'd be the perfect model for one of my clients. You have a presence that can't be taught or faked, while you're real enough to connect with the average man."

He laughed. Not a good sign.

"I'm not interested, but thanks for asking."

"It's a major national campaign. The exposure would be excellent."

"Doesn't matter."

She reached into her purse, pulled out a business card and held it out to him. "You could get a free trip to New York out of the deal."

"Right now all I'm interested in is getting this horse taken care of," he said as he reached for the reins.

Her stubbornness kicked up a notch. She couldn't

give up when so much rode on this campaign and Rory's participation.

"Elizabeth, hurry up," Janice yelled from the parking lot.

"Lady, the rest of your party's ready to go."

Let 'em wait. "Did I mention the job will pay around thirty thousand dollars? Surely a ranch hand like you could use the money."

Rory pushed his hat off his forehead a bit. Now she had his attention.

Dark coffee-colored eyes peered down at her. The look in those eyes could sell refrigerators to Eskimos. Or hopefully, designer jeans to the average man. Or the average man's significant other.

Then gravel crunched under car tires, drawing his gaze away from her. When his attention returned a moment later, his interest had vanished.

"Lady, the next tour group has pulled into the parking lot, and I don't have time for this."

She held out her card again. "If I agree to leave, will you take my contact info, and consider my business proposal?"

"Deal." Rory snatched the card out of her hand and shoved it in his shirt pocket. "But don't count on hearing from me."

That was okay. She believed in positive thinking. If she sent good karma into the world, good things would return to her. Now if she could only collect by getting Rory to agree to model—because she needed this cowboy or she was out of a job.

THREE DAYS LATER Rory sat in his worn leather desk chair as the banker he'd known all his life told him he couldn't approve a second mortgage.

"Rory, if things were different, if we were still a family-owned bank, maybe I could approve this, but I've got stockholders to answer to. Twin Creeks carries too much debt to justify another loan."

He thanked John, reassured him that he understood it was simply a business decision, and hung up the phone.

Rory's chin sank to his chest. He'd already tried to sell some of their horses, but most folks were having financial difficulties, too. He'd looked for extra work, but there were too many unemployed people out there and no one was adding on help anyway. The second mortgage had been his last palatable choice to get the cash his mom needed. There had to be something he could do—his mom's life depended on it.

The McAlister family had gone through their savings to pay for the medical bills when Rory's dad had suffered a heart attack behind the wheel and sent his truck into a ditch, putting him and Rory's younger brother, Griffin, into the hospital. Then two years ago, when his dad's heart finally gave out, Rory cashed in most of their stocks to pay for those bills and his dad's funeral. Now, their mom had gone as far as she could with her cancer treatments and was left with one alternative, which turned out to be experimental—and expensive.

You have another alternative. You just don't like it.

He pulled open his middle desk drawer, shoved aside some papers and located Elizabeth Harrington-Smyth's business card.

He twirled it between his fingers as he stared out the window. The snow-capped Rocky Mountains filled his view. Though he'd seen them every day of his life, their beauty never failed to amaze him. Some people thought they had a magnificent view when they looked out at a city skyline. Personally, he didn't understand the appeal. Give him what God had created any day. Man's creations were strictly amateur in comparison.

His hands tightened around the chair arm and the worn leather creaked in protest. Visions of his dad sitting in this same chair flashed in Rory's mind. He still missed the old man every day. More so lately, since the doctor had found the inoperable tumor on his mother's brain. How he wished he could talk to his dad about what to do, even though he knew what his dad would say. *Do whatever's necessary to get the money for your mother. She's a good woman, the rock of this family, and she damned well deserves every shot to beat cancer.*

Knowing his mom had only one alternative didn't make this call any easier. Rory willed his hand to reach for the phone.

Nothing.

Not even a twitch.

Picking up a phone. Such a simple action, so why couldn't he?

Because this call would change his life irrevocably. But at least it was his choice, as opposed to bankers and doctors calling the shots. Life was full of choices. Some turned out well and some sucked pond water. All a body could do was think things through, make a careful decision and deal with any fallout.

The last thing Rory wanted to do was leave this ranch, even short-term. He loved the land, the horses and the hard work that made his muscles ache at the end of the day. He loved the mental challenge of managing the ranching business.

A quiet knock sounded on his office door. "Come in, Mom."

"How'd you know it was me?"

He smiled. "The ranch hands and Griff knock loud enough to break down the door. Avery rarely bothers to knock."

His mom grinned, but weariness filled her eyes, twisting his gut as she walked across the office. Until the last year she'd been active and energetic. Then she'd started chemo. The constant nausea had almost killed her, but hadn't done anything to shrink the tumor. Now, thanks to the steroids the doctor prescribed and her lack of energy for the long walks she enjoyed, her weight had ballooned. At least her hair had grown out enough for her to wear it in a short, spiky style. Despite all that, she hadn't given up. Talk about strong.

Her quiet strength always amazed him. She never complained, and remained positive. He'd always loved his mom, but now he admired her in a different way.

Rory said a silent prayer that this experimental treatment would work.

"Griffin is ready to take me and Avery to the airport." His mom stopped in front of his desk. Her frail hand rested on his forearm. "Are you sure we can afford this treatment, since insurance isn't covering it? It's so expensive."

Thank goodness for Avery. His little sister, who'd always driven him crazy, wanting to tag along with him and his friends, had turned out okay. Since their mother's diagnosis, she'd stepped into the family caretaker role. Avery coordinating their mom's appointments and accompanying her had allowed Rory to focus on putting food on the table and keeping the ranch afloat. He couldn't ask for a better sister.

"Don't worry about the money, Mom. I've got the situation under control."

She squeezed his arm and peered down at him. For a moment he worried that she'd read the lie in his eyes.

"If you're absolutely sure."

"I'll worry about the finances. You concentrate on getting well." He stood, walked around his desk and enveloped her in a hug, wishing he could take on this fight for her.

He couldn't bear to lose her, too. Not so soon after losing his dad.

She kissed him on the cheek, and he pulled away. "Now, get out of here. I don't want you to miss your flight."

Once his mother had closed the door behind her, Rory returned to his desk. He picked up the business card, flipped open his cell phone and dialed.

CHAPTER TWO

"ELIZABETH HARRINGTON-SMYTH."

Her voice sounded exactly as Rory remembered—pushy, businesslike and New York City. At the ranch she'd been like a defensive lineman, single-minded in pursuit of her goal, intent on getting to him, the quarterback. The lady definitely didn't acknowledge the word *no*. Not exactly his favorite type of woman.

"It's Rory McAlister. We met when you were at Twin Creeks Ranch in Estes Park last weekend. I was your guide on the horseback ride."

"I remember, though I'm surprised to hear from you."

That made two of them.

He swallowed hard and barreled forward. "The modeling job you said you could get me, is it still available?"

"Yes, it is."

"And it'll pay thirty thousand dollars?"

"Over the course of the campaign, yes."

"What does that mean?"

"You'll get paid when we do the photo shoots. Then you get paid again whenever the material is used for an aspect of the campaign."

He needed to do some research to see if he could work a deal to get more money up front. "Are you interested?"

"Yes." He forced the word past the lump in his throat.

"Email me a photograph of yourself as soon as we get off the phone. My address is on my card."

"I don't have anything taken by a professional photographer." Nor would he, if he had to pay for them.

"I don't care. Send me what you've got, even if it's family photos. If you have ones showing your face clearly, that would be great."

"I'll send what I can find."

"Have you gotten an agent yet?"

Forget that. An agent would take a percentage of what he made. No way would he give anyone a part of his money, when he needed every penny so desperately. Surely with an MBA he could negotiate the deal. "I'm representing myself."

"I want you on the first available flight to New York."

"You expecting me to pay for the flight?"

"We'll reimburse you. Put the ticket on your credit card and turn in your receipt to me. I'll send it on to Accounting, and they'll cut you a check within two weeks."

"I can't do that." He'd hit his credit limit paying for the two plane tickets to Portland.

"If that's a problem, I'll contact our travel person to book your flight."

"You do that."

"I'll email you the details."

"What about a hotel? I'm not paying for that, either."

She paused, and he imagined her sitting at a clean desk in an efficiently organized office, trying to decide if he'd be this big a pain about everything. He made a mental note not to push her too much on anything but money. That issue was nonnegotiable. He had to pinch pennies.

"I'll book you at a hotel near our office. I'll email you the details. Is that to your satisfaction?"

"I'll see you tomorrow."

For better or worse, his life was about to change.

ELIZABETH HUNG UP HER PHONE, jumped out of her chair, took two quick steps across her office, then stopped. A management supervisor who planned on becoming a vice president did not dash into the hallway because she was excited. She sucked in a calming breath, smoothing the front of her black pencil skirt, and headed for her friend Chloe Walsh's office.

Reaching it, Elizabeth shuddered at the clutter surrounding her. Piles of paper dotted the room. She couldn't even see the top of Chloe's desk because of the stacks of portfolios and pictures on it. Elizabeth shook her head. How did her best friend find anything or get any work done? This office would drive her past the brink of insanity.

"I heard from cowboy hottie," Elizabeth said as she sank into the chair in front of Chloe's desk—once she'd transferred a stack of photos from the seat to the floor.

"The gorgeous ranch hand from Colorado?" Chloe pointed to the picture Janice had taken of Rory during the week of a million bridesmaid events.

"That's our guy," Elizabeth said. "A real-life cowboy dream, if you liked the rough outdoorsman type. He called me back."

Chloe swiveled her chair around and glanced out her tenth-floor Madison Avenue window.

"What're you doing?"

"I'm checking for pigs. I swore they'd be flying if that cowboy ever called you back."

"Me, too. Thankfully, we were both wrong." Elizabeth plucked a piece of lint off her skirt. "We've got to get moving full blast on finalizing the idea. We need to finish storyboards, ideas for TV commercials, print ad mock-ups, billboard ideas, and have everything ready ASAP. Then when we do Rory's photo shoot we'll be set to present everything to Micah Devlin."

"What'll we do if Devlin doesn't go for this idea?"

"Don't even think it. Be positive. We have to believe in this campaign and sell him on it."

"Got it, Chief. I'll be Little Miss Sunshine."

"Let's not go overboard. The guy's smart. Devlin won't buy a snow job. We'll believe in the campaign because it's going to be wonderful."

"I'll make a note of that." Chloe grabbed a scrap of paper and pen off the nearest pile and started writing. "Be positive, but not delusional."

Elizabeth smiled. What would she do without Chloe? Her friend always made her laugh when she needed to most. "It's scary how much rides on this idea."

"You didn't tell our cowboy that, did you?"

"Do I look stupid? If he knew how important this campaign is, and how central he is to pulling it off, who knows how much he'd want to get paid."

Chloe held up her hands in mock defeat. "Excuse me for losing my mind and forgetting you're all business no matter what the situation or how gorgeous the guy. Surely if he wanted too much money we could find another cowboy."

Elizabeth took another calming breath, needing to channel her nervousness. "I've tried. It's not as easy as it sounds. Believe it or not, most cowboys just want to spend time on their horses riding the range, or whatever it is they do. Plus there's something about this guy."

"Other than good looks?"

"There's something about the way he moves. He exudes confidence."

"If he's a real cowboy, and all they want to do is ride the range, why's this guy willing to model?"

Elizabeth had asked herself the same question since Rory's call. "I don't care, as long as he is."

When she'd given him her card he'd been polite, but she'd seen the you've-got-to-be-kidding look in his eyes. She'd suspected modeling was the last thing he would do, right after moving away from Colorado.

So why the major about-face?

Well, there was no reason to borrow trouble when what had changed his mind wasn't important. All that mattered was that she got what she needed for the campaign.

"We better hope he doesn't change his mind," Chloe said.

"Again, I say, don't even think it. Think positive, because I don't know about you, but I don't want to be on the unemployment line."

"You think Devlin's that close to pulling his business?"

"He made it quite clear when I talked to him yesterday that his patience has run out. He's given me to the end of the week to find a spokesman, so we're doing whatever we have to in order to get this done. We've got to finalize this campaign fast or we'll all be out of a job."

ELIZABETH STARED AT Rory's face displayed on her computer monitor. No doubt about it, he was a natural. Despite the amateur photos, the camera loved him. His maleness oozed through the screen. He would be the perfect spokesman.

Women would take one look at Rory in Devlin's designer jeans and buy a pair for their guy. Men would wear the jeans hoping they'd look like Rory, and have women falling at their feet. Exactly what the client wanted. Their jeans sold well in New York and Los Angeles, but hadn't broken into other major markets. Devlin wanted to get the guys who wore Levi's and Wranglers to spend their hard-earned cash on his expensive product. Rory could pry open those wallets.

She spun around in her desk chair, giddy over how things were coming together. She couldn't wait to show Devlin the mock-up. If he didn't like Rory and the campaign, then fine, let him take his business elsewhere, because nothing would please the man.

She considered sending Devlin Rory's photos, but her practical nature balked at the idea. Instinct told her to wait until she had the campaign completely outlined and professional photographs of Rory. God forbid she sold Devlin on the cowboy, and then discovered Rory froze in front of a camera.

Needing to stretch her legs and energize her mind, Elizabeth decided to take a quick bathroom break and then grab a fresh cup of coffee before she dived into the details for Rory's photo session.

She weaved her way through the maze of offices and cubicles until she reached the woman's restroom, where quiet sobs floated toward her from the middle stall. She knocked gently on the door. "You okay?"

"I'm fine." More sobs contradicted the words.

"Nancy? What's wrong?"

The door latch clicked free, and Nancy, a friend and fellow management supervisor, exited the stall. The middle-aged woman clutched a wad of toilet paper in each hand, and her eyes were red and swollen.

"Everything's not fine. Tell me what's wrong."

Racking sobs consumed her. Not sure of what else to do, Elizabeth enveloped the woman in an embrace.

"I found out yesterday that I have breast cancer," Nancy choked out, once her crying subsided.

You have breast cancer. One of the most feared phrases a woman could hear. Tears pooled in Elizabeth's own eyes for this woman, and what she was facing. "I'm so sorry, Nancy." She tightened her hold on her friend. "If you want to go home, I'll say you weren't feeling well."

Nancy stepped out of Elizabeth's embrace and dabbed at her eyes with the toilet paper. "Let me think about it. I'm not sure I want to go home. It's so lonely there. I kept saying there was time for me to have a family. I said I'd focus on that once I felt secure in my career." Her voice cracked. "Now I've got nothing but my career, and because of the cancer, I may never have the chance to get married."

"They've made great strides in breast cancer treatment. It's not the death sentence it once was." Elizabeth's words sounded so hollow, when women still died of breast cancer every day.

"From your mouth to God's ears. They want me to have surgery next week and start chemo soon after that."

"Do you need someone to go with you?"

"I'll let you know. Right now I'm in shock." She sighed deeply. "I think I will take the day off. I'll call my best friend and see if she wants to go out for lunch. Then we can do some shopping therapy."

As Elizabeth returned to her office, she heard her blaring phone from halfway down the hall. Once seated at her desk, she glanced at caller ID. Micah Devlin. So much for having everything in order before she talked to him. Taking a deep breath, she picked up her phone.

"I'm glad you called, Micah." She tried not to wince over her white lie. "I've found the perfect man for your campaign, but I won't have photos for you until after the shoot tomorrow."

"Send me what you have."

"They're family pictures. I'd prefer to wait for the professional shots."

"Send them. I want to see this guy to make sure we're on the right track this time."

Elizabeth winced at Devlin's reminder of her previous suggestions for a spokesperson. Ones he had immediately, and not so politely, shot down. Some clients were dreams to work with. She had plenty of those, and they kept her sane and confident. Micah Devlin could benefit from a class on how to tactfully get his point across without incinerating those who worked for him.

"I have every confidence you'll be as pleased with this choice as I am."

She retrieved Rory's message from her email, hit Forward and typed Devlin's name. After saying a quick prayer, she hit Send.

Here goes everything.

"I'm emailing his photos to you right now. Keep in mind these aren't professionally done, but I believe his essence, his personality, comes through nonetheless."

She heard Devlin's computer keys clicking as he retrieved her message. She couldn't breathe. Thoughts bounced around in her brain. She hadn't updated her résumé in years. How would she tell her parents if she lost her job? She had mortgage payments....

"Now that's what I'm talking about. He's somebody the average man can relate to. He's not one of those pretty boy models. Before I sign him, I want to see how he comes off in a professional shoot."

Air rushed into Elizabeth's lungs, and she smiled over passing the first hurdle. "Rory will be in town tomorrow, and by Friday's meeting we'll have photos for you."

"I've contacted Harms and Finn."

Devlin's little tact problem reared its ugly head again. So that's why he'd called—to drop that bomb. Her firm, Rayzor Sharp Media, had lost an account to them six months ago. The agency was top-notch and hungry. "They're good."

"I meet with them tomorrow."

"Then I look forward to showing you what we've got on Friday."

She could pull this campaign together. If she didn't sleep until after the meeting, lived on Starbucks with double shots, and the rest of her team did the same, they'd be fine.

No problem.

Except that they were working with a cowboy, not a professional model. A total unknown who'd never modeled before. The unknown made Elizabeth nervous. It was always so unpredictable.

Rory sat in his office waiting for his brother. Things were moving much faster than he'd expected. When he'd called Elizabeth he'd never dreamed she would expect him to be on the first flight to New York. She was probably one of those people who stayed attached to the office via her iPhone so she never missed a message, even when she was supposed to be on vacation. Life was way too short to spend it that attached to anything but family.

He smiled. At least he wouldn't be the only one miserable. Having to manage the ranch would severely cramp Griff's style. The life of the party, his kid brother never turned down an invitation, but would soon discover he couldn't be out all night and sleep until noon while running the ranch.

Rory glanced up as he sauntered in and flung himself into the leather wing chair in the corner of the office. Griffin had a gift with animals, especially horses. He had a way of calming them, sensing when something was wrong. Business was an entirely different matter. Despite his ability in math, Griffin hadn't shown any interest in learning that side of the ranch. All that was about to change. Little brother was going to have to step up.

"I couldn't get the second mortgage."

"Why?"

"The downturn in the economy has caused a drop in tourism. Pair that with the amount of debt Twin Creeks already carries, and John couldn't justify it."

"You'd think since he was dad's best friend, he'd cut us a little slack."

"John's a smart businessman, and this was purely a business decision."

"Wait a minute. Mom and Avery left for Portland yesterday. How did you pay for their flights?"

"I put it on a credit card." One charging a fortune in interest. The hole Rory was digging kept getting deeper. "I need to get additional cash coming in before we start receiving Mom's medical bills."

"Did you tell her?"

Rory shook his head. "I didn't tell Avery, either. She isn't to know anything about this. No one is, for that matter. This stays between you and me. Are you clear on that?"

"But if—"

"Avery's got to take care of Mom. That's her job, keeping her calm and positive. You mention any of this, and I'll beat you to within an inch of your life. You got that, little brother?"

Griffin nodded.

"I've got the money situation under control, but I need you to take over the ranch's day-to-day operations."

"I'm obviously missing something. How did you find a way to come up with that kind of cash?"

"I'm going to New York City to model."

Griffin laughed. "No, seriously, Rory. What're we going to do?"

"This isn't a joke. I called the advertising executive who was here last week. She's got a client I can work for who will pay thirty grand for me to do an advertising campaign. I'm leaving tonight."

"What? Are you sure about this? You hate being in the spotlight, and you hate having your picture taken. If anything, you've always tried to blend into the background."

"What choice do I have? If Mom doesn't get this treatment, she'll die."

Griffin nodded, and for a moment the weight of their worry hung in the air.

"You have to hold things together here while I'm in New York."

"Tell me what to do."

Some of the heaviness pressing on Rory's chest lifted. He picked up a three-ring binder and gave Griff a crash course on Twin Creeks' finances.

"Don't spend money on anything but the essentials, Griff. I've cut expenses to the bone. In doing that I haven't had to let anyone go."

"It's that bad?"

"We're not on the verge of bankruptcy, but things are tight." Rory handed over a file. "Jameson is interested in buying Star's foal. Follow up with him next week. He's been lowballing us. I've given him the best price possible. Don't let him haggle with you. Another copy of the quote I gave him is in his file."

"Everything sounds simple enough."

"Stick to the budget." Rory flipped to another section in the binder.

"Thank goodness for cell phones. You're only a call away if I have questions," Griffin murmured.

"I may have to call you back, since I'll be working."

"How are you going to stand being away from here? You break out in a cold sweat when you have to go to Denver. Being in a big city like New York will drive you crazy."

That's exactly what worried Rory the most.

WHEN RORY WALKED INTO Rayzor Sharp Media's reception area, the first thing that hit him was how sterile the place felt. The desk was a sleek chrome-and-glass contraption with lines and angles and no warmth. A big black sign with the company name hung above it. The white walls added to the lifeless environment. He suddenly found himself missing the warm wood and earthy colors he saw everywhere at home.

A pretty little brunette dressed in black, who looked as if she hadn't eaten a decent meal in a month, glanced up and flashed him a perfect, blinding-white smile. "Hello..." She stretched out the word and looked him up and down, making him feel like a bright red apple held out to a horse. "What can I do for you?"

Man, he was out of his element. Fingering the brim of his Sunday Stetson, which he held in his hands, he said, "I'm here to see Ms. Harrington-Smyth."

"Lucky Elizabeth. Is there anything I can get you? Coffee? Bottled water? My phone number?"

For a moment he didn't know what to say. Strong women didn't scare him, but he wanted a woman to at least give him a chance to show interest before she made an all-out play for him, and he wasn't used to being pounced on the minute he walked into a place of business.

"I'm good."

"You sure are." The receptionist pointed to a cluster of ridiculously flimsy metal chairs. "Have a seat. I'll let Elizabeth know you're here."

As he sat, he hoped the chair would hold his weight. He didn't belong here. Elizabeth's client would take one look at him, laugh and ask her if she was crazy to put this cowboy in an ad campaign to sell clothes.

Now if the client was Ford or Chevy, that he could see. Man, he wished she wanted him to sell trucks instead of jeans. That wouldn't be a bad deal. He could chuck a saddle and some grain sacks in the back of a flatbed, crawl in the cab and drive off into the sunset. Yup, that would be a sweet deal.

But he hadn't gotten that lucky.

A minute later Elizabeth walked into the reception area. She was tinier than he remembered. Heck, she couldn't be more than five-two, because she barely reached the middle of his chest, even wearing high heels. He grinned. Those spiky shoes sure made her calves look fantastic. How could such a little thing have legs that were longer than an Alaskan night?

"I'm glad you're here. I hope your flight was pleasant." She held out her hand.

He shook it, surprised at the softness of her skin. "The flight was fine."

"Thanks for getting here on such short notice. Today we're going to take some photos. I've got a meeting tomorrow with the client. You and I both work for him. Unfortunately, until we have professional shots he's unwilling to sign a contract with you or the agency."

"I can't sign the contract and have him cut me a check today?"

"Mr. Devlin insists on seeing the professional photographs first."

Rory nodded, trying to shove aside his nervousness and unease. The sooner he got to work, the sooner he'd get paid. "Then we'd best get started."

"Follow me." Elizabeth started walking. "Let me tell you a couple of things about today's shoot. We're doing this one in-house since the photos are to show the client how wonderful you'll be to showcase his jeans. When he signs the contract, we'll do the commercial and print shoots elsewhere."

She glanced at Rory as if she expected him to say something, so he replied, "Makes sense."

"I coordinate the shoot. It's my job to make sure everyone else is doing his or hers, and that we have everything we need. We've got a small set, and once you change, our photographer will take pictures of you there. But the first thing we need to do is get you into our client's designer jeans."

Designer jeans. Probably uncomfortable, tight and way too fancy. Rory followed Elizabeth down a series of hallways to a big open room, where she picked up a pair of dark blue jeans off a table.

When she held them out to him, he realized this job was going to be worse than he'd expected. Way worse.

CHAPTER THREE

"No REAL MAN would be caught dead in these."

"Excuse me?" Elizabeth couldn't believe what Rory had just said about the client's jeans.

"I didn't mean to say that loud enough for anyone to hear."

Not an ounce of remorse showed in his clear, coffee-colored eyes, annoying her further. Her campaign rested on this cowboy, and he needed to take this job seriously. She'd fix that problem right now. "The first rule of being a spokesperson for a product, which is what we intend for you to be, is to always sing the product's praises. Never, in public or private, make any negative comments about the company, its employees or their products."

"Do I have to check with you before I say anything to anyone?"

"That might not be a bad idea until you get the hang of this business."

"I was joking."

She stared at him, not quite sure how to respond. "I know a lot of people don't value advertising, but this is a serious, competitive business."

"Lighten up. It isn't brain surgery."

Bullheaded man. Elizabeth pinched her lips together and counted to ten. If she didn't need him so desperately, she'd fire him, because obviously her words weren't hitting home.

"No, it's not brain surgery or rocket science, but that doesn't mean what we do here isn't important. We're a crucial part of the economy. If we create an ineffective campaign, company sales go down, which means people get laid off. It also means a possible fall in stock prices and less dividends for stockholders. That creates other repercussions in the economy, which I won't go into here." Mainly because Rory probably wouldn't grasp the fine nuances. "Mistakes like criticizing the company's product can cause a lot of people, you included, to lose their jobs. Are we clear on that?"

"Where do I change?"

She ignored his question for a minute, trying to determine if she'd made her point. Finally deciding the man would have to be a complete idiot not to have understood her, she pointed to a door on the opposite side of the studio. "You'll find a shirt in there. You can wear your own boots for this shoot."

While Rory changed, Elizabeth surveyed the scene around her, checking the details for the photo shoot. Micah Devlin was a perfectionist with a keen eye, and expected the same from everyone he worked with. He had to like Rory; otherwise the whole concept was a loss.

Think positively, Elizabeth. That breeds good energy, and good energy brings about good results.

The lighting was perfect. The background clean white. A saddle was propped on a hay bale, a rope casually wrapped around the saddle horn. Rats. She'd forgotten about requesting hay bales. She glanced at the set assistant. "Kudos on the set, especially on such short notice."

The young woman beamed.

Elizabeth rubbed her itching eyes. The sneezing would start soon. She dug in her purse, searching for a Claritin to stem her allergy symptoms, but came up empty. No getting around it, she'd have to suffer through.

Two more hay bales sat beside the saddle, completing the scene. Enough props to let people know Rory was a cowboy, but not enough to detract from the jeans or the cowboy. For the actual campaign she planned outdoor shots in upstate New York at a barn, on a horse, working around the place. But right now she needed to sell Rory to Devlin.

Please let him look good in the jeans.

The coffee she'd gulped an hour earlier sloshed in her nervous stomach.

Wait a minute. What was she thinking? As long as the jeans fit, he'd look terrific in them. A man that gorgeous could make anything look good. A mental picture of Rory shirtless in a pair of jeans, his chest slick as he poured water over his sweaty skin after a long day of fixing fences, flashed in her mind.

Note to self—get shots of Rory with his shirt off.

She fanned her face, though that wasn't the only place she was warm. What was she thinking? This was business. She never mixed business with pleasure, and besides that, Rory wasn't her type.

The click of stilettos on the hardwood floor interrupted Elizabeth's daydreaming. She turned to find Stephanie Jones, her black leather makeup case slung over her shoulder, sauntering toward her.

The leggy brunette stopped in front of Elizabeth. "Where's our model?"

Before she could answer, she sneezed. Not one of those polite feminine sneezes, but one with hurricane force. Darn allergies. "He's changing," Elizabeth said, after two more sneezes. "Let me explain what I'm looking for today. Just play up his natural good looks. I want him to stay real, like the cowboy he is."

"You're kidding! He's really a cowboy?" Stephanie's blue eyes sparkled as if she'd snatched up the last fifty-percent-off cashmere sweater at Barney's.

What was it about cowboys? Stephanie hadn't even seen Rory and she was drooling. Mark, the lighting tech, had about stepped on his tongue when Rory walked in.

"He's the real deal, and I want his pictures to reflect that. I want him to look like he's just stepped out of the ranch house and is heading toward the barn to work."

"In designer jeans?"

Elizabeth bristled at Stephanie's skepticism about her ad campaign.

Breathe. Don't let her negativity invade your space and make you doubt your decision. This is the right way to go with this campaign.

A big smile on her face, Elizabeth said, "Devlin Designs wants to crack the Western and middle-American market with their men's jeans."

"Okay, now using the cowboy makes sense."

"I hope the public sees it the same way. I won't keep you any longer. You need to set up, and I need to check other details of the shoot."

While the stylist traipsed across the room to the makeup table and chair, Elizabeth went to talk to Chloe.

"I can't wait to get this guy on film," she said the minute Elizabeth stopped beside her.

Just then, Rory strolled out of the dressing room. The client's designer jeans fit him perfectly, emphasizing his strong thighs. Ones he'd no doubt obtained from riding. Who'd have thought horseback riding was such a workout? But her quads and glutes had been sore for two days after her horse excursion.

Rory's tanned skin contrasted nicely with the crisp, white, snap-front, Western-style shirt she'd picked out. Denim and white. Classic, clean. One never went wrong with the basics.

She smiled at the personal touches he'd added—his belt buckle, a royal flush fanned-out poker hand, plus his boots and his cowboy hat. Rugged, but accessible.

Absolutely delicious. Absolutely perfect. Absolutely wrong for her.

"If he's any indication, they sure raise them handsome in Colorado." A sinful grin spread across Chloe's face.

Elizabeth continued staring at Rory. Before meeting him she'd have said her ideal man was more comfortable in a Brooks Brothers suit than jeans. Rory put those immaculately groomed men in their thousand-dollar suits to shame.

She started to move toward him, but Stephanie reached Rory first, introduced herself and led him to the makeup chair.

"Our model is too delectable for words," Mark said as he joined them.

This was getting a little ridiculous. "Has everyone forgotten why we're here? And no, it isn't to ogle Rory."

She was beginning to think she needed to hire a body-guard for the cowboy.

"There's no harm in looking," Mark said, glancing at him longingly.

"But with you it doesn't stop there," Chloe reminded the lighting tech.

"Plus I'm pretty sure he's heterosexual," Elizabeth added, trying to end the subject without having to give a lecture on professionalism.

"But you don't know for sure."

Elizabeth leaned toward him as if sharing a confidence. "I'm counting on you to help me out. This guy isn't a model. He doesn't understand the game. We all have to be careful that we don't scare him off. I think this might be his first visit to New York."

"All right. I'll back off. Just for you."

"I appreciate your sacrifice, Mark." She smiled in relief. "You've done a super job with the lighting, by the way. You're the best."

"Can I have that in writing for when review time rolls around?"

"Absolutely."

He glanced toward the set. "I'm off to be wonderful. I need to reposition one of the lights."

"You sure you didn't tell him to back off so you can have Rory all to yourself?" Chloe asked once Mark had left.

"Oh, please. You know my type, and Rory's not it."

"A guy doesn't have to be a Mensa candidate to be worth spending time with."

"That's the difference between us. You can be involved with someone for right now. I don't see the point in that."

"Fun and great sex." Chloe nodded toward Rory. "Look at him. I bet he's amazing in bed."

"There's more to a relationship than hot sex."

"Maybe, but that's a pretty good place to start."

"Now's not the time to talk about this," Elizabeth said, realizing how far they'd strayed off course. "Nothing can interfere with today's shoot. Be the epitome of professional."

"What he does for those jeans is amazing."

"Thank goodness."

"Not to stress you out more," Chloe said as she adjusted the height of her tripod, "but we're all counting on you to pull this one out. Word is Devlin's agency-shopping."

"This time the rumor mill's right, but I've got everything under control." Maybe if she said that enough times she'd believe it. The whole self-fulfilling prophecy thing. "Rory will help us change two crucial opinions. One, that only gay men wear designer jeans, and two, wearing designer jeans will make a man look like a pretty boy. I want the average, red-blooded, straight male to think that if a cowboy will wear these jeans, he can wear them, too."

"Then let's get this show on the road."

WITH A ROOMFUL of people, all with their gazes glued on his every move, Rory felt like a piece of meat. Prime choice, grade A, but meat nonetheless.

The stylist opened her black case, revealing small bottles and other containers. His stomach tightened when he recognized it was makeup. He'd figured she might have a hair dryer and hair gel in the thing. He sat horrified as she stared at him, and then selected one

bottle. She dumped some of the liquid on a foam triangle and leaned toward him.

"Whoa, hold on a minute. Is that makeup?" Sissy
city jeans were one thing, but no way was he wearing
makeup.

The stylist nodded. The triangle moved closer.

He leaned away. "Cowboys don't wear makeup."

High-pitched giggles greeted his response. "This
cowboy needs to, because if you don't wear base
makeup and blush—"

Blush. Wasn't that the pink stuff women swiped over
their cheeks? He resisted the urge to hang his head in
shame.

"If you don't wear makeup, you'll look washed out
under the lights."

"Better that than wearing that stuff. If any of my
friends find out, I'll never live it down." He shuddered.
"Next thing you'll be telling me I need mascara."

"It would—"

"No mascara. A man's got to draw the line somewhere."

The stylist lightly swatted his arm and giggled again.
The sound grated on his nerves. "There's no need for
you to worry. No one will be able to see you've got
makeup on, and I swear I won't tell anyone."

Her words failed to reassure him. Something in his
gut told him that his wearing makeup would get out—
that was the kind of luck he had. But what choice did
he have? He needed this job, and photos were the first
step to landing the gig. The things he did for his mom.
"I've died and gone to hell, and this is my punishment."

The woman used the sponge to dab makeup on his

skin. The oily liquid slid across his face, sending ripples of revulsion through him.

"See, that's not so bad."

He gritted his teeth at the comment and refused to look in the mirror. He'd wear the blasted stuff, but no way did he want the sight of him in makeup burned into his memory.

"This doesn't detract from your masculinity at all," she declared.

He suspected she was a woman who thought a man wouldn't be interested unless she agreed with everything he said, and complimented him nonstop.

Now little Lizzie—Elizabeth, he'd decided, didn't fit her—didn't appear to let anyone tell her what to think. In an effort to tune out Stephanie's incessant chatter as she fussed with his hair, he'd watched Lizzie out of the corner of his eye.

Dressed in a black skirt and white blouse that showed off her knockout curves, she efficiently circled the room, checking lighting and the setup. What was it with all the women here wearing black? Hadn't they heard of color in New York?

As if thinking about her pulled her to him, Lizzie walked his way. "Is he ready to go, Stephanie?"

"He's perfect."

Rory almost laughed. Perfect? Not in his universe. He looked like a sissy in these tight, fancy stitched jeans. "Anybody gonna ask me if I'm ready?"

Both women turned to him, their mouths hanging open. Guess he'd broken another photo shoot protocol.

Lizzie recovered first. "I'm sorry, Rory. I didn't mean to appear rude. I need to make sure Stephanie's finished her job, which is to make sure you look your best under the lights." She turned to the stylist. "Once again, you've done super work. Now, Rory, if you'd come this way. I'd like to introduce you to the photographer before we start shooting."

Rory stood, thankful to put distance between him and Stephanie before she jumped him in the chair. "Lead on."

He liked the white shirt Lizzie had picked out for him, but the jeans wouldn't last a week on the ranch. "Just out of curiosity, how much do these pants cost?"

"The pair you're wearing retails for two hundred dollars."

He whistled. "Men actually spend their hard-earned money on these?"

"Devlin's men's jeans are among the hottest in the upscale market."

Guilt swirled inside him at the thought of playing a part in convincing people to waste money on high-priced jeans, when a pair of Wranglers or Levi's worked fine. The world was so out of whack. Kids got killed over expensive sneakers. People who couldn't pay their rent found money to get tattoos. Stuff didn't make a person. Didn't people get that?

Lizzie led him to a tall, slender woman with shoulder-length black hair, dressed in a long, flowing purple skirt and a red T-shirt with a baggy white sweater thrown over that. Big chunky beads hung around her neck. Finally, a female who wasn't dressed as if she was heading to a funeral.

She introduced herself and tossed him a look that said she was interested in more than taking his picture. What was the deal with everyone at this agency?

"Are you ready to get started?" Elizabeth asked.

"Tell me what you need me to do."

Chloe smiled. "Just be you. I'll do all the hard work. Let's start with some simple shots of you sitting here on the hay. That'll give us both a chance to warm up. I hope you don't have allergies like Elizabeth. She's been sneezing since she arrived."

"Thanks, Chloe, for pointing out the obvious." Elizabeth punctuated her statement with an unladylike sneeze, followed by a delicate "excuse me."

"The hay won't bother me. I'm around it all day long."

"Good. Chloe, you get behind the camera and see how everything looks. Rory, come with me. I'll position you."

Position him? A very intimate picture of him and Lizzie tangled together in bed popped into his head. "Excuse me?"

"I'll show you where to sit on the set, which way to look, that kind of thing. That's what we call positioning. What were you thinking?"

"I had a more intimate picture in mind." As Rory followed her he couldn't keep his gaze off the way her little black high-heeled shoes made her hips sway, causing his blood to pump.

She froze and a pretty pink blush spread across her face. "I'm sorry you were confused."

He leaned toward her to rattle her chain a little more. After all, if he was going to be on display, he had no intention of being the only one uncomfortable. "Lizzie, if we get together, there won't be any confusion."

For a second her eyes widened and her pupils dilated. Then she swallowed hard. "My name's Elizabeth."

"You don't look like an Elizabeth. It's too long a name for such a little thing like you."

She snapped her lips together. He expected to see steam coming out her ears any minute. This job could be fun, after all.

"My parents named me Elizabeth. That's what they called me, and that's the name I go by." She crossed her arms over her chest, pulling her blouse open farther at the neck. She had a pretty neck. He'd love to kiss that spot where the vein throbbed wildly beneath her skin. "Now, if we're through with the discussion regarding my name, we both have work to do."

He smiled, way more at ease than when he'd arrived. "All set."

"Have a seat on the hay bale there." Lizzie pointed to the one closet to the saddle.

He sank onto the hay, braced his hands on his knees and leaned forward. "Now what?"

That pretty pink color still tingeing her cheeks, Lizzie turned to Chloe. "How's it look from your angle?"

"Good from here. Now, get out of the shot and let me work."

The rapid-fire click of the camera shutter filled the studio. During a momentary lull, Stephanie buzzed around him, more annoying and persistent than the horseflies at home. "I think he's getting a little shiny. Let me add some powder."

Rory tried not to wince. Just what he needed, more makeup. Pretty soon he'd look like Bozo the Clown.

She swiped a brush across his face, tossed him a big smile and fluttered away. She wasn't any better at getting the leave-me-alone signals than the horseflies.

More clicking.

This was every bit the torture he'd expected, except for the short diversion with Lizzie.

"Relax, Rory, you look like you've got a dentist appointment later today," Chloe said.

"Relax? How's a man supposed to do that with everyone staring at him, watching his every move? I feel like the turkey on Thanksgiving, sitting there in the middle of the table."

"That's an interesting point of view," Lizzie said. "It's not that everyone's watching what you do so much as ensuring nothing needs their attention."

"Try to forget everyone's here, Rory. Concentrate on one thing, and tune out everything else," Chloe suggested.

He focused on Lizzie. All straitlaced and in charge, but he'd seen a fire flash in her eyes when he'd called her that. There was definitely something there. All she needed to do was let go and channel that energy. Now that would be a job worth taking on.

"Hold that pose."

More clicking.

Lizzie leaned toward the photographer and the women whispered back and forth for a minute, before Lizzie said, "Rory, let's try some shots with you standing."

He stood, but wasn't quite sure what to do with his hands. That wasn't exactly true. Right now he'd like to have his hands on Lizzie, caressing her dynamite curves and those long legs of hers. Heat shot through him. If he didn't think about something other than her legs, these fancy jeans would get even tighter. "What do you want me to do with my hands?"

"Stand like you would if you were hanging around the ranch with friends."

When he hooked his thumbs in his front pockets, Lizzie smiled.

She seemed different when she smiled. Softer. More approachable, more womanly.

"Fabulous. Keep looking like that." The camera clicked away as Chloe rattled on. "Whatever you're thinking about, it's doing wonders for you."

Rory's gaze locked with Lizzie's. He imagined holding her, exploring her full curves. He could almost hear her excited sigh in his ears as his hands glided over her breasts and hips.

Then his phone, which he'd instinctively shoved in his back pocket, rang. Lizzie's smile evaporated, replaced with a scowl.

"Whose phone is that?" she asked. "Everyone here knows my policy on cell phones interrupting a photo shoot."

"It's mine." Rory pulled it out of his back pocket and answered the call.

He *answered* the call? Elizabeth stormed toward him. The man possessed no work ethic. "I forgot to mention that when we're at a photo shoot, everyone turns off their cell phones."

Ignoring her, he said, "I know he's trying to make it sound that way, but don't worry about it. He'll cool down."

"Get off the phone now."

"Got to go. I'll call you back later." Rory ended the call.

"I can't believe you answered that call."

"I had a life and responsibilities before this job came along. I still have things that need my attention."

"I realize that. However, I expect you to deal with those things on your own time, not on the client's." Elizabeth held out her hand.

"I'll turn it on vibrate."

"Give it to me. I'll hold on to it until we're done with the shoot." When he opened his mouth, she suspected to protest, she explained, "You can't have your phone in your back pocket. It'll ruin the line of the jeans."

Reluctantly, he handed over his BlackBerry.

"Let's get back to work." She returned to her position beside Chloe. "Where were we?"

The photographer stepped out from behind the camera. "If our focus is to sell jeans, we might want to see more of them."

"You're absolutely right, Chloe." Elizabeth tapped a manicured nail against her watch. "Got any ideas?"

"Rory, do you mind turning to the side and lifting that saddle?"

"Finally something I feel comfortable doing." He lifted the saddle and balanced the leather against his thigh, as if he'd done so every day since he was strong enough to pick it up.

Rory's gaze locked with Elizabeth's and held. Electricity shot through her. Strong. Hot. Baffling. The look in his eyes mesmerized her, making her more confident that she'd chosen the right man for the campaign.

As she watched Rory's biceps flex under his shirt, heat coursed through her. Then she glanced at his thighs. No doubt about his strength there, and his butt did amazing things for those jeans.

Oh, yeah, this shot was more than perfect.

If Micah Devlin didn't like this picture and believe the campaign would sell jeans, then there was no pleasing him.

Remembering the campaign put things back into perspective for Elizabeth. She appreciated the sight of an attractive man as much as the next woman, but this was business. She couldn't let irrational pheromones on overdrive interfere with her work.

"Angle behind him," she whispered to Chloe. No way did she want Rory hearing this conversation. "I want shots from behind."

"Butt shots coming up."

She blushed, surprised at her reaction, since she and Chloe discussed models' body parts all the time in shoots. "We're selling jeans. The client will want to see how they look on our model from every angle."

"No need to get defensive," Chloe said as she moved to get the shots.

Elizabeth remained rooted in place, staring at Rory. The cowboy was absolutely mesmerizing. Stalwart. Confident. Any girl's best dream. Elizabeth could barely breathe. Now if Chloe could get the heat radiating from him on film...

"Rory, would you mind putting down the saddle and taking off your shirt?"

"Yes, I'd mind."

Elizabeth couldn't have heard him. Either that or he misunderstood her question. "Excuse me?"

"I don't mind putting the saddle down, but I'm not taking off my shirt."

She stood there for a moment trying to regroup.

She was in charge. She told everyone what to do and

they did as requested. No one at a photo shoot questioned her decision. Not even Chloe.

This cowboy *so* pushed her buttons.

For a minute she considered ordering Rory to take off his shirt, but the glint in his eyes stopped her. He flashed her a look similar to her first boss's I'm-not-discussing-this expression. Sure, she was in charge, but her job hinged on two men's whims right now, Micah Devlin and Rory McAlister. She couldn't risk angering Rory enough that he hopped on the next plane to Colorado.

She could do this. Finesse and charm time. "Everyone take five."

The crew scooted away, though not far, in case she and Rory put on a show.

She walked to where he stood beside the hay, wanting to make their conversation as private as possible. "Rory, what's the problem?"

"There's no problem, because I'm keeping my shirt on."

She stared at him, trying to fathom what the hang-up could be. It wasn't as if she was asking him to pose for a pinup poster. Granted, she hoped this shot would have the same effect and drive women wild for him and the jeans, but they were primarily selling the product.

Maybe he was embarrassed about his chest? It couldn't be because he wasn't in shape. No way could he be hiding a beer belly under that formfitting shirt. Okay, so what else could it be? He was a cowboy. They got thrown from horses. "Do you have some kind of injury or scar that's making this uncomfortable for you?"

"No."

"Then what's going on?"

"You told me I'd be modeling jeans, not posing for beefcake shots."

"Shots of you without your shirt will highlight the jeans, and it's what the client wants."

"We don't always get what we want."

She crossed her arms over her chest. The guy was one huge piece of granite, hard and unmoving. Needing a chance to cool off, she walked to the table with bottled water by the dressing room. She grabbed one, surprised that the top didn't pop off the way she squeezed the thing, and stormed back to Rory.

"Here, have some water." She shoved the bottle into his hands. Hopefully, the water would cool him off, too. "I need a minute."

Then she walked to the opposite side of the studio to talk to Chloe.

"I gather he's still refusing to take off his shirt?"

Elizabeth nodded. "I think he's just being stubborn."

"We've got to get the shots of him in just the jeans."

What about Rory made her want to dig in her heels? She felt as if she were six years old again, fighting with Angela Simmons. *I dare you. No, I double dare you,* and the next thing she knew, they were both sitting in Principal Mathews's office.

"You may have to pull rank." Chloe glanced toward Rory. "Look at him. How else do you think you're going to get him to cooperate?"

She followed her friend's gaze. The cowboy was leaning against the wall, his arms crossed over his strong chest. His lips formed a thin line. Nope, he hadn't let go of his anger, either.

His gaze locked with hers again. Then his chin tilted up ever so slightly and he smiled.

No way was he backing down.

She'd never been a gambler, especially when the costs were so high, and not just for her, but those who worked with her. So much rode on the campaign's success, and she needed those shots of Rory in just the jeans.

If he wanted to lock horns about this issue, he'd chosen the wrong person to mess with, because she couldn't afford to lose.

She stalked across the floor and stopped in front of Rory. She looked into his chiseled features, unmoved by his gorgeous face or his angry scowl. "I need shots of you with your shirt off. You either do as requested or you're fired."

CHAPTER FOUR

RORY, A DAMNED GOOD poker player, could bluff with the best of 'em, but Lizzie won this hand fair and square. Not that he would let her see how much the fact bothered him.

He unscrewed the plastic cap off his water bottle, kept his gaze focused on her and took a long drink. Then he set the bottle on the nearby table and tugged the shirttails out of his jeans. He grabbed one side in each hand and pulled. The snaps popping as they came loose broke the silence. Next, he peeled off his shirt and tossed the garment on the table.

His gaze still locked with Lizzie's, he leaned back, crossed his arms over his bare chest and said, "How's this work for you, sweetheart? Does what you see get your engine racing?"

Her cheeks immediately turned the same shade of pink as his mother's favorite roses. Lizzie blinked and swallowed.

Point to him.

"Let's get this done," he said as he walked away.

Her high heels clicked on the wood floor as she scrambled to catch up with him. "Break over, everyone."

He stopped beside the hay bales and turned toward her, deciding to have a bit more fun teasing her. "How do you want me positioned? I'm all yours."

The pulse in her neck throbbed wildly. Her eyes dilated. He smiled, knowing he'd chipped a piece out of her in-control businesswoman facade. What would Lizzie be like if she loosened up a bit? She'd be a handful who could give a man a wild ride. Now that he'd like to see.

"I'm not quite sure." After clearing her throat, she faced the photographer. "What do you think, Chloe? How should we position Rory?"

"Yes, ladies, by all means—what do you think would be my best position?"

Lizzie choked on the water she'd been about to swallow. He thumped her on the back. "You okay?"

She nodded, and he sank onto a hay bale.

"What you're doing looks amazing, Rory," Chloe said, the camera held to her eye. "Hold that pose."

As the photographer swarmed around him, clicking, his gaze never wavered from Lizzie. For all her confidence, put things on a man-woman level and she apparently didn't know what to do.

"Now cross your arms," Chloe said.

Rory started fantasizing, imagining taking Lizzie's hair out of the tight ponytail and running his fingers through the blond, curly strands. His imagination wandered further. Would the texture be as silky as he suspected? He pictured her golden hair falling around her face as she leaned over him in bed.

"Pick up the saddle." Her voice cut through his fantasy.

He stood and did as requested, but pretended he was lifting her instead. Heck, she probably weighed less than the saddle. Then an image of them flashed in his mind: of her sliding down his body and wrapping her legs around his waist. Her beautiful hair spilled down her back as she tilted her face upward, exposing her graceful neck. What kind of sounds would she make when he explored her skin with his lips?

He lowered the saddle a little to cover his rising excitement.

How long had it been since he'd had a date? Over six months. Talk about the date from hell. Their dinner conversation had consisted of her telling him all about her last boyfriend, who she'd dated for five years, and how he'd dumped her. Rory's previous relationship had been over a year ago, and since he wasn't a casual sex kind of guy, that was the last time he'd been intimate.

He stared long and hard at Lizzie. Something about her reached out to him. Danged if he knew what, because a lot of women were prettier.

"Stephanie, mist Rory." Lizzie tossed the request over her shoulder. "I want him to look like he's been working up a sweat."

Confidence. She had an air about her. Maybe that was what appealed to him. Such a tiny woman and yet she looked as if she'd stand up to a grizzly. Had to be either her assurance or his dry spell that accounted for his body's unusual reaction.

The stylist popped up in front of him with a water bottle. The moisture sprayed on his chest instantly reminded him that he stood half-naked in front of a group of people, and that Lizzie had threatened to fire him unless he agreed to comply. His daydreams burned like dry kindling tossed on a campfire.

"You're doing a fantastic job." Stephanie batted her long eyelashes. "Once this campaign hits the street, Devlin jeans are going to fly off the shelf."

He didn't care whether or not the jeans sold well. All

that mattered was that he earned thirty grand. Then he'd kiss this big city and modeling goodbye.

"Rory, set down the saddle and put on your hat," Chloe said.

Bossy city women. *Rory, do this. Rory, turn and look at me. Rory, you need to focus.* He felt like an elementary schoolkid having a bad day.

"Push your hat back a little. We need to see more of your face." This order came from Lizzie. "Cross your arms over your chest," she called out next.

Good thing, because he was about to put his hands around her pretty little throat.

"I think we have everything we need," she finally said. "Let's call it a day, everyone."

He walked past her to where he'd left his shirt, slipped the garment on and returned to her. He leaned down, not wanting anyone to overhear. "Next time we have a disagreement—" and based on today's events, future disagreements were a sure thing "—we work them out in private. Don't ever pull rank on me again. I don't perform on command."

"Neither do I," she called out to his back.

Damned if the little minx wasn't a spitfire, and damned if he didn't admire her for that.

RORY'S WORDS HAMMERED in Elizabeth's head as she walked to her office. How dare he speak to her like that? Then to top things off, he'd walked away without allowing her to say anything but the lamest of comebacks.

She'd definitely needed to set ground rules with the cowboy. He wasn't in Colorado anymore, and the New York business world ran differently than a horse ranch. His open defiance of her authority had to stop. Otherwise, they'd butt heads constantly and make everyone miserable. An uncomfortable environment bred negativity, which led to poor work performance and an unhappy client.

When she arrived in her office, she found Chloe at her desk, downloading photos. Her friend glanced upward. "I don't know how you work in this office. It's too ordered. Doesn't that stifle your creativity?"

"An orderly work space leads to an orderly mind." Her grandmother's pet phrase popped out before Elizabeth could stop it. She slid the chair from in front of her desk to the other side, close to the computer, and threw herself into the seat. "Sleep deprivation's warping my mind, and turning me into my grandmother."

"It could be worse."

"How?"

Chloe shrugged. "I'm not sure. That just sounded like the thing to say. Wait a minute, I've got it. The good news is getting sleep will fix the problem."

"I wish that would work on my problem with Rory. I hope he's not going to continue to be so difficult."

"What was with you two, anyway?" Chloe asked. "Playing referee is not in my job description, and if it's going to be in the future, I want more money."

"He pushed every one of my buttons today. The man could write a book on how to become the world's biggest pain in the ass."

"Apparently the sparks are still flying."

"Can you believe he refused to take off his shirt? I don't get what the big deal was. It wasn't like I was asking him to pose in his underwear."

"If I could figure guys out, do you think I'd be here?" Chloe pulled up the first set of photos onto the computer screen, the ones of Rory sitting on the hay bale. "No, I wouldn't. I'd be in the Caribbean living off the money I made from my *New York Times* bestseller on how to understand men."

"Wouldn't that be nice?"

Chloe pointed to the monitor. "Check these out."

Elizabeth stared at the photos. Rory had a presence. Incredible, steamy, make-a-woman's-insides-tingle-with-a-look presence. "The shots are fantastic, but they don't showcase the jeans."

"I agree, but do you want to put one of these in a portfolio to show Devlin how well Rory photographs?"

"Couldn't hurt."

Chloe clicked computer keys and a second later the printer hummed to life. "Now, about you and Rory, I wasn't talking about the arguing type of sparks. I was talking about the making-you-all-hot-and-bothered ones."

Elizabeth stood and retrieved the photo from the printer. "I don't know what you mean."

Good comeback. That'll make her drop the subject.

She laughed. "You never were a good liar."

"So, I admit it. The guy drives me crazy."

Chloe flashed her an annoying best-friend, know-it-all smile.

"I didn't mean that in a good way," Elizabeth stated. "He's stubborn, inflexible, and refuses to take directions or criticism well."

"One person's fighting is another person's dancing."

"That's the silliest thing I've ever heard." After tossing the photo onto the desk blotter, Elizabeth sank back into her chair. "If you're trying to say I enjoyed arguing with him today, you're way off base."

"You may not have had fun, but he was having a blast

seeing your temper flare. Think about what it would be like making up with him. Oooh!"

"You think Rory was being difficult on purpose? Why would he do that?"

Chloe shrugged and pulled up more photos on the computer screen. These of Rory holding the saddle.

"If he was, he has a sick sense of humor," Elizabeth declared. "A man with self-respect and a decent work ethic wouldn't enjoy making his boss uncomfortable." She tapped the monitor. "Print out that one."

Chloe nodded. "Think about it from his point of view. He's a strong, assertive man, a lone cowboy. I'm guessing Rory doesn't take orders from too many people."

"Then he's going to have to start learning who's at the top of the food chain."

"When Devlin signs the contract and you center the jeans campaign on Rory, you're going to have to find a way to coexist."

"It'll be easy. I plan for this campaign to do major things for my career." That is, if Rory didn't drive her completely insane first. Elizabeth paced the length of her office, stopping at her credenza to straighten the silver Effie Award she'd received for the Tug-Ups training pants ad she'd created last year.

Courage and self-esteem bolstered, she reasoned she could work with Rory. After all, she worked with Micah Devlin.

"Saving the Devlin account and creating a nationwide campaign can turn management supervisors into vice presidents. When Rory's driving me insane, I'll visualize my new, spacious, vice-presidential office."

"Ah, yes. Your ten-year plan."

Elizabeth ignored her friend's sarcasm. Chloe wasn't a big believer in planning, preferring to remain open to life's opportunities because goals stifled her. Elizabeth believed that to achieve what she wanted took goal setting, strategic planning and a lot of visualization.

Chloe leaned forward in her chair and whistled. "Look at these photos. Cowboy here just might take both our careers places."

Elizabeth gazed at the pictures. Rory stared back at her, his boots firmly planted on the ground, the white shirt pulled taut across his pecs, his biceps bulging as he held the saddle. The man would become the stuff women dreamed of. "Print that one."

Chloe nodded, and scrolled through more photos. A few seconds later, she clicked on an image to enlarge it, then leaned back in her chair and sighed dreamily. "One of the perks of my job, butt shots of gorgeous men." She tapped the computer screen with her dark purple nail. "And that man has one fine butt."

Glancing at the photo, Elizabeth kept her lips pinned together for fear she'd start drooling. Once she had her emotions well under control, she said, "Remember the focus of our campaign is the jeans, not on how good the model's butt is."

"Are you saying you disagree with my assessment?"

She'd have to be blind to disagree. Not that she'd admit the fact to Chloe, for fear of eternal taunting. "My job is to focus on how the jeans look."

"Which is pretty damn good on his butt."

"Print the first one and the shot where he's looking over his shoulder at us."

"You mean the one where he looks like he's ready to carry you off into the sunset?"

"If that's the third shot, then yes. We'll add that to the portfolio." Elizabeth stared at the photo. Rory's eyes had darkened to a deep walnut color, and he had the slightest smile on his face. "What makes you say he was thinking of me? Maybe he was thinking about you."

"Don't I wish." Chloe sighed again. "But alas, his gaze followed you around the room."

That information should've made Elizabeth warm in all kinds of places, but instead the fact worried her. She couldn't afford having Rory see her as anything but his boss. "He can't be interested in me. Can he?"

"Why's that so unbelievable?"

"We're ill-suited."

"Opposites attract."

"You're full of clichés today."

"You're just ticked because I'm right, and don't try to change the subject. It's true. Opposites do attract."

"They may have instant chemistry, but those relationships don't last. The ones that do are based on things like similar values and interests." Needing something to busy her hands and control her nervousness, Elizabeth grabbed a pen and fiddled with it. "Pull up the shots of him shirtless."

"You'd give a guy up because you worked together? Even if you thought he was your soul mate?"

"There's no such thing. In a world of over six billion people, there has to be more than one man I could have a lasting relationship with."

Chloe shook her head. "If I thought a guy was the one, I wouldn't let anything get in the way."

The last shots of Rory popped onto the screen. Chloe whistled through her teeth. "Be still my heart. These are the best yet. Look at those six-pack abs."

Elizabeth stared at the photo, speechless. Rory could make a nun think twice about her vow of chastity. Hell, think three times about it. "Make that one poster-size. I'll put it on an easel. Put the rest in a portfolio. I'm off to make sure the mock-ups are ready for tomorrow."

Pointing at the picture displayed on the computer monitor, Chloe said, "That's all you've got to say about this?"

"I think it's excellent. It should accomplish exactly what we need it to."

Her friend flopped back in her chair and threw her hands in the air. "And that's why you don't date much."

"Can we stick to the job here, and stay off the topic of my love life?"

"What love life?"

Elizabeth pointedly ignored her jibe, mainly because she lacked a good comeback. Tough to argue with the truth.

Her dating had been a little sparse lately, but that was because she had standards. If she let her friends set her up she could have three dates a week, but what was the point of dating if the candidates fell below par? On top of that, her job's long hours left little time for a social life. But more importantly, she had no intention of letting dating sidetrack her from what mattered—saving Devlin's accounts and advancing her career. That required work and sacrifice. Everything worthwhile did.

"How can looking at this gorgeous guy, one you'll be working in close contact with, not make your body sing?"

"I'm tone-deaf."

Listening to her body, being ruled by her hormones, led down a scary path. Going against common sense led to caring, wanting, expectations and possibly loving. All of those things, in her experience, led to heartbreak. No, thanks. Been there, done that. Gave away the T-shirt.

"I don't have time for anything except getting ready for tomorrow's meeting." Elizabeth glanced at her watch. Eight o'clock. The night was zooming by at warp speed. "I still have to come up with a slogan before the morning meeting."

"Got any ideas?"

"I have a bunch written down, but now that we've got Rory's pictures they don't seem right." She rubbed her throbbing temples. "I want something memorable, like the Calvin Klein ad with Brooke Shields. 'Nothing gets between me and my Calvins.'"

"Think about Rory's qualities."

"He's stubborn to the point of pigheadedness."

"His good qualities."

She thought for a minute. "He's strong. He's authentic."

"He sure is a real man, and very delectable."

Rory's comment that no real man would wear designer jeans popped into Elizabeth's head. She grabbed a Post-it note and scribbled out a line as adrenaline gushed through her system, invigorating her. "I've got the slogan, Chloe, and it's perfect."

BY THE MORNING MEETING in the agency's conference room, Elizabeth was running on stress and caffeine. The stuff that fueled corporate America. Once she presented a hopefully coherent campaign to Micah Devlin and answered his questions, which if past meetings were any indication would be many, she planned on collapsing and sleeping for two days straight.

When she escorted Devlin, dressed in a pair of his own jeans and a pin-striped button-down shirt, into the conference room, he sat at the long mahogany table and pulled out his iPad.

She smoothed the skirt of her charcoal-gray Ellen Tracy suit and glanced down at her red stiletto pumps. Chloe called them her ruby slippers, because Elizabeth felt invincible when she wore then.

Ruby slippers, do your magic. "We believe Rory McAlister is the perfect person to represent Devlin Designs' men's jeans."

Elizabeth pulled the cover off the poster on the easel, revealing Rory—naked from the waist up, his arms crossed over his wide chest, his biceps bulging, his skin slick with sweat—wearing the company's jeans and his cowboy hat. Below the picture ran the words *Devlin men's jeans. Strong enough to stand up to a real man.*

Her breath stuck in her throat as she waited for her client to respond. When she'd first met Micah Devlin she'd been attracted to him. In his mid to late thirties, he was approximately five or so years older than her, and she liked that. He had an MBA from Harvard Business School. Was the CEO of the family business—a Fortune 500 company, no less. He was tall, in shape without being overly muscular. His company contributed to numerous charities. He'd seemed like her dream man. At least on paper.

Then she'd gotten to know him. His controlling personality and micromanaging had effectively incinerated her attraction.

No worries about mixing business and pleasure there.

"I like him," Devlin said. "He's strong and fit, but doesn't look like he spends all day in the gym."

Relief burst through her, making her knees weak, but Elizabeth clamped down on the emotion. There would be time to celebrate later, once the contracts were signed, her agency's with Devlin and his with Rory.

"That's exactly what we were trying to portray. His strength comes from working with his hands and his back, like so many Americans."

"Do you plan to weave that hardworking attitude into the campaign?"

"Definitely."

Devlin jotted down notes on the iPad. "What're the rest of your plans?"

"I thought we'd start with the Times Square billboard, since Devlin Designs has it booked for the next three months. We'd pair that with ads in the *New York Times,* the *Chicago Tribune* and *USA Today.*"

"I understand the newspapers' appeal, but I'm not so certain about the billboard. Sure, it'll be seen by millions of tourists, but other than that, how will it help us appeal to middle America?"

His question momentarily threw her off stride. Her grandmother's voice rang in her head. *Is that really the decision you want to make? Have you thought this through thoroughly, Elizabeth?*

Shaking herself mentally, she tuned out her grandmother. Elizabeth refused to be intimidated, when she'd prepared for this meeting until three in the morning, and this was one of the questions she'd anticipated. "I think showcasing Rory on June's billboard is the quickest way to create a buzz while we're finalizing magazine ads and shooting the TV commercial. When people see Rory's picture, they'll want to know who he is. Women will hit your website en masse to find out more about him. We'll add a new page to the site—meet Devlin De-signs' newest model. We'll get him tweeting, to add to the buzz. That excitement should help me book spots for him on the morning show circuit."

Devlin tapped his pen on the table. "Plus the bill-board should give us a boost to our East Coast sales."

Elizabeth nodded, the knot between her shoulder blades loosening. What was it about Devlin that cracked her self-confidence? "The average man is going to want to look like Rory. Women will think if their man wears your jeans he'll look like Rory. The gay man is going to want to date him. No matter what, they're going to check out Devlin jeans. I think we'll get an excellent return on the investment. Even though we're targeting a different market, everything fashionwise starts here in New York."

"Since we can't use the ad we'd planned on for the May billboard because of that model's scandal, let's showcase the jeans and introduce Rory instead."

Elizabeth stared at Devlin, momentarily stunned. A billboard took a minimum of two weeks to put together, and today was April 16.

What did this guy think? That she twitched her nose like Samantha on *Bewitched,* and billboards magically appeared?

"If we go with this shot—" Elizabeth pointed to the easel and Rory's gorgeous beefcake photo "—we might be able to pull it off."

"I like it. An outdoor scene on a billboard will clut-ter up the message anyway. I don't want anything dis-tracting from the cowboy, the slogan and the company name." Devlin clicked his pen as he thought. "Do what you have to, within reason, to get the job done. If you think the budget needs to be revised, let me know."

Elizabeth nodded. So much for sleeping for two days after this meeting.

"What's this cowboy's voice like?" Devlin asked. "Can he do the commercial work or will we need to hire a voice-over actor?"

"Rory has a pleasant voice with a slight Western drawl, which will work perfectly for the campaign."

"Pleasant? We need more than that for our spokesman."

"Forgive me. That was a poor choice of words. His voice is hardly average." She couldn't tell this Fortune 500 CEO that Rory's voice sent ripples of excitement through her and made her lace panties damp. Or could she? "The women at the shoot commented that his voice was as good as his looks."

"I've got a lot riding on this. Before I sign this cowboy and the agency contract I want to know what he sounds like."

Warning bells clanged in Elizabeth's head. Considering Rory's unpredictable behavior at the photo shoot, the thought of him meeting Devlin sent dread snaking down her spine. She counted to ten.

Never let a client see uncertainty. It's the kiss of death.

She smiled at Devlin. "Do you want to meet him in person or would a demo CD work?"

Please say the latter.

Devlin had been about to answer her when his cell phone played "I Could've Danced All Night." He grabbed it out of his briefcase. "Excuse me. I have to take this."

Phone to his ear, he stepped outside the conference room.

She couldn't believe that Micah Devlin, who chastised her when she took a call from another client with an "emergency," had answered his phone. Obviously, he subscribed to the do-as-I-say, not-as-I-do philosophy.

"What's up?" his surprisingly gentle voice floated in through the open door. "Can it wait? My day is full of meetings."

While Elizabeth longed to scoot her chair to where she could actually see him as he talked on the phone, she resisted the urge. Innocently overhearing a conversation and openly eavesdropping were two different things, and she had no desire to be caught doing the latter.

"Don't do that," Devlin almost pleaded. "You know the doctor told you not to drive for three weeks. Please wait." Frustration crept into his voice. "I'll run by the pharmacy after this meeting. I'll be there in a half an hour tops." Again he paused. "I love you, too, Nana."

Elizabeth hoped she'd concealed her shock when he returned to the conference table, phone in hand, the softness she'd heard in his voice only seconds ago nowhere visible in his eyes. Who would've thought he actually had relatives, much less one he cared about?

"Since Rory McAlister will be a company spokesperson, I want to talk to him face-to-face. I need to make sure he can have a coherent conversation."

Elizabeth swallowed hard. Sure she knew Rory's voice sent a women's happy hormones into overdrive, but how would he do when a reporter tossed questions at him? How could she have forgotten that when she'd developed the campaign? Details mattered, especially to Devlin.

"I met Rory on a ranch in Colorado. He's used to interacting with tourists. He was quite engaging with facts and local-color tidbits." At least he'd appeared to be, from the bits and pieces of stories she'd heard, riding at the end of the line of horses.

"He'd better be able to handle interviews."

"I assure you he will." Elizabeth smiled. By his first interview she'd be certain he was prepared. She could make a fortune in Vegas playing high stakes poker with her bluffing skills.

"Once I've talked with this cowboy and am convinced he'll suit our needs, I'll sign him to a contract. Then I'll sign the jeans contract with your agency. Set up the meeting for tomorrow."

She noted he hadn't mentioned renewing the other lines' contracts. He probably still wanted that leverage to hold over her.

Devlin pulled his iPhone out of his pocket and punched a couple of buttons. "Ten works for me. I don't want to see his face everywhere, by the way. When the public sees him, I want them to think of Devlin Designs."

"I agree. I suggest you have your legal department add an exclusivity clause to the standard contract."

"You don't think his agent will balk?"

"He's currently representing himself."

Devlin smiled openly for the first time. "Then there's no need to pay him thirty grand over the course of this campaign. What do you think we can get him for?"

Sleep deprivation had to be playing tricks with her hearing, or had rotted her brain cells, because they'd extensively discussed what to pay a spokesman, even an unknown, before she'd started her search. "I told Rory he'd make thirty thousand, as per our discussions."

Devlin picked a piece of lint off his spotless shirt. "When we talked, we discussed a lot of options, from models to rodeo cowboys. That amount seems a little steep for an unknown with no experience."

Elizabeth swas seated and folded her hands in front of her to keep from shaking the man silly. Glancing into his eyes, she realized the truth. He'd changed his mind about the money when he'd discovered Rory lacked an agent.

"Offer him twenty thousand," Devlin stated.

"This puts me in an awkward position. Rory and I had a verbal agreement."

Devlin folded his arms across his chest. His sharp gaze bore through her. "I pay your agency to negotiate with models on my behalf."

What was it lately, with men drawing a line in the sand with her? "I'll inform Rory of your wishes, and will do everything in my power to get him to agree to the new terms."

"Make sure you've dealt with the money issue by the time we meet tomorrow."

"I'd feel more comfortable taking a day or two to prepare before I discuss the subject with Rory."

"I want him signed to a contract so we can move forward with this campaign." Devlin's icy tone and granite gaze left no room for further discussion.

"I'll talk to him today."

CHAPTER FIVE

ELIZABETH WALKED DOWN the hallway to Chloe's office and suppressed the urge to bang her head against the wall.

"Shoot me now and put me out of my misery. I've lost the will to live," she said as she sank into the wooden chair in front of her friend's desk. Now that the adrenaline and caffeine had worn off, exhaustion claimed her.

Chloe paled. "Do I need to update my résumé for the next round of layoffs?"

"No, but you might want to measure me for a straitjacket, because I'm going to lose my mind working with Devlin."

"What happened?"

"I have two new problems. The first being Devlin wants to meet with Rory before he'll sign the contract."

"Why is that a problem? Rory's perfect."

"He's a cowboy, and his mystical cowboy charm won't work on Micah Devlin."

"Rory will do fine."

"I'm not so sure. When I first gave him the jeans for the shoot, he said no real man would be caught dead in them. Can you believe that?"

"Since you're still talking about Rory in the present tense, I assume you didn't kill him. But what did you do after he said that?"

She glared at her friend. "I'm not the Wicked Witch of the East, you know."

"I didn't say you were. It's just you get a little over-zealous sometimes, especially when people make mistakes in their job."

"I very calmly and professionally pointed out the important points of being a company spokesperson."

"I bet that went over like a lead balloon. Guys love having a woman tell them they screwed up."

"I think he took it well, but after the jeans comment, you can see why I'm concerned about him talking with Devlin. All I need is for Rory to say something negative about the product."

"He won't, since you set him straight."

"You're just saying that because he's good-looking. In an interview situation, he'll have to think on his feet, and who knows what someone might ask him? What if he doesn't stop to think before he answers, and blurts out the first thing that pops into his head?" Once Elizabeth started voicing her concerns, she couldn't hold them back. "Sure, he's photogenic, but I have no idea what kind of education Rory has, or whether he can hold an intelligent conversation. What if he can't talk about anything but horses, mucking out a stall and fixing fences?"

"Whoa. Can we slow down this runaway train? Rory doesn't need to be a Rhodes scholar to do well on the morning show circuit. He's got a great personality and charisma. Those two things can't be taught, and will go a long way in an interview. Plus you'll prep him."

When Elizabeth opened her mouth to speak, Chloe held up her hand. "If you're worried about anything else, talk to Rory. Find out about his education and background. Ask him how he feels about doing interviews."

"Men have such fragile egos. What if he hasn't graduated high school, and my asking about his education embarrasses him? There has to be a reason he's a cowboy and not a white-collar businessman. He might get mad enough to quit."

"How much sleep have you gotten this week?"

"Not much."

"You must be dead-tired, Elizabeth. This kind of situation never flusters you. In fact, you thrive on a challenge."

"I'm beginning to understand why sleep deprivation is so effective in breaking down prisoners of war." Elizabeth walked to the small refrigerator in the corner of Chloe's office, pulled out a can of Red Bull, popped the top open and took a long drink. Within seconds the caffeine bolted through her system, reviving her brain cells. "You're right. I can do this. I can use Rory's male ego to my advantage. I'll tell him I need his opinion on Devlin's concerns and the rest of the campaign."

"Guys like that. They're fixers."

"While we're talking, I can identify any weaknesses he might have in a business meeting or an interview situation."

"Good, problem number one under control. What's the second problem?"

Elizabeth squeezed the Red Bull can. The sound of crumpling aluminum filled the room. "Devlin has decided the money I quoted Rory, the price we discussed at length beforehand, is too much to pay. He wants me to renegotiate the deal."

Chloe leaned back in her chair and threw her hands in the air. "You're going down in flames."

"What happened to playing the encouraging best friend and colleague?"

"Sorry, I can't lie that well. No way is Rory going to take your news well. Not that I blame him. If someone quoted me one amount for a job, and then wanted to lowball me, I'd throw a fit, too."

"That's what I'm afraid of." Elizabeth resisted the urge to pick at her nail polish. "Devlin wants me to have renegotiated Rory's contract by tomorrow's meeting."

"Push the meeting back."

"I tried. Devlin refused."

"Sure sucks to be you."

Elizabeth grabbed a scrap of paper off the desk, wadded it up and tossed it at her friend. The shot fell short, landing in Chloe's lap. "I don't need you pointing out the obvious. What I need are suggestions on how to keep Rory from strangling me when I talk to him."

"The best you can hope for is avoiding a major scene and/or violence."

Elizabeth laid her head on the desk. "You're right. I'm going down in flames." She peeked up at Chloe. "Where did you go the last time you were going to break up with a guy and you were worried he'd make a scene?"

"I'll chalk up that comment as a stress-induced insensitivity." Chloe tossed the wad of paper at Elizabeth, and it bounced off her head. "When I was worried Jason would make a scene when I broke up with him, I did the deed at Bar American."

"Brilliant idea." Elizabeth straightened. "Hope

springs eternal. No one makes a scene at a restaurant, especially one of Bobby Flay's."

"That idea will cost two white peach margaritas from Mesa Grill."

"Well worth the price, and speaking of Mesa Grill, I think we'll eat there. The Southwestern food and atmosphere are more Rory's style." Elizabeth stood and walked across the room. "I'm off to call him. Hopefully he hasn't eaten yet. I've got the making-a-scene issue under control, but how am I going to convince him to take a pay cut?"

"I have no idea. You're on your own there."

"That's what I'm afraid of."

As she walked out of Chloe's office, she told herself to think positive and pray, because that was her only hope—divine intervention.

ELIZABETH ARRIVED at the restaurant fifteen minutes early, in the hopes that by the time Rory showed up she'd have developed a strategy to convince him to agree to the pay reduction. As she waited, she told herself she wasn't doing anything wrong. Rory hadn't been signed to a contract. She acted on behalf of the client with the model. Despite all those logical reasons, the thought of renegotiating his contract left her feeling a little sleazy.

She'd think positive. Would convince him this setback wasn't permanent. He could turn this into an opportunity to impress the client, and get a huge raise on the next contract.

Elizabeth thought for a minute. How lame was that? Unless Rory was comatose, no way would he buy it.

She glanced around the restaurant. Hanging on one

wall was a picture of a cow. Another had a picture of John Wayne in classic cowboy pose and dress. The booth upholstery was a print of cowboys on horses. Rory would fit right in. The restaurant should remind him of hearth and home, and hopefully put him in a good mood.

By the time he arrived, ten minutes late, she hadn't come up with a better option. After the maître d' showed him to the table, Elizabeth bit her lip and resisted the urge to lecture him about the importance of promptness for business meetings.

His hair was damp, as if he'd just crawled out of the shower, and curled at the collar of his plain white shirt. With that he wore a pair of navy slacks. She smiled when she noticed he still had on his cowboy boots and the royal flush belt buckle. Cowboy *GQ*. Not bad. Her pulse jumped. Seeing him now made her realize what a fool Devlin was to risk losing Rory by haggling over money.

"I appreciate you meeting with me after such a long day." She looked pointedly at her watch once he sat across from her.

"I had to eat. This way you're picking up the tab."

Elizabeth winced. If Rory was worrying about the cost of dinner, Chloe was right. She would go down in flames once she brought up renegotiating his salary.

For a moment she focused on the menu, not quite sure where to begin. Business meetings usually never bothered her, so why was this one making her uncomfortable? And it was more than the fact that she had to renegotiate his contract. Maybe because across the table from her sat one gorgeous man. She scoffed at the idea.

She'd been alone at similar meetings before with way better-looking male models.

Gay models. Big deal.

From the red-hot glance he'd tossed her when he'd pulled off his shirt this afternoon, the man had to be straight. No gay man could look a woman in the eyes like that and nearly singe her eyebrows.

The waiter took their drink orders, pulling her away from her unsettling thoughts. Deciding her brain was fuddled enough from lack of sleep, and this was a business meeting, she stuck with water. Rory ordered a beer.

To repair any damage she'd done to their karma that afternoon, Elizabeth said, "First of all, I wanted to apologize if I offended you in any way at the shoot today. I'm afraid I may have come off a little harsh. There's so much riding on this campaign, and it's put me a bit on edge."

"I'm a big boy. I can take it."

His words, coupled with his sultry gaze, sent tremors rippling through Elizabeth. She grabbed her water glass and took a long sip, not quite sure what to make of his comment. The man either loved playing word games or was clueless about how what he said sounded to other people.

Since ignoring the comment provided the wisest course, Elizabeth barreled onward. "I wanted to apprise you of what transpired today in my meeting with Micah Devlin." Start with the positives. She sucked in a deep breath and smiled. "He was very happy with your photos. He thinks you definitely have the image and the presence he's looking for to represent his company's jeans."

Rory nodded, grabbed a slice of sourdough bread and slathered it with butter. "What's our next step?"

Out of the corner of her eye Elizabeth noticed an attractive redhead with perfect teeth flashing a smile Rory's way.

"We hope to get you on some morning shows."

He nodded again, revealing no signs of panic in his voice or his facial expression. Good. Elizabeth relaxed her grip on her water glass.

The redhead continued to stare. A stunning blonde at the bar looked at Rory as if she wanted to skip dinner and go straight to him for dessert.

On the good-news side, he garnered exactly the reaction Elizabeth had hoped for with women. On the negative side, having them openly drooling over him set off a feeling alarmingly close to jealousy in her.

"How do you feel about doing interviews?" she asked. "Have you had any experience with that kind of situation?"

"I've been interviewed for the local paper a time or two."

"Good." That was better than nothing. Barely. "Then you're used to having a reporter ask you questions." Elizabeth almost stumbled over her words. What kind of tough questions could a local reporter ask? *What do you think of the price of grain at the feed store?* "Sometimes a reporter will put you on the spot. If you think it'll make you more comfortable, we could do some practice interviews."

"Whatever you say."

Why was he being so agreeable? Nervousness tickled her spine. This couldn't be the same man who'd refused to take off his shirt earlier today. Something was up, and from her interactions with Rory so far, she reasoned it couldn't be good. Either that or the man had undergone a stubbornectomy since their photo shoot.

She shook herself mentally. Quit borrowing trouble.

The waiter placed a glass in front of Rory, then poured the bottled beer and asked if he could take their orders.

"The ancho chile-honey glazed salmon is superb. I highly recommend it." She turned to the waiter. "In fact, that's what I'll have tonight."

He nodded and turned to Rory.

"I'll have the rib eye, rare, and a side of mashed potatoes."

It figured he was a meat-and-potatoes guy. She took a drink of water and focused on her goal.

"Back to the interviews," Elizabeth said, once the waiter departed. "When I met you in Colorado, you seemed fairly comfortable talking to people."

"I hold my own."

"On the guided tours you talk about your local community and its history. Are you comfortable talking about other things?"

His right eyebrow inched upward. "I'm aware of what's going on in the world. We get cable and everything in Estes Park."

She mentally cringed. How did she keep managing to say the wrong thing? She'd never been prone to that before. "I didn't mean to imply you didn't. I was wondering what topics you felt comfortable talking about in an interview."

"I can talk about most anything. Being in the tourist industry has taught me to think on my feet. You wouldn't believe some of the situations that come up."

Then he smiled. She almost reached into her purse for her sunglasses. "Or maybe you would, considering our first meeting."

Her mouth went dry. His smile could make Mother Teresa sin. Elizabeth had to get that smile on film.

"The main thing to remember in interviews is to be upbeat and personable."

"And to be positive about the client's product. See, I can be taught."

She laughed. The man possessed quite a sense of humor. "I forget that this is all new to you, and you're not a professional model. I also proposed television commercials to Devlin as part of the campaign. He wants to meet you before we go further. He's a bit of a control freak."

"Takes one to know one."

She bristled until she looked at him. Humor shone in his sparkling brown eyes. "I could say the same for you."

"Sure could. That's what made today's photo session hard for me. Seemed like everyone was telling me what to do. I'm not used to that."

She made a mental note to slow down and explain things to him on future shoots.

"FYI, the only one you need to listen to is me, unless the client's present."

"I'll keep that in mind."

She liked this easygoing man a lot better than the pain-in-the-ass model from earlier in the day. Too bad she had to spoil things by bringing up salary issues.

"Devlin wants to meet you tomorrow at ten. Will that work for you?"

"I'm at your service."

Rory's slow drawl wrapped around her, sending a rush of heat through her system. If he used that voice in TV commercials, women would cause a stampede on their way to department stores to buy Devlin's men's jeans.

"I appreciate your flexibility," she said as their waiter placed their entrées in front of them.

The redhead who'd been eyeing Rory since he arrived, now finished with her meal, sauntered toward their table on a roundabout way to the front door. All the while she eyed Rory like an air force pilot preparing for a precision strike. She slowed down beside their table and then "accidentally" dropped her purse right at Rory's feet.

He reached down, picked up the woman's crimson leather bag and held it out to her. When she accepted it, she none too subtly slipped a piece of paper into his hand, smiled and strutted away.

How could she hit on a guy when he was with another woman? Elizabeth was amazed at such tackiness. She stared at Rory and waited. What straight man under the age of eighty wouldn't take this gorgeous woman up on what she so obviously offered?

He tossed the paper on his bread plate without even glancing at the note.

Wonders never ceased. Elizabeth scooped up a piece of salmon. Knowing her time was running out, she found the expertly cooked fish tasted like paper in her mouth. She needed to get to the money issue before they finished their entrées. "Is there anything you're concerned about with our meeting tomorrow with Devlin?"

"Should I be?"

No, I'm the one who should be worried, since Devlin wanted me to renegotiate your salary.

She shook her head. "Devlin wants to meet you before he officially puts his stamp of approval on the campaign and signs the contracts, but we shouldn't have any problems. You're the right person for the job."

She knew she should bring up the subject of money, but couldn't. The topic change would bring their pleasant dinner to a quick and deadly end. "How long have you lived in Colorado?"

"All my life. I'm third-generation. All my family's there."

She couldn't imagine living where her parents and grandparents lived. Probably because her parents never stayed very long in one place.

"How 'bout you?"

"I've lived in New York state all my life, but I've only lived here in the city since I graduated from college."

She paused, hoping he would share his educational background with her. When he didn't, she gathered it was probably because he lacked a college education.

When the waiter cleared away their dinner plates, Elizabeth knew she couldn't avoid the salary issue any longer. She took a long drink of water and then forced the words past her tight throat before she chickened out. "There was one thing Devlin wanted me to discuss with you before tomorrow's meeting." She swallowed hard, struggling to choose the correct words. Hell, there weren't words that would make this any easier. "Seeing as you have no name recognition and no experience—"

"You said that made me interesting."

He remembered that, huh? Figured. He possessed the most inconvenient memory. "Name recognition and

experience are vital in the modeling industry, and fac-
tor into what a company is willing to pay. Because you
lack those two things Mr. Devlin feels thirty thousand
for the campaign is a little high. He thinks twenty thousand is more reasonable."

There. She'd gotten the words out. She waited for
the hurricane to hit.

"We agreed to thirty thousand," Rory said, his voice
low and unexpectedly calm, like the air before the storm
hit and tossed trees and buildings around.

"Yes, that's what we discussed, but we haven't signed
a contract."

She considered telling Rory to get an agent to watch
out for his best interest, but her conscience balked at
the idea. She and Rory worked for Devlin Designs. In
this situation she represented her agency and her client, not the model.

Rory crossed his arms over his chest. His gaze
drilled into her. "I can head right on back to Colorado.
My job there's waiting for me. It's no skin off my nose."

CHAPTER SIX

AFTER DELIVERING HIS ULTIMATUM, Rory took a long swallow of beer, hoping the icy liquid would calm his rising temper. He should've known better than to trust Lizzie. Obviously, he hadn't learned the don't-trust-career-driven-city-women lesson well enough from Melissa.

Memories rushed back. They'd met at Harvard, and he, young idealistic fool that he'd been, had fallen madly in love. They'd made plans for a future together, or least he thought they had.

He'd believed Melissa loved him enough to follow him to Colorado. When she accepted his proposal she'd agreed to live with him on the ranch, but the closer the wedding date loomed on the calendar, the more she waffled, until she finally admitted she'd changed her mind. She wanted him to move to Boston instead, and if he wouldn't the engagement was off.

Now here he sat across the table from another bossy city woman, and apparently Lizzie thought him a complete idiot. What did she expect him to say when she announced the client wanted to throw their deal out the window and renegotiate?

Sure, you can screw me over. I'll let you.

No way would he roll over and play dead. He wouldn't go down without one helluva fight. Not when his mom's life was at stake.

Rory carefully folded his napkin and placed it on the table. A deal was a deal. "I specifically asked you what this job would pay, and you told me thirty thousand. If there was a chance the job would pay less, that was the time to tell me."

Elizabeth paled.

Good. No way would he make this comfortable or easy for her.

"In my own defense, I discussed the issue with Devlin, and thought we were clear on this." She shifted uncomfortably in her chair. "Yesterday was the first time he mentioned not wanting to pay you that amount."

"He needs to honor our agreement, and so do you."

Rory prided himself on conducting his business honestly and above reproach. Obviously, Devlin possessed fewer scruples.

"While you and I had discussed your monetary compensation, until a contract is signed there isn't a formal agreement in place with the client, and renegotiation is possible."

"Is this how he does business?"

"I've never had a problem like this with him before."

"I'm just lucky then."

"I don't blame you for being upset."

He couldn't let her know how important this job was to him, but he couldn't let her and Devlin screw him on the deal, either. "I'm past upset. I'm about ready to tell the guy to go to hell."

"Then we'll both be out of a job."

"And Devlin will be out of a spokesperson." Rory leaned back in his chair. "He'll have to start his search all over."

"Everybody loses then. What good does that do?"

"It'll make me feel damn good. I won't play the fool."

"No one is doing that. This is a business decision. You have to prove to Devlin that you'll increase sales enough to justify what he's paying you. If you had modeling experience, you could point to previous campaigns, and what they'd done for the company."

"Just because I don't have the numbers to prove it doesn't mean I won't bring in money."

"I agree. In fact, I'm banking on that very fact, but Micah Devlin is a numbers man. If he can't see it on paper, it doesn't exist."

"Is this a deal breaker for Devlin?"

"I honestly don't know, but it very well could be. He mentioned that cowboys had to be a dime a dozen."

"I don't see a whole lot of them in New York City." Rory waved his arm around the room. "You see a lot of cowboys here?"

"I tried all these arguments with Devlin. Between you and me, and if you mention this to anyone I'll deny it, I don't agree with what he's doing."

"But here you are, asking me to work for less."

"Devlin Designs is my client. I have to respect the CEO's wishes." Her finger drew lines in the condensation on her water glass. "If you want to keep your job, the best thing to do is agree to Devlin's demands."

"I've met this kind of businessman before. He doesn't care who he plows over as long as the deal works out well for him."

"Help me out here." Elizabeth leaned forward and placed her small hand on his forearm.

Her simple touch sent off shock waves through his system stronger than a kick from an unbroken horse, momentarily sending him into a giant fog.

"I sense we both want to find a solution to this problem," she continued. "I don't want to see you get screwed, but Devlin's met with other agencies. He could go with someone else."

"I can't take less money." If Rory gave in now, Devlin would try to screw him again somewhere down the road. "I do more than give tours. I breed horses. Sometimes on paper a foal doesn't look like he'll be anything out of the ordinary. Then when I work with him I see something special, something I can't put a finger on. You know those intangibles you were talking about."

She nodded.

"When I come across a horse like that, I'm going to drive a hard bargain when I sell him. What I'm saying is I'm an experienced horse trader. No one's going to take advantage of me."

AT NINE-FIFTY the next morning, Elizabeth met Rory in the agency reception area and ushered him to her office, closing the door behind them. A night of worry and anger threatened to choke her. "Please tell me you've changed your mind about your salary demands."

Rory shook his head. "The man told you he'd pay me thirty. That's what you told me. A deal's a deal."

She hated stubborn men. She ought to put Rory and Devlin in a room and let them fight it out, because she'd had enough of both of them.

"There's nothing I can do to talk you out of this?"

"Nope."

She reminded herself to breathe. Maybe when faced with Rory's defiance, Devlin would back down.

Sure, and as Chloe often said, pigs would fly.

At least Rory was dressed like the cowboy spokesman Devlin wanted. He wore the same navy shirt he'd worn when they'd met, plus his boots and his royal flush belt buckle. "I'm glad you had the common sense to wear the client's jeans."

"Don't give up, Lizzie." He reached out to her, but at the last minute pulled back and shoved his hand in his pocket. "You might be surprised how this meeting turns out."

His smooth, cool voice wrapped around her, and the confidence in his eyes almost had her believing him. Wait a minute. How could he remain this calm and collected unless he was up to something?

"Tell me you don't have some harebrained scheme planned."

"Would I do that?"

"I don't know you well enough to answer that question." Elizabeth shook her head. "No, that's not true. I suspect you'd try just about anything to get your way."

"Harebrained ideas aren't my style."

These two men were going to kill her. Either that or drive her completely insane if she didn't rein them in. But before she could respond, her office phone buzzed. She reached around Rory, grabbed her phone and answered the inside line.

After ending the call, she picked up her Netbook off her desk. "Devlin's waiting. Don't try anything we'll both regret. He's a very astute businessman and doesn't like to be questioned."

"I wouldn't dream of it."

"I recognize sarcasm when I hear it, and I don't appreciate it. At least listen to what the man has to say. He's always been reasonable in the past."

"I have to do what's right."

"Please…" She reached out and placed her hand on his forearm. Muscles rippled under her palm, sending corresponding waves ricocheting through her. "Remain open-minded."

A second later he broke the contact. As she and Rory walked toward the conference room, she couldn't help but think she was heading into a business meeting that would end in a pissing match. As the only non-testosterone-filled party present, she'd be utterly doomed.

When they entered the conference room, she introduced the two men and they shook hands.

"I don't believe in running around the mountain," Rory said as he sank into a leather chair across from Devlin at the conference table. "I climb straight to the top. I heard you had concerns about the campaign."

Elizabeth cringed as she sat beside Devlin and booted up her Netbook. Hadn't the cowboy ever heard of small talk and tact? She turned to Devlin. "Rory and I met last night." She tossed him an I-talked-with-him-like-you-told-me-to look. "I shared some of your concerns regarding the campaign."

"My first concern has been addressed," Devlin said. "I wanted to make sure your voice will work in commercials and in public appearances."

"I'm glad we have that settled." Elizabeth retrieved the file containing her notes. "Rory and I discussed him doing spots on morning shows." She glanced at her file to refresh her fuzzy, sleep-deprived brain, then swiveled her chair toward Devlin. "Rory's had experience with the local media. Morning shows won't be his first interview situation. Also, his work with tourists from all over the world has taught him to deal with unusual situations and to think on his feet."

She smiled. Could she spin a situation or what?

"National morning shows are very different from being interviewed by local reporters," Devlin said.

Rory leaned forward in his chair and braced his elbows on the table. "People are people. I figure if I treat these high-priced morning show hosts with respect, I ought to do fine."

Respect? Sirens blared in Elizabeth's head, sensing where Rory's thoughts had turned. Her mind scrambled to determine a way to derail him before he blasted Devlin. *Say anything. Just get the words out before Rory does.* "That attitude will definitely come across on TV, and people will relate to Rory for that. Don't you agree, Micah?"

"I have a lot riding on this campaign," Devlin said to Rory.

"As long as I represent your company, in public no one will see me in jeans other than yours."

"As it should be."

Rory nodded. "I'll talk up the product. I can tour the rodeo circuit. I know a few boys that might be able to get us some publicity in that market. What you see here is what you get. I pride myself on honesty."

Elizabeth opened her mouth to say something, but snapped it shut instead, deciding to sit back and watch the show. Rory had said he was an experienced horse trader. He hadn't been joking. The cowboy was holding his own with Devlin. No small accomplishment, considering Devlin held an MBA.

"I expect the same from you," Rory added. "Which brings me to the issue of money. We had a verbal agreement regarding my payment, and now you're going back on your word."

"This is business, and until there's a signed contract, everything is negotiable." Devlin straightened in his chair. "With your experience, thirty thousand for a campaign is a bit high."

"I'm worth every penny." Rory leaned forward.

The man's confidence astounded her, and was in fact a thing of beauty to watch.

"There's a fine line between confidence and arrogance." Devlin's hands tightened around the upholstered chair arms as he glared at him.

"I have a proposition for you," Rory said, clearly unfazed by Devlin's harsh look. "I did some checking on the internet last night. From what I gathered, a spokesman is usually paid every time pictures are taken or a commercial is shot. Then he gets paid again when ads run in magazines, newspapers or on TV. He also gets paid more for interviews."

Devlin nodded.

Elizabeth sat back, somewhat shocked. Sure, people could discover just about anything on the web, but that didn't mean they understood what they read. Rory actually sounded as if he knew what he was talking about.

"From what I read, the spokesman makes more money that way than with a flat fee, but I read about something called a buyout. I'll sign a contract today for thirty grand."

Thin lines formed around Devlin's mouth. "I have no guarantee you can pull off interviews or a TV commercial. I'm taking all the risk here."

"Then I'll have my agent call you."

Rory's little gem of news hit Elizabeth right between the eyes. Anger clogged her throat. Agent? How dare he not mention he'd signed with someone?

Wait a minute. Rory couldn't have gotten an agent in the last two days. She relaxed. He was bluffing, and doing a damned good job of it.

Devlin's angry eyes pinned Elizabeth like a butterfly in a child's science project. "You said he was representing himself."

"That's what I was told."

"If money's going to be an issue, we can stop things right here. I'll get an agent, and you can deal with him." Rory crossed his arms over his broad chest. His determined gaze drilled into Devlin. "Who would you rather negotiate with? I'm guessing it's me, but the choice is up to you."

Elizabeth held her breath and waited. She'd just witnessed horse trading at its finest.

"I'm willing to go as high as twenty-five, but I want the payments made in thirds over the course of the contract."

"I want half up front forty-eight hours after I sign the contract."

"Deal, but I want everything we've agreed to today put into the contract." Devlin held out his hand, and he and Rory shook on it.

Miracles did happen. Elizabeth closed her eyes to hide her relief. When she opened them, she reached for her Netbook. "I'll write up the contract terms as negotiated, and let you both review it. Then you can send it to your legal department, Micah."

Both men nodded.

"I'll have the agency's contract to you later today," Devlin told Elizabeth. He turned to Rory. "If you give me your email address, I'll send you our contract with you. I'd like to have it signed by early next week so we can proceed with the campaign."

"I'll sign it as soon as I have a lawyer look over it."

Ten minutes later, a slightly shell-shocked Elizabeth escorted both men to the reception area. Once Devlin left, she faced Rory. "You should have told me what you intended to do."

"If I had, would you have trusted me?"

"No."

"That's why I didn't tell you."

"While your show was entertaining, and you came up with a good solution that benefited everyone, don't ever pull something like that again."

A WEEK LATER Rory thought he'd lost his mind. All he did was stand around and let people take pictures of him all day, and sit around the hotel watching any sports event he could find on TV all night.

He'd talked to Griff a few times. The first time, he'd called to get an update and make sure Devlin's check cleared. So far, his little brother was doing a fine job managing the ranch in his absence. Not being missed there had been a tough pill to get down.

Restless and needing to see the sky above his head, Rory decided to take a walk. He missed being outside, being active. He'd tried working out in the hotel gym, and that helped some, but he needed to feel fresh air and the sun on his skin. Remembering his agreement with Devlin, he pulled off his worn Wranglers and tossed on the designer jeans before grabbing his hat and heading out.

The list of reasons he'd be happy once this gig was over kept growing, starting with the jeans. He'd never liked the blasted things no matter how much he wore them, and they still made him feel like a sissy.

He hadn't walked a block when his cell phone rang.

"Thought I'd let you know we signed the papers for Jameson to buy Star's foal."

Good. That would help the ranch's cash flow. "Don't let him pick up the foal until you've got confirmation the money's been transferred into our accounts."

"Got it."

"You're doing a good job, little brother."

Had he made it too easy for his siblings, always stepping in to take care of things when the situation got the slightest bit tough? Rory had thought he was helping. Being the oldest, he'd learn everything the hard way. He hadn't wanted his younger siblings to go the same route.

"I don't know how you do it. Managing this place is sure cramping my style. I was so damned tired last night I fell asleep at ten o'clock."

Rory laughed. "Not so easy to be the life of the party when you've got to get up at dawn."

"How are things going on your end?"

"It's been a long week." Rory rubbed his stiff neck.

"So modeling's not all bright lights and pretty girls?"

"It's hard work. I'm already tired of people telling me what to do."

Griff chuckled. "Getting a chance to see how the other half lives, huh?"

"Can't say I like it a whole lot." Rory stopped at the corner of Broadway and Forty-ninth and waited for the light to change. He'd learned early on that these New York City drivers would just as soon run someone over as stop to avoid him. "You heard from Mom? I called last night, but she was asleep. Avery says she's holding her own, but the treatment's tough on her."

"Avery said it's worse than chemo."

As long as the treatment didn't kill her, but killed the cancer.

"Keep me posted."

He ended the call. People rushed past him. Everyone here lived in such a hurry. No wonder Elizabeth fit right in. The woman was a whirlwind. Would she act like that in everything she did—that is, if she ever loosened up? If she focused that energy on a man, she could burn him to cinders in the bed. Rory smiled. What a way to go.

Someone bumped into him, mumbled a quick apology and scooted off. This walk wasn't accomplishing what he'd hoped. Instead of releasing his pent-up energy, being out on the streets had spiked his blood pressure.

He missed the quiet at home. When he hiked in the mountains, he could think. The solitude cleared his head. Whenever he took a walk here, he returned to the hotel with a headache.

He'd hoped the streets might be quiet this early in the morning, but no such luck. Neon lights flashed. Horns honked constantly. People hurried by. He glanced upward, hoping a glimpse of the sky would calm his nerves. Instead, the Times Square billboard caught his gaze. He froze.

No. It couldn't be.

Lizzie never mentioned anything about a billboard. He stared. No matter how hard he tried, he couldn't deny the reality slapping him in the face.

CHAPTER SEVEN

THERE HE WAS, big as the Rocky Mountains, wearing nothing but the blasted fancy designer jeans and his cowboy hat, his arms crossed over his chest for all the world to see. The words *Devlin jeans, strong enough for a real man* ran along the bottom of the billboard.

He scoffed. Leave it to Lizzie to come up with that slogan. As if any real man would wear these jeans....

And how in the heck did she get the blasted billboard done so fast?

He'd thought the photo shoot had been embarrassing. Seeing himself staring down from a billboard sent him skyrocketing to new heights of humiliation. How would he ever handle television commercials airing on stations in his neck of the woods? At least no one he knew would see this.

Think about the money and Mom. That would get him through.

"Is that you up there?"

He turned to find a twentysomething brunette, her hair pulled into a ponytail and a Texas Rangers baseball hat perched on her head, ping-ponging between him and the billboard.

"It is," her friend, dressed in jeans and an I love NY T-shirt, said. "He's wearing the same jeans, and look, he's got the same poker hand belt buckle."

"Yup, it's me." Unfortunately.

"Are you famous?"

"No." *Please, Lord, let this be the extent of my fame. Don't even give me fifteen minutes. That's way too much.*

"I bet you'll be famous soon," I Love NY said, her eyes glued on him as if he were the only stallion in the pasture.

Some men would think this scenario was a dream come true. "That's kind of you to say so," he mumbled.

I Love NY dug through her purse. A second later she handed him a Starbucks receipt and a pen. "Can I have your autograph?"

He almost asked her if she was kidding, before the manners his mother had drilled into his thick skull kicked in. "I'd be happy to. What's your name?"

"Lindsay."

He wrote "To Lindsay, thanks for being my first fan," and signed his name. This autograph stuff wasn't so bad. He might even grow to like it. "You ladies from New York?"

"We're here on a girls' vacation. We're from Texas."

"I should've guessed that." He pointed to the baseball cap.

The other woman handed him a scrap of paper. "My name's Judy."

He stood there trying to figure out something clever to write. Signing autographs was harder than a person would think unless he simply scrawled his name, or wrote something generic. He thought doing that was kind of a raw deal. Everybody liked to feel special. He finally settled on "Judy, enjoyed meeting you in NYC" and signed his name.

When he looked up from the scrap of paper, a crowd

of women had gathered and started tossing questions at him.

"Are you married?"

"No." Someone else shoved paper and pen into his hand. "Who should I make—"

"Seeing anyone?"

An image of Lizzie flashed before his eyes. How insane was that? The last thing he needed was a relationship with another city woman. "Not right now."

He scrawled his name on the paper and held it out. To heck with making them feel special. He just wanted to get out of here. This many women, all focused on him, couldn't be good. One woman was unpredictable—a gaggle of them downright scary.

"Do you have any pictures?"

"Not right—"

"Do you live in New York?"

These women could teach police interrogation classes.

"I live in Colorado."

"Here's my business card," a tall blonde dressed in black pants and a blouse said. "Call me. We can go out to dinner."

"Would you like me to show you around the city? Here's *my* business card."

Wonderful, he could start a collection. He managed to toss a smile in the general direction from which the card came.

The circle around him grew tighter. He backed up, bumped into a woman and mumbled a quick apology. A tall redhead leaned toward him. "You and I could have a lot of fun. Let's get out of here."

He considered telling her he was gay, just to get rid

of her. But with the way his luck was going, she'd club him over the head and kidnap him to prove he wasn't, that he just hadn't met the right woman.

Before he could answer, the ladies all started talking at once, creating quite a noise. To the general crowd he blurted out, "Excuse me, I've got to go."

But when he stepped forward to leave, the circle didn't budge, and someone grabbed his arm. Fear shot through him. The women had him so surrounded that if he pulled away, he'd knock half of them down.

He turned to the heavyset woman at his elbow and smiled. "Would you mind letting go of my arm? I'm thinking I might need it later today."

She leaned closer, and the bitter smell of coffee assailed him. "I'm from Littleton. Where in Colorado are you from?"

"I'm from Estes Park."

Another woman grabbed his left arm. His fear spiked up a notch. "Ladies, if you don't let go, you're going to pull me apart like a wishbone."

"Only if you agree not to go anywhere."

Right now he'd agree to just about anything to get these two to free him. "I can stick around awhile."

Apparently satisfied with his promise to stay, the women released him.

But when an escape route presented itself he'd be outta here faster than a jackrabbit with a coyote on its tail. Only who knew how long one would take to appear?

Then someone pinched him on the ass. He jumped and spun around, looking for the guilty party, not quite sure what to do if he identified her.

He drew the line at grabby women. His chest tightened and his heart banged painfully against his ribs. It was either him or them, because he couldn't take this anymore. Deciding to call in reinforcements rather than trample the women as he broke free, he grabbed his cell phone and called Lizzie. "I need your help."

"What's wrong?"

A woman shoved a Wal-Mart receipt and a pen into his hand. "Will you sign an autograph for me?"

"Do you have any pictures like the one on the billboard to sign?" someone else yelled. "I'd love one of those."

He tried to tune out the barrage of questions. "They've got me surrounded. You have to help me get back to the hotel."

"Who?"

"What hotel are you staying at?" someone shouted at him.

They could torture him for days, but no way would he give out that information.

"Women have me surrounded," he said, cupping his hand, still clutching the now sweaty pen and paper, around his ear in an attempt to hear better. "There's a whole herd of them. They're asking for my autograph. They're asking if I have pictures like the billboard. I don't know what to do, and they won't let me leave."

"This is fantastic!"

"No, it's not." A camera flash went off in his face, momentarily blinding him. Great. Now he was completely defenseless.

"We have a few photos of the billboard shot. I'll be there with them in ten minutes. This is exactly the kind of reaction we want."

this kind of thing and had experience dealing with public appearances. Rory was completely out of his element. She made a mental note to prep him for these types of public situations. Her instincts told her this wouldn't be the last time someone recognized him.

"Ladies, Rory will be glad to talk to all of you. If you could just move back a little bit to give him some breathing room, that would be great."

While he signed autographs and answered personal questions, she told everyone they could find Devlin's men's jeans at most department stores. She and Rory made a pretty good team. Once they returned to the office, she'd call Devlin to tell him Rory had been recognized from the billboard, and that the reaction he'd received had been exactly what they'd hoped for.

The situation went great for about ten minutes. Then suddenly, a fortysomething woman dressed in skintight jeans and a rhinestone T-shirt cupped her hand around Rory's magnificent butt and goosed him. He jumped, his panicked gaze locking with Elizabeth's.

She placed her palm gently on the diva's arm. "Please treat Rory with respect."

"Are you accusing me of something?"

The woman tugged her arm free at the same time Elizabeth removed her hand. Elizabeth flew backward, knocking into part of the crowd. Coffee rained down.

Another woman grabbed Rory. The brittle sound of tearing material filled Elizabeth's ears. Glancing at him, she saw his shirtfront was ripped from the pocket to the waist, revealing his bronzed, toned chest.

The noise grew deafening. Women yelled about getting splashed with coffee. Some screamed as they fell to the sidewalk. Others threatened to trample them. Women lunged at Rory.

Elizabeth reached for the fallen ones. "Watch out. Don't step on anyone," Rory said as he helped a middle-aged lady to her feet.

Women shoved each other, trying to get away or to get to Rory. An even bigger crowd grew as passersby stopped to watch the scene. It looked like one of those old films, with the blundering cops falling over each other.

What had she done?

"This wasn't what I had in mind," Elizabeth said as she helped another woman to her feet.

"You didn't mean to start a catfight?" Rory asked.

She shook her head. "What do we do? How do I stop this?" She had experience creating buzz, not shutting it down.

"Running comes to mind."

A whistle blew, immediately halting the chaos.

"Who started all this?" a policeman asked as he approached.

Every person except Rory pointed to Elizabeth.

"Officer, this is all a terrible misunderstanding," she said, desperate to diffuse the situation and pacify the cop. "A crowd had gathered. People got a little close. Someone bumped into someone else, and then everything went crazy."

"Everything was fine until she got here," the woman in the rhinestone T-shirt yelled.

What was it with her? Did she wake up this morning intent on destroying someone's life, and Elizabeth held the lucky ticket?

"Everyone seems pretty clear you're the instigator.

Start at the beginning with why a crowd had gathered," the officer told Elizabeth.

She paused, not quite sure what to say. Police frowned on impromptu advertising events. They were sticklers for permits and advance notice. Both of which she'd forgotten in her excitement.

"Women started asking me for autographs when they recognized me from this," Rory said, pointing upward.

The officer glanced at the billboard. "Nice photo." He turned to Elizabeth. "Were you one of the autograph seekers?"

"I work with Rory."

"In what capacity? Are you his agent?" The man glared at her disapprovingly.

What she wouldn't give to be beamed out of this situation. Or to have the ability to erase everyone's memory, starting with this cop and the question he'd just asked. Because unless she lied, her answer would not make him happy.

She swallowed hard and prayed she could talk her way out of this sticky situation. "I'm not his agent. I'm the executive in charge of the ad campaign."

"You decided to stage an impromptu advertising event," the officer accused. "You thought you could get some free publicity without the hassle of getting the proper permits. When are you ad people going to realize you can't do that?"

"I absolutely did not stage this."

"I was feeling a little cooped up this morning, so I took a walk," Rory said. "When the crowd gathered I called Elizabeth to help me."

"What happened when you arrived?"

"She passed out pictures for him to sign, and started

bossing everyone around," one woman, probably the diva, said.

"She bumped into me and spilled coffee all over me," another added.

The officer raised his hands, silencing everyone. "I've heard enough. I'm giving you and cowboy guy tickets for disturbing the peace, unlawful assemblage, failure to obtain the proper permits, and anything else I can think of. This little stunt is going to cost your company a bundle, little lady."

"That's all you're going to do?" someone called out.

"You should arrest her for assault," another woman added.

"That might not be a bad idea."

If this kept up these women would get her life in prison. Talk about a mob mentality.

Rory glanced at the officer. "Can I speak to you alone, man to man?"

The cop nodded and motioned to the crowd. "The rest of you, break it up. If your clothes were damaged, get a business card from her."

When he pointed at Elizabeth, she said, "I'll be happy to pay for dry cleaning or replace any garments that can't be cleaned."

As she handed out business cards and the crowd dispersed, Rory said, "This is my fault. I'm new to all this stuff. A few weeks ago I was in Colorado giving horseback riding tours. Now here, today, I was surrounded by a group of women wanting my autograph. It's a little much for a simple cowboy to handle. They got very close, if you know what I mean."

The officer laughed. "I can see that from your shirt."

"That wasn't the only place they got grabby." Rory

shuddered. "They damn near scared me to death. I tried to leave, but they circled around me. The only way I could've escaped was to run the ladies over, but I was raised to treat women right."

Elizabeth watched in amazement as the officer's posture relaxed the longer he spoke with Rory. Give them five more minutes and they'd probably be fast friends.

The cop tilted his head toward Elizabeth. "What about her?"

"I called her. The crowd kept asking me for pictures, and I figured that if she brought some, they'd take the photos and go."

"You promise me nothing like this will ever happen again?"

"It won't, because if it did, it'd probably kill me."

The officer nodded and then turned to Elizabeth. "I want one of your business cards, because if I hear you've been involved in something like this again, I won't just ticket you. I'll haul you off to jail."

As LIZZIE AND RORY walked into her office, his anger threatened to boil over. If he was back home, he'd saddle Blaze and head for the mountains, hoping a long ride would clear his head and cool his temper. If that didn't work, he'd muck out a few stalls to burn off steam. Unfortunately, none of those options were available.

As Lizzie sank into her leather desk chair, he realized his best alternative would be putting his fist through her office wall.

She, on the other hand, had been a little ball of excited energy once she'd found out they weren't going to jail or getting ticketed.

"Tell me this kind of thing doesn't happen a lot," he finally said, once he'd calmed down enough to speak.

"Why are you so upset? Everything turned out fine, but you look like you're ready to hit something."

"Don't tempt me." Rory rested his fists on her desk. "You're wondering why I'm upset? We nearly got arrested. I don't know about you, but that's never happened to me before."

"But thanks to you, we weren't."

Only because he'd aw-shucked his way out of trouble. Not one of his proudest moments. He'd handled the situation only because he was doing this for his mom. If he wanted to live in a big city and be in crowds all the time, he'd have gone to Boston with Melissa.

Elizabeth swiveled toward her computer and punched a few keys.

"Did you see all the people videoing the scene on their phones? This is wonderful." She typed something on her keyboard. "I'm checking to see if it's on YouTube yet."

Rory shook his head. Had he heard her right? She couldn't have described the horror they'd just experienced as wonderful. "You're saying that there's no such thing as bad publicity?"

"Exactly." She spun her chair back around to face him. "It's not on YouTube yet, but I bet it will be tonight."

The sparkle in her ocean-blue eyes captivated him and took his anger down a notch or two. "Promise me this will never happen again."

"Gee, now I'll have to cancel the near riot I had scheduled for tomorrow."

He glared at her, more out of principle than genuine

anger. "Very funny. It's easy for you to joke about this. You didn't almost get your clothes ripped off."

"I'm sorry. I should've anticipated someone recognizing you from the billboard. If I had prepared you more, the situation wouldn't have gotten so out of hand."

"Next time I head out I'm either taking a guard dog or going on horseback for a quick getaway."

When she laughed, the warm rich sound filled him, evaporating the last of his irritation. "I'm sorry there's no room in the campaign budget for those items."

"If I'd known the risks, I'd have added them to my contract demands."

His gaze locked with hers. Something passed between them. Something Rory hadn't expected and didn't want to examine. Lizzie was wrong for him in so many ways, and the timing couldn't be worse.

Her cell phone rang, thankfully breaking the spell. He'd been just about to make a very wrong turn.

Elizabeth could barely contain her excitement when caller ID revealed her contact from *Wake Up America* on the line. While she wouldn't have planned a scenario like the one in Times Square, she certainly planned to make the most of the free publicity.

"I heard your new model is so hot he caused a riot," Brooke said.

"I told you he was going to be big. What can I say? Women go wild for this guy."

"We'd love to interview your cowboy. Have him at the studio by 5:00 a.m."

Between prepping him and proofing the material for the print ads that had to go out first thing in the morning, Elizabeth would be up all night. The things she gave up for the job. But who needed sleep, anyway? Getting more than four hours a night was highly overrated.

"He'll be there." She ended the call. "*Wake Up America* wants to interview you. Their studios are at Times Square. It seems everyone's talking about you."

"Will they expect me to talk about what happened? If they do, I'm not too clear on things. All I remember is all these women surrounding me, and let me tell you, there's nothing scarier than a herd of angry, grabby women. My whole life flashed before my eyes."

"My first tip is not to refer to the women as an angry herd, or you might find yourself facing another one." For the first time since she'd met Rory, uncertainty briefly flashed in his eyes. How surprising that a group of women put a kink in his armor. "Just remember to utilize that cowboy charm I've seen you wield so often."

"Cowboy charm?" He flashed her a grin that could sell whiskey to a teetotaler.

"Give Brooke that look that mesmerizes a woman, and makes her think you're going to grab her, toss her on your horse and ride off into the sunset."

"Do I do that for you?"

His warm, husky voice rippled through Elizabeth as he leaned forward in his chair and peered into her eyes. He had the slightest smile on his face. Oh, yeah, that was the look.

Horse and sunset, here I come.

"Apparently I have cowboy immunity. Must've been included in my childhood shots, because I don't get why women go all wild for you cowboys."

"If you took a chance, you might be surprised."

Her mouth went dry. Her mind went blank. Her heart

raced. This man was dangerous. He could get her to forget everything, including her own name.

Sometimes in the middle of the night when she couldn't sleep, she imagined letting go, of not living her life so tied to rules. She dreamed of finding a man—lately more often than not, Rory—to love her, but then reality crashed down.

"It takes a lot to surprise me."

"Is that a challenge?"

Sirens blared in her head. This game had gotten way out of control. The last thing she wanted was him thinking she'd challenged his manhood. Talk about waving a red cape in front of a bull. "We have a professional relationship, nothing more."

Maybe if she told herself that enough, she'd believe it.

He grinned. "If you say so, Lizzie."

"It's Elizabeth," she snapped, angry more over his comment than the use of his nickname for her. But the way he said it, combined with the way he looked at her, as if she were the scoop of ice cream on a slice of apple pie, made her toes curl. "Why do you persist in calling me Lizzie when I've asked you repeatedly not to?"

"It lights a fire in you, and puts the prettiest pink color in your cheeks."

Lit a fire in her? More toe curling. How could she be mad at him when he said that? "Of course it puts color in my cheeks. Calling me Lizzie makes me angry, or haven't you noticed?"

"I've noticed. It just doesn't bother me."

This man refused to be put in his place, scaring the hell out of her.

She stiffened, and reached for a file on her desk to keep her hands from shaking.

He stood and moved closer to her desk. His large body filled her vision. His musky scent wrapped around her. She inhaled deeply, then stopped herself, remembering that Rory didn't fit any of the criteria on her ideal-man checklist. In fact, he'd top her don't-date-this-kind-of-man list. So why did she find herself thinking about him way more than she should, and not in a businesslike manner, but in a very intimate way?

"You know what John Lennon said?" he asked.

"No, but obviously you're dying to enlighten me."

"Life is what happens while you're busy making other plans." Rory braced his hands on her desk and leaned close enough for her to notice he had the longest eyelashes she'd ever seen. "You're so busy making plans that you're missing out on life, Lizzie."

"I am not," she insisted lamely.

Terrific comeback, Elizabeth. That'll put him in his place.

"Saying it doesn't make it so."

"We need to prep for your interview tomorrow on *Wake Up America*," she said, pointedly ignoring his comment and desperately needing to reclaim control of the discussion. "What I think is—"

He straightened. "I need a hot shower after all those women pawed me."

"This can't wait—"

"Sure it can. Meet me at my hotel room at six. We can order room service and deal with the interview stuff over dinner."

"Meet me in front of your hotel at six. I'll drop by

in a taxi. We can pick up dinner and then head to my house to work."

No way would she be alone with him in a hotel room, where the only furniture would be a couple of tiny desk chairs and a king-size bed. Talk about risky business.

As ELIZABETH AND RORY sat in the cab on their way to her neighborhood deli, she questioned the wisdom of taking him to her town house. That was her personal space, her haven, and while she worked at home a lot, this felt like crossing the streams in *Ghostbusters*— something unknown and probably not good.

"How about we pick up takeout and head back to the office to work?"

"I've had enough of that place. If I'm working tonight, I want to kick back and relax."

"My office is—"

"It's your place, my hotel or nothing." He crossed his arms over his chest and flashed her the stubborn look she'd come to detest.

"My place it is."

She could handle the situation. They'd eat and discuss tomorrow's interview. She'd talk to him about what to expect and how he should respond. Same business meeting, just different location.

By the time the cab let them off in her neighborhood, she felt more relaxed, more under control.

"Guess I can say I now know how sardines feel," Rory said when they walked inside the deli and the cluster of people closed around them.

"The crowd's actually a little light tonight."

"I'd hate to see the place on a busy night. How do people keep from getting trampled?"

"There's an elaborate set of rules guiding traffic flow. I had to take a course when I moved to the city."

Rory froze and stared at her wide-eyed.

"What?"

"Was that a joke?"

She nodded. "Why is that so surprising?"

That right eyebrow rose. "I'd begun to think you had your funny bone surgically removed."

A woman bumped into Rory and mumbled a hasty apology. He cringed. "I'm having flashbacks." Then he sniffed the air and held out his arm to Elizabeth. "Do I smell like women's perfume?"

She stepped closer, careful not to get too close, and inhaled. Nothing but clean, musky, intoxicating maleness filled her senses. Now that was a fragrance to drive women crazy.

"You definitely don't smell like perfume. Why?"

"Some of those grabby women must've bathed in the stuff. Even though I've taken a shower, I can still smell their perfume on me."

Visions of Rory in the shower, his hard body wet and glistening, flashed in Elizabeth's mind. Fantasies bombarded her. So much for being in control.

The man behind the counter asked what they wanted. What a loaded question, with Rory standing beside her and desire thrumming through her system. She couldn't think.

She'd thought being alone with him in his hotel room was risky business. As they walked out of the deli, Elizabeth realized she had no idea what she'd ordered for dinner. Apparently just being with Rory was dangerous, and she was taking him home.

CHAPTER EIGHT

ELIZABETH HAD NEVER thought of her town house as small until Rory walked in. He more than physically filled the space; his essence overwhelmed it. And he looked so comfortable, so at ease.

So much for her town house feeling less risky than his hotel room.

Trying desperately to harness her raging hormones, she headed for the safety of her kitchen. "You'll have to excuse the mess," she said as they entered. "I'm in the process of remodeling."

She deposited the deli sack containing their dinners on the black granite counter, and shook her head in disgust. Only half the glass-and-stone backsplash had been installed. Except for the top one, the boxes of slate flooring hadn't been opened, and that was to have been installed today, as well. The project was already a week behind schedule. What had the tile guy done all day? Watch ESPN? "I can't believe it. They told me the backsplash and the floor would be done by now."

"You hired someone? They charge a fortune. Tiling isn't tough. You could've done the installation yourself."

No way would she do that kind of physical labor. "I went to college so I could make a good salary and pay people to do things like this for me." She stopped, embarrassed over what she'd said. Could she sound any more condescending to someone who worked with his hands? How much did ranch hands make, anyway? Probably not much. Maybe he only earned enough to scrape by. "That didn't come out right. I'm no good with power tools, and there's the whole learning curve thing, and time's an issue for me. I hired someone so the project would be done in a timely manner."

"If you did the work yourself you'd save a ton of money."

"You're obsessed with money," she countered. "I see it as my way of helping the economy by creating jobs."

Maybe Rory had grown up poor. People with his kind of money obsession often had. Even when they crawled out of poverty, they worried that one misstep would send them tumbling back.

"Your contractors left the tile adhesive." Rory pointed to a tub in the corner of the kitchen. "I could finish the backsplash in no time."

"I'm paying someone to do this."

"Fire him. He said he'd have the work done today, and he didn't. Did he call to say why he didn't finish?"

"I'm capable of managing this job."

"I'll take that as a no."

"Okay, so I need to stay a little more on top of things. I'll call the tile man tomorrow and find out what happened."

She pulled a bottle of cabernet out of the metal wine rack on the corner of her counter. "Want a glass of wine?" She definitely needed one. The man was driving her crazy, and she hadn't even started prepping him for the interview.

Rory nodded.

After opening the wine, she filled two crystal wineglasses and handed one to him. She took a big swallow before setting her glass on the counter. Scanning the directions on the lid of their entrées, she discovered they were having chicken Parmesan and bowtie pasta. "I don't cook much."

"Technically, you're not cooking now. You're reheating."

"I'm using the oven. As far as I'm concerned, that constitutes cooking." Elizabeth turned the dial to Bake and set the temperature for three hundred fifty degrees. "Do you want dinner or not? Keep in mind, those who criticize don't eat."

"Cooking it is."

A strange metallic odor filled the kitchen. "What's that awful smell?"

Rory smiled. What did he know that she didn't?

"Have you used the oven before?"

"No, it's new." Or was, three months ago.

"The oven gives off that smell the first time it's turned on."

She glared, annoyed at him for pointing out her ignorance. "How do you know that's what it is? Maybe I've got a gas leak or something."

"We bought my mom a new oven a couple years back. It gave off the same awful smell the first time she turned it on."

He had Elizabeth there. Her only culinary experience had occurred before the age of thirteen, with her grandmother, and those appliances had been ancient.

"Is it okay to use?"

"It's fine, but it'll stink for a while. Did you take the instruction manual out?"

"Damn." She grabbed the oven door and pulled, but it wouldn't budge. She tugged harder. Nothing. Now what?

Rory materialized beside her and peeled off the clear tape that held the oven door closed. Then he pulled out a plastic bag of paperwork. After tossing the packet into the sink, he stepped back.

Feeling like a complete fool, and thinking she should try out for the Food Network show *Worst Cooks in America,* she tossed the aluminum containers holding their dinners into the oven and slammed the door. "I've never gotten new appliances before."

"It sounds like you've done a lot to the place. How much of an equity boost will you get?"

"What do you know about that?"

"I know you have to make sure you don't put more money into a house than you'll get out when you sell it."

"I'll check with my designer on that."

"Check with a Realtor. The designer makes money off your remodeling. The more renovations, the more money she makes."

As Elizabeth moved around the kitchen, setting the table, the fact that he'd considered things she hadn't stung her pride. She was smart, and yet hadn't considered how much she was raising the value of her town house versus the renovation costs. She hadn't shopped around to get the best price on materials, either. How had she strayed so far from her usual thoroughness?

She'd forgotten those things because she'd been so desperate to make a home, a place that reflected her personality. A sanctuary that soothed her soul after a long day, and was truly hers. Something she'd missed since her grandmother died.

"You're so organized and in control in your job," Rory said. "You need to be the same with this project."

She smiled. "Was that a compliment?"

"Guess so."

Despite downplaying his praise, she found his words set off a warm glow inside her. He admired her as a businesswoman, but what did he think of her as a woman? *Don't go there.* Doing so would be like the dumb blonde in every horror movie that heard a funny noise, went to investigate and got killed by the psychopath. "Thank you. That means a lot to me, especially after today."

The oven timer beeped. She opened three drawers before locating the oven mitt Chloe had given her three years ago as a housewarming gift. Carefully, Elizabeth removed their dinners, plated them and placed them on her kitchen table.

"I thought we'd go over strategies for your interview while we eat."

"Woman, don't you ever take time off?"

"Tomorrow is important." She forced her voice to remain level and not to go into lecture mode, despite her annoyance. "It's your first national TV appearance. You need to be prepared."

"There's more to life than work. When do you loosen up and have fun?"

"I enjoy what I do."

"It's not the same thing. What about going out with friends? Spending time with family?"

His simple question unleashed that nagging little voice that had plagued her way too often lately. A picture of Nancy's tear-streaked face flashed in Elizabeth's mind. No, she wouldn't end up alone like that. She had time to find a good man, and weren't a lot of women doing just fine waiting until their late thirties before having children? So if that was true, why had his words caused her chest to tighten up?

"I have friends I socialize with," she insisted, though the words sounded hollow even to her.

She raised her chin in defiance, refusing to allow him to make her doubt her life. Two could play twenty questions. Time for Rory to be on the defensive. "You say all I care about is work, but all you seem to care about is money. What about that?"

"That is none of your business."

"Hurts to look in the mirror, doesn't it?"

"Since neither of us is perfect, how about we call it a draw?"

"Deal." She smiled. How could he so effortlessly pushed her buttons, and then equally as effortlessly deflate her irritation? Shaking herself mentally and remembering her goal for tonight, she said, "I know the situation today was hard for you personally, but don't you realize how amazing it was?"

Rory visibly shuddered. "I think what happened is going to give me nightmares."

"The reaction today means we can create an association in people's minds between the product and you. When people see your face they'll think of Devlin jeans."

"Kind of like when people see Morris the Cat they think of Nine Lives cat food."

She laughed. "That's an interesting comparison. Wonder what that says about you?"

"I didn't say *I* was like Morris the Cat."

No way would she compare him to anything as tame

as a house cat. A panther maybe, because all stretched out he appeared disinterested in the world, but in reality was keenly alert and ready to strike.

When they'd finished dinner and cleared the table, Elizabeth said, "To prepare, I thought I'd ask you possible interview questions. Then we'd go over ways you could answer."

"What a great way to spend an evening."

After refilling their wineglasses, they moved into the living room. As she sank onto her upholstered white couch and waited for Rory to get settled, she glanced around the room. The white sofa paired with the black chairs and a touch of red accents suited her minimalistic style perfectly. Then her gaze focused on Rory, and she found herself biting her lip to keep from laughing.

His muscular frame looked so ridiculously powerful as he squeezed into a small armchair. "Join me over here. That way we'll be closer, like you'll be with Brooke when she interviews you tomorrow."

Even though he sat on the other end of the couch, Rory's presence overwhelmed Elizabeth. His earthy scent swirled around her. What would her life be like with him there all the time?

What was she thinking? They worked together. Taking a deep breath and focusing on tonight's purpose, preparing him for tomorrow's interview, she said, "Today's journalism leans toward sensationalism. Don't be surprised if a lot of the questions are filled with sexual innuendos."

"What happened to serious journalism?"

"That's reserved for political leaders and crime victims."

"What kind of things will she ask?"

"She'll probably ask you things like what it felt like to have all those women wanting your attention."

"It felt damned scary."

"You can't say that. Say it was like nothing you'd ever experienced before."

He laughed. "That's for sure."

"She also might ask you about your pecs. What size they are, for example."

Rory's eyebrow rose at her comment. "Why would she do that?"

Elizabeth licked her lips. She couldn't say because his pecs were more intoxicating than Chloe's killer margaritas. "She'll probably ask about them because it's apparent from the billboard that you're in very good shape."

"This interview sounds like it'll be as much fun as dealing with those women in Times Square."

THE NEXT MORNING Elizabeth stood beside Rory in the *Wake Up America* studio for his first television interview. While bats had set up residence in her stomach and were playing a rousing game of tag, Rory appeared completely relaxed. Nothing seemed to bother the man. Elizabeth smiled to herself. *Except the crowd of women in Times Square.*

They'd met at four this morning for breakfast. While Rory shoveled down scrambled eggs, pancakes and bacon, she'd tossed out questions for him to answer. He'd done well, but would he do as well when the cameras were rolling? He wouldn't be the first person to freeze up in front of a TV camera.

Think positive. Send out good energy, Elizabeth. If you believe in him, he'll believe in himself.

"You'll do a great job in this interview. Be yourself, cowboy. When you do that you effortlessly captivate women."

He looked down at her. His brown eyes sparkled. "Do I captivate you, Lizzie?"

Her breath caught in her chest. When he focused on her as he was now, she felt she was the only woman in the world. If only it were true, and not that he looked at every woman that way. Where did reality begin and end with this man?

Then she realized he'd called her Lizzie.

She decided to ignore the name issue, since correcting him had become an exercise in futility. Maybe ignoring it would take the fun out of the game. "Remember, I said I'm immune to your cowboy charm."

Though she might need a booster shot soon. Very soon.

A production assistant informed Rory his interview was up after the next set of commercials. "Remember to be positive," Elizabeth whispered before the assistant ushered him onto the set.

Her iPhone rang. Pulling it out of her purse, Elizabeth checked the screen and noticed Nancy's name.

"I was going to call you later to tell you I've been saying extra prayers today." Her friend had another chemo treatment this morning.

"I need all the prayers I can get today," Nancy's weak voice whispered over the phone lines.

"Are you okay?" Elizabeth's heart tightened.

"That's why I'm calling. This is a bit of a rough day. Could you make sure Mark gets his art for the Hamlin furniture ad to the printer by five?"

"No problem. I'll see to it. You rest as much as you can."

"I keep repeating what you told me, that this is just a speed bump, but some days it's harder to believe than others."

"How about I bring you some dinner later?"

"I'd love some chicken soup from Cohen's."

"You got it." Elizabeth glanced at the set and noticed Brooke had joined Rory. "I've got to go. Rory's interview is about to start."

With his dark good looks and her tall golden appeal, the pair made a striking couple. An odd feeling twisted inside Elizabeth.

Once seated on the sofa, Rory started to remove his Stetson.

"Leave your hat on." Brooke placed her graceful hand on Rory's arm. "It makes you so much more cowboy."

Elizabeth rolled her eyes at how Brooke drew out the word *cowboy*. "I have to say, Rory, you're as attractive in person as you are on the Times Square billboard."

Then the reporter actually blushed.

Oh, please. How obvious could she be? She might as well ask Rory if he'd like to have a roll in the hay.

"That's kind of you to say, Brooke." Rory flashed the reporter his million-dollar smile.

Elizabeth shook her head. The man was a walking pheromone, mesmerizing any woman within twenty feet of him. He should wear a warning label. *Caution— may cause women to lose their faculties after prolonged exposure.*

The red camera lights came on. "If you've been in Times Square lately you've probably seen our next guest staring down at you from a billboard. He's the bare-chested cowboy wearing Devlin Designs' men's jeans," Brooke said. She turned to Rory. "You caused quite a stir yesterday."

"I was walking around right outside your studio and a couple of women recognized me from the Devlin Designs jeans billboard in Times Square. They asked me for my autograph, and then next thing I knew I was surrounded by women."

Elizabeth smiled, pleased that Rory remembered her instruction to mention the company name as often as possible.

"I hear a couple of the women got a little touchy-feely, if you know what I mean. Not that I blame them."

"I got to say, I'm not used to all this female attention. I'm just a simple cowboy from Colorado."

Elizabeth almost laughed again. Simple cowboy? After last night's discussion on home equity and remodeling, she suspected Rory was anything but. That man, however, had disappeared once they arrived at the studio. The Rory on the set was all aw-shucks. A regular good old boy. Which man was the real one?

"I noticed you didn't answer my question." Brooke's voice broke through Elizabeth's thoughts.

Red spread across Rory's cheeks. Elizabeth covered her mouth to hold back her laughter, unable to believe he actually blushed.

"I did receive a pinch or two, and my shirt got torn some."

"Did you know video of what happened yesterday has been posted on YouTube?"

After glancing at the floor for a few seconds, Rory

returned his attention to Brooke and smiled. "Now that is something. I never thought I'd end up on YouTube."

Lizzie cringed. His posture had stiffened slightly and the smile didn't reach his eyes. He was truly embarrassed being on display. Part of her wished she could run onto the set and rescue him. Now that she'd seen him genuinely happy, as he'd been when he'd joked about her cooking skills, or lack thereof last night, watching him now bordered on painful.

"I've seen the clip," Brooke continued. "I think you're being modest about the reaction you received. Let's see what our viewers think."

A second later the sight of Rory surrounded by women popped up on the monitor. Elizabeth glanced at Rory, who stared at everything in the studio but the monitor as the scene played out. Seeing the video gave Elizabeth an entirely different perspective on the incident. While they'd been in the thick of things, she'd concentrated on making the most of the opportunity. For the first time she actually put herself in Rory's shoes, a man new to the city and the ad game.

The women touched his arm. A few placed their hands on his chest when they asked for his autograph. More than a couple had pinched his butt. One woman goosed him. Of course, Elizabeth had known all that had happened, but seeing it in a more detached way and all together, she realized how degrading the women's actions had been toward Rory.

And yet, through it all, he'd remained polite. A complete gentleman.

The YouTube clip ended, and Brooke turned to Rory, an impish grin on her face. "The women almost ripped your shirt completely off. Good thing you work for a clothing company. You might go through a lot of shirts."

Rory chuckled, the slightly harsh sound grating on Elizabeth's ears. "Who would've thought I should've asked for a replacement shirt clause in my contract with Devlin Designs?"

"How about you take off your shirt and show us your wonderful abs so our viewers can see what all the excitement was about?"

Rory froze. Brooke looked him up and down like a woman about to pounce.

Then his gaze sought out Elizabeth.

She shook her head and mouthed the words *you don't have to do this*. The last thing she wanted him to do was humiliate himself on national TV.

The humor that usually sparkled in his eyes had vanished, replaced with iron resolve as he stood and peeled off his shirt. Then he hooked his thumbs in his front pockets, leaned back on his heels, raised his chin a bit and stared straight at the camera. Nothing but confidence shone in his eyes. "Is this what you wanted to see?"

"Women across the country are certainly getting all hot and bothered right about now."

Rory flashed the reporter a forced smile and said, "I don't know about that."

"I do." Brooke cleared her throat. "That's all the time we have. Thanks for stopping by, Rory."

After she plugged the upcoming story and they went to commercial, Brooke said, "Interviewing you was a pleasure. If you want to get together and see some of the city's sights, call me." She pulled a business card out of her suit coat pocket and handed it to Rory once he'd shrugged on his shirt. "I'd be happy to play tour guide."

For Elizabeth the interview had been a triumph, but the success was bittersweet, because despite the charm and bravado he'd displayed, Elizabeth suspected the interview had cost Rory a large chunk of his pride.

As HE WALKED out of the *Wake Up America* studio, Rory didn't know how he could keep working for Devlin Designs and retain any semblance of who he was.

He'd do it because he loved his mother, of course, and she needed the money.

But he'd been wrong about the interview being as bad as the incident in Times Square. Yesterday's humiliation had been limited to under a hundred people. The interview had been far worse because he'd been treated like a sex object on national TV. People at home would see that show, and he'd never hear the end of it. He'd be the butt of jokes for years to come. Hell, he'd probably be in the old folks' home one day, and people would still be razzing him about appearing half-naked on *Wake Up America*.

"That was an experience," he said once they reached the street. Then he glanced at Lizzie. Her face glowed. The on-camera embarrassment had been worth it, to see the joy on her face now, and to know he'd put that look there.

"You were amazing." Lizzie threw her arms around him and hugged the stuffing out of him. Her unexpected praise combined with her luscious curves molded against his body had him alive and humming.

Her eyes shone with pride. In him. He felt himself

drowning in her beautiful blue eyes. He'd slain her dragon for her. Power surged through him.

Desire scored a direct hit to his groin.

He lowered his lips to hers. One taste. What could that hurt? Yeah, and the captain of the *Titanic* probably said, "Don't worry. That's a small iceberg." Right before they hit the thing and sank.

CHAPTER NINE

RORY'S LIPS COVERED HERS, sending shock waves through her entire body. But that wasn't what excited Elizabeth the most. The shy man who'd bluffed his way through the interview and yet remained the perfect spokesman, polite and enthusiastic—had revealed an intoxicating strength of character far sexier than his great body.

His strong arms wrapped around her. She clutched his shirt, fearing her knees would give out.

Rory filled her senses. Her toes curled inside her Coach python printed pumps.

But immediately following those fantastic feelings, alarms blasted in her head. She tossed them and her never-mix-business-and-pleasure rule aside until her cell phone belted out Darth Vader's theme, and reality crashed down on her.

She jumped out of Rory's arms, her heart hammering as if she'd run three blocks, her body throbbing with desire. How had she gotten so completely lost in him? How could she have forgotten they were standing on the sidewalk in the middle of Times Square? This was so not good.

"Devlin's calling. Cross your fingers that he's as happy with the interview as we were." She avoided Rory's gaze as she said, "Hello, Micah. Did you see it?"

She tried to focus on his response, but her mind kept

wandering back to Rory's kiss. How would she face him, work with him, now that they'd crossed that work-personal life boundary?

Right after her call with Devlin she needed to explain to Rory how she'd gotten carried away over his interview's success. She'd say they needed to keep things in perspective and remain professional.

"Our cowboy did a great job. He struck the right balance of country boy and confidence."

Elizabeth hailed a passing cab, and when Rory opened the door for her, she dived in. He sat in silence beside her, while she gave the driver her office address. "We set Rory up with a Twitter account a few days ago. I'll have him post a couple of tweets today." The cabdriver blasted his horn at a couple pedestrians sauntering through the crosswalk.

"I hope this female fervor translates into jeans sales."

"I think it will. Women will be talking about the gorgeous guy they saw on *Wake Up America,* and they'll be heading to the nearest department stores to buy their guy a pair of Devlin's men's jeans."

"If the number of hits the video and our website have gotten since the interview are any indication, this campaign should be do well." Devlin paused. "I've been thinking."

Elizabeth cringed. Good things never happened for her when Micah Devlin said he'd been thinking. His ruminations invariably led to more work that needed to be accomplished immediately, or disastrous ideas she had to talk him out of. "What about?"

"Since meeting Rory, I've wondered about shooting the commercial in upstate New York. The setting doesn't seem to fit him. I checked out Estes Park on the internet. It's the perfect place to shoot the commercial."

She should have thought of that. Colorado and the Rocky Mountains were so a part of who Rory was. It added to his ruggedness, his appeal.

"Shooting the commercial in Colorado would increase the production cost. When I'm back at the office, I'll run the numbers to see exactly what the change in location would add to the budget. We could go over everything tomorrow."

"No need. I want the commercial shot in Colorado on the ranch where Rory works. It'll add authenticity to the campaign. As soon as you get the details ironed out, I want to head to Colorado. I don't want to let the excitement wane. I want to get this commercial on the air as quickly as possible."

Sure, the major work for the commercial was done, but didn't he realize the script would need changes, and negotiating with the ranch owner would take time? She briefly considered mentioning those facts, but knew from past experience he'd only tell her to do whatever was necessary, within reason, of course, to get the job done. The man must think he owned her, body and soul. Either that or he thought she had nothing to do but work twenty-four hours a day on his campaign. "I'll get to work on hammering out the details once I get back to the office."

She gazed out the cab window, watching people bustle along the busy city sidewalks as the taxi sat stuck in traffic. The irony of the situation slapped her in the face. The pedestrians were moving faster than she was. Not only was she stuck in the cab, her entire life seemed stalled right now.

She worked her tail off for Rayzor Sharp Media, and in turn, for Devlin Designs, and all it seemed to get her was higher expectations, a pat on the head and no social life.

After Devlin instructed Elizabeth to email the shoot details the minute plans were finalized, he ended the call, and she threw her phone into her purse.

"Bad news?" Rory asked.

She still couldn't look him in the face. If she saw his lips she'd start thinking about how they felt against hers. She'd remember how he made her forget everything but him. She cleared her throat. "Remember how I said next week we'd shoot the TV commercial in upstate New York?" Rory nodded, and she continued, "Not anymore. Though Devlin approved all the plans, now he wants the commercial shot in Estes Park at the ranch where you work."

Rory's expression darkened and his back straightened as if someone had stuck a broom handle up his shirt. "I'm not shooting the commercial there."

Okay, that was an unexpected reaction. Something didn't fit. "I thought you'd be thrilled to go home."

"I want to keep my personal life and this job separate." A muscle in his jaw twitched, the only evidence of his irritation other than the storm brewing in his eyes. "I'm not sure I can do this job, do things like I did in the interview or the photo shoot, at home with half the town watching."

Her heart twisted for him, and his embarrassment. He always seemed so confident, so comfortable in his skin that she'd never considered posing shirtless might bother him. Guilt swirled through her. She'd been so condescending when they'd met. She'd assumed he understood what doing a national jeans campaign entailed. The thought that he might not realize there would be beefcake shots had never occurred to her.

"How did you plan to keep everyone at home from finding out, when this is a national campaign?"

"When you said that, I thought there'd be ads in magazines like *GQ*. My neighbors don't read that kind of stuff."

"Guess you hadn't considered TV commercials and spots on national morning shows."

"I didn't think I'd be working half-naked, that's for sure," he said in a strained voice. "The news is probably all over town by now. The phone calls and text messages from friends and neighbors will start rolling in soon. I'm going to be a bigger joke than old man Jenkins when he got locked out in the middle of the night in his underwear and had to go to the neighbors to call his wife to let him back in."

"If the interviews and photo shoots bother you so much, then why did you take this job?"

"It's all about the money." Pain flashed in his eyes before he turned away.

"Why do you need the money?" What could drive a proud man like Rory to go against his obviously private nature and accept a nationwide modeling campaign? Nothing but the most desperate of situations. "Do you want to talk about it?"

"I'm fine."

"I'm sorry. I wish there was something I could do. I suggested discussing the shoot location more, but Devlin wasn't open to it."

She didn't dare push Devlin on the issue. In a couple of months it would be time to gear up for the women's spring campaign. If she fumbled things on this one, Devlin wouldn't renew the contract, and she'd be in the same spot she'd been in when she met Rory—facing company layoffs. Unfortunately, if she had to choose between pleasing Devlin and easing Rory's embarrassment, she had to choose the first, but the decision left a bitter taste in her mouth.

"What about if I say I won't do the shoot in Colorado?" he asked at last.

"You'll be in breech of contract. Devlin could sue you, and if you need money, I'm guessing that's not an option."

"You're right about that."

Something dire had forced Rory to take this job. She considered asking him again what was wrong, but it was clear he wasn't interested in confiding in her. So instead she focused on work. "We originally planned on shooting the commercial in a barn. I assume there's one at the ranch." When he nodded, she out pulled her iPhone. "What's the owner's name so I can contact him about shooting the commercial at Twin Creeks?"

"The owner is funny about letting other people use the land. It's been in the family for generations. How about I contact her for you?"

Rory worked for a woman? Interesting, considering his reaction to having Elizabeth as a boss. She frowned. Maybe it was just her he had a problem working for.

"I'd prefer to contact her myself."

"The fact that you're a New York City woman will be a drawback where the owner's concerned."

"You think she'll say no to me because of that?"

"She might, and I don't think you want to risk it."

"You're right."

"I work there. Tell me what you want to spend, and I'll cut the deal for you."

"Are you sure?"

"Trust me. I'll get the job done."

Rory had always been up front with her. If he was upset about something, he told her outright. She'd never pegged him as the kind of man who played games, so why did she have an odd feeling twisting her stomach into one big knot? "Okay, contact the owner for me."

Please don't let me down.

One issue dealt with, the tougher one still to tackle. Their kiss. The mind numbing, all-consuming kiss. "We need to talk about what happened between us after the interview."

"When what happened?"

The cad. Mischief sparkled in his deep brown eyes. He knew exactly what she meant, but he wanted to hear her say the words.

"I want to discuss our kiss."

"It was damn fine."

Heat rushed through her from head to toe as if he'd kissed her again. Why did she have to start feeling something for a man now? And why this man, who was so wrong for her? Shutting off the emotions Rory aroused in her, she said, "I got carried away in the moment. I want to make it clear that there is nothing between us but a professional relationship."

Rory grinned infuriatingly, as if he thought she'd just lied through her teeth. "Sounds to me like you're trying to close the barn door after the horse is long gone."

ELIZABETH HAD MANAGED to pretty much avoid Rory since their kiss four days ago. The few times he'd caught her on the phone, she'd kept their conversations short and centered on business. She'd insisted she was busy finishing the details for the commercial shoot. Since she preferred to have a cameraman familiar with the West, she needed to hire one from Denver. That took more time than she'd anticipated. She contacted the Chamber of Commerce to get the names of caterers. She worked with the creative team to tweak the commercial copy. After finalizing the plans, she'd met with Devlin so he could approve everything and clear his calendar to join them in Colorado. When Rory asked if she was avoiding him, she hid behind her work.

What a lie. She'd been amazed God didn't strike her down for that whopper.

Everything reminded her of Rory and how marvelous it felt to be in his arms. Now, as the Denver city sights gave way to small towns and farms, she wondered how she could turn off the emotions he'd dredged up in her. Since Devlin still held the remainder of his business over her head, she couldn't let anything get in the way of her job.

"Make sure you drink lots of water and load up on carbs so altitude sickness doesn't hit you," Rory said.

"The joys of being in the mountains. I'd manage to put the unpleasantness of altitude sickness behind me."

"You had trouble with it the last time you were here?"

"Not a bad case, but I was a little sick the entire time."

"You should've told me. We could've spent the night in Denver to let you get acclimated before we went higher into the mountains."

She shook her head. "We don't have time. I've got to

get the details for the commercial hammered out before everyone else arrives tomorrow."

"How many people are we talking about?"

"The agency's art director and copywriter will be there. Devlin will be at the shoot. I've got a cameraman and director from Denver who will be joining us. I think that's about it."

He whistled. "I never knew it took that many people to make a commercial."

"Very few people realize how much time and manpower it takes to produce a one-minute spot. You thought the photo shoot took a long time. Shooting the commercial could take days."

After about an hour, the road grew snakelike. How could she have forgotten how awful the drive up into the mountains was? Must be that she'd suppressed the bad memory.

The road consisted of one curve after another, and they weren't big, slow curves. No, they were those tight, turn-on-a-dime ones that made her clench her teeth and sent her stomach into her throat. Why would anyone want to live up here?

She gulped another swig of water to clear her popping ears, and said a quick prayer that she'd avoid altitude sickness this trip. That is, if she survived the hairpin turns and actually arrived in Estes Park.

Think positive, Elizabeth. You'll make it to the ranch. You'll shoot the commercial, which will be brilliant, and then you'll hightail it out of here, never to return.

Trees zoomed past her line of vision. Her stomach roiled.

"You're looking a little green," Rory commented as

he took another sharp curve at what she felt was a ridiculously high speed. "You okay?"

"Could you slow down a bit? The curves and everything zooming past me is not agreeing with my stomach."

"Focus on the horizon instead of what you see out your window. That should help."

His suggestion calmed her stomach a little, but then claustrophobia kicked in. The mountains towered over them no matter where she looked. If she opened her window she swore she could touch the huge trees.

"And people say it's scary to drive in New York? Obviously they've never driven on highways where a mistake could send them plunging off the road to a fiery car crash."

"You're safe with me."

Safe was the last thing she was with him around.

Rory glanced at Lizzie. He'd spent the last four days trying to figure out how he felt about her, and yet he still didn't have a clue. Things had been pretty simple until he'd kissed her. She was his boss and a fun diversion to break up the monotony and tension of the job from hell.

All he knew was things had changed between them when he'd kissed her. Not that little Lizzie would admit it.

That thought kicked him hard in the stomach like an angry mule. Lizzie wasn't half-bad at all. She was pretty as a picture, and he had to admit he enjoyed their verbal sparing. A man had to stay on his toes with her around. He sure liked a woman who had a brain and made him use his.

Too bad she was a city woman who'd made her dislike of his neck of the woods quite clear. And she was his boss to boot.

The woman had created more havoc in his life than a winter blizzard, but she only topped off his current list of problems.

He was going home. Talk about a mess.

"Thanks for handling things with the ranch's owner."

Rory's hands tightened around the steering wheel, his knuckles whitening. No way would he be able to keep his new job a secret. His stomach clenched as he thought about the ribbing his friends and neighbors would give him. Sure, he had a tough skin, but he guessed not thick enough to get through the next few days.

"She's out of town." Thankfully. Dealing with his mother wouldn't be fun. She'd always been able to spot when he was lying. She would confront him about why he'd taken a job he hated, why he'd stepped into the spotlight when he'd spent his life avoiding it. But dealing with that would be easier than explaining Lizzie to his mother.

She'd wonder what was between them, and damned if he knew. Even if he explained he and Lizzie had primarily a professional relationship, that detail wouldn't stop his mother from going into matchmaking mode. Since her cancer diagnosis, she'd started dropping hints about how she wanted to see him "happy and settled down," as she put it.

"She doesn't mind us being there when she's not?"

"She knows I'll watch out for the ranch's interests." Uncomfortable with the conversation, he asked, "What do you think about returning to Colorado?"

"Will you two hurry up? I'm not getting any younger."

Unwilling to offend Rory's mom, Elizabeth headed up the walkway to the sprawling, reddish-brown ranch house. The huge place would house at least four families in Manhattan.

When she reached the porch, she shook hands with Rory's mother. "Hello, Mrs. McAlister, I'm Elizabeth Harrington-Smyth. I'm a management supervisor at the advertising agency Rory's working for."

Beside her, Rory grew very interested in his boots.

Mrs. McAlister's hands went to her hips, and she flashed him a glance similar to one Elizabeth's grandmother gave her when she was particularly annoyed. Not that Rory noticed, with his current boot fascination. "Rory Alan McAlister, what have you been up to? I expect an explanation." Then she turned around and walked into the house.

"You didn't tell your mother about your job with Devlin Designs?"

"Must've slipped my mind."

"Sure, this from the guy who remembered every part of our initial phone conversation."

He shrugged, but said nothing.

"Why didn't you tell your mother?"

He glanced at her feet and her Coach stiletto pumps, which had clumps of dirt stuck to the heels. "I hope you have some sensible shoes."

"I brought flats."

"Are they cute little dainty women's shoes?"

"I wouldn't call them—"

"If they're not work boots or sturdy tennis shoes, they'll be ruined after five minutes of walking in the dirt and grass, and manure if you're not careful."

"I'll be working here, but I won't be *working* here. I'll be fine." After all, how different could this commercial shoot be from the ones she'd done in rural, upstate New York?

"Tell me you brought something other than skirts like you've got on now. It's pretty on you, and sure shows off your great legs, but it'll be damned hard to work in around here."

He thought she had great legs? Feminine vanity had her blushing and going warm all the way to her toes.

"I've got slacks."

"You should've brought jeans."

That comment erased her glow from his compliment, leaving her irritated at his scolding. She'd packed for this shoot like she would any other, with what she considered practical but fashionable shoes, slacks and blouses. Maybe she wasn't thinking straight, but that didn't mean he had to point out the fact.

She started to fire off an explanation, but then realized how effortlessly Rory had sidetracked her. Again.

The man continually turned her world upside down with steamy looks that got her so hot she thought she'd melt her shoes, or he made her head spin with his word games. Whatever the method, he pulled a fast one when he wanted to change the subject.

Inside the house, a large winding staircase stood to her left. The openness and the sheer size of the space amazed Elizabeth. Glancing right, she spotted an office the size of her living room in New York. She followed Rory into the living room, where his mother sat in a big leather chair beside an equally supersize leather couch. A large picture window filled the one wall with a breathtaking view of the mountains.

While enormous, the home wasn't elaborate. Western, rustic and warm: that's how she would describe it. Thankfully, the place wasn't rustic enough to have dead animal heads tacked up on the walls.

While Elizabeth sank onto the couch, Rory crossed the room, bent down and kissed his mother on the cheek. His large, tanned hand rested on her forearm. "How are you, Momma? You doing okay?"

The tenderness in his voice surprised Elizabeth. He truly loved his mother. Not like she loved her parents because they were her parents. He loved his mother because he admired her and respected her, and something in his strained features and voice told Elizabeth he was worried about his mom.

"I'm hanging in there." Mrs. McAlister's right hand caressed Rory's stubbled cheek.

The apparent love between them filled the room. Affection so tangible between mother and son that Elizabeth could almost touch it. She looked away.

When she'd last seen her parents, over a year ago, they'd met at a restaurant. There hadn't been any hugs or kisses, merely a mutual exchange of information. Once they'd finished eating, her parents had left for Cairo and she'd gone back to her town house.

Uncomplicated. Unattached. Unemotional. So unlike the scene in front of her.

"Now sit down, and tell me what you've been up to." Mrs. McAlister's gentle voice as she shooed Rory away pulled Elizabeth from her thoughts. "Elizabeth, how did you meet my son?"

She detailed her first trip to Estes Park.

"And now Rory's working for your agency?"

Out of her peripheral vision, Elizabeth glanced at

him. From the glower on his face, he wasn't happy that his mother had found out about his moonlighting.

"That right, Mrs. McAlister. Rory's modeling for a client of mine."

"Call me Nannette."

"Rory negotiated an amazing deal with the client. He—"

"No need to bore Mom with the details." Rory pinned Elizabeth with a be-quiet stare. Okay, not only hadn't he told his mother about his job, he didn't want her knowing the details of the deal, either. Why wouldn't he want to tell her how he'd stood up to a Fortune 500 CEO who wanted to lowball him, and negotiated a sweet contract?

"That was how you got the money I needed, wasn't it?" Nannette's low voice dripped with regret.

Rory nodded. "No big deal."

"You didn't have to do that. We could've found another way."

"Can we discuss this later?"

Elizabeth glanced from mother to son. What was going on? She felt as if she was watching a foreign film without subtitles.

"I'll let it go for now," Nannette said. "But we will talk about this."

"I never doubted we would."

Her parents had shown concern over her being successful and dedicated in her career, but not concern for *her,* as Nannette showed for Rory.

"Tell me you're not modeling underwear," she pleaded as she stared at her son, whose face had suddenly turned beet-red. "That wouldn't be right, and I don't like underwear ads. We all wear underwear and know what it looks like."

Elizabeth opened her mouth to respond, but Rory shook his head, as if to say this, too, would pass.

"Lord knows when the average person wears underwear it doesn't look like it does on a model," Nannette continued. "The ads always do something silly, like showing a man sitting at the breakfast table drinking his morning coffee and reading the paper in his underwear." She paused, then laughed. "Wait a minute. I recall your father doing that a time or two."

"He sure did. Guess that wasn't a good example," Rory teased back.

"How about when they show a woman dancing around the house in her bra and panties. I don't know any woman who does that." Her gazed locked on Elizabeth. "Have you ever done it?"

Elizabeth couldn't contain her smile. She liked this down-to-earth woman with her sharp sense of humor. "I have to admit I never have, and I think those ads are silly, too."

"No son of mine should—"

"I get the point, Mom. You don't have to worry. I'm modeling jeans."

"Thank the good Lord. I can still look Reverend Klockers in the face on Sunday morning," Nannette said, her hand splayed across her chest.

Again Elizabeth laughed. Rory just shook his head, his cheeks still ruddy.

"You're modeling jeans. So that's why you're wearing those fancy britches." Nannette turned to Elizabeth. "No offense, since your client makes those jeans, but they wouldn't last a week here on the ranch. They aren't working jeans."

Note to self. The campaign needs to address the issue that Western people view Devlin's jeans as too fancy.

"That's what I told her, Mom."

"I guess they'd be fine for a night out dancing, though." She flashed Elizabeth an apologetic smile. "This can't be easy for you, Rory. You've never liked being in front of a camera." Nannette turned to her. "When he turned ten he wouldn't let us take his picture. Whenever we brought out a camera he refused to look at us. Once when a friend's mom wanted a picture of the team after they won the Whiz Quiz competition, Rory hid behind another boy."

Guilt over giving him an ultimatum during their first photo shoot sprouted inside Elizabeth.

"Where are my manners? You've been here ten minutes, and had a long trip to boot, and I haven't offered you anything. Can I get you some iced tea or water?"

Elizabeth shook her head. "I need to be going. I want to check into the hotel."

"Nonsense, I won't hear of it." Nannette waved her hand in the air. "That's a waste of hard-earned money when we have plenty of room here."

Elizabeth smiled, realizing where Rory got his frugal nature. "The client is paying for my hotel."

"Doesn't matter. We'd be happy to have you stay here," Nannette said.

"It's not that simple. I have other people joining me tomorrow. Six, in fact, including the CEO of Devlin Designs, and they're all staying at the hotel."

"We're shooting a TV commercial here," Rory interjected.

"Your mother doesn't know about the commercial?" Elizabeth glared at him, trying to control her rising temper. He'd said her being a New York City woman would be a problem for the owner, when in reality he'd talked her into letting him negotiate the right to use the ranch so she wouldn't contact his mother. He'd lied to her twice now. Elizabeth's stomach tightened. What other little surprises waited for her here in Colorado?

"When were you planning on mentioning this?" Nannette stared at him with a look only an irritated mother could deliver.

"I'm sorry, Nannette. Ultimately, this is my fault. I should've seen to the negotiations myself." Elizabeth turned to Rory, struggling not to punch him in the nose for making her look incompetent. "You told me you would clear everything with the ranch's owner. In fact, when I asked you about that very fact on the plane, you told me everything was fine."

Rory ignored her. "Do you trust my decision on this deal, Mom?"

"Of course," she said.

He turned to Elizabeth. "See? Everything's fine. You worry too much."

Nannette laughed. "You're one to talk, young man. That's like the mule calling the donkey stubborn."

"Isn't that the truth." Elizabeth turned to Rory's mom. "I'm sorry that us filming the commercial here has come as a surprise. I'll make sure to keep you updated. I assure you this isn't the way I do business."

"I'd appreciate that. Rory's gotten a little overprotective lately where I'm concerned. He's failed to clue me in on some important details." Exasperation laced Nannette's voice.

"I know what you mean. He's forgotten to tell me a few important things lately, like the fact that his family owns this ranch." She smiled at Nannette. "He can be a bit controlling. Dare I say overbearing?"

The older woman nodded, looked at her son and shook her head.

"You two realize I'm still here, right?"

"When he was little," Nannette said, completely ignoring his comment, "his father and I joked that he would be a great dictator of a small country."

"Thanks for sharing that fact, Mom. Sure makes me look like a fabulous guy." Beside Elizabeth, Rory sat back, his arms crossed over his chest and his jaw clenched. Any minute smoke would roll out of his ears. He liked to tease her, but wasn't so crazy about being on the receiving end.

"Don't get your nose all out of joint. We wouldn't give you such a hard time if we didn't care. Would we, Elizabeth?"

Wait a minute. Now things weren't so funny. Rory's mom thought she cared about him? Major wrong turn. Elizabeth drew a deep breath to slow her racing heart. "I care for Rory like I care for everyone I work with."

That should put things in perspective for Nannette. The last thing Elizabeth needed was a matchmaking mother.

Wise brown eyes focused on her. Elizabeth held her breath as she prayed the woman would buy her fib. Not fib, actually. What she'd said was technically true.

Sure, you care for Rory the same way you care for Chloe, or Jerry, the copywriter. Why don't you try to sell his mom the Brooklyn Bridge while you're at it?

"Rory, take Elizabeth's suitcase upstairs," his mother finally said, breaking the awkward silence.

"I can't stay—"

"Nonsense. If you're shooting a TV commercial here, you might as well coordinate things from the ranch," Nannette said.

Staying here, being able to see Rory anytime, wouldn't be good. Avoiding him for the last week hadn't helped her put their relationship back on a professional track. No matter how busy she stayed, whenever someone mentioned his name or she saw his picture, her body reminded her how wonderful it felt to be in his arms and have his lips covering hers. Worse was the fact that she'd started wondering what a personal relationship with Rory would be like.

She couldn't stay at Twin Creeks. She needed to put physical distance between them.

"If I cancel my reservation now the company will still have to pay for the room."

"Stephen, the owner, is a friend of mine. He'll overlook that if I say you're staying here."

So much for that escape route. Elizabeth's mind scrambled to find another excuse.

"Stay. I'd like to get to know you better, since you're my son's boss." When Elizabeth opened her mouth to speak, Nannette added with a twinkle in her eyes, "This is my ranch. You need to keep me happy or there won't be any commercial."

That, she realized, settled the issue.

"Rory, get Elizabeth settled upstairs, and join me in the kitchen. You and I need to talk."

Elizabeth resisted the urge to smile. Things could be worse. She could be in Rory's shoes.

AFTER RETRIEVING HER SUITCASE, Rory escorted Lizzie up the winding oak staircase to the second floor. He'd been surprised how well his mom took the news about his latest career endeavor. Of course, with Elizabeth present, how much could she say? Nannette McAlister was a lady through and through, and ladies didn't scold their adult children in public.

Which meant he'd better hold on tight during the storm he'd find in the kitchen. To say his mom wouldn't be pleased that he'd put himself on display for her was like calling the Rocky Mountains a few hills.

"Is your mother always so persuasive?"

"Pretty much." He laughed. His mother could get the entire U.S Congress to vote her way if she put her mind to it. "Dad used to call her the family rock, and said once she'd decided something there was no moving her."

Lizzie chuckled. "I like her."

Before he could respond, Lizzie's cell phone rang. "Hello, Micah," she said as she looked at Rory and rolled her eyes. "Yes, Rory and I are at the ranch." She paused and listened.

Poor Lizzie. Devlin and his micromanaging never let her have a moment's peace. At least he would be at the hotel while she'd be here at the house.

Rory frowned, not sure what he thought about Lizzie staying here. In the short time he'd known her, she'd gotten under his skin, becoming the itch in the middle of his back that he couldn't reach to scratch, and wouldn't go away if he ignored it.

He hadn't found a woman so stimulating, both mentally and physically, in years, probably because he'd shut himself off emotionally since Melissa. But Lizzie had sneaked up on him. Every time he thought he had her figured out, she threw him another curve. As she had downstairs with his mom. The two of them had ribbed him pretty good. He'd given a good show of being upset, but in truth, he'd enjoyed seeing Lizzie have fun. Her pretty blue eyes had sparkled like the little creek out in their eastern pasture when the morning sun hit it. The water looked like it was sprinkled with diamonds.

All those feelings scared him to death.

On the other hand, if she stayed at the ranch, maybe he'd figure out if what he felt for her was real. He opened the guest room door, stepped inside and deposited Lizzie's suitcase by the foot of the bed.

"I plan on familiarizing myself with the ranch as soon as we get off the phone. I'll have any minor changes that need to be made done by the time you arrive tomorrow." Lizzie ended the call. "That man is going to nitpick me to death."

"Don't let him get to you."

"Things are still pretty dicey with Devlin until he renews the agency's other contracts. Until then he can pull the remainder of his business, and I'd be in big trouble."

"You spend a lot of time worrying about losing your job."

"My career is very important to me, and who wants to be unemployed anytime, much less in this economy?"

"Your job isn't who you are, Lizzie."

"I've worked very hard to get where I am. You, on the other hand, don't seem to care about work at all."

"I care. I'm just not obsessed. There are other things that mean more to me, like my family and friends. What else do you have in your life?"

The fact that Lizzie never talked about anything but work hadn't escaped him. She stood before him now, her eyes wide as she tried to figure out how to respond.

"Don't bother. I see the answer in your eyes." How could she live like that? When he stood in front of the pearly gates, Rory figured no one would ask him about his job. They'd ask about the people he loved, and what he'd done for them during his life.

"My life is full and I'm very happy."

He considered asking her who she wanted to convince, him or herself, but decided not to push his luck. He'd need all the luck he could get when he talked to his mother. "I'm off to explain things to Mom."

"Is it true you don't like having your picture taken?"

"I've never liked the spotlight. When I was in Little League the coach wanted me to pitch because I could throw hard and was a lefty. The last thing I wanted was to stand on the mound with everyone's attention focused on me."

"You should have told me."

"Would you have hired me if I had?"

They both knew the answer to that without her answering. Probably not. "But I'd have done things differently at the shoot. I would've cleared the set of nonessential people. I could've made the experience easier for you."

Rory hooked his thumbs in his front pockets, trying desperately to look as if the conversation hadn't hit a nerve. "What's done is done."

"Is that what bothers Nanette about what you're doing?"

If his mom thought he'd taken the job because he'd wanted to, she'd be all for the idea. What made her mad was that he'd set aside his life to get the money she needed for treatment. And to top it off, he hadn't informed her of his plans.

"What about your dad? Does he know?"

That little arrow shot straight out of the blue and

hit him right in the heart, almost knocking him to his knees. "My dad died two years ago."

"I'm sorry. I didn't know. What happened?"

"He and Griff were out fixing fences when Dad had a massive heart attack. By the time Griffin got Dad back to the house and the paramedics arrived, it was too late." Shutting off the painful memories, Rory said, "Mom's upset because our life is ranching. She knows that's all I've ever wanted to do."

Lizzie peered up at him as if she was trying to read his mind. Then she tilted her head slightly to the left. He'd come to realize that meant she was thinking, and that couldn't be good for him. "Is that the only reason she's upset?"

He nodded. "That, and I didn't tell her about it."

"Then why do I feel like there's something that everyone else but me knows?"

Rory kept his features blank, refusing to tell her the truth. No way did he want Lizzie looking at his mom with pity or thinking he couldn't pay for his mother's cancer treatment. "You're seeing things that aren't there. Meet you downstairs at six for dinner."

He turned and rushed out of the room, fearing that if he spent another moment with Lizzie, if she looked at him with those clear blue, understanding eyes, he'd buckle. He'd tell her how weary he was of carrying the family's burdens. He'd tell her how much he longed for a woman to share those worries with him. He'd tell her he wondered if she could be that woman.

Yup, he'd escaped just in time.

As Rory walked into the kitchen, his favorite room, he remembered how it had always sent tempting aromas wafting through the house. Baking bread, apple pies, a good beef roast were among his favorites. During the last few months those smells had been absent.

Today he found his mother seated in a chair at the oak table. A paring knife, ceramic bowl and unpeeled apples sat on the table in front of her. She looked up at him with tears in her eyes. "I'd hoped to make an apple pie, but now I don't seem to have the energy to get it done."

"We'll live without pie." He sank into the chair next to her.

"I hate what this disease has done to our lives."

Then damn it, they'd have pie. At least that one little piece of normalcy. "Is the crust done?"

She nodded and dabbed at her eyes with a tissue.

"You tell me what to do, and we'll get 'er done." He picked up the knife and started peeling apples.

She smiled briefly at his use of Larry the Cable Guy's favorite saying.

"This new treatment's going to change things for the better." From his mouth to God's ears. "What did the doctor say before you left Portland?"

"He said we'd know more when I go back next month. They'll do another CT scan to check the tumor's size, and then I'll have another round of treatment." Her long fingers picked at the fancy side stitching on his jeans. "What do you think of modeling?"

He sliced the apple he'd peeled into the bowl. "Can't say it's a whole lot of fun, or that it's much of a profession, but it's worth it."

She flashed him a weak smile, and another tear ran down her cheek. "Why didn't you tell me?"

"What would you have said if I had?"

"I'd have told you not to do it."

"Exactly why I didn't say anything." He wiped away her tears with his thumb and picked up another apple. "They're going to pay us good money to shoot the commercial here." Then he told her about the deal he'd negotiated with Devlin.

"I'm glad you're getting to do some business deals. That should make you happy." Nannette covered his hand with hers. "You always put everyone else first."

"It's not that bad, Mom. I'll be done modeling in a couple months."

Then he could put his life back together.

"Now tell me about Elizabeth."

His mom's question hit him right between the eyes, momentarily stunning him. "There's nothing to tell, Mom. She's my boss."

Nannette chuckled. "You can't fool me. The looks you two were throwing each other had nothing to do with work."

He should've known he wouldn't get that half-truth past his mother. She always knew when he was lying. "To tell you the truth, I don't really know what's going on. She's a pistol, and she makes me laugh."

"About time you found a woman who can do that. I'd like to have grandchildren while I'm still young enough to enjoy them."

He wished she hadn't said that. Once the words left her mouth, a picture of Lizzie, his child in her arms, sitting in the rocker his grandfather made for his grandmother by the stone fireplace in the living room, flashed in his mind. Surprisingly, the image didn't scare the daylights out of him.

His lack of concern, however, worried him. A lot.

CHAPTER ELEVEN

AFTER TAKING A Claritin to head off her allergies now that she was forced into the great outdoors again, and two ibuprofen for her nagging headache, Elizabeth headed outside to explore the ranch.

As she wandered, she texted Nancy. I'm in the Colorado wilderness. Saying extra prayers. Stay strong.

She wished she could do more than sit with her friend during treatments, or buy her a pretty scarf now that she'd started losing her hair.

As she walked toward the barn across the gravel parking lot, kicking up clouds of dust in her wake, Elizabeth admitted Rory had been right. Her cute little pink Coach flats wouldn't make it out of this shoot alive. She sighed. The things she sacrificed for work.

The thought drew her back to the conversation with Rory. Had she sacrificed too much for work?

Lately, she'd started to think she had. His comment about how life was what happened when you were busy making other plans... Had her ten-year goal kept her from seeing what else her life could be?

After tossing her phone back in her purse, Elizabeth swatted the flies away from her face. Obviously, they hadn't gotten any less persistent since her last visit. Ever since Rory had galloped into her well-ordered life, she'd started questioning where she wanted it to go, and more often wondered if he could fit in somehow.

No, she couldn't go there. She and Rory were too different. Opposites.

She had to remain focused on the commercial. Too many jobs, hers included, still balanced precariously on Devlin's happiness with the jeans campaign.

Clearing her mind, she focused on the scenery around her, studying it in context of the TV commercial. Trees taller than her town house created a canopy around her. Wildflowers decorated the fields. She peered toward the horizon and saw a cluster of animals, elk or deer, munching on grass.

Instead of honking cabs and cell phone chimes, the neighing of horses and the chirping of birds rang in her ears. While that was still a shock, on this visit she could appreciate the beauty around her. She could see how the serenity called to Rory.

Rory. What was she going to do about her growing feelings for him?

Adding him to list of things she needed to sort out, but couldn't deal with now, she grabbed the barn door and pulled, discovering it was locked.

Ever since she'd learned about his camera shyness and his fear of the spotlight, she felt a compassion for him and an admiration she found intoxicating. Neither of which she seemed able to shut off. And there was the kiss they'd shared. What she'd felt when he'd held her and his lips covered hers left her wanting more. Much more.

Stop it, Elizabeth. You're asking for trouble thinking like that.

Assured that the outdoor aspects of the commercial

would work and didn't need retooling, she returned to the house. Once inside, her shoes tapped across the hardwood floors as she walked through the living room toward the kitchen in search of Rory's mom. She wanted to ask her to recommend a caterer for tomorrow. Glancing out the windows, Elizabeth marveled at the beauty of the mountains towering outside. They reminded her of Rory—strong, constant and a force to be reckoned with.

In the kitchen she found Nannette at the sink, peering out the window. A view like that would take a lot of the sting out of washing dishes. The enticing smells of roast beef and apple pie wafting in the air made Elizabeth's stomach growl. "Mrs. McAlister, I'm sorry to bother you."

She spun around, a bright smile so like her son's on her face. "You're not bothering me. In fact I'm glad you're here, Elizabeth. I could use a hand."

"I'm not sure I'll be any help." Elizabeth joined her at the sink. "My idea of cooking is reheating leftovers from last night's takeout."

"You've got a pair of hands, so you'll do." Nannette patted her shoulder.

Elizabeth glanced around the open and inviting room. This was a kitchen a family congregated in to share the joys and trials of the day. The kind of room that housed parties with friends.

"A kitchen like this might inspire even me to cook."

"This is my favorite room in the house. When the kids were little, they'd sit at the table doing their homework while I cooked dinner."

She pointed to a spacious alcove off the kitchen with a table for six and large picture windows with another breathtaking view. "I could trust Rory, but I had to keep an eye on Griffin. He'd tell me he'd do his homework in his room, but he'd sneak out to spend time with his friends."

A mother should be there to help with homework and to give kisses for skinned knees, not be traveling around the world digging up the possessions of dead people. The rip in Elizabeth's heart widened.

"But not Rory?"

"He was the opposite extreme. He worked too hard. He'd spend hours studying for a test. I had to make that boy take breaks."

Elizabeth envisioned a younger Rory studying at the kitchen table, his dark head bent over textbooks. "Has he always been so stubborn and driven?"

When she first met him, she'd never dreamed that would be something they had in common.

Nannette laughed and nodded. "One time when I told him no about something, I can't remember what, he accused me of not listening. I said I'd heard him, but he couldn't believe it. He swore if I listened to him I'd see he was right, and change my mind."

"That certainly sounds like the Rory I know."

"The good thing about that was if someone had a harebrained idea, Rory told him so, and was confident enough not to get involved."

Elizabeth glanced at the family pictures on the black granite counter and picked up the one of a boy of no more than four on a horse. Rory. No mistaking that strong jaw and determined look. "You have a lovely home." And this house *was* a home.

Her town house would be perfectly decorated, but would it still lack the warmth she felt in every room in the McAlister house? Everyone who walked in the door to her grandmother's tiny house had been welcome and was immediately enveloped in the love. This house felt the same.

"Dinner smells wonderful. I hope you didn't go to any trouble."

"We all have to eat. You can finish the mashed potatoes while I get the roast out and make the gravy."

The thought of a home-cooked meal had Elizabeth's mouth watering, and pulled up memories of Sunday dinners with her grandmother. They'd sit and talk about the upcoming week. Then her grandma would tell her tales of her childhood in Ireland. Elizabeth frowned, remembering how they'd talked about one day visiting there together. Yet another missed opportunity.

Elizabeth walked to the cooktop and stared at the huge pot filled with enough potatoes to feed all of Manhattan, trying to remember what her grandmother had taught her about making mashed potatoes. "Where's the strainer?"

"It's in the cupboard to your left," Nannette said.

"I did warn you that I don't cook, didn't I?"

She smiled. "Mashed potatoes isn't cooking. It's demolition."

"I like your thinking." Elizabeth located the large plastic strainer. After hooking the colander on the faucet, and locating pot holders, she grabbed the pot and walked toward the sink.

"What do you think of my son?" Nannette asked.

Elizabeth jerked, sending a handful of potatoes tumbling into the sink. "He's hardworking. The client and I have been very pleased with the work Rory's done so far."

Nannette shook her head as she retrieved the butter and half-and-half from the refrigerator. She placed them on the counter and told Elizabeth where to find the mixer.

While Elizabeth rummaged in the lower cabinet to her left, Nannette continued, "I didn't ask what you thought of my son's work. I'm sure he's doing a fine job. That's how he is. He puts one hundred and ten percent into whatever he does. I wanted to know what you think of Rory as a man."

Elizabeth bumped her head on the counter as she stood, the mixer clutched to her chest. Nannette should warn a girl before asking such a loaded question. Rory made her want to scream one minute and kiss him the next, and the man sure could kiss. The one he'd given her outside the *Wake Up America* studio had nearly singed her eyebrows. "I don't know him well, but he seems very honest and responsible."

"'Honest and responsible'? Poor Rory. That hurts."

Elizabeth turned toward the young woman who floated into the kitchen. She had to be related to Rory; her smile and her good looks were dead giveaways. "I'm Avery, his little sister. He'd say meddling little sister, but don't you believe it."

"A woman could do a lot worse in a man than honest and responsible," Nannette said.

"I agree," Elizabeth echoed.

Avery glanced at her mother. "Mom, have a seat. I'll get dinner on the table."

The two exchanged a look, Avery's filled with concern, her mother's filled with stubbornness.

"I'm fine, dear," Nannette said.

"You sure?"

Something passed between mother and daughter as Elizabeth watched the pair. Something she couldn't identify, though she recognized its importance. First Rory hadn't shared the news about his job with his family, and now this. What was going on?

"Women often make the mistake of wanting to change a man." Nannette retrieved a knife from the butcher block and started slicing the meat. "I loved and accepted your father as he was. If a woman can't do that, all she'll have is a house full of misery."

How different would Elizabeth's life have been if she'd shared similar moments with her mom? One where a mother taught her daughter the things a woman should know. In junior high, Elizabeth had spent a week walking around looking like a clown before a teacher took her aside and showed her how to apply makeup.

"I'm not saying honesty and being responsible are bad things," Avery said as she tossed a hunk of butter and some half-and-half into the potatoes. "But it's not how a man wants a woman to describe him. When women describe Rory usually the first thing they say is how gorgeous he is."

Elizabeth would have to be blind to miss Rory's good looks. Every time she looked at the man, her insides melted like chocolate in a five-year-old's hands. "I noticed how good-looking he is, but we work together. I have a strict don't-mix-business-and-pleasure rule." However, that rule grew harder to follow all the time, but not because of his gorgeous face and rock-hard body. His confidence, his quiet strength, drew her more.

The mixer's whir as Elizabeth mashed the potatoes stalled their conversation.

"You work with Rory?" Avery asked, her eyebrows lowered in confusion. "Are you a horse breeder?"

Nannette saved her from answering. "Elizabeth's in advertising."

"I've been telling Rory for over a year to hire someone to revamp the ranch's advertising. He never wanted to spend the money. How did you get him to dust off the company checkbook?"

Elizabeth swallowed hard and tried to formulate a response that wasn't a massive lie. "I didn't—"

"Dinner's ready. Avery, grab the potatoes, and show Elizabeth into the dining room," Nannette interrupted, once again rescuing Elizabeth from the awkward conversation.

In the dining room, Avery sank into a chair across from Rory. "Elizabeth, you can sit beside Rory. As kids he and Griffin couldn't sit together because they picked on each other, and the next thing we all knew, they were fighting. They still can't sit beside each other, for the same reason."

"You make me sound like I've got the self-control of a ten-year-old," Rory said.

"That's because you and Griff do." Avery flashed her brother a brilliant smile, obviously another McAlister genetic trait. "I was always the good one."

"Talk about rewriting history. I seem to remember Mom and Dad getting called into Principal Johnson's office more than once because you'd stirred up trouble."

"I did not stir up trouble." Avery glanced at Elizabeth. "Mr. Johnson didn't understand my enthusiasm for causes. Instead of seeing me as a forward-thinking youth, he labeled me a troublemaker."

Rory laughed and turned to Elizabeth. "Avery spins a situation almost as well as you do, Lizzie."

"Do you really want to tick both of us off?" Elizabeth said, unable to resist joining in the teasing.

"Elizabeth, I think we can take him." Avery grinned.

"No doubt about it."

He threw his hands in the air. "I surrender, and humbly apologize."

As Elizabeth sat beside him, she understood why she'd felt outclassed when he teased her. An only child, she'd never learned the fine art, while Rory had spent years honing his skills with his siblings.

He leaned closer, his warm breath tickling her skin. "Why didn't you want to sit by me? Were you worried I'd bite? I don't unless I'm invited to."

Her tongue stuck to the roof of her mouth. The man was a first-class flirt. How much of what he did was for show, though, and how much was real? Just for her?

She swallowed hard and thought over the times she'd seen Rory with other women. He been polite, but reserved. Very different than the way he acted with her.

Don't go there. Hoping never led to anything good. It was a direct route to disappointment.

"Stop it. Don't say things like that."

He bent toward her, his lips next to her ear. "If I start nibbling on you, the last thing you'll want me to do is stop."

Elizabeth, her body tingling, her heart hammering as if she'd just finished a Pilates class, glanced at Avery to see if she'd heard his comment.

"Rory, it's rude to whisper when other people are in the room," Avery teased, glancing pointedly between her and Rory, her crystal blue eyes shining with mischief.

"Mind your own business, little sister."

"You're really pushing your luck. I might need to start sharing some of your finer childhood moments. How about the time you dared Griff to—"

"You win!"

"Avery, get Griffin," Nannette said as she entered the room and placed a bowl of asparagus on the table.

"No need, Mom." The smooth drawl, so similar to Rory's, came from the living room.

Elizabeth turned that way. While Rory possessed short dark hair and dark eyes, his brother had shoulder-length, light blond hair and blue eyes. Maybe an inch taller than Rory, he strolled toward the table, a lazy grin on his face. "Hello, pretty lady. I'm Griffin. If you've spent time with big brother here, you're probably about to die of boredom. If you're interested, we could go see what fun we can find around town later."

Another charmer? Obviously the trait was attached to the McAlister Y chromosome. But Griffin left her unmoved. Something in his eyes told her he tossed out compliments like most people tossed pennies into a fountain, and forgot them just as quickly.

Elizabeth had learned early on that some people had personalities they put on like a winter coat when they left the house. Her father was that way. Everyone liked and respected him because he could be counted on to step up and offer assistance to his business associates. Things were very different at home when she'd needed help with her homework. He was either too busy, or was brusque and quick to show his frustration if she didn't immediately grasp a concept.

Elizabeth caught sight of Rory out of the corner of her eye. He wouldn't be that kind of father. He'd be there for his children, and she suspected he would show endless patience, no matter what.

Her stomach tightened. Where had that thought come from?

Her hand shook as she reached for her water glass. This bordered on disaster. Her well-constructed wall between work and pleasure had a big hole in it.

"BACK OFF, GRIFF. Elizabeth already has a tour guide if she needs one." Rory stared at his little brother. If he looked in the mirror right now, he'd probably discover his complexion Kermit the Frog green.

When had he started thinking of Lizzie as his? Rewind and change that scene, because it was as dangerous as driving down the mountains during a blinding snowstorm, with seven inches already on the roads.

"So that's the way it is?" Griff taunted.

"That is none of your business."

"Stop it, you two, or take it outside," Nannette snapped. "I don't care which."

Griffin walked to the head of the table, bent and kissed his mother's cheek. "Don't get riled up, Mom. I'm just having a little fun. You know there's nothing I like better than getting a rise out of Rory."

"We have a guest. Pull out your company manners so she doesn't think you were raised in a barn." Nannette took a slice of beef and passed the platter to Griffin, who sat beside his sister.

"Rory, I hear Elizabeth got you to revamp our advertising," Avery blurted out.

"Where'd you get that idea?" he asked as he accepted the platter from her.

"Elizabeth said she worked with you, and Mom said she's in advertising."

Rory clenched his fork. *So it begins.* "We work together, but I'm working for a client of Elizabeth's who makes designer jeans."

"Doing what?"

"I'm the company's jeans spokesman."

Avery laughed so hard tears streamed down her face. When she finally could speak, she said, "You're modeling jeans? My brother who there are a handful of decent pictures of after the age of ten, is willingly getting in front of a camera? What the heck would make you do that?"

Rory stiffened. Who would've thought he needed to wear armor to dinner? "I couldn't pass up the opportunity."

Elizabeth laughed. "You really think anyone who knows you is going to buy that?"

"Now they won't." He glared at her. "You could've backed me up."

"Backup wouldn't have helped you pull off that whopper," Griff stated.

When faced with unwavering opposition and imminent defeat, a smart man turned to diversion. "What's the plan for tomorrow's TV commercial?"

"The crew should arrive somewhere around noon," Lizzie said, rising to the bait like a hungry trout. "We'll start shooting in the barn if that's all right with you, Nannette."

"That's fine. We have some tours scheduled, but we won't be using the barn."

"You're shooting a TV commercial here?" Avery leaned back in her chair. "I've stepped into the *Twilight Zone.*"

"Does feel like that, doesn't it?" Griffin mused.

After helping himself to a hefty pile of mashed potatoes, Rory passed Lizzie the bowl. She deposited a dainty scoop onto her plate.

"You need to load up on carbs." He picked up the bowl of potatoes and held them out to her again.

"I have some, thanks."

"Not near enough." When she didn't take the bowl, he dug out a healthy spoonful and plopped it on her plate.

"I can take care of myself."

"I'm not so sure. Remember what happened when you took charge in Times Square?"

"What happened?" Griff asked.

Rory froze. He'd actually forgotten where they were—the family dinner table with his mother and siblings watching. For a moment all he'd thought of was Lizzie and how she'd had altitude sickness before, and the fact that she wasn't taking care of herself.

He glanced around the table. Three sets of McAlister eyes were trained on him. Avery stared in complete bewilderment. Griff shook his head with pity. His mother tried to hide her smile behind her water glass. "You're looking at me like I've sprouted a second head. What's the deal?"

"Nothing, dear." His mother's smile brightened. "Now what's this about Times Square?"

"Elizabeth stirred up all kinds of trouble."

"I'm not taking all the blame for that mess." She folded her arms over her chest.

"One of you tell us what happened."

"I'm pleading the fifth," Rory said as he stared at his plate. Maybe if he ignored the question, the issue would go away.

"We're not going to stop asking until you tell us," Griff taunted. "You might as well give in."

That worked as well with his family as it usually did, about once every time hell froze over. Rory looked at his mother, hoping to find an ally.

She smiled sweetly at him and said, "Yes, tell us what happened."

He threw his hands in the air and turned to Lizzie. "I give up. You tell 'em."

"Rory was walking around New York City one morning. Some women recognized him from the Times Square billboard, and asked him for his autograph. A crowd of women gathered, then they went a little crazy."

"Crazy I could've handled, but they got grabby." Rory shuddered at the memory. "Talk about assertive women."

Griff laughed. "You never could handle women."

"I'll admit I'm not the master juggler you are. I called Elizabeth for help, but when she arrived she decided I should stick around to sign autographs." Rory turned to her. "Your turn."

"Suddenly everyone was pushing. Coffee went flying. Things were a blur after that." She sipped her water. "The good news was we got an interview with *Wake Up America* out of the mess."

"Wow, I go to Portland and the whole world changes." Avery shook her head.

His sister's comment hit Rory right between the eyes. Lizzie had changed his world.

BEING PART OF a true family dinner had been a new experience for Elizabeth, and she'd enjoyed herself. This was how family meals should be—warm, caring, joking with each other, but with love.

She marveled at the differences in the McAlister siblings' personalities. Rory was the serious one, the manager, the get-it-done guy. Griffin was his polar opposite—carefree, go with the flow, there's plenty of time for work later. The youngest, and only girl, Avery appeared to be the nurturer of the group, and yet could hold her own with her big brothers, trading jibe for jibe.

When she stood and began clearing away the dishes, Elizabeth grabbed her plate and Rory's.

"Put those down," Nannette insisted. "Griffin and Avery are on dish duty. You and Rory head into the living room and talk things over for tomorrow."

After she thanked Nannette for the excellent meal, she and Rory left for the living room. His warm brown eyes gazed at her with concern. "Are you okay? You skipped lunch, but you hardly ate anything at dinner tonight."

"Everything tasted wonderful, but my stomach's a little queasy."

"You need to take it easy, and get a good night's sleep." His thumb brushed her cheek. "You've got dark circles under your eyes."

Her stomach somersaulted. How did he so effortlessly get through her defenses when she least expected it? Desperately needing to get the situation back on a business level, she stepped away. "I need to see the barn before we start taping the commercial. It was locked when I checked earlier. Other than that, we're ready to go for tomorrow."

"You up to it?"

She nodded. Once on the front porch, she glanced skyward. Stars, too many to count, dusted the inky sky like diamonds poured out on black velvet. Rory's cowboy boots rattled across the wood porch as he joined her. "The sky is so beautiful. I can't remember the last time I noticed stars."

"That was one thing that was hard for me when I was in New York." He stood close behind her. While he didn't touch her, his presence enveloped her just the same. "It's so bright and so loud at night. I missed the quiet and the stars."

She laughed. "When I was here before, I had trouble sleeping because it was too quiet. I guess it's all about what you're used to."

Gravel crunched under their feet as they headed from the house to the barn. Rory pulled open one of the large double doors, reached in and turned on the lights. The musty smell of hay tickled Elizabeth's nose as she stepped inside. Thank goodness for Claritin.

Stalls lined each side of the barn, with a wide hall running down the middle. Rory leaned against a wall, his thumbs hooked in his pockets. Casual confidence radiated from him. Sure, he had good looks, but his confidence skyrocketed his appeal. "What's the plan for tomorrow?"

Keep your mind on business.

She needed to impress Devlin on the jeans campaign. Any problems or disappointments on his part put in jeopardy her agency getting him to renew his contract for his other business. She couldn't afford emotions sidetracking her or clouding her professional judgment. Getting involved with Rory was a train wreck waiting to happen, with her livelihood, not to mention her heart, as likely casualties. Though they could have a lot of fun before the crash.

"You mean what do I have planned if Devlin hasn't had more brainstorms since I talked to him last?"

"You think he'll change something at this stage?"

"Without a second thought. The man's a major pain in the ass. He's even more stubborn than you are."

"The bastard. We ought to string him up."

Laughter bubbled out of her. How long had she kept a lock on her emotions? She'd shut down in so many ways, and she hadn't realized that until Rory barreled into her life. How could she let him be a part of it when he'd ride out as fast as he'd come? She couldn't afford to get attached, because righting her world once he left would then be that much harder. Childhood had taught her that painful truth. Now, eyes wide open, she'd been forced to acknowledge that lesson rather than brush it off.

For years, every time her parents visited, she'd prayed they would stay. She'd pulled out her best manners, trying to show them she wouldn't be any trouble. She'd hinted how amazing it would be for them to be a more conventional family. But they always left, leaving her devastated, lonely and wondering what she'd done wrong.

"It's good to hear you laugh. You should do that more often." Rory pushed away from the wall and strode toward her, his gaze penetrating her defenses. Sparks of electricity raced through her. "You work too hard. You need to have some fun, learn to let go."

He kept advancing.

"This is my job." That was what they were talking

about, wasn't it? When he looked at her like she was the only woman in the world, her brain turned to mush. "I have to take it seriously. When I'm more established in my career, than I can worry about the rest of my life."

But did she risk putting her life on hold so long she'd wake up one day and realize she'd waited too long? Was that what she wanted for her life?

Rory stopped in front of her, and for a moment looked as if he might touch her. "None of us knows how much time we have. We can't afford to waste any of it."

"This campaign is crucial. I've got to anticipate Devlin having suggestions," Elizabeth said, desperate to get the conversation on safer ground.

When Rory stepped away, regret flashed in his eyes. "Let's say he realizes the brilliance of your commercial concept and doesn't change a thing. What'll I be doing tomorrow?"

"I know you and your mom say these aren't working jeans, but I think showing you wearing them around the ranch is the best way to convince men that anybody would be comfortable in them." Though she'd turned their conversation to a safer topic, Rory's presence still overwhelmed Elizabeth. "I thought we'd film you riding around the ranch, taking care of your horse and tossing some hay bales around."

"Sounds easy enough."

"Where's your horse?"

Rory motioned for her to follow him. They stopped by a stall across the barn. A beautiful chocolate-colored horse trotted over and shoved its nose under Rory's palm. He stroked the animal's neck. Such beautiful hands and such a gentle touch. Elizabeth bet his hands could do magical things to a woman's body. Her pulse quickened at the sensual images flooding her brain.

Warning bells clanged in her head.

"Don't let Devlin intimidate you," Rory advised. "If he says he's changing something, don't assume it's a done deal. Tell him what you think about the idea."

"He doesn't *intimidate* me. I give him my opinion. He doesn't listen, and when I can't change his mind, I defer to him because he's the client."

"Looks to me like you roll over and play dead if he pushes you hard."

"He's threatened to pull the rest of his business. The agency's already had one round of layoffs recently. Losing Devlin's business would mean more, with me heading the list because I'm in charge of his account."

Rory smiled. "That's the no-nonsense management supervisor who puts me in my place. Be that person with Devlin. Assertive, but calm and factual. He'll respect that."

"Is that how you see me?" Calm, assertive and factual. Ouch. Not exactly how a woman dreamed of having a sexy man describe her.

Elizabeth held her breath, waiting for his answer, refusing to examine why she cared what Rory thought of her. She wanted him to see her as more than a driven career woman, but what did she want him to see?

A woman he could fall hard for.

Damn that nagging little voice. Especially when it hit the target dead center.

"That's what I see on the surface, the tough, no-nonsense businesswoman. Down deep, I suspect, there's an incredibly sexy woman dying to let loose."

Sexy? The thought burst inside her like fireworks on

the Fourth of July, all brilliant, hot and dangerous. Part of her longed to let go and feel something, connect with another human being. Her worst fear was that she'd turn around and become a bitter old lady living alone. Truly alone. No parents. No spouse. No children. Only some distant cousins she hadn't seen or spoken to in years.

"You think you could help that woman get out?" The words escaped before she could snatch them back. Then she realized she wouldn't take them back even if she could.

Rory's callused hands framed her face. "Count on it."

She couldn't think. Blood pounded in her ears as her heart beat at a frantic pace. He was all wrong for her; her head knew that. He wouldn't score a two on her ideal-man checklist, and yet all she could think about was him kissing her. Now. She leaned into him and placed her hands on his cotton shirt. His heart hammered below her palms, matching the frenzied pace of hers.

His lips covered hers, demanding and intoxicating. His hands moved to her hips.

To hell with being responsible. She wrapped her arms around his neck, pulling him closer, until his erection was pressing against her stomach, sending her body into overdrive. His palm covered her breast, kneading and searching. A moan echoed through the barn.

In the back of her mind she heard footsteps, a voice calling Rory's name. But she didn't care.

The next thing she knew, Rory had pried her arms from around his neck and stepped away from her.

Through a haze of frustrated sexual desire, she saw Avery approaching.

"Hey, you two," his sister said, a knowing grin on

her face. "Mom has a couple of questions about tomorrow. She sent me to find you."

Elizabeth stared at Avery as the reality of how close she'd come to disaster sank in.

She'd gone beyond breaking one of her cardinal rules—never mix business and pleasure—and had been about to shatter it.

AROUND ONE IN THE MORNING, Elizabeth lay on the ceramic tile bathroom floor, wishing the earth would open up and swallow her. Her head throbbed. The world spun. Her stomach rolled. She hauled herself over the toilet seconds before what little dinner she'd eaten came up.

"Oh, dear, looks like altitude sickness strikes again."

From her position clutching the porcelain god, she discovered Nannette standing beside her.

Elizabeth closed her eyes. Add acute embarrassment to feeling like death warmed over. Now would be an even better time for the earth-swallowing-her-up thing. "I'm fine," she croaked. "I'm sorry I bothered you."

"You didn't wake me. I was up wandering the halls, and saw the light. I don't sleep well lately." Nannette reached over and flushed the toilet.

"I'm sorry."

"No need to apologize. I had three babies within five years. For a while someone was always throwing up. It got so bad once that I didn't feel like I was properly dressed if I wasn't wearing baby barf."

"If I wasn't half-dead, I'd smile."

"Now let's see what I can do for you." Nannette reached into the vanity and pulled out a washcloth. She held it under the faucet, wrung the cloth out, handed it to Elizabeth and then scooted out of the bathroom.

Alone once more, Elizabeth felt her insides pitch. Not again! She fought to keep down what little remained in her stomach. Minutes later a hand started rubbing her back. Focusing on the gentle caress helped her relax. The nausea eased.

A glass of water appeared before her face. Held by a tan, masculine hand. She recognized that hand. It belonged to the man who'd earlier said she was sexy. This scene would certainly change his mind.

"Thank you," she mumbled to Rory. To hell with her embarrassment. She was grateful for the comfort. She accepted the glass, sipped and rinsed out her mouth. Then she took a small drink. All the while his hand rested on her back, offering support and solace. Despite all their differences, all their squabbles, he'd given her more comfort than anyone had in years.

"I'm sorry to be a burden."

"I'm glad you're here instead of at a hotel. There's nothing worse than being sick away from home, except being sick away from home alone. Here we can take care of you."

When was the last time someone had done that? Probably when her grandmother was alive. When she'd gotten the flu last year, Elizabeth had suffered through alone on ibuprofen and chicken soup delivered from the deli down the block.

"What other symptoms do you have?" Concern rang in Rory's voice. "Do we need to head to the emergency room?"

"My head hurts."

"Let me see your fingernails."

Elizabeth raised her hand in his general direction. "Now's a weird time to check my manicure."

He chuckled. "Good. Your mind's clear enough for you to come up with a decent joke. I'm checking to see if your nails are blue, but they're fine. Confusion and blue nails are two symptoms of severe altitude sickness. Is your breathing okay?"

"It's fine."

Rory open the medicine cabinet. Pills rattled in a bottle. A minute later two Advil appeared under her nose.

"Take these. It'll help with your headache."

Elizabeth washed the pills down with the water he'd given her earlier.

"If you're not feeling better tomorrow, I'm taking you to Dr. Harper."

"I have to be better. The crew arrives in the morning, and we're shooting the commercial in the afternoon. All I need is some sleep."

"You need to take this seriously. Altitude sickness can be life threatening."

"Thanks. That makes me feel better." No way would her life end out here in the middle of nowhere. She had plans. Goals to achieve.

There had to be more to life than this. Something longer-lasting. Something that would leave a mark on the world after she turned to dust.

She wanted to be remembered for more than being a hard worker who created ad campaigns to sell jeans and Tug-Ups.

Those thoughts sucker punched her right in the gut.

At least before she met Rory she'd been content. Being with him and his family made her realize how alone she was. How empty her life had become. How could she go back to that?

Super. Altitude sickness mixed with a dose of self-pity. Could the night get any worse?

"You need to take it easy for a couple of days. Altitude sickness leaves someone pretty weak."

She grabbed the toilet, trying to use it for leverage to stand. Immediately, Rory's strong arms wrapped around her, helping her to her feet. For a second she gave in to the urge to rest her head on his arm. His warmth seeped into her. He felt so good. Too good.

She could get very used to having him around.

Now that was something to worry about.

CHAPTER TWELVE

RORY WOKE THE next morning with a crick in his neck from sleeping in the chair in Lizzie's room. He'd been afraid to leave her alone in case her symptoms worsened.

She'd scared the daylights out of him last night. People died from altitude sickness. Granted, not very often, but it happened. Then his fear of losing her had scared him even worse. Just what he needed in his life, one more person to worry about and take care of. But no getting around it, he cared about Lizzie. The question was how much did he care, and what should he do about how he felt?

There couldn't be anything more than a fling between them. Their lives wouldn't allow it. He couldn't see himself in New York any more than Elizabeth could see herself in Colorado, and he wouldn't make the mistake of begging a woman to stay here with him again.

He'd never been big on short-term relationships, but now he was rethinking that policy. A bug bite became all someone thought about when he didn't scratch it. If Rory didn't explore what was between him and Lizzie, he'd wonder about it forever. If he gave in, their relationship would run its course and he could move on. That would work. And if he laid out his expectations before they got involved, no one would get hurt.

We're adults. There's something between us. We both

*know we can't have anything permanent, but how about
we enjoy each other while it lasts?*

Okay, so the laying-it-out-on-the-table speech needed
some work.

Lizzie groaned.

"Feeling that good, huh?"

"I feel better than I did last night." Her gaze flicked
in his general direction. "Thank you for helping me."

"No problem."

"Please tell me you didn't sleep in that chair all night."

"I planned on staying awhile to make sure you were
okay, but then I dozed off."

"You have to look good for the shoot today. You
needed your rest."

"Woman, you've got to learn to think about something other than work." He leaned forward and brushed
a stray curl off her cheek. "Do you need to bump the
shoot back a day?"

"I can't."

Her soft whisper wrapped around him, and for a minute he lost himself in her clear blue eyes.

"I'll have to thank your mother for helping me last
night. She's a terrific woman. Your whole family is
pretty amazing. You're very lucky."

He didn't miss the wistfulness that slipped into her
voice. "They're okay most of the time. What's your
family like?"

"There's not much to tell. My parents are archeolo-
gists. They travel all over the world."

"Did you go with them as a kid?"

Her lips tightened into a thin line. "I stayed with my
grandmother when they were on their digs. When she
died my parents gave me the choice of living with my

aunt and uncle or going to a boarding school. I chose the boarding school."

Why would a child choose living at a boarding school over moving in with relatives? Then he thought about the situation from a kid's point of view. If her parents didn't want to spend time with her, why would she trust anyone else? The only reason he could think of for a child making that choice was because she wanted to insulate herself from being rejected again.

No wonder Lizzie kept everyone at arm's length. An image of her as she must've been as a child flashed in his mind. Same honey-blond hair, same curiosity filling her eyes. Same keen mind searching for a challenge. How could parents walk away from a gift like that?

"That must've been rough."

She shrugged, but he glimpsed the pain in her eyes. "I survived."

Her quiet strength wormed its way into his heart. The woman had grit. Nothing got the best of her. "I bet you were a terrific kid. They missed out."

She closed down right before his eyes. The vulnerability in her face vanished, as her jaw tipped up.

"I've got to get ready for the shoot." She clutched the blankets to her chin. "You need to leave."

He crawled out of the chair and stood beside her bed. "When you're feeling better, Lizzie, we're going to talk. Things have changed between us."

"No, they haven't. I'm the boss. You're the employee." Her gaze hardened. The closeness they'd shared a minute ago disappeared.

Rory rubbed his thumb along her jawline. "There's been a slow fire burning under us for a while now, and I'm not the only one who feels it."

"I have a rule about never mixing business and pleasure."

"Every rule is meant to be broken." Rory smiled. If Griff heard him say that he'd laugh himself silly. Of the two of them, Rory was the rule follower. He now knew he just hadn't met a rule worth breaking. He intended to smash this one of Lizzie's to pieces.

LATER THAT AFTERNOON, Rory cringed when he walked out of the house to find a good portion of Estes Park's sixty-five hundred residents milling around the ranch. He'd known the juicy news of a commercial being shot at Twin Creeks would whip through town faster than stampeding cattle. He'd told himself he was ready to face everyone, but seeing his neighbors and friends now, he realized nothing could prepare him for everyone he knew turning out to watch him make an ass of himself.

He spotted Joshua Stone and Cade Jacobson, his friends since kindergarten, among the crowd. Damn. Those two wouldn't let an opportunity to harass him pass them by. Rory always gave as good as he got, but today's jokes wouldn't be so easily ignored.

"Mom saw you on *Wake Up America,*" Cade called out. "She said you're on a billboard in New York City. Why would anyone want to see your ugly mug on something that big? Have they gotten complaints about it scaring children?"

Joshua punched Cade in the arm, and the pair laughed. Rory gritted his teeth. They'd tossed insults like this since the moment they'd learned to talk, but today's jibes pricked his skin. Damned if he'd let them see his humiliation, though.

"Your dad still using that picture of you to scare the coyotes off your ranch, Cade?"

"Rory's got you there, Cade. You are damn ugly."

"He's probably all high and mighty now that he's been on national TV, and can't talk to us," Joshua taunted when Rory turned to leave.

"Just look at those fancy jeans he has on," Cade added.

Their loud guffaws bruised his eardrums. "I could pencil you in later, and we could grab a couple of beers at Lonigan's, but now I'm working." Rory tossed this over his shoulder as he started walking toward the barn.

He'd told Lizzie no self-respecting man would wear these blasted jeans. Now he had proof. Knowing he'd been right didn't make wearing them any easier to stomach.

"Working?" Joshua goaded. "Is that what you call it? Doreen sure loved your little striptease on *Wake Up America*."

That zinger dug deep under Rory's skin, drawing blood. He stopped dead and spun around. "You're just jealous because even Doreen hollers for you to put your shirt back on, not take it off." Rory plastered an I-don't-give-a-damn-what-you're-saying look on his face, the one he'd perfected from years of trading insults with his mouthy younger brother.

Cade pulled out his iPhone and pointed the thing at Rory. "How about you strike a pose for us? We can print the pictures and sell them on eBay. If you'd autograph them, that is."

His patience stretched thin, he was about ready to punch his buddies in the nose, lifelong friends or not, when Lizzie materialized at his side.

"I'm sorry, gentlemen. You can't take pictures, since this is a commercial shoot. You're welcome to stay in the parking lot, but this area is closed to the public." She placed her hand on Rory's forearm. Despite the weariness in her eyes and her pale complexion, she emitted her customary take-charge attitude. "I'm sorry to drag you away from your friends, but we need to get started."

"Those two should send you flowers," Rory muttered as he and Elizabeth walked away.

"I know. You were about to take a swing at them."

He froze. "How'd you know?"

"Intuition. I figured you needed an out. I've situated a spot for you and the stylist in a far corner of the barn. No one can see you from there. I'm off to check the lightning."

Her concern for him, for his embarrassment, and her attempt to help him salvage his pride, wrapped around his heart and squeezed.

Minutes later, as he sat having his makeup done—no way would he ever get used to that—he couldn't get his thoughts off Lizzie and how she'd sensed what he needed and rescued him. That had always been *his* role in the family. Damned if being on the receiving end didn't feel good.

His gaze sought her out where she was talking to the cameraman. She looked like she'd been dragged behind a truck for a mile or two. He noticed she didn't have any water on hand. He needed to remind her to keep hydrated, and he needed to get her a chair, too. She appeared ready to topple over any minute.

"Why didn't you tell Joshua and Cade why you're doing this?" Avery asked as she stopped beside him.

"Yeah, that would be better, telling them I can't afford to pay for Mom's medical treatment."

"Everyone knows how expensive health care is these

days." His sister put her hands on her hips. "They'd want to help. The whole town would. You're not Superman, so quit trying to pretend you are."

"We don't need handouts."

"Pride is a good thing, to a point."

"I can handle our finances."

"I know that." Avery nodded in the direction of Rory's friends. "They know that. I know how hard this job is for you. You're not a spotlight kind of guy like Griff is."

"If I hadn't found a way to pay for Mom's treatment, I'd ask for help. But since I've got this wonderful gig, I don't need to."

"What can I do to help you?"

"Keep an eye on Elizabeth. She had a rough night with altitude sickness."

"I'd be happy to, but won't you be with her all day?"

"I won't be able to make sure she takes care of herself while I'm working." Rory glanced toward Lizzie. "She doesn't have any water, and she needs a chair. She can't stand all day. Plus this client of hers is a real pain in the ass. If he gets too irritating, distract him so she can get the commercial done."

Avery smiled like she had when they were younger and she knew a secret. He braced for her latest revelation.

"Wow. You've got it bad."

He scoffed. "I'm just concerned about her welfare. She's my boss."

"I saw how you two looked at each other last night in the barn, so no way am I buying that fish story." Avery rubbed his arm. "I'm thrilled. It's about time you found someone. You worry too much about everyone else. You need someone to worry about you. I like her, especially since she doesn't bow down to you."

"It can't go anywhere between us."

"You don't know that."

"Yes, I do. She lives in New York. I live here. My idea of a relationship isn't a long-distance one. I'm not big on phone sex."

"You never know what fate has planned." Avery smiled and nodded toward Elizabeth. "Don't wait too long before you let her know you're interested. You're not getting any younger."

"You're acting like I'll be getting my AARP card any day now."

Elizabeth called his name and motioned for him to join her and Devlin. "Gotta go," Rory said to Avery. "I'm on the clock."

As Elizabeth watched Rory stroll toward her, she remembered how she'd woken to find him sitting beside her bed. His concern for her had been touching, but then he'd spoiled everything by talking about their relationship.

The man could be so impossible, but so unexpectedly kindhearted, and oh so delicious. She should be mad at him for wanting to talk about how their relationship had changed, but how could she when he was right? Things were different between them, but she wasn't yet sure what she wanted to do about the fact.

"We're starting with you in the barn," she said when Rory joined her and Devlin. "We'll shoot you getting your horse ready, then ushering it out of the barn. Then we'll film you riding around the ranch."

"How's that going to fit in with our real-man slogan?" Devlin asked.

Elizabeth bit her lip. They'd been on the set for only thirty minutes, and the man had already maxed her out with questions. Every one of which sent of rockets of pain through her throbbing head. Soon she'd be popping Advil like they were Altoids. How many ibuprofen could a person take without risking overdosing?

"I emailed you a copy of the voice-over dialogue," she said with as much politeness as she could muster.

"I haven't had the chance to read it," Devlin admitted.

Why would he take time out of his schedule to read the copy himself? Not when he could take time he'd set aside for the shoot and have her explain it to him.

Sure, he could waste *her* time. "The voice-over will talk about Rory's day, then end with the line, 'no matter where your day takes you, Devlin's men's jeans can handle the job.'"

Devlin nodded in approval.

"Rory," Elizabeth began, "go about your business like you would any day. The camera's here to film what you're doing. It's not like the still photo shoot, where I wanted you to look at the camera."

"Got it."

A few minutes after the filming started, Avery materialized beside Elizabeth with a canvas collapsible chair and a refillable water bottle.

"Sit," she whispered in her ear. "You won't make it through the day if you don't."

Realizing the truth in what she said, Elizabeth gratefully sank into the chair as Avery shoved the water bottle into her hand. Smiling, Elizabeth mouthed *thank you* and sipped the water.

Luckily, she felt better than when she'd woken up. This morning when she'd swung her legs to the floor to get out of bed, the small motion set her world spinning. It took a few minutes for the dizziness to pass, and twice as long as usual for her to shower and dress. Now if she could just make it through the shoot today without collapsing, she'd be happy.

"I'm not sure about Rory's shirt," Devlin began.

Add *or killing her client* to her list.

What problem could he have with a simple beige, button-down shirt?

"It's one of your shirts." Elizabeth smiled. What she wouldn't give for a muzzle. Hey, maybe one of those bridle things scattered around the barn would work.

"I like the shirt. Rory looks super in it," Avery interjected. "The light cream color accentuates his complexion and his brown eyes without detracting from the jeans."

Elizabeth smiled, thankful for the unexpected support. "You should be in advertising. That was very well put."

"I think he'd look better in a darker color," Devlin insisted, and crossed his arms over his chest.

"Let's go with what he has on," Elizabeth said with as much assertiveness as she could muster, considering her throbbing head. "We'll review the film before dinner, and if you're not happy with what you see, we'll try a darker shirt tomorrow."

Devlin thought for a moment, and at one point seemed as if he might argue, but finally nodded, momentarily pacified.

One bullet dodged. How many other details would he question before the day was over?

Maybe she'd get lucky and he'd be struck mute. She smiled at the thought. A girl could dream.

Turning her attention back to the commercial, she watched Rory. His biceps rippled as he tossed the saddle onto the horse's back. Definitely eye candy, but she'd come to realize how much more there was to him. She admired his honesty and his work ethic. Though he didn't exactly admire the advertising business, he gave this job all he had.

He looked so comfortable, so at ease here at the ranch. Had she ever been this comfortable in her own skin?

No.

She longed for the contentment, the peace she sensed in Rory. She longed for a family like his. She longed for him.

Damn. She couldn't fall for Rory. Talk about a doomed relationship.

"Cut," the director called out.

"Great job, Rory," Elizabeth said, shaken over her recent thoughts. "We're going to do it again so we can get closer shots of the jeans and your face." She turned to the cameraman. "How's that sound to you?"

"I'm not sure about this horse," Devlin said before he could answer.

The man had to be kidding. He had problems with the horse she'd cast? Wasn't the animal horsey enough?

No way would both she and Devlin survive the day.

"The animal's fine. It's Rory's horse. That adds a familiarity, a relationship element, to the commercial," Elizabeth snapped. "You need to let me do my job."

"Wait a minute," Devlin countered.

She'd opened her mouth to tell him to keep his insane questions, comments and ideas to himself when Avery placed a hand on his arm. "Mr. Devlin," she said as she flashed him a dazzling smile.

"Call me Micah." He turned his attention to Avery, and if his mouth hadn't been closed, his tongue would've scraped the floor. Not that Elizabeth blamed him. No woman in a plain pink tee, khaki shorts and no makeup should look as good as Avery did.

"Micah, how about I show you some of our other horses?" She linked her arm through his. "Then if you aren't happy with Blaze—that's Rory's horse's name—you'll know what other animals you have to choose from."

"That's an excellent idea," Elizabeth said.

As she stood there, slightly stunned at the masterful way Avery managed Devlin, the pair strolled off. Of course, it helped when a woman looked like a cover model. After a couple steps, Avery looked over her shoulder, smiled and winked.

Elizabeth smiled back. Avery had just saved Devlin's life, because a minute more and she'd have strangled the man.

Rory's family amazed her, accepting and helping her more than her parents ever had, making her soul ache, knowing she'd have to leave.

Forcing back ridiculous, pointless tears, Elizabeth turned to the crew. "Okay, everyone, let's get those close-ups shot."

Later, when they broke for dinner, she turned to Avery. "Thanks for running interference with Devlin."

"Is he always that big a pain?"

"Pretty much."

"How do you stand working with him? I'd tell him to take a hike, and hope he got lost on the trail."

"I wish I could, but his company is responsible for over half my agency's business. Otherwise I'd have told him that a long time ago."

"I hope all your clients aren't like that."

"They all have their moments, but he's the worst." Elizabeth thought back over the last couple years since

Rayzor Sharp Media had landed Devlin's account. Had she truly been happy? *Hell, no.* The answer burst through her. She hadn't realized until now, but the joy had been missing in her work lately. Every day it became harder and harder to get up, knowing what she'd find when she went into the office—messages from Devlin questioning something she'd done, or informing her of his latest brainstorm. If she didn't have him to deal with, then invariably, another client had a problem needing her attention.

Was this how she wanted to spend the rest of her life, working with pain-in-the-ass clients?

Rory had turned her world upside down. Now his family added to the emotional chaos churning inside her, making her want what she couldn't have. She'd been way happier, or at least thought she was, before she'd met him.

She wished she could turn back the clock, because ignorance was definitely bliss.

PEOPLE HAD NO IDEA how hard and monotonous modeling was. Rory had spent the day doing the same thing over and over until he thought he'd go crazy. If people knew what the job really entailed they'd never say it was a glamorous profession.

At eight, Elizabeth finally wrapped up the shoot and told everyone they'd start back at six tomorrow.

Rory stood in a stall brushing Blaze after he'd unsaddled the poor horse for the last of countless times today. The animal snorted and shook his head.

"I know, fella, you don't get why I saddled you so much and we never went anywhere. Welcome to the wonderful world of modeling."

The horse snorted again.

"That's what I think. It's a real blast."

"Commercial filming days are long," Lizzie said as she came up behind him. "Unfortunately, it'll be another long day tomorrow, too."

"We're tough. We can take it." He patted Blaze's neck, then turned to Lizzie. He'd been so busy concentrating on following directions during the shoot, he hadn't gotten a chance to really look at her. While some color had returned to her cheeks and she seemed steadier on her feet, she still had dark circles under her eyes. "You hold up okay today? I'm tired, so you must be exhausted."

Terrific line. Real romantic. Tell the woman you've got the hots for that she looks tired.

"I made it through relatively unscathed, thanks to Avery. She had Devlin following her around like a little lapdog."

"She has a way of doing that with men."

"I can't imagine why. Just because she's tall, blonde and gorgeous. Do you think she'd consider modeling?"

Rory shook his head. "Avery's in vet school."

"Wow, she's got brains, too. God was way too generous with your sister."

He reached out and tucked a strand of hair that had escaped from Lizzie's ponytail behind her ear. "You're every bit as pretty and as smart as she is."

A pink blush spread across her cheeks. "I wasn't fishing for a compliment."

"I didn't say you were." He moved closer, wanting to explore the attraction boiling between them. Since he'd met Lizzie he'd been thinking about things he hadn't in years—marriage, kids, building a house of his own on his patch of land.

Blaze whinnied and shoved his muzzle into Rory's back. Glancing over his shoulder, he said, "Can't stand not being the center of attention, can you, boy?"

"He's a beautiful horse."

Blaze stepped toward Lizzie.

"He's a sucker for a pretty woman."

She reached out as if she wanted to touch the horse, but pulled back at the last minute. Rory moved behind her, took her hand in his and placed her palm against Blaze's neck.

Her pretty flowery scent filled his senses. Hell, everything about her filled his senses. Her fast, shallow breathing echoed in his ears. Her tight little butt brushed his thighs. Electricity from the simple contact shot through him, threatening to incinerate him from the inside out, and bringing him immediately to half staff.

Lizzie stroked Blaze's neck. The image of her stroking Rory in an entirely different manner materialized in his mind.

"He loves being scratched behind the ears."

She glanced over her shoulder. "How about you?"

"Honey, you can touch me any way you want."

He bent down and kissed the sensitive spot where her neck met her shoulders. Her moan filled his ears. She leaned back into him, and her hands clutched his thighs.

While everyone thought making love to a woman in a barn was romantic, it wasn't. Hay got in all kinds of awkward places, and the stuff itched like crazy. He wanted more for his first time with Lizzie. She deserved more.

"Your room or mine?"

CHAPTER THIRTEEN

"RORY, ELIZABETH, YOU STILL in here?" Devlin shouted from somewhere in the barn.

Elizabeth flinched. Rory rested his forehead against hers.

"Damn. Talk about bad timing," he said, his voice and body tight. "If we ignore him maybe he'll leave."

"No way. He'll search the place until he finds us." Elizabeth pulled away and straightened her clothes. "We're in here, Micah."

Rory picked up the brush and moved to the opposite side of the stall, behind his horse. She smiled when she caught sight of the evidence of his desire.

"Micah, I thought you'd left," she said, when he entered the stall. "Rory and I were going over the day's events, and discussing the plans for tomorrow."

While her body still hummed from Rory's touch, she clamped down on those emotions, trying desperately to slip back into business mode.

"I need to talk to you both before I leave for the hotel," Devlin said.

"I'm off the clock," Rory barked. "We can talk first thing in the morning."

"I agree," Elizabeth stated. "It's been a long day for all of us."

"What I want to discuss affects tomorrow's shoot."

When Elizabeth glanced at Rory, he looked as if steam would roll out his ears any minute. "Doesn't matter. I'll talk to you in the morning," he insisted.

"You and I can talk in the house," she told Devlin as she headed out of the stall.

"I need to talk to *both* of you."

The CEO's words halted her. She spun around and glanced back at Rory with a please-help-me-out-here look.

"You've got five minutes. No more," Rory conceded as he stormed out of the stall toward the barn door, Elizabeth and Devlin scurrying after him.

A couple minutes later Rory ushered them into the living room.

"I'm getting some water. Either of you want some?" He looked directly at Elizabeth.

"I'm fine," she mumbled as she sank into the nearest armchair.

"Me, too," Devlin echoed from his spot on the couch.

When Rory returned with two glasses of water, he handed one to Elizabeth. "You need to keep hydrated because of the altitude sickness."

Devlin turned toward her. "You're sick?"

"I'm fine. I've got a mild case of altitude sickness."

"It's more than a mild case," Rory said as he glared at Devlin. "You're lucky she's so dedicated. She should've spent the day in bed."

"I've always admired Elizabeth's dedication. That was one of the reasons I signed with Rayzor Sharp Media." Devlin cleared his throat. "Which brings me to the opportunity I have for you two and the agency. Based on response to the billboard and the *Wake Up America* interview, indications are this campaign will be a real winner. Because of that, I want to expand it to include other aspects of our men's line. We've recently added boxers and boxer briefs to our product line."

Elizabeth glanced at Rory. He sat with arms crossed, jaw clenched, staring at Devlin.

Rushing to prevent Rory from exploding like Mount Saint Helen's, she said, "Right now we need to concentrate on shooting this commercial. Once we're back in New York we can discuss expanding the campaign."

"Elizabeth, I want you to develop a campaign to showcase our other products, especially our underwear line," Devlin continued, a big smile on his face. He was apparently unaware of the storm brewing around him. "The average man is the perfect market and, Rory, I want you to be the product spokesperson for all our men's products."

"I'll model pants, shirts, shoes, even ties, but no way in hell am I modeling underwear."

Devlin's smiled faded, replaced with a scowl. "Let's discuss this."

"There's nothing to discuss, because I'm not changing my mind." Rory stood and stalked out of the living room.

Elizabeth wished she could escape, too, but she had to pacify Devlin.

Rory's outright refusal put her in an awkward spot. Again. Smack-dab in the middle between him and the client. She wasn't cut out to be a peacekeeper. How did UN ambassadors do this kind of thing for a living and not end up in a rubber room?

With the jeans campaign under way, they'd already started their branding strategy. A new model would confuse the consumer.

"You need to change his mind," Devlin said to her.

All she wanted to do was crawl into bed and pray the whole mess evaporated by the time she woke up.

"If there's one thing I've learned working with Rory, it's that there's no talking him into anything."

"Since his contract covers only the jeans campaign, I'm willing to make it financially worthwhile for his participation in this new endeavor."

"He's a proud, private man. Modeling underwear crosses a line for him."

"Convince him otherwise."

"Let me do some thinking tonight. There may be a way we can get Rory to advertise the product without him having to be photographed wearing them."

"My assistant is sending boxers Fed-Ex. I want to get photos of Rory in the underwear here at his ranch. Maybe we could shoot another commercial if you wrap this first one up quickly."

Sure, she could whip up commercial shoot details on twelve hours notice. She'd have to be David Copperfield to pull off that trick.

And what did the guy think they'd do? Put Rory in a pair of boxers and video him riding his horse around his ranch? That'd be classy.

Elizabeth dug her fingers into the leather couch arms and struggled to control her rising temper. "Micah, creating a commercial isn't something we want to do on the fly. It takes careful thought and a lot of planning to be a successful part of a coordinated campaign. We're smarter to finish this commercial and work out a new campaign strategy to include other items from your product line once we're in New York."

As she struggled to decide how to deal with this latest harebrained idea, Devlin continued. "How difficult could shooting an underwear commercial be? We put Rory in the boxers, and film the commercial in his bedroom and his bathroom, showing him getting ready for a day working around his ranch."

Yeah, that's all there was to it. Elizabeth closed her eyes and counted to ten, then counted to twenty. When she opened them she still wanted to strangle Devlin. Maybe if she explained the situation the jury would see the crime as justifiable homicide. She inhaled deeply and pushed aside her murderous thoughts. Calm and factual. That's how Rory said she should deal with Devlin. "It may seem that simple, but it's not."

"Elizabeth, there you are."

She looked up and discovered Avery standing in the doorway.

A savior. Thank you, Lord.

Rory's sister glided across the room and stopped in front of Devlin. "I'm sorry to interrupt." She flashed him a contrite look.

"No need to apologize," Devlin answered, his eyes glued to Avery's beautiful face.

Elizabeth bit her lip to keep from grinning. Forgive her? What man wouldn't be thrilled that a goddess like her was interrupting?

"I've been looking all over for Elizabeth," Avery continued sweetly. "Mom sent me to find her. She has a question about tomorrow's shooting schedule. I'm afraid I'll have to steal her for a while."

"That's no problem." Devlin turned to Elizabeth. "I'll give you until tomorrow afternoon to get that idea to me. Then we go with mine."

Yippee, a last minute reprieve from the warden.

Elizabeth nodded, stood and followed Avery out of the room. Once in the kitchen and out of Devlin's hearing, she said, "What's your mom's question?"

"She doesn't have one. I was rescuing you."

"Once again you're a lifesaver, but how did you know I needed help?"

"When I saw Rory a minute ago, he said if you and Devlin were still meeting, I was to get you out of there."

Elizabeth smiled. Rory playing her knight in shining armor? Who would've thought?

"Where is he? I need to thank him."

"He's in his office, and for the record, he's the one who asked me to keep an eye on you today."

A minute later Elizabeth stood in front of Rory's office door, suddenly unsure of herself. She'd come to thank him for sending Avery to rescue her, but found herself wanting more.

Somewhere along the way she'd quit caring about their differences. Even if the relationship couldn't last, she wanted to feel his strong arms around her. It had been so long since she'd cared about a man. She wanted him holding her close, exploring her body. She wanted *him*.

That was enough for right now.

With courage, hope and longing filling her, she knocked on the door. When he called out for her to enter, she opened it and walked in, having decided to seduce her employee. To hell with not mixing business and pleasure.

RORY LOOKED UP from the pile of invoices on his desk to see Lizzie walking into his office. He'd been amazed how well she'd held up today, considering the rough night she'd had. In fact, if he hadn't known she was sick, he wasn't sure he'd even noticed anything different in her work performance today. She'd been focused, demanding. The same little slave-driving perfectionist.

So much grit and strength in such a compact package.

One he'd like to spend a lifetime unwrapping.

Whoa, back up that train.

Even if he asked her, which he wouldn't, Lizzie wouldn't give up her career in New York to start all over in Colorado.

"Thanks for sending Avery to rescue me." She glided across the room toward him, a look he'd never seen before—hot, intense, determined—filling her eyes. Something more scorching than a raging Colorado brush fire blasted through him. He leaned back in his chair. If any other woman but Lizzie looked at him like that he'd think she was about to seduce him, but Lizzie had a clear-cut hands-off policy regarding coworkers.

She stopped in front of him and placed her dainty hands on his knees.

Gently, she pushed his legs apart and stepped between them. She licked her lips and looked at him as if he were the last piece of prize-winning apple pie at the county fair. Trying to wrangle in his raging desire, he grabbed a deep breath before he dared open his mouth. "Lizzie, you need to step back."

She smiled, but didn't move. "I'm bothering you?"

"That's an understatement, and if you don't put some distance between us right now, we're gonna end up a lot closer."

"I don't have a problem with that."

Every nerve in his system went on high alert. Before they continued, he had to make sure she understood where things were going. "If you don't take your pretty little hands off me, in about ten seconds you'll find yourself under me on that couch over there, my hands exploring every inch of your beautiful body."

She licked her lips and her palms moved to his thighs. The fire raging in him scorched another ten acres.

"What about your not mixing business and pleasure rule?" His hollow voice bounced off the office walls.

"I've decided you're right. Every rule is meant to be broken."

"That's all I needed to hear." Rory pulled her into his arms and his mouth captured hers. His body kicked into high gear. Passion gnawed at him.

Her fingers clutched his chest as she leaned into him. He deepened his kiss. His tongue mated with hers as his hand covered her breast, caressing and exploring. Her passionate moan thrilled him.

When Lizzie ground her pelvis against his erection, he nearly exploded. "Damn. I never should've moved back home."

"What are you talking about?" Her husky whisper fanned his heated skin.

"One, you deserve a bed, not to be tumbled on a couch. Two, my mother lives in this house."

"I want you. Now." Lizzie reached for the zipper on his jeans. The scrape of metal filled the room.

He sucked in a breath as her hand slid inside his waistband, gently caressing his heated flesh. Sweat broke out on his forehead as he fought to not explode right then and there.

"I don't mind being quiet, and beds are overrated."

CHAPTER FOURTEEN

ELIZABETH'S CELL PHONE alarm blasted her awake at four.
Rory, curled around her, his incredibly talented hand
cupping her breast, slept through the noise.

As she shut off her alarm, she felt her face flame
with embarrassment. She'd made love with Rory in his
office. Then they'd sneaked up to his room. Propriety
might have ruled her life with an iron fist before, but
not once Rory wrapped his arms around her. When she
broke the rules, she broke them with a passion. A passion she'd never felt before.

At least she'd had the presence of mind to set an
alarm for an early escape. The last thing she wanted
was someone in Rory's family seeing her slinking out
of his room in the morning.

She spent a few precious moments watching him,
remembering how she'd discovered the man possessed
unbelievable stamina and skill in bed. He'd also been
surprisingly tender the second time they made love.
He'd explored every inch of her as if he'd been trying
to file the details away.

What had she done? Sure, she had amazing memories to hold on to now, but how would she ever go back
to New York and leave him here in Colorado?

She leaned over and kissed his forehead, longing to

fight reality's rude advance. Then she sighed and slid out of bed.

"Where you going?"

She snatched up her blouse and threw on the garment.

"Don't you think it's a little late for modesty?" He flashed her that million-dollar smile, and her heart melted. She'd see that smile in her dreams forever.

"You've got a point, but I've got to go."

"The sun's not even up. Come back to bed."

"I don't want anyone to see me coming out of your room."

Resignation replaced desire in his warm brown eyes. "I'll stand guard."

He tossed off the covers and stood. Her resolve wavered at the sight of him.

She had to get out of here fast, before she threw away common sense and her heart. His future lay here in Colorado. Hers resided in New York.

He joined her at the door and kissed her tenderly. She knew she needed to say something, but the right words eluded her. Finally she forced out, "I'll see you at work in a little while."

How lame was that?

"This is the first time I've looked forward to coming to work since I left the ranch."

Rory opened the bedroom door and scanned the hallway. "All clear."

After giving him a quick kiss, she scooted out of his room.

Her reality had spiraled so out of control since meeting Rory, and yet she now realized her life needed mixing up. While she'd thought herself happy, she'd been barely content, more numb than anything. Rory had showed her what life could be if she opened up to the possibilities. No going back now, but the scarier question was if she went back, what would she be going back to?

ALL DURING THE SHOOT, Elizabeth struggled to keep her focus on work. She couldn't help melting every time Rory sent her a steamy glance. She hoped no one noticed. How would she leave him tomorrow after what had happened between them last night?

They finished shooting the commercial just before dinner. Both she and Devlin survived, thanks again to Avery's distractions. Once the crew had packed up and left for the hotel, Elizabeth asked Devlin to join her in the McAlister living room. He sank onto the caramel-colored couch while Elizabeth sat in the chair to his right and resisted the urge to wring her hands.

"I hope you're as happy with what we've accomplished here as I am," she said as an icebreaker.

"Rory is the perfect spokesperson for our new markets."

"Speaking of Rory, I've come up with an idea that I think will please both of you regarding the underwear campaign." She cleared her throat, kept thinking positive and sent out good energy. Maybe it would work, provided the good vibes bored through Devlin's thick skull and actually hit brain cells. Hey, stranger things had happened. Look at Elton John and Eminem performing together at the Grammys.

"Imagine Rory answering the ranch house door. Standing on the other side is a gorgeous woman. Dangling from her index finger is a pair of Devlin Designs' boxers. I haven't completely worked out the dialogue, but she could say something like, 'You left these at my place.' We could also do a shot with Rory in bed. He's leaning against the headboard. The sheets are pooled at his waist."

Elizabeth paused and reminded herself to remain assertive and focused. "Another idea I had has a woman coming out of the bathroom. She walks toward Rory, wearing his boxers. She smiles and asks if they look as good on her as they do on him."

For the first time since she'd started talking, Elizabeth glanced at Devlin.

He wasn't doing cartwheels over her ideas, but his thoughtful gaze told her he was considering them. Better results than she'd expected.

His contemplation and openmindedness lasted only another minute before he frowned. So much for visualizing the outcome. She was definitely asking for a refund on the positive thinking course she'd taken.

"Your idea won't work because it pulls the focus off Rory. With him wearing the product the focus remains clearly on him and underwear."

"If the camera remains on him, I think the viewer will stay focused on Rory as well, and with him in bed shirtless, what woman would take her eyes off his gorgeous body?"

"Surely you can convince him to change his mind." Devlin paused, gazing pointedly at her. The look in his eyes soured her stomach. "You two seem like you've become close."

Damn. Devlin had noticed. Elizabeth swallowed hard. *Remain calm. Don't show any reaction to what he said, because no way could he know exactly what had happened between them.*

Sure, she and Rory had acted differently at the shoot today, but the changes were subtle. He didn't question her directions as often. A couple times she'd asked what he thought about how she envisioned a shot. A few times she'd caught him staring at her with a look that would melt the polar cap. But Devlin couldn't know *how* close she and Rory had actually become.

"Rory and I have settled into a comfortable working relationship."

"Good. That should help when you talk to him."

She clenched her hands together so tightly her fingers went numb. How could this man even suggest she use her relationship to strong-arm Rory into changing his mind? Devlin proposing she do so left her needing a hot shower to scrub off the scum.

Then realization dawned. He expected that because in the past she'd compromised her principles to keep his business. Every time he threatened to agency shop, she knuckled under, so why wouldn't he expect her to do so now?

"You don't know Rory if you think anyone can talk him into doing something."

As if on cue, Devlin's eyes narrowed and he folded his arms across his chest. "I can take the remainder of my business elsewhere."

She was so tired of him holding that over her head. She thought about her town house—the first real home she'd had since her grandmother died—along with its mortgage payment. She'd saved enough to survive a couple months, but to avoid losing her home she couldn't be out of work longer than that.

Her career and her town house were all she had. Her chest tightened from the weight of her decision. What a lousy choice. Her pride and principles, or keeping her home and everything else she'd worked for.

No, that wasn't true. If she lost her job and her town house, she'd still have her self-respect and her dignity.

She was done with Devlin's ultimatums. No longer would she compromise her principles and give up bits of her soul to keep his business. She'd hit her breaking point.

"I won't try to talk Rory into doing something he doesn't want to do. If you want his arm twisted, you'll have to do it yourself." She straightened, vowing to not let him bully her. "I do value your business, and I've worked very hard for your company, but I won't play on his trust and respect for me, or our personal relationship."

"I'll be contacting Ms. Rayzor about ending our association."

"I'm sorry to hear that." Elizabeth stood, shook Devlin's hand and lied through her teeth saying it had been a pleasure working with him. Then she turned and walked away.

But now that the worst thing she could imagine, losing the Devlin Designs account and probably her job, had happened, the incapacitating panic she'd anticipated didn't come.

An unexpected sense of freedom flooded her system as the world opened up to her. She could pursue any of the career options she'd dreamed of! But what did she want, deep down in a corner of her heart? Realization burst inside her. She wanted to be in charge of her life, not at the mercy of pain-in-the-ass clients she hadn't chosen to work for.

Now all she needed to do was find a way to turn that dream into an income before she lost her town house, her shirt and her mind.

Rory sat in the kitchen with his mother. Last night, after Lizzie had fallen asleep, he'd mentally replayed his discussion with Devlin. Then his mind fixated on the ranch's financial state. He'd started modeling because he needed money. That hadn't changed. In fact, he needed more, because his mom had told him she'd require more treatments than the doctor originally thought. Unable to sleep, Rory had gone to his office and crunched the numbers.

He'd examined the ranch's expenses and income. He'd pulled up his mother's medical treatment and prescription costs. Then he added in Avery's vet school tuition. He ran the numbers three times, each time hoping for a different result.

No matter how he worked them, without added income he came up in the red. Bright red.

As he sat at the kitchen table now, with memories of his happy childhood swirling around him, he knew what he had to do.

"Devlin wants me to model underwear." He tossed out the statement, hoping his mother wouldn't immediately string him up before he had the chance to explain.

"Absolutely not. Under no circumstances." She glared at him. "Am I making myself clear?"

Yup, expected reaction right on cue. "The contract I signed only covers jeans. Devlin will have to negotiate a new one to cover other products. To do the underwear, I'd make him pay some serious money."

"It's not worth it." His mother rubbed his arm, her initial storm subsided. "It's not worth your pride. I know how much you've sacrificed already."

Sure, doing so was at the expense of his pride, but he could take the hit. "Lizzie's always telling me I have more than my fair share of pride." His joke fell flat. Instead of coaxing a smile from his mom, he received another glare. "I could earn enough for your treatment, anything else you need, and Avery's tuition."

His mother pulled her hand away from his arm. "I won't let you humiliate yourself. We'll be fine."

Rory rubbed his neck, fatigue suddenly overtaking him.

"No, Mom, we won't." His mother, the eternal optimist. His words twisted his gut, because he hated being so blunt, but she needed to know the truth. "I ran the numbers last night. With all the expenses, unless we increase our income, we're running in the red."

"Then we'll cash in some stocks or annuities."

"What we've got left for stocks won't put a dent in your medical bills. Dad and Griff's bills from Dad's first heart attack and the accident wiped out our savings." Now that he'd actually started talking about their financial state, he couldn't stop the flow of words. "We'd started recovering, but then Dad had another heart attack. I sold almost all the stocks and cashed in whatever I could to pay for those medical bills and his funeral. There's nothing to draw from, Mom. Our income is down because people aren't vacationing as much or for as long as they once did. People don't have the disposable income to buy our horses or to board them here at the ranch. We need more money."

"He's right, Mom," Griff said. Entering the kitchen, he went straight for the refrigerator, where he grabbed a can of Pepsi, popped the top and took a long drink. Then he joined them at the table, tilting his chair back.

His mother turned to him, tapping a manicured nail on the oak tabletop—a screaming indication of her irritation. "You knew we didn't have money for my treatment, Griffin Ryan, and you didn't tell me?"

Griff's chair hit the floor with a loud thunk. "He threatened to beat the crap out of me if I told anyone, and let's face it, he's bigger than you are."

"You should have told me," their mother said in a soft, iron-filled voice.

Griff paled, and Rory knew if he looked in the mirror right now, he'd find his own complexion a similar light color. As children, he and Griff had learned that the quieter their mom became, the greater her anger. They might outweigh her and tower over her now, but they both knew to take cover when Momma got mad, and she was red-hot furious at the moment.

Her piercing brown eyes focused on Rory. So much for his short reprieve. "You took this job to pay for my treatment without telling me we didn't have the money to pay for it. This is a family problem, and we'll deal with it as a family. I will not be kept in the dark about finances. Is that clear?"

Both he and Griff mumbled, "Yes, ma'am," as if they were ten years old again.

Nannette turned to Griff. "They want Rory to model underwear, and he's considering the idea. Tell Rory a man with an MBA from Harvard Business School can't do that." His mom's voice broke and tears filled her eyes when she looked back at Rory. "You worked too hard in school to do this. Surely we can find some other way."

"We've been trying." Rory's heart ached for the truth he'd forced his mother to face.

"I could help. You shouldn't have kept this from me. I'm not some child that needs to be protected."

"Mom, take it easy. It's not good for you to get so upset," Rory pleaded. "I didn't tell you about this because I knew you'd overreact."

"You're right about that."

"Rory was doing what he thought was best, Mom. Cut him some slack," Griff added.

Nannette stood, her face flushed. She was obviously madder than he'd ever seen her. This much stress couldn't be good for her system, which was already taxed to the limit, coping with her latest treatment.

She needed to calm down. As Rory rose, his mother swayed. He and Griff raced around the table toward her. Rory caught her before she hit the floor. "Call 911, Griff."

"Already am!" his brother yelled.

"What's wrong?" Avery rushed into the kitchen. "Oh, God, no. Mom. Is she unconscious?"

"Go meet the paramedics, Avery." Rory's voice cracked. He swallowed hard. "Hang in there, Mom. Don't leave us."

CHAPTER FIFTEEN

AVERY TORE THROUGH the house toward the front door, almost knocking Elizabeth over on the way through the living room.

"Avery, what's wrong?"

"Mom collapsed. We've called 911. I've got to meet the paramedics."

"Where is she?"

"The kitchen."

"Stay with your mom. I'll meet the paramedics."

Avery nodded and ran back toward the kitchen. Elizabeth raced out of the house onto the front porch, with what she'd overheard when she went to talk to Rory swirling in her head. Treatment? Nannette appeared healthy, but obviously she had some condition requiring medical care. Apparently expensive enough to drive Rory to model to earn the money. Elizabeth took a deep breath as the answer to why Rory had changed his mind about her offer sank in. He needed the money to pay for his mother's medical bills.

He'd put aside his pride, his privacy, his dreams, to help his mom.

What a man. What an incredibly magnificent man. A man who'd sacrifice whatever he had to because of his love for another person.

And Elizabeth had derided him over being interested

in nothing but money. Of course the job had been all about the money for him. He could have so easily put her in her place by telling her he needed cash for his mother's treatment. Elizabeth had been a fool, and she owed him an apology.

Then what his mother had said sank in. *Tell Rory a man with an MBA from Harvard Business School can't do that.*

Shame washed over her as she recalled various conversations she'd had with Rory. She'd lectured him on the ripple effect business downturns had on the overall economy.

She'd met him on a horse ranch and assumed he wasn't college-educated. She'd misjudged him and looked down on him because of her assumptions.

At any time he could've put her in her place by throwing his Harvard education in her face, but he hadn't. Tears filled her eyes. She, on the other hand, had repeatedly tossed her education and business sense right in his. He'd shown his true character in every interaction with her.

Her heart melted. No woman could ask for a better man.

She'd been able to deny how much she loved Rory before. Now there was no escaping the fact. She'd finally fallen head over heels in love, despite trying to guard against the fickle emotion. She'd found a man she wanted to spend her life with, only to discover herself unworthy of him.

As she stared into the darkness enveloping her, she prayed the paramedics would arrive in time. She prayed that Nannette's collapse had been caused by something other than whatever disease she was fighting. Nannette

leaned against her, just the littlest bit. Not enough for anyone else to notice, but close enough that his pain radiated through her.

"I hate feeling helpless," he murmured, as they watched Brandon start an IV on Nannette.

That done, the medic walked toward them. Rory stiffened and moved away from her, all the vulnerability she'd seen in his eyes earlier, gone.

"She's stable, Rory, so that's a good sign." Brandon returned his BlackBerry. "Her oncologist said as long as she's stable, the best thing to do is get her to the hospital. He's calling the E.R. doctor to update him on Nannette's treatment."

"Thanks, Brandon."

"We'll meet you at the hospital."

Rory joined his mother, knelt beside her and kissed her forehead before the EMTs loaded her on the gurney. "If you wanted a little attention, Mom, all you had to do was ask."

"There are some things you need to know—" Nannette began weakly.

Avery's sniffles echoed in the room.

"Tell me tomorrow," Rory said, and then turned to his friend. "Take good care of her."

"You got it." Brandon walked to the head of the gurney. "Now, Mrs. McAlister, I don't want to hear any complaints about my driving. I'm a more responsible driver now than when Rory and I were in high school."

After his mother and the EMTs left, Rory looked at Griffin. "We should have two cars at the hospital. You and Avery ride together, and I'll drive there in my truck."

"See you at the hospital," Griffin called as he and Avery left the kitchen.

Once they were alone, Elizabeth stared at Rory. His hands shook as he pulled his keys out of his jeans pocket. She joined him and held out her hand. "Give me the keys."

"I've got to go to the hospital. Will you be all right here?"

"You're in no shape to drive."

"I'm fine."

"No, you're not." She caressed his cheek with her hand. "Let me help you."

He handed her his keys, fatigue and worry causing his broad shoulders to slump. "You drive. I'll navigate."

As she and Rory made their way through Estes Park's darkened streets toward the hospital, she longed to tell him that everything would be okay, that his mom would be fine. She glanced at him in the passenger seat, and her heart froze. The strongest, most capable man she'd ever known had tears in his eyes.

"When was your mom diagnosed with cancer?"

"Around a year after my dad died." Rory's voice broke. "I don't know how she did it—going through chemo while still dealing with dad's death. Sheer force of will, I guess."

"She's an amazing woman." Elizabeth's hands tightened around the steering wheel. "That's why you changed your mind about modeling, isn't it? You needed the money to pay for her treatment."

"Who told you?"

"I overheard part of your family powwow."

"I wouldn't have pegged you as an eavesdropper."

"I'm not. I was coming to talk to you. Devlin wanted me to talk you into doing the underwear gig."

"I'm not changing my mind."

"I'm not asking you to." Elizabeth pulled into the hospital parking lot and followed the signs directing her to the emergency room entrance. "I told Devlin if he wanted your arm twisted, he'd have to do the job himself."

"I may have to give in."

"You can't compromise. Not when you're so adamantly opposed to it."

"If you heard the discussion earlier, then you know that without additional income, the ranch is running in the red."

Elizabeth pulled into a parking place. "What's your advertising plan?"

"There's the website, and we've got brochures in the hotels and the tourist bureau."

"Maybe that's part of your cash flow problem."

"Now's not a good time for me to talk business."

"Sorry, old habits are hard to break." Elizabeth turned off the engine and handed Rory his keys. Then she crawled out of the truck. She couldn't help him with his business issues right now, but she could help him in other ways. "Who do I need to call about your mother? Does she have family other than you kids who need to be notified? How about a pastor?"

"I haven't even thought about that."

Elizabeth reached into her purse and pulled out her iPhone. "Tell me who needs to be called."

Rory rattled off names as they strode toward the emergency room entrance, and she compiled a list. The hospital's giant motion sensor door swooshed open as they approached. Griffin and Avery stood to one side of the reception area, Avery's shoulders shaking with the force of her emotion as she cried in her brother's arms.

"Has something happened to Mom?" Rory asked, his voice filled with panic.

Avery stopped crying and gazed at them through red, swollen eyes. "We haven't heard anything yet."

Deep worry lines etched Griffin's forehead. "I'm hoping no news is good news."

"I'll find out what's going on." Rory stalked toward the reception window. "Lucy, how's Mom doing?"

The nurse behind the desk smiled at him. "They're running tests now, but she's conscious and coherent. In fact, she's giving Dr. Greer a tough time. She keeps insisting she's fine and wants to go home. He says no matter what, she's spending the night."

Rory laughed, but not his normal full-bodied laugh. This one held a brittle quality. "Sounds like Mom."

"She's one tough lady." Elizabeth joined him and rubbed his arm. "That will help her get through this."

"You need to register her," Lucy said.

As Rory reached in his back pocket for his wallet, another nurse rushed out a door to the left. "Dr. Greer wants to talk to all of you. He needs to do a CT scan, but your mother says she hates 'those damn things' because they're noisy and claustrophobic."

"You two go," Rory said to his siblings. "I'll join you once I get Mom registered."

"We've got your mother's information on file." Lucy nodded toward Elizabeth. "We'll get her paperwork taken care of. You can sign any necessary forms later."

Elizabeth held out her hand. "If you give me your

phone, after I'm done with that, I'll call the people we talked about."

Rory leaned toward her, kissed her on the cheek and handed her his BlackBerry. "Remind me to thank you later."

After he and the others left, Elizabeth turned to Lucy. "Would you point me in the direction of registration?"

"I'll take you there," Lucy said as she came around her desk. "That boy has always carried more than his fair share of the family burden. He needs a woman who's strong enough to take some of that weight off his shoulders."

"Rory and I work together. I'm his boss," Elizabeth said, hoping to clear up the receptionist's misconception before it spread through the town. "We're not involved."

No. They were just sleeping together, but only for now. And she loved him more than she'd ever imagined possible.

Lucy laughed. "Honey, you're not fooling anyone. My guess is not even yourself."

No kidding.

Fifteen minutes later, Elizabeth made her way to the waiting room and sat with Avery and Griffin. "I've called Reverend Klockers. He's on his way. I've also called your uncle. He'll take care of everything at the ranch. He figured that was the best way he could help. If you want him to come to the hospital, you're to call him. I checked Rory's BlackBerry. There are tours scheduled for tomorrow." She glanced at Griffin. "Do I need to reschedule them?"

"Uncle David and I can see to them."

Elizabeth checked off the item on the to-do list she'd compiled while registering Nannette.

Avery linked her arm through Elizabeth's. A fresh batch of tears pooled in her eyes. "Mom has been through so much, and now this. What if the tumor's growing? What if the experimental treatment doesn't work? What if—"

"Avery, don't even think those things. Take a deep breath." Elizabeth clasped her hand, then breathed deeply, encouraging the younger woman to breathe with her. Once Avery appeared more under control, Elizabeth said, "Show me where the cafeteria is. I could use some coffee."

Rory's sister hesitated.

"I could use a cup myself," Griffin stated. "Go on. I'll talk with Uncle David about the tours while you're gone."

"You'll call if…" Avery stopped, unable to continue. She bit her lip.

Griffin patted her arm. "Mom's tough. She's going to be okay."

"We won't be gone long." Elizabeth stood and gently coaxed Avery to her feet. "I hear you're in vet school. What's that like?"

As they left the waiting room, Elizabeth glanced over her shoulder at Griffin. Phone to his ear, he mouthed the words *thank you.*

RORY LOOKED UP to find Lizzie and Avery entering the waiting room, their hands filled with coffee cups. He'd joined Griff a few minutes ago with a list of things to take care of, only to discover Lizzie had seen to most of them. Without his asking. Without him having to lead her through things step by step. All his life he'd been the one everyone looked to during a crisis. He figured that was part of the oldest-child job description, but sometimes, like tonight, the role weighed him down.

Accepting a coffee cup from Lizzie, he smiled. What a woman. She could hold her own in the business world. She could laugh with him and trade zingers point for point. Now she'd taken care of things he hadn't even realized needed to be done, like checking tomorrow's tour schedule.

He could get used to having her around. Someone who worried about him every once in a while. Someone he could count on. Someone he could love and grow old with.

Realization hit him as hard as running headfirst into a ten-point elk.

He'd fallen in love with his little Lizzie.

Now the question was what the hell should he do about it?

One thing he knew, he wouldn't beg her to stay. He'd made that mistake before.

"How's your mom?" Elizabeth asked as she sank into the chair beside him.

He twined his fingers with hers, sending little ripples of heat through her. "Dr. Greer thinks she collapsed because of fatigue and stress, but he's doing more tests to be sure. When he's got all the results, he'll fax them to Mom's oncologist in Portland, and they'll talk over the results."

"If I'd known she was sick, I would've talked Devlin out of doing the commercial at Twin Creeks." Tears pooled in Elizabeth's eyes. When she sniffled a bit, Rory traced circles on her palm with his thumb.

His actions confused her. He'd never given any indication that he wanted a permanent relationship with her, yet here he was, turning to her for comfort. Was that all this was, him needing comfort and her being convenient?

Please, let him think we had more than that.

"Don't beat yourself up over it. If anyone's to blame it's me. I should've checked to make sure she was still in Portland."

Lizzie squeezed his hand. "I guess we're both at fault."

"Stop it, you two. It doesn't matter, and feeling guilty won't help. We need to focus our energy on helping Mom," Avery stated, her gaze and her voice filled with censure.

Both brothers stared wide-eyed at their sister. Rory nodded. "You're right. You always manage to keep things in perspective, Avery." He smiled weakly. "Mom's stable. We don't know how long she'll be in the hospital. All of you need to go home and get some sleep."

Both Griff and Avery shook their heads.

"What if Mom's situation changes?" Avery blurted out, then her eyes widened in horror, as if her saying the words could bring about the event.

"Us being here won't keep that from happening." Rory released Elizabeth's hand. "I'll take the night shift. Then tomorrow, when I'm sleeping, you can stay here with Mom, Avery, while Griffin takes Elizabeth to the airport."

Rory's words, said so calmly and without regret, crushed Elizabeth. Her heart shriveled and then she went numb.

What had she expected when she'd thrown herself at Rory? That he would declare his undying love for her and beg her to stay, because he couldn't bear for her to leave him?

Obviously unaware of the turmoil churning inside her, Griff turned to her. "What time's your flight?"

"It's at one-twenty, but you don't have to take me. I turned in my rental car when we arrived, but I can rent another one."

She sat there wishing Rory would ask her to stay. She longed to tell him how much she loved him and that she wanted to spend the rest of her life with him, but she couldn't. Right now she had nothing to offer him, and he had enough problems. She refused to add to his burdens.

And he would worry about her. He was that kind of man. One who shouldered his family's problems and worked to ease their situation. He'd feel partly responsible for her unemployment because it resulted from her unwillingness to talk him into modeling underwear. Not that she believed that, but Rory would feel obligated to her, and she'd never be sure if he was with her out of love or not.

Relationships started when one person's life lay in ruins never went well.

"I'll take you." Griffin's voice broke through her thoughts. "We can drop Avery off here in the morning and then head to Denver."

Flashing what she hoped was a no-my-heart-isn't-in-pieces smile at Griffin, she said, "That would be perfect."

CHAPTER SIXTEEN

RORY STARED OUT one of the hospital's huge picture windows, watching for Griff and Avery. When he'd received Griff's text saying they were on the way, Rory had left their mom sleeping in her room, and headed for the hospital entrance. A minute later Griff's dark blue Chevy truck pulled into the parking lot.

When Rory saw Lizzie, as well as his brother and sister, crawl out of the truck, his heart fell. He'd hoped she wouldn't come to the hospital today. Letting her go last night had been hard enough. Seeing her now was like pouring rubbing alcohol on an open wound. When he'd tossed out the comment about Griff taking her to the airport, he'd held his breath. He'd prayed she would say she couldn't bear to leave him.

When she didn't, he unsuccessfully tried to force the words asking her to stay past the lump in his throat. He'd traveled that road before, begging a woman to stay, to love him, and he'd crashed and burned. A smart man never made the same mistake twice.

The hospital door whooshed open and Rory smiled, trying to pretend his stomach wasn't full of knots. His gaze remained locked on his siblings as he updated them on their mom's condition. If he looked at Lizzie, he feared he'd beg her to stay in Colorado. With him. Forever.

The hospital door slid open behind them, ushering in a gust of fresh Colorado air and Micah Devlin. Lizzie stiffened and moved away slightly as he approached.

Rory glanced from one to the other. What was up there?

When Devlin reached them, his adoring gaze locked on to Avery. "How's your mother? When I checked out this morning the front desk manager told me she collapsed last night."

Not happy with Devlin's interest in his baby sister, Rory said, "We're waiting for test results. Then Dr. Greer and Mom's oncologist in Portland will go over everything in a phone conference."

Devlin reluctantly turned toward Rory. "If it would help, I'll send the company jet to Portland and fly your mother's oncologist here. Or if they'd have better treatment for her in Portland, I can fly her there."

For a minute Rory stood there regrouping. Talk about a shot out of the blue. Once he recovered from his shock over Devlin's unexpected offer, he murmured, "Why would you do that? If it's to get me to do the underwear campaign, it won't work."

"My grandmother had cancer."

It made sense now. He belonged to the cancer-patient's-family club. That explained why Devlin made the offer, but did Rory want to accept? He'd given up bits and pieces of his pride over the last months. How much more could he lose before the well was tapped out?

He had to draw the line somewhere. "Thanks for the offer, but we're doing fine."

Lizzie turned to Griff and whispered something.

"What did you say, Elizabeth?" Rory scowled at his brother. "What's going on?"

"I asked Griff for his keys." Lizzie shifted awkwardly. "I thought I'd wait in the car while all of you talked."

Was she that eager to get away from him? Rory stared into her eyes, trying to determine what she was thinking.

Please. Tell me you want to stay. That you can't bear to walk out of my life.

She held out her hand to Griffin.

Avery glanced between Rory and Elizabeth as if she wanted to say something, or hit him. Rory couldn't tell which. Griffin tossed him a what-do-you-want-me-to-do-bro look.

Rory wouldn't beg her to stay. He couldn't. If he asked Lizzie to remain in Colorado with him and she turned him down, how could he survive her rejection? Letting her go was safer. "Griff, take Elizabeth to the airport so she doesn't miss her flight."

A WEEK LATER, Rory sat in his office, staring at the mountains, still reeling from Lizzie's departure. He'd felt connected to her in a way he'd never imagined possible, especially after she'd gotten him through the scare with his mother. The love he felt for her made what he'd shared with Melissa seem like a childhood crush.

He'd thought about calling Lizzie, but she hadn't given him any indication she wanted anything to do with him. He'd hoped when he mentioned her going to the airport, she'd say something about wanting to stay, but apparently, they'd scratched each other's itches and now the fling was over.

At least he hadn't begged her to stay. This way, while he hurt like hell, he still had his pride. Granted, that wasn't much, but as his dad used to say, it was better than a kick in the teeth.

How could he have thought he could have a brief affair with Lizzie? He wasn't a love 'em and leave 'em guy like Griff. Rory wanted—hell, needed—that emotional connection, and the minute he'd touched Lizzie, deep inside he'd known he never wanted to let her go. He'd been a fool. Making love to her hadn't gotten Lizzie out of his system. Instead he'd fallen even more in love with her.

His cell phone rang. Hoping to find Lizzie on the line, he glanced at the caller ID. Disappointment crashed over him when he instead saw Devlin's name. Rory had to stop wishing she'd call. A man could handle only so many letdowns before he became a masochist.

He answered the phone, and again thanked Devlin for offering the use of the corporate jet.

"Avery said she and your mom fly to Portland once a month. If you email me the treatment dates, I'd be happy to send the jet for them."

While Rory's pride wanted him to say he could get his mother and sister to Portland, his financial common sense won out. Eliminating airfare costs would save a chunk of change, and he'd come to realize there was no shame in accepting help. "Thanks. I'll send you the dates."

"Now on a business note, I need to inform you of a change I've made," Devlin said, his voice oddly strained. "I've signed with another agency for the rest of the men's campaign."

"You fired Elizabeth?"

"I parted company with her agency on the rest of my business. Her firm will still be handling the advertising for our men's jeans."

Rory had taken business speak 101 at Harvard. No way was he buying Devlin's whitewashed version. "What happened to Elizabeth when you pulled the rest of your business?"

"There's no point to this line of discussion."

"There is to me."

"I heard she was part of the layoffs Rayzor Sharp Media recently went through."

Elizabeth had lost her job, the thing that meant the most to her, because she wouldn't talk him into modeling underwear. She was a single woman trying to support herself in New York. Not an easy thing to do considering the cost of living. Damned if he'd let her lose her job because she wouldn't twist his arm.

"I've signed with Harms and Finn," Devlin continued, after an awkward silence. "The new management supervisor will contact you regarding advertising plans for other products in our line."

"Hold on there. I don't have a contract for anything other than jeans." Rory smiled. Turnabout wasn't only fair play, it felt damned good.

"I'm sure we can come to an understanding regarding further ventures."

"Not if it doesn't include Elizabeth."

"This is business. Don't let your feelings for a woman cloud your judgment."

Rory's hand tightened around his cell phone. "I'll say this once. My personal life is none of your concern."

"I didn't mean to offend you. I should have said that

we can make this a profitable business relationship for both of us."

"I'm not modeling underwear. Not even if hell freezes over."

"We'll put that on the back burner."

Devlin's twinge of desperation raced across the phone lines. Rory smiled. Being in the driver's seat was the only way to travel.

"The new management supervisor and I will fly to Estes Park," Devlin continued. "We can discuss plans for the rest of the clothing line."

"I don't work with anyone but Elizabeth."

"I'm sure once you meet Matthew, you'll like him."

"It's not a matter of liking the guy or not." Rory leaned back in his desk chair and stretched his legs out. "Elizabeth earned my trust and respect. If the deal doesn't include her, forget it."

"That's not the best decision for my company."

"You aren't the only one who has news to share. The billboard and *Wake Up America* interview created quite a buzz. I've had other major men's clothing companies contact me about acting as a spokesman for their lines," Rory bluffed.

"We have an exclusive contract."

"For jeans." Rory paused. "I bet any one of those companies would be willing to hire Elizabeth, too."

"We agreed that you'd be Devlin Designs' men's spokesperson."

"Until a contract is signed regarding the rest of the clothing lines, everything is negotiable." Throwing Devlin's words back at him went down as smoothly as Johnny Walker Blue. "This is a business decision.

I'm sure you understand that I have to look out for my best interests."

Silence. Rory waited. He wished he could see the look on Devlin's face. The man wouldn't like being on the disadvantaged side of the negotiation process.

"If I agree to hire Elizabeth, will you sign a contract to act as our spokesperson exclusively for all of our men's clothes?"

"Hire Elizabeth and we'll discuss the issue."

ONCE INSIDE HER town house, Elizabeth kicked off her red pumps and collapsed onto her couch. Not even her ruby slippers had helped with today's interview.

A sadist had to have invented the job search process. That was the only explanation for the torture involved.

She picked up her phone and called Nancy. "How'd the chemo go this week?"

"Not too bad. The new antinausea medicine is helping a lot." Nancy's voice sounded much stronger than it had in weeks.

"Thank goodness for modern pharmaceuticals. And congrats. You've passed the halfway mark in your treatment."

"That does feel good. I love the Fight Like a Girl T-shirt you gave me, by the way."

"I thought it was fitting, since you're one of the toughest—and I mean that in a positive way—women I've ever known. You will kick this." Nancy's battle put Elizabeth's job situation into perspective. Her problems were insignificant compared to her friend's. "What time do you want me to bring over the soup from Cohen's Deli?"

"Will six-thirty work?"

"My schedule is wide open."

"Speaking of that, how's the job search going?"

After telling Nancy the job situation was going well, Elizabeth ended her call.

If only the search was going as well as the picture she'd painted for her friend.

The interview she'd had today with a small but stable agency had gone passably well by most standards. Rhea and Kayse primarily dealt with food service companies. Not the best fit, considering Elizabeth's culinary skills, and the salary wouldn't come close to covering her mortgage payment, let alone her other expenses. But she didn't have a lot of options.

The more she interviewed, the less enthusiastic she became. She wanted to choose her clients. The thought of getting people to buy luxuries and useless products to increase sales for huge corporations left her feeling hollow. She wanted to help people like Rory, who needed to increase their family business to pay for life's necessities.

Thinking of him sent an ache chasing through her system. She'd tried to stop this exercise in futility and focus on her future, but everything reminded her of him. Today, when she'd seen him staring down at her from the Times Square billboard, her eyes had teared up, blurring her vision so badly she'd stumbled off the curb.

After her interview she'd transferred money from her emergency savings to cover this month's mortgage payment. Then, after seeing her account balance in stark reality, she'd called a Realtor about putting the town house on the market. If she lived off boxed mac and cheese, ramen noodles and PB&J sandwiches, she could last another two months tops. No getting around the brutal fact that she had to get out from under her mortgage payments. So much for a permanent home.

She inhaled deeply. No big deal. She'd survived before she purchased the town house, she'd survive after she sold it.

Darth Vader's theme rang out from her cell phone. Hell must have frozen over if Devlin was calling. How had she missed that happening when she'd read the paper this morning, and why hadn't she deleted him from her contact list? "Hello, Micah. What a surprise to hear from you."

No kidding. That was like saying snow in June was a surprise.

"I've been reconsidering our working relationship. For cohesiveness's sake, I'd like you to continue being part of the team on the new men's line campaign."

Good thing she was sitting down because otherwise she would've fainted. Yup, hell had definitely frozen over. "You signed with Harms and Finn." Chloe had relayed that bit of information yesterday.

"Jack Finn will be contacting you about a position with them."

Considering how she'd pretty much told Devlin to go to hell the last time they'd talked, the job offer made no sense, setting off Elizabeth's if-something-appears-too-good-to-be-true-it-usually-is radar. "What would my position be?"

"You'd work exclusively coordinating Rory's shoots and appearances."

"Does he know about this?"

The man's silence spoke volumes. Rory knew. Devlin was simply trying to figure out how to spin the truth.

He cleared his throat. "When I told Rory we'd signed with another agency, he refused to consider any further ventures if you weren't involved."

While thrilled that Rory cared enough to fight to get her job back, she wanted to land a position on her own merits. She didn't want something handed to her because she was involved with the campaign's model.

But if she accepted the job she could probably keep her town house, and she could see Rory again.

However, accepting Devlin's offer also meant working with pain-in-the-ass clients. She would go back to having no control over her career and convincing people to buy high-priced designer clothes to make themselves feel better instead of concentrating on the things in life that really mattered. Family. Friends. Honesty. Creating a legacy.

And the thought of returning to that life left her cold and surprisingly depressed. She desperately needed more.

Her earlier thoughts flitted through her mind. Small family-owned firms needed, but couldn't afford, quality advertising. Why couldn't she work with people like Rory to increase their business and make their lives better? The idea blossomed within her, leaving her more excited about her career than she'd been in years.

"Micah, while I appreciate your offer, my answer is no, thank you."

A WEEK LATER, Elizabeth stood on the McAlister front porch, her purse full of Claritin, and wished her knees would quit knocking. What if Rory didn't feel the same way she did? After all, he hadn't called her since she'd left Colorado. Maybe he hadn't felt the same connection. Maybe he didn't want a long-term relationship with her. Maybe he didn't love her like she loved him.

But he cared enough to strong-arm Devlin to hire her.

Okay, say he didn't love her. She still had an advantageous business proposal for him. They could both benefit from her advertising suggestions whether they had a personal relationship or not.

Who was she kidding? That would never be enough for her.

"Never thought I'd see you here again."

Her breath caught in her throat at Rory's low, husky voice coming from behind her. With her heart banging against her ribs, she turned to find him standing there on the walkway. He looked almost exactly as he had the day they'd met. Dark blue snap-front shirt, fringed chaps, the crazy royal flush belt buckle and his ever present Stetson. The reality of how much she'd missed him, of how much she loved him, of how much rode on his response to her proposition slammed into her, leaving her weak. "I have a business proposal for you."

"Other than the twenty-five grand I made, our last business deal didn't work out so well. At least the money will get us through a few months."

Since his hat shaded his eyes, she couldn't tell if he was kidding. Didn't matter. She barreled forward. Big gains required big risks. "I'm unemployed, in large part because of you and your stubbornness. The least you can do is hear me out. I think you owe me that."

That's it, Elizabeth, get off to a good start by blaming the guy. That'll make him want to talk to you.

"That didn't come out right." She clutched her briefcase tighter to control her shaking hands. "I'd appreciate the opportunity to present my ideas to you."

His gaze softened as he sauntered toward her. For a minute she thought he might pull her into his arms. She wished he would. That way she'd know he cared.

"Come on in and tell me about this business proposal."

He opened the front door and stepped aside for her to enter. Once inside, the house's warmth and comfort enveloped her. Somehow in the short time she'd spent here, this house had become a home to her, more so than any other place she'd lived.

She walked into the living room and sank onto the couch. Not knowing what else to say, she asked about Nannette's health.

"She's doing better. The oncologist confirmed her collapse was from stress and exhaustion. He's ordered her to take it easier."

"Bet you're having fun trying to get her to follow that order." Elizabeth stared out the window at the mountains, which were so like the man she loved—sturdy, constant, providing shelter to the valleys below.

"Every day or so I lock her in her room so she has to rest."

Elizabeth laughed. She loved his humor, and how he made her smile.

"Mom and Avery are in Portland for another round of treatment. The last CT scan showed her tumor hasn't grown."

"That's wonderful news." Elizabeth took a deep breath and plunged ahead, while she had the courage and he'd given her an opening. "That's part of what brings me here. You need to increase your business to pay for her treatment. I can help you do that." She unzipped her briefcase and pulled out a black binder.

Through working on this idea for Rory's ranch, she'd rediscovered what had brought her to the advertising field—the joy of creating something she felt passionate about.

She held out the proposal, and when he failed to take it, she placed it on the coffee table in front of them.

"You haven't been able to find another job?"

"I'm tired of being part of a large agency. I want to choose my clients, and do work that excites me. I want to make a difference for people who need to increase their business to improve their lives."

"Is that why you turned Devlin down?"

"He told you?"

Rory nodded.

"While I appreciate what you did for me, I want to get a job on my own merits."

"I thought that's how you'd feel, but I wanted you to have a choice." Rory picked up the binder and flipped through the pages.

Her gaze remained locked on his hands. Such strong hands, capable of creating such incredible passion. She blushed, remembering what he'd done to her body when they'd made love. And yet his hands could offer such compassion, as they had when she'd been sick.

Suddenly, warmth coursed through her. Damn pheromones. She had to remain clear-headed. Her future was at stake.

Turning her attention to Rory's face, she scrutinized his features for reactions as he studied her proposal. She hadn't poured bits of herself into a campaign as she had in this one for years. She'd laid out a new website design, coordinated it with an updated brochure, then outlined a marketing strategy.

No reaction. Not good. How could he not love what she'd done?

"I appreciate all the trouble you've gone to, but us working together isn't a good idea."

She ignored the painful twinge in her heart and charged forward, refusing to take no for an answer. "Even if I didn't know how much you dislike dealing with the advertising aspects of your business, looking at your website, your brochures and the ranch's signage would tell me that. If you hire me, I can coordinate those things for you."

"I don't want a business relationship with you."

Her stomach fell and she fought back tears. She hadn't expected such a quick and brutal rejection. "I can increase this ranch's business. I can help you tap into new markets. Give me a chance."

She bit her lip, hating that she danced precariously close to begging.

"You don't get it, Lizzie. I want a personal relationship with you."

Her heart stopped. Just for a second, as his words sank in. She closed her eyes, fearing she was dreaming.

The leather couch scrunched under Rory's movements. When she peeked out from under her lashes, she found him kneeling in front of her. Tears pooled in her eyes.

"You think you could get used to living here?" His large warm hands covered her icy ones.

"I've been exploring the possibilities. I've stocked up on Claritin. I'm considering buying stock in the company." Her gaze remained focused on her ruby slippers. *Please let their magic work this time.*

"Elizabeth." He released her hands. His thumb gently

tilted her chin upward, forcing her gaze to meet his. The look in his eyes, one of tenderness and desire, rendered her speechless. "I want you here. In my house. In my bed. In my life."

"You want us to live together?"

"For a smart businesswoman, you're being awfully dense."

"I'm not being dense. You're being vague."

He flashed her a blinding smile. "I say I want you in my bed and in my life, and that's how you respond?"

"I want to be clear on where you see our relationship going."

"Do I have to spell it out?"

"Apparently."

"I love you. Marry me." His voice wavered the tiniest bit.

Tears stung her eyes. "How can you love me after all I've done? After how I treated you? I looked down on you because I thought you were just a ranch hand, while you treated me with respect. I don't deserve you."

"That doesn't matter now. I can't live without you. Please marry me."

"Yes, I'll marry you."

"Won't you miss the big city?"

"I'd miss you more." Elizabeth smiled. Her cousin Janice had been right. It was amazing what no longer mattered once she found the right man.

Strong hands lifted her. She wrapped her arms around Rory's shoulders as he sank onto the couch, settling her on his lap. He kissed her with a reverence that warmed her all the way to her toes. "There is so much to love about you. You're confident, funny, caring and sexy as hell."

His words reached deep inside her, sewing together the hole in her heart her parents had created. "I love you so much." She looked into his mesmerizing brown eyes. "I'll have to send my cousin Janice a thank-you gift. Coming to her wedding was the best thing that ever happened to me. I'd never have met you otherwise." She bit her lip, deciding to truly test her shoes' magic. "Will you be the Harrington-Smyth Agency's first client? I want to help you increase your business."

"As long as you don't make me model for the ranch's website."

"Are you giving up modeling?"

"I'm finishing out my contract with Devlin for the jeans campaign. He wants me to model other clothing items, but I haven't given him an answer yet. If he kicks in enough bucks I might consider it, but no way in hell am I modeling underwear."

"The women of the world will be so disappointed. What if I need you to model for one of my future clients?"

"No way, sweetheart. The only modeling I'll do is for you in the privacy of our bedroom. There I'll model anything you want."

"Even underwear?"

"Honey, for you I'll model nude."

She chewed on her lower lip and looked him up and down. "I don't know. I'll need to take preliminary photos, kind of like a screen test for a movie."

He stood, still cradling her in his arms. "How about we go upstairs and you can see if you think I'm up for the job."

* * * * *

C.C. COBURN

married the first man who asked her and hasn't regretted a day since—well, not many of them. She grew up in Australia's Outback, moved to its sun-drenched Pacific coast, then traveled the world. A keen skier, she discovered Colorado's majestic Rocky Mountains and now spends part of the year in that beautiful state.

Currently she's living in England with her husband, as well as a Labrador retriever and three cats. Her first book, *Colorado Christmas*, received glowing reviews and a number of awards. She loves hearing from readers; you can visit her at cccoburn.com.

Books by C.C. Coburn

Colorado Christmas
The Sheriff and the Baby
Colorado Cowboy
Colorado Fireman
Sweet Home Colorado

COLORADO COWBOY

C.C. Coburn

Acknowledgments

Many thanks to:
My fellow Harlequin American Romance author
Cathy McDavid for her invaluable assistance
in all matters to do with accounting.

Authors Karen Templeton and Katharine Swartz
for their help with New York City.

Rancher Phil Craven of Texas.
And George Meyers of the spectacular
Santa Maria Ranch in Colorado—a true romantic,
working hard to preserve the traditions of the
West. Theoretical mathematician and sometime
ranch hand and burro racer Daniel McCarl,
for introducing me to George and
showing me around the Santa Maria.

Sergeant Cale Osborn of
Summit County Search and Rescue for his help
with mountain rescue procedures.

And my dear friends equine veterinarian
Dr. Holly Wendell and horse rescuer Helen Lacey
for patiently educating me about horses.

Any errors or discrepancies in this story are the
fault of the author and in no way reflect the
expertise of the aforementioned.

CHAPTER ONE

LUKE O'MALLEY DIDN'T LIKE the look of New York City one little bit. And he didn't like the look of his son any better.

The young street tough lounged in the judge's chambers, chewing gum and wearing an insolent expression. His contempt for everyone in the room extended to his unlaced sneakers braced against the judge's desk as he leaned back on the legs of his chair.

Last night, after receiving the call from the judge summoning him to New York to meet the son he'd fathered by Megan Montgomery, Luke couldn't help wondering: *Is this some sort of scam?*

Now a successful rancher, Luke employed innovative techniques at Two Elk, his ranch in the Colorado Rockies, which had ensured that his herds were among the best in the state, if not the West. And the horses he bred were of superior quality and in demand by ranchers and riders alike.

Had Megan seen the article about him in *Cowboys and Indians* a couple of months ago? He'd been swamped with letters from women looking for a rich husband, and he'd tossed them all in the trash. He wasn't interested in marrying a gold digger. He'd already been there, done that. Had no desire to repeat the experience.

For fifteen years, Luke had wondered about Megan,

where she was, who she was with. Was she married? When he'd gotten the call from Judge Benson summoning him to New York, he'd gone. Even if the kid proved not to be his, he'd wanted to see Megan again with a need he couldn't explain. Ask her why she'd left so suddenly. Why she'd never answered the letter he'd sent to Wellesley.

Now she was back, and he wanted to touch her, kiss her, hold her. Make up for fifteen years without her. Fifteen years of trying not to long for her.

If there was any doubt in Luke's mind as to whether he had a son *before* he and his brother Matt walked into the judge's chambers this morning, they'd been dispelled the moment he laid eyes on Cody Montgomery. The kid was the spitting image of him and his brothers at the same age. Only the O'Malley boys hadn't dared wear their hair so long on one side that it covered their eyes. And on the other side…what the heck was with that buzz cut and the lightning strike shaved into it?

The O'Malley boys sure wouldn't have sported a thing like that miniature dumbbell stuck through their lip, chewed gum or peppered their conversation liberally with four-letter words, either. Their pop, Mac, had seen to that.

Nope. He didn't much like the look of Cody Montgomery, fourteen-year-old runaway and criminal-in-the-making. How had Megan let it come to this?

THIS IS MY so-called father? Cody thought. The guy acted like he had a pole stuck up his butt and Cody resented like the way he stared at him…especially his hair. And his lip piercing. Like he was some sort of freak. Okay, Cody wasn't so crazy about the lip piercing, either, but you needed it to look tough. To be part of the gang. Well, they weren't technically a gang—not yet, anyway. But the guys were checking around for one to join.

He hated the way the guy was looking at his mom, too. Like he didn't believe her. Like he didn't believe he was his son.

That just irritated Cody even more. How could *he* know who his father was? Whenever he'd tried to talk about it with his mom, she'd clammed up. Once, she'd said, "It was a mistake," but that only made it sound like she thought Cody was a mistake. *Worthless. Like trash.*

What else could he think? For all he knew, his real dad could be doing time. Or maybe what he'd done was even worse, though he couldn't think of anything much worse than having a criminal for a dad.

All the guys had fathers who were doing time, so Cody had pretended his was, too. He'd muttered something about armed robbery at a gas station when they asked about it.

Secretly, he hoped that if his father *was* doing time, it'd be for some minor crime, maybe some white-collar offense. That didn't hurt anyone—not physically, anyway. He wondered how many years you got for a white-collar crime. Probably less than fourteen…

He supposed it was okay if his father turned out to be some rancher from Colorado, like this guy claimed to be—as long as the guys didn't find out.

Cody had always liked the idea of Colorado. He wondered if the guy lived anywhere near the Rockies. He'd enjoyed reading *National Geographic* magazines in the school library—when he was a kid. The pictures of the Rocky Mountains were spectacular and somewhere he'd always wanted to go. Not that he'd ever admit it.

Now he didn't have time for that. Now he hung out with the guys....

And now the judge was talkin' again! Sheesh! Couldn't she just mind her own business for a change? He was doing fine. He was surviving.

"...I therefore believe, Mr. O'Malley," she said, "that it would be in Cody's best interests if he could be removed from the environment he's living in at present—"

THE FRONT LEGS of Cody's chair hit the floor with a thud as his feet came off the desk, and he spewed forth a stream of invective that turned the air blue and had Megan cringing in her seat. What must Luke think of his son? What must he think of *her* for letting things get this bad?

Judge Gloria Benson, as usual, was unperturbed. She'd assured Megan at an earlier meeting that she'd dealt with her share of juvenile offenders, plenty of them a lot more hardened than Cody. A bit of bad language didn't faze her. She'd told Megan that most of those children—due to having families who didn't give a damn—were beyond rescue, but she felt Cody had the option of leading a better life.

The judge believed that with his father's intervention, Cody had a good chance of making it to his next birthday—unlike so many kids who came through her court and didn't live past their teens.

That bald admission had been sobering for Megan. The thought that her precious son might die before he reached adulthood... She'd wanted to pack them both up and catch a train or bus to anywhere that wasn't the Bronx or even New York City. Judge Benson had said, "I hope Mr. O'Malley has the courage to accept the challenge and follow through. Because right now, Cody's future is very precarious."

Considering the expression on Luke's face, he'd rather be anywhere than here with his son.

"Your honor," Megan said. "If you'd just give me another chance, I know I can put his life together and get him back into school."

"Ms. Montgomery...Megan..." Gloria sighed. Then she seemed to gather herself and said, "I can't tell you how many mothers have begged me for just one more chance before I send their child to juvenile detention. How many I've yielded to, and then weeks later heard their child had died in a gang fight, or from an overdose of whatever drug was on the streets that day. I'm determined that's not going to happen to Cody. You're a good mom and I know you love your son. But unless you can afford to move out of your neighborhood to a better part of town, where Cody stands a chance of living a healthier—and longer—life, or we can find a solution here today, then I have no alternative but to send him to juvenile detention."

She turned her attention to Luke. "Cody's been in my court three times in as many weeks. His behavior is worsening. He's no longer attending school regularly. He's run away from home more than once, been caught joyriding in a stolen vehicle and I'm concerned he's on the brink of becoming part of the street gang culture of this city. Once that happens, he'll be lost to us."

Megan felt she had to explain, so Luke wouldn't see her as a complete deadbeat. "I'm working two jobs and in my final year of studying to be an accountant. I can't be there to watch him all the time," she said. But even as the words left Megan's mouth, she guessed the judge had heard that excuse far too often. In Megan's case, it was true.

"I understand all of that and your intentions are honorable," Judge Benson said. "But I'm afraid continuing the way things are will result in losing your son to crime and I know you don't want that."

Megan's tiny shake of her head was her only concession to her bald statement. She fought the tears that threatened and then lost the battle as they spilled down her cheeks and dropped onto her blouse.

The judge was right; she needed help with Cody, needed someone to take part in his care and discipline. "That's the reason I wanted to meet Cody's father and see if we could find a solution," Gloria explained. Obviously noticing Megan's distress, she opened a drawer, removed a box of tissues and offered them to Megan.

Megan's hands shook as she pulled several tissues from the box. Feeling thoroughly humiliated in front of Luke and his brother, she blew her nose and wiped her eyes and cheeks.

She wanted to turn her back on everyone. Protect herself from all the bad things in her life. Megan had never stopped loving Luke, in spite of his betrayal. She'd spent too many nights dreaming of seeing him again, being held, being kissed by him. Hearing him declare his love. Never once in those dreams had she imagined they'd meet under such humiliating circumstances.

Megan bit her lip, unable to meet the eyes of the rest of the room's occupants, knowing everyone was staring at her. This would have to be about the lowest point in her life.

And then a warm hand covered hers.

How Megan had changed in fifteen years! Luke thought as he covered her hand, needing to reassure her she wasn't alone anymore.

He'd been a twenty-four-year-old ski-instructor attracted to the college junior with the twinkling blue eyes. She was on spring break in his hometown of Spruce Lake and, within days, they were dating. And then they'd made love. Several times. He'd guessed she was a virgin, but she'd been every bit as enthusiastic as he was. He'd fallen for Megan from the moment they met. It was only later that he wondered if she'd done it as a dare. A city-girl college bet—losing her virginity to the first cowpoke who came along.

She'd left Spruce Lake abruptly without even saying goodbye. He'd tried to contact her, but failed. Back then, cell phones weren't that common, not for college students, anyway.

Weeks later, he'd married his ex-girlfriend, Tory, because she'd claimed to be pregnant by him. He'd tried not to think about Megan for the past fifteen years.

Yesterday, when he'd received a phone call from the New York City judge informing him he had a son, he'd been shocked—disbelieving. To learn not only that he'd fathered Megan's child, but that his son was in trouble with the law, had left him numb and confused. Judge Benson had requested a meeting in her office. Her tone had brooked no argument.

He'd assured the judge that if the child was his, he'd take responsibility and agreed to a meeting at noon the following day, anxious to resolve the matter, anxious to meet his son—if indeed this was his child. Anxious to see Megan again.

Paralyzed with shock, he'd turned to his brother, Matt, sheriff of Peaks County, for support. Matt had immediately agreed when Luke asked him to come to New York. They'd spent a sleepless night on the plane, discussing why Megan had never told him about the kid. How ironic that Tory had claimed to be pregnant with his child but wasn't, while Megan apparently *was*. How deeply he regretted allowing himself to be tricked by Tory, but at the time what was he to believe? They'd split up a few weeks before he'd met Megan. He had no reason not to believe her. If only he'd had the sense to demand a pregnancy test. But Tory had seemed so fragile, so lost.... She'd taken their breakup so badly he hadn't wanted to upset her any further.

He half wished Matt had worn his sheriff's uniform; maybe the kid would watch his language in the presence of an officer of the law.

And in spite of Matt's even-tempered counseling, Luke was still pretty steamed up by the time he'd arrived in the judge's chambers today. He wanted to know why Megan had kept something so important a secret. And how had things gotten to the point that his son was such a delinquent he was on a one-way trip to juvenile detention?

Most young women wouldn't hesitate to contact the father of their child, either to get money out of him— or pressure him to marry them—just as Tory had done. Yet Megan hadn't said a word.

He'd fallen so hard and so fast that, within a week of meeting Megan, he'd wanted to make her his wife. She'd left him waiting at a restaurant with a diamond ring burning a hole in his pocket, feeling like every kind of fool when she hadn't shown up for their date that evening. Instead, Tory had. The woman was obsessed with him. Could find him anywhere in their small town. At first Luke was flattered, but he'd soon found it suffocating. That was why he'd broken up with Tory. However, the news she'd delivered that night guaranteed he'd be tied to her for a very long time. Bile rose in his throat at the memory and he made an effort to push all thought of his ex-wife firmly aside.

Megan had kept his son's existence a secret for more than fourteen years. Why? Luke had so many questions he needed answers to. He studied Megan, trying to gauge how she felt about being here. It was hard to tell, since she wouldn't meet his eyes. She sure seemed worn down by life. Her light brown hair had lost its shine and there were dark smudges beneath her once-vibrant blue eyes. She'd lost a lot of weight, too; her clothes almost hung off her thin frame.

"Luke?" Matt nudged him. "Judge Benson was speaking to you."

Luke turned back to the judge. "I'm sorry, Your Honor. I have to confess, this situation… Well, it's taking me a while to come to grips with it."

"Redneck!" Cody sneered.

"Cody, please?" his mother pleaded. "Don't speak to your fa—*Mr. O'Malley* like that."

That about sums it up, Luke thought. She's scared of the kid. Begging with him, for Pete's sake. So the kid figured his father was a bumpkin because he lived on a ranch, did he?

"I was saying, Mr. O'Malley, that it's taken a great deal of courage on Ms. Montgomery's part to reveal the name of Cody's father and allow me to get in touch with you.

"When I saw Cody here in court again the other day on yet another misdemeanor, I was deeply saddened. His mom is doing the best she can, but raising a child in a city like New York can be hard enough with two parents in the home. It's often almost impossible with one. And when that parent is finding it difficult to make ends meet, their children sometimes shoplift to get the things their parent can't afford to buy them. They're also easy prey for the street gangs. That will be Cody's future if I don't act now. My only alternative is to put him into juvenile detention—"

Cody swore, leaping to his feet, his chair clattering backward onto the floor.

"Cody! Don't use that sort of language. Apologize to the judge."

"No way!" he mumbled, picked up his chair and sat back down with a thud.

Luke was transfixed by the exchange. This kid didn't give a damn who he offended—or hurt—especially his mom. No wonder the kid assumed he could do what he wanted. She was incapable of disciplining him.

Cody leaned back in his chair, and Luke had a clear view of Megan. Tears were welling in her eyes as she looked at him, then glanced away.

She needed him. Needed someone to take charge— if only for a while.

Suspecting most of Cody's behavior was bravado— showing his father and uncle how tough he was—Luke knew one thing for sure: it was long past time to put a stop to it by starting to act like the kid's father.

He leaned toward Cody and said in a low growl, "A word. Outside." He stood and walked toward the door. The kid didn't move. *"Now!"* he said more harshly.

After several long beats, the kid got up and sauntered over to the door. He pushed past Luke and walked out into the foyer.

Thankful the area was deserted, Luke watched as Cody slumped against a column, crossed his arms and fixed a smirk on his face.

It took all of Luke's willpower not to grab his son by the shoulders and shake him. Instead, he took a deep breath and said, "I understand how angry you might be about the situation, but you won't speak to women in that way—*especially* your mother. Treat me how you want, but I will not allow you to *ever* treat your mother like that again."

"Yeah? How're gonna stop me?"

Apparently, the kid was expecting a physical threat, but that had never been Luke's way of disciplining his children. "Because I'm going to be your father from now on. You have a problem, you take it out on me, not your mom. Understand?"

He caught the flare of surprise in Cody's expression, then it became guarded again as he shrugged and said, "Whatever," and strode back into the judge's chambers.

He stood in front of the desk, arms still folded. "Can we go now?" he asked his mother.

"No, Cody, we're not leaving here until we've come to an agreement about your future."

Luke wanted to cheer. At last Megan had said *no*. Up until now, all she'd done was try to placate her—*their*, he corrected himself—son.

"I think we're all agreed we don't want you in juvenile detention," the judge continued. "So now we need to decide on a solution. Sit down, Cody," she said firmly.

Cody hesitated for a moment and then complied,

throwing himself into the chair and slouching in it, a sour look on his face.

Luke wasn't so sure juvenile detention *wasn't* the place for Cody. At juvie, they'd soon sort him out. His mom wouldn't have to constantly worry about where he was. Or maybe Luke could provide them with financial support. Then Megan wouldn't have to work; she could go to school full-time if she wanted. And he'd buy her a place in a better neighborhood.

"...my suggestion, therefore," the judge was saying.

Luke gave himself a mental shake.

"...is that for Cody's sake, he go and live with you on your ranch in Colorado—"

"No!" Megan cried.

Cody's predictable response was another four-letter word.

"You've got to be joking!" Luke exploded, incredulous the judge could suggest this young tough belonged on the ranch with his three innocent daughters.

She calmly folded her hands on her desk. "No, Mr. O'Malley, I'm deadly serious."

Luke shifted forward to emphasize his point. "I can support Cody *and* his mother. I'm more than willing to compensate her for the child support I should've contributed over the past fourteen years. Money isn't a problem."

"Oh, yeah! How much you gonna give me, *Dad?*" The last word was loaded with derision.

"Cody!" Megan made eye contact with Luke for only the second time since meeting again after so many years. "I don't want your money," she snapped. "I can manage." She turned desperate eyes to the judge and asked, her voice trembling, "Are you saying you're giving Luke custody of my son?"

The judge held up her hands and smiled compassionately at Megan. "No, I'm not giving custody to Mr. O'Malley."

Megan released a sigh of relief.

"I'm awarding you both custody. Joint custody."

There was another outburst from his son.

"Cody!"

Unflappable, the judge said, "Cody, if nothing else, moving you to another environment might broaden your vocabulary." She nodded at Luke. "Is this solution acceptable to you, Mr. O'Malley?"

Luke was horrified. It certainly was not. "Judge, I've got three little girls. I don't want them exposed to this sort of behavior—"

"Luke!" Matt muttered beside him.

His brother's caution made Luke realize how selfish he was sounding. "I can pay to send him to boarding school—get him out of this environment. That's what you really want, isn't it? To get him away from the street gangs? There are good boarding schools in Connecticut. His mom could visit him on the weekends." He looked at Megan, pleading for her agreement.

MEGAN WAS APPALLED by Luke's suggestion that they send her son away to boarding school. But then she'd relaxed when he mentioned she'd be close enough to visit Cody every weekend. Certainly a lot closer than Colorado. Maybe when Cody had settled down he could visit with Luke in Colorado. Get to know his father. It would tear her apart not seeing Cody every day, but this might be the only thing that would save him.

"I don't have any objection to an arrangement like that," she said, and glanced at Luke, then wished she hadn't. Feeling the familiar tug of attraction—but stronger now—she silently cursed her desire for this man. Fifteen years had only added to his dark good looks, but it was his willingness to bear some of the burden of raising Cody that had her reacting to him on such an elemental level.

She'd fallen for Luke within days of meeting him. She was so captivated by him, she'd gladly given up her virginity. He'd been charming and funny, with old-fashioned manners and beguiling brown eyes that made her heart melt and her common sense fly out the window. And what had her lapse in rationality gotten her in return?

The conversation she'd overheard at the recreation center the evening she was to meet Luke at the Victorian Inn for dinner had proven what a fool she'd been. He'd toyed with her emotions, stringing her along to believe they were in an exclusive relationship, when, in fact, the woman she'd overheard talking to a friend was pregnant with Luke's child.

She forced the anger—at herself and at Luke—aside and said, "I will agree to any solution that will get Cody away from the environment he's in at present. Somewhere safer, like a boarding school in Connecticut, would be acceptable to me—"

"I'm afraid that's not going to work," the judge cut in, then addressed Cody. "Would you excuse us for a moment, Cody? Your parents and I have things to discuss. You'll find refreshments and a television in the next room." She indicated a small door leading off her office.

Cody leaped to his feet. "Fine! Talk about me behind my back, why don't you? But I'm tellin' you now,

I'm not goin' to any boarding school!" He stalked out, slamming the door behind him, causing Megan to jump with fright.

"I think as you can gather from that little tirade, Cody would only abscond from boarding school," the judge said. "And then we wouldn't know *where* he was."

Megan's earlier hope of getting Cody away from New York and the bad influences surrounding him plummeted. Judge Benson was right, of course. Short of enclosing him in ten-foot walls topped by razor wire, Cody would take off the second his supervisors' backs were turned.

CODY FOOLED AROUND, switching channels on the TV, his mind elsewhere, wondering what the adults in the next room were deciding about his life.

His *father* had other kids? Why hadn't his mom told him that? Maybe she didn't know until today, although by the look on her face, she wasn't that shocked. Maybe that was why his mom didn't want to talk about it whenever he'd asked. He was a married man and she'd had an affair with him. Yeah, that had to be it. His mom wouldn't do anything like that knowingly, so the guy must've lied.

He wondered what happened to his dad's wife, since apparently she wasn't in the picture. Maybe he killed her and buried her on the ranch somewhere. He looked tough enough to kill someone. Judging by the death stare he kept giving him. *Yeah, you might think you're tough, old man, but you don't scare me!*

"CODY NEEDS A FATHER'S influence, and presence, badly," Judge Benson said. "Megan has spent fourteen years raising your son. It's now your turn to help with his up-bringing. I appreciate your suggestion about the boarding school, but I think the best place for Cody right now is on your ranch in Colorado."

"No!" Megan cried. How could she even suggest such a thing? She'd never get to see Cody! It was as if her baby was being wrenched from her arms. Fighting tears, she appealed to the judge. "Cody is my life. My *only* family. You can't take him away from me, Judge Benson. Please don't do this to me."

"I'm not suggesting you stay here without Cody. I think it's best if you both move to Colorado."

The judge had to joking! "I can't do that. My life is here, in New York. I have job obligations and my study—"

Gloria Benson shook her head. "There's nothing to keep you here, Megan. No family, no worthwhile job. You can further your studies in Colorado. I'm suggesting that both of you try and make a go of being a family for Cody."

"But Luke has a wife. I'm sure she wouldn't want him spending his time between two families." She beseeched him with her eyes to tell the judge her plan wouldn't work. Why had the man been so silent throughout this discussion? Surely he was as upset as she was?

"I'm divorced," Luke said in a tone that had her staring at him in disbelief. Judge Benson hadn't said anything about that in the few minutes they'd had together before Luke arrived at the meeting. But she'd obviously been aware of it since she'd made such an outrageous suggestion. And then the impact of Luke's statement hit her. Luke was *divorced?* Somehow, that complicated things even more, but Megan couldn't put her finger on just why.

Matt cleared his throat and said, "I realize this is very difficult for you, Megan, but I'd like to say something on my family's behalf. We can all offer Cody a lot of support. We're a big, close-knit family with lots of positive male role models. I think Judge Benson's proposal is the ideal solution. There's plenty of room at the ranch for you and Cody, and you'd be most welcome there."

Luke rounded on him. "Hold it right there! I haven't agreed to anything. Can you honestly tell me that you want that...that—" he pointed toward the room Cody was in, glanced at Megan, then back at Matt, lowering his voice to a harsh whisper "—*juvenile delinquent* living under the same roof as your nieces?"

"He's not a *delinquent*," Megan protested, her anger rising. How could Luke say that about his son? Be so callous about his own flesh and blood? If only he knew Cody better, he'd know he was a great kid. But since he didn't, she appealed to the judge. "Tell him Cody's a good kid. Please?"

"She's right, Luke. Cody *is* a good kid. He was getting excellent grades in school until a few months ago, but a bad element has moved into the area and it's negatively affecting some of the kids. That display he subjected you to is simply bravado. It's going to take some work to get him back again. Hard work." She played her trump card. "I was hoping you'd be up to it."

Megan felt her lip curl. Luke hadn't been man enough to acknowledge he had a son fourteen years ago when she'd sent him a letter just after Cody's birth, telling him she'd had his child. If he couldn't accept then that he had a baby, he certainly wouldn't be up to the challenge of raising a difficult teen now.

She blinked back tears as she remembered that sad time. The letter going unanswered. The phone call she'd made to the ranch a month later—just in case he hadn't gotten her letter. It had been answered by a woman. Megan had given her name and asked to speak to Luke, but the woman had said, "Luke's away at a convention. I'm his wife. Shall I tell him you called?"

Shocked to the point of gasping for air, Megan had hung up. *Luke was married.* So the conversation she'd overheard hadn't been a mistake or a figment of her imagination. Megan had never felt lonelier than at that moment. Nor had she ever felt more foolish. She wasn't contacting Luke to get money out of him, and she didn't expect him to play a part in their son's life—not if he didn't want to. She'd written the letter as a courtesy. Whether he'd received it or not, there was no point in leaving a message with Luke's wife.

"Megan, are you all right?"

Judge Benson's voice broke into her thoughts and Megan made an effort to control her emotions. She didn't want anyone in this room to know how vulnerable she felt, to know the truth of how stupid and gullible she'd been. Or how angry she was with Luke for denying their son back then.

LUKE TRIED TO CONVINCE himself it was worth risking the stable family life he'd worked so hard to restore since Tory deserted them, only to turn it upside down by letting Cody into it. He wished he'd known about his son all those years ago. Megan was seriously delusional if she thought Cody wasn't a delinquent. Otherwise, why were they all here?

"I know my brother is more than able to rise to the challenge, Judge." Matt's foot connected with Luke's ankle. "I think he's just a little stunned to find out he's a father again. Aren't you, Luke?"

Luke sent his interfering brother a glare. He was perfectly capable of making up his own mind; he didn't need Matt making it up for him. "I'm prepared to give it a try…if Megan is." He looked across at her, his eyes begging her to disagree. She lifted her head defiantly. If he wasn't mistaken, that was pure loathing in her eyes.

As if to thwart him, she gave an almost imperceptible nod.

"I don't want you going into this halfheartedly, Mr. O'Malley." The judge's voice held steel. "What we have here is a boy in desperate need of a father's influence and a strong family relationship—and a mother who's willing to agree to that."

Luke shot another glance at Megan. She didn't look too willing.

"What I need from you is a commitment to your son. A commitment that you will *not* fail him. He needs you, more than he's ever needed anything in his life. And believe me, we *are* talking about his life."

The judge's sobering words brought Luke up short. If Cody continued as he was, his life could be in danger. Sending him away to boarding school wasn't the answer.

He squared his shoulders. "You have my promise, Judge. I'll do everything within my power to help Cody. I'm committed to being his father in every way possible."

The judge nodded and sat back, visibly more relaxed. "Good. So you'll move to Colorado, Megan?"

"If that's what you think is best," Megan said stiffly. Hands clasped, she avoided Luke's gaze.

"Yes," Judge Benson said. "But now we have to face the hard part." She picked up the phone and addressed her assistant. "Would you ask Cody to step back in, please?"

CODY SAUNTERED BACK into the room after a good two minutes of making them all sit and wait on the edges of their seats. It was this sort of insolence that Luke would never tolerate from his daughters. The kid really needed straightening out. Luke only hoped he was as ready for the challenge as Matt claimed he was. He had enough stress in his life, and adding a troubled child to the mix wasn't going to help.

When Judge Benson explained to Cody what the adults had decided, he scrambled to his feet and let loose with a string of colorful adjectives that had Megan blushing and begging him to stop, Luke ready to leap from his chair, drag him to the bathroom to wash out his mouth and both Matt and the judge sitting sagely, waiting for the tirade to end.

Eventually it did, and Cody threw himself back into his chair. The room fell silent. "I'm not goin' anywhere," he snarled.

The judge sighed. "Then I'm afraid you give me no other choice, Cody." She picked up her phone and said, "I'll have to send you to juve—"

"I'll do it on one condition," he interrupted. Obviously, there was room for negotiation where juvenile detention was concerned.

"And what might that be?"

"That he—" Cody pointed at Luke "—marries my mom."

It was harder to tell who gasped louder, Luke or Megan.

MEGAN FOUND HER voice first. "Cody! What are you saying?"

He glared at her, chilling Megan to the bone. What had become of her once sweet-natured son?

"If you want us to play 'happy families,' then he's going to have to marry you. And I mean *right now.*" He gestured dismissively at Luke. "I want him to be committed to us. I don't want him hanging around and pretending to be my dad, like what happens to the other kids in the neighborhood, and then have him run off when somethin' better comes along."

"We'll be living in Luke's home, Cody," she reminded him. "He won't be going anywhere."

"You know what I mean!" he cried, jumping up and overturning his chair. "Everyone in our neighborhood's had dozens of 'dads' or 'uncles' living with them. None of 'em ever stay around for long 'cause they're not married to the kids' moms. They don't care. They're only there for the sex!"

"Cody!" Megan was horrified. Yes, it *was* like that in their neighborhood, but she'd never had another man stay the night, let alone *live* with them. She hadn't even dated. She glanced at Luke to guess what he must be thinking. Did he believe she'd had a succession of men through the door like some of the other single moms in their neighborhood? The men got all the fringe benefits but took none of the responsibility, and they left when things got hard. Or they went to prison.

Luke was watching her carefully, as though considering her reaction, but Megan couldn't think of a thing to say to dispel the notion that she was one of those unfortunate women.

LUKE SEARCHED CODY'S FEATURES. Was the kid trying to manipulate the adults in the room? Or did he genuinely feel that without a marriage certificate, their "family" wouldn't be a valid one?

"It's not going to be like that, Cody. I have a big house. Your mom and you can have your own space. What I'm offering is the security of a home and family who'll love you and care about you."

"How can I know you mean that if you don't care enough about me to marry my mom?"

Luke could see through the bravado to the pain in Cody's eyes. The kid had been through the wringer. Lord knows what kind of men must've been in his life for him to question Luke's commitment like this. Cody wasn't asking them to live as husband and wife and sleep in the same bedroom—and judging by the sparks of anger emanating from Megan, that wasn't even a remote possibility.

What his son was doing was asking Luke to prove he cared about *him,* to prove he'd stick around—by marrying his mom. It was a hell of a big demand, but his son's immediate future was more important than Luke's need for a wife he loved, a wife who'd warm his bed at night. And by marrying Megan, that was what he'd be doing—sentencing himself to a loveless, celibate marriage.

Cody was too young to understand how complex marriage was, how deep the commitment needed to be for both parties to make it work. He'd been twenty-four when he'd married Tory, and at that age he hadn't understood it himself.

"You can't make demands like that Cody," he said as gently as he could. "What you're asking isn't fair to either of us. Your mom has agreed to Judge Benson's suggestion that you both come and live on my ranch. Let's leave it at that."

Cody crossed his arms and nestled further into his chair. "If you won't marry her, I'd rather go to juvie than live on your hick ranch."

"No!" Megan cried, turning to him. "Don't joke about that."

"I'm not joking, Mom. I *mean* it. I need to know he cares enough about me to marry you. He should've done it fifteen years ago."

Luke winced at that. If he'd known about Cody, he would've married Megan. But she hadn't given him that chance and he'd been robbed of knowing his son, of guiding him toward becoming a man. He looked at Cody. The kid was truly hurting. Hurting inside and hurting his mom in the process.

Megan's eyes held terror as she appealed to him. "Please…*do something*," she begged. "He means what he says. He'll go to juvenile detention and I'll lose him forever!" Megan covered her face and turned away.

Luke watched Cody's reaction to his mom. Initially, the kid seemed upset that his mother was in so much pain, and then he got a grip on himself and set his mouth in a firm line—a look Luke associated with his younger brothers at a similar age, when they'd decided they were going to do something and nothing and no one was going to stop them. Cody glared back at Luke as though it was all his fault Megan was crying. All Luke's fault that he hadn't given him his name and his birthright.The love of a father and a family.

Cody was fourteen now, far from being a man. Luke determined there and then that by the time Cody was eighteen, he'd have turned the boy's life turned around, instilled in him what it was to be a responsible member of the community. A man. By then Cody would be graduating from high school and heading off to college. So what was sacrificing four years of his life for the betterment of his son's? If he married Megan now, in four years, they could divorce, move on, find other partners. But in the meantime, Cody would have time and space to grow up and become a contributing member of society. If he went to juvenile detention, his son's life could be in more danger than Luke would allow himself to imagine.

Megan sat with her head down. She looked so vulnerable, so desperate to do the best for their son, but would she agree to such an outrageous proposal? Luke knew he was probably going to make the second biggest mistake of his life—but it might be the only decision that would save Cody.

Sick with fear for his son, Luke got up and went to stand in front of Megan. She refused to lift her gaze to his, so he crouched down.

"Megan," he murmured, waiting until her head came up and she'd focused her sad, defeated eyes on him. Then he asked, "Will you marry me?"

CHAPTER TWO

LUKE STARED OUT the window of the airplane as it flew west, home to Colorado. He couldn't believe what he'd done. Within minutes of proposing to Megan, the judge had them standing before her, reciting their vows.

He'd taken along his birth certificate and ID to the meeting as requested. Apparently the judge had asked the same of Megan. Gloria Benson had issued a marriage license and then, using her judicial powers, had waived the normal thirty-day waiting period required in New York State.

Matt wore a grin from ear to ear throughout the short ceremony. Megan frowned at Luke and chewed her lip while Cody had looked totally bewildered that they'd gone along with his ultimatum. The fact that they'd managed to completely catch him off guard was the only high point of the ceremony. Megan had turned her cheek aside when the judge had pronounced them husband and wife and invited Luke to kiss his bride.

If Luke had thought his marriage to Tory was a living hell, he was having genuine misgivings about marrying a woman who loathed him so much. At least Tory had pretended to like him—for a while.

Four hours later, after arranging to have Megan's and Cody's possessions packed by a moving company and sent to the ranch, they were on the flight to Denver.

Cody had protested that he wanted to go home and get some things, but Luke had refused to let him anywhere near their old neighborhood and instead had taken him shopping for new clothes. That, if nothing else, had earned Cody's grudging agreement. Megan had purchased a few items to tide her over, too.

"Thank you," she'd said quietly as they waited at the curb outside the department store for the cab to take them to the airport. It was the first time she'd spoken to him since the ceremony.

Luke looked at her, puzzled.

"Thank you for giving my son a chance." For once she wasn't looking at him with barely disguised hatred in her eyes.

"He's *our* son," he'd said. "We *will* make this work—together." And then he'd spotted the jeweler's window, turned to Matt and said, "Can we meet you back here in fifteen minutes?" He took Megan's elbow and led her to the window. This might be a marriage of convenience and Megan might hate his guts—although Luke was at a loss to understand why—but a ring was symbolic and, right now, that was all this marriage had going for it.

"Choose a ring," he'd said.

"Luke, this isn't necessary. We've been through the motions. I think that's all Cody really wanted." She smiled tightly. "In fact, I think he's as shocked as we are."

Luke couldn't help grinning. "He is, isn't he? Maybe we should surprise him every so often by agreeing to some outrageous idea."

"Careful," she warned. "He's got an active imagination."

Luke hadn't let go of her elbow and he gave it a little squeeze, needing to impart a sense of mutual purpose. "I'm sure at heart he's a good kid, Megan. We can do this."

She nodded as though resigned to their situation. "I'm determined to."

Luke had followed her into the jewelry store. An assistant showed them the wedding rings, and Megan selected a plain gold band for Luke. "The girls will like this," he said. "Okay, let's get something special for you."

"I'd completely forgotten about your little girls. How are they going to feel about this? You coming home with a wife *and* a son. It's going to be an awful shock for them."

"They'll probably insist we get married all over again for their benefit."

Megan bit her lip. Luke didn't want to find it endearing, but it reminded him of her so long ago....

"Never fear, we have our very own judge in the family. Becky will rise to the occasion with a far more romantic event than our first wedding. If that's what you'd like."

Megan blushed and looked back at the rings, and Luke drew his cell phone out of his pocket. "You keep doing that. I'm just going to call my girls and let them know what's going on."

Luke had turned away from Megan to make his call in private. Fortunately, he got hold of Matt's wife, Beth, rather than one of his daughters. Matt had apparently called Beth already and explained the situation. "Congratulations, Luke! I don't know anyone who's gained both a son and a wife in one day before."

"Very funny," he said. "Can you put one of the girls on, please? I feel I need to warn them."

"Lucky for you, Sash isn't home at the moment. But Daisy's here. I'll put her on."

Luke grimaced as he waited for Daisy. Beth was right, Sash probably wasn't going to be happy at the news of his marriage. She was full of teenage angst and hormones, and these days it was more likely she'd be in a bad mood than a good one.

"Hi, Daddy!"

"Hey, squirt," he greeted his middle daughter, Daisy.

"When are you comin' home?"

"Tonight, honey, but first I need to tell you something."

THE CALL COMPLETED, Luke had closed his phone and turned to Megan. He hoped he hadn't said anything on his end to give any indication that things mightn't be rosy back at the ranch at the news of their marriage.

"How about that one?" she asked.

He shook his head. "Too plain. Hey, that's nice." He pointed to a diamond-encrusted gold band.

"It looks like an engagement ring," Megan said.

"No, madam," the assistant remarked. "It's a special design that incorporates the engagement and wedding rings in one design."

"I like it," Luke said. "It suits us. We got engaged and married at the same time."

When Megan had looked up at him and blinked, Luke experienced a rush of protectiveness toward her. She seemed as full of wide-eyed innocence now as she had nearly fifteen years ago. If only he'd realized back then how much their actions would change their lives…

"I guess you're right. Okay," she said.

The assistant had removed the ring and passed it to Luke, who raised Megan's hand and placed it on her finger, holding his breath and hoping it fit. It really was a beautiful ring and symbolic of their hasty engagement and marriage. "Perfect," he said when it fit. He looked into her eyes, trying to see what was hidden there.

She'd blushed and pulled her hand away. "We'd better get back. They'll be wondering what's happened to us."

Luke nodded. There'd been something in her eyes, something strange and unreadable. He planned to get answers when they were alone at the ranch—starting with why she'd kept Cody's existence a secret.

He'd quickly paid for the rings and, as they didn't need wrapping, headed outside to find Matt and Cody still waiting, only now Cody was wearing headphones attached to a handheld gaming device he was absorbed in playing.

"Cody! Where did you get that?" Megan cried, as though fearing he'd stolen them.

"Relax." Matt placed a restraining hand on her arm before she pulled the headphones off and repeated her question. "Cody suggested we pop back into the store. Somehow I got talked into buying him that."

"I'm so sorry, Matt," Megan said. "I...I'll pay you back as soon as I can."

"Megan, he's my nephew and I owe him a bunch of birthday and Christmas presents. Besides, it's a long trip back to Denver and this is a small price to pay for some peace and quiet. He hasn't uttered a single curse since he put them on."

"Really?" Megan's frown turned into a smile, lighting up her face. Luke liked the effect.

Luke hailed a cab, which whisked them to the airport. Since it was a Friday, the flight was full, but fortunately there were seats available in first class. Luke purchased them without batting an eye.

Cody had seemed impressed and set about devouring every item of food offered to him. He'd then downed a couple of sodas and fallen asleep.

Luke glanced across the aisle at his sleeping son and felt a pull of recognition. He was an O'Malley all right. In spite of the hair and the piercing, he resembled the O'Malley males. He was already pushing six feet and would no doubt end up at least as tall as Matt, who at six-four was the tallest of the five brothers and two inches taller than Luke. Matt, too, was sleeping. How alike his son and his brother looked. Cody had the square, sometimes stubbornly set jaw and straight nose that characterized the O'Malleys.

It was so strange to discover he had another child. A son. He wondered how the girls were going to take it. Twelve-year-old Sasha would probably hate him on sight—and not hesitate to say so! She was at that difficult age—no longer a girl, not yet a woman—with a mass of confused hormonal behavior to back it up. Nine-year-old Daisy, in spite of her feminine name, would challenge him to an arm wrestling or calf-tying contest. She was a real tomboy and loved ranch life. Sweet four-year-old Celeste would have him wrapped around her little finger in minutes.

A pang of conscience gripped him. Was he taking a huge risk by exposing his very innocent, country-raised daughters to his tough, streetwise son? He hoped not and then wondered what Cody would make of his half sisters.

He looked at Megan, dozing beside him, her seat reclined. With her face relaxed in sleep, he could see the beauty that had first attracted him fifteen years ago.

Whoa there, fella! Megan Montgomery might be his wife of a couple of hours, but he hadn't thought about her *that* way in a very long time. She'd been a holiday fling that had turned into something deeper—or so he'd believed until she'd run out on him. He'd had a lot of flings while working as a ski instructor. The job had provided an income over the winter months while his father tended the ranch. Luke was well aware when he started dating Tory that she'd had several lovers. But so had he. She was a willing bed-partner and he didn't think beyond that because he didn't intend to make their relationship permanent. When Luke married Tory a month after Megan left town, he'd hung up his instructor's jacket and given up the carefree bachelor life for good.

Megan stirred and shifted, moving her head closer to him. She breathed in deeply, then exhaled a tiny sigh and buried her head against his arm.

Luke sat stiffly, waiting for her to settle, fighting his reaction to the sound of that tiny, innocent sigh and the feel of her nose pressing against his arm.

This wasn't what he'd planned. He'd assumed he could remain cool and aloof, treat Megan with the respect due the mother of his child and not get involved.

He stood and made his way to the bathroom.

MEGAN FELT LUKE LEAVE his seat, felt the warmth leave her body where her face had nestled against him. She'd woken herself up with that sigh of contentment. Woken up after having a wonderful, slightly erotic dream that even *smelled* good. And then she'd opened her eyes and realized where she was—on an airplane with her face right up against Luke's arm. He was wearing a polo shirt so she'd been burrowed against his bare, muscled flesh. She hadn't dared move, in case he saw she was awake.

"Would you care for a drink?" the flight attendant asked.

Startled, she sat up. "What? Um, I guess so." Unaccustomed to the luxury of flying first class, Megan was a little intimidated by the attentive service. Once, a lifetime ago, such treatment was what she'd been raised to expect.

"We'll have a bottle of your best champagne," she heard Luke saying as he returned to his seat.

The flight attendant turned toward Luke and stepped a little too close for Megan's liking. "Celebrating something?"

"We just got married today."

"Oh, that's lovely," she said, although it sounded to Megan like she didn't really think that was lovely at all. "Congratulations." She encompassed Megan in her already faded smile. "I'll get a bottle and two flutes immediately, sir," she assured Luke.

Luke stretched and then sat down. "I hope you don't mind. It seemed appropriate. We haven't had a chance to toast each other and our future together."

Our future. She wondered how long that future could possibly last. Luke wouldn't be satisfied with hanging around home and hearth indefinitely. He'd soon be out seeking the company of other women. Willing women like the young flight attendant. Sadness engulfed her. Sadness and confusion. She could never hope to compete for Luke's affections with such a smorgasbord on offer. But was that what she actually wanted? Luke's affections? A real marriage—to him? Too much had happened in too short a time; her life had changed in a matter of hours and she hadn't caught up to it yet.

"Is everything okay?" Luke asked.

"What? Oh, yes. Fine. Why?"

"You look a little peaked. I hope you're not having regrets already."

Not yet, but I know I soon will, she thought.

"You're afraid of heights. Are you also afraid of flying?" he asked, reminding them of their first date.

Luke had packed a picnic and driven them to Inspiration Point, a local beauty spot above the town of Spruce Lake. The location would've been ideal—if it didn't plunge nearly a thousand feet to the valley floor. As soon as she'd stepped from his vehicle and noticed how high they were and just how close the cliff face was, she'd suffered an attack of vertigo and nearly passed out.

Interesting that he'd remembered that date…and how afraid of heights she was.

To purge the memory of Inspiration Point from her mind, she said, "Tell me about your daughters, Luke, and the rest of your family. I remember you're the oldest of five boys and that you were all raised on a ranch, but I guess in the few weeks we…knew each other, that's all I ever found out about you."

The champagne arrived, and Luke allowed the flight attendant to pour the sparkling liquid into two chilled flutes.

He turned toward Megan and touched his glass to hers. "To us."

She lifted the glass to her lips, took a sip, then crinkled her nose and sneezed. "Oh! The bubbles got to me," she said. "I'm sorry. I didn't mean to spoil your toast."

He touched his glass to hers a second time and said, "Let's try that again."

They did, and Megan managed to keep her ticklish nose under control.

She settled back against the seat and listened while Luke filled her in on his family, loving the sound of his voice, deep and sure. She'd done the right thing letting the judge get in contact with Luke. Who was she kidding? She hadn't had any choice. Judge Benson had practically blackmailed her into it! Either she gave her Luke's details, or Cody would be sent to juvenile detention that very night.

It'd been easy to get Luke's number. He'd been at the ranch his family had lived on for four generations. Megan had asked to leave before the judge spoke to him. She didn't want to be in the room and hear Judge Benson going through a long explanation of who Megan was and hearing him deny that he knew her, hearing him insist he couldn't possibly have fathered her child. The denial would've hurt too much.

When Judge Benson called Megan that night, she'd told her Luke was arriving the next day and they'd be meeting in her chambers. Stunned by the swiftness of his response, she'd asked, "Did he remember me?" and instantly cursed herself for sounding so desperate, so *adolescent*.

It gave her a tiny thrill when the judge said, "Of course he does, Megan. He seems like a very pleasant man, if a little dazed at the news that he has a son. He'll be in my chambers tomorrow at noon. Please be there with Cody."

"Of course I will. And, Judge Benson, thank you so much for taking the time to care about Cody."

"It's my pleasure, Megan," the judge had told her. "At this point, as I explained to you earlier, I think the best thing for him is to meet his father. I'll take it from there."

"H-how do you know that's the best thing. You haven't met Luke. He could be an ax murderer or... or—"

The judge had laughed heartily. "An ax murderer with a voice like that and a glowing character reference from both the local sheriff *and* a county judge? I don't think so. See you at noon tomorrow."

The judge had hung up before Megan got a chance to question her further. Megan hadn't slept a wink.

"...then there's Matt. He's married to Beth."

Megan was brought back to the present, wondering how much she'd missed of what Luke had said.

"Are you sure you're okay?" Luke asked. "You were looking at me, but I don't think you were taking much in."

"I...I guess I'm just tired." She shrugged. "Jet lag."

"It's only 6:00 p.m. New York time. You can't be *that* tired."

Luke held his hand to her forehead. She told herself not to think anything of it. His apparent concern probably meant as much now as it had back then. *Nothing.*

Luke took the champagne glass out of her hand and pressed the flight attendant call button. When the woman appeared, he handed her the glass and said, "My wife isn't feeling well. Could you get her a cool compress."

My wife. The words had Megan's heart pounding.

They sounded so good. So…*possessive*. Normally, she would've backed away from such a notion. But those words—coming from Luke—had sounded…like something she very much needed to hear.

"I'm fine," she assured him. "I'm just a little tired. I didn't sleep well last night." Megan wished she could take that statement back, not wanting Luke to know she'd been terrified about today's meeting.

But if she was honest with herself, she'd liked his take-charge attitude. She'd especially appreciated it when he'd dealt with her boss at the supermarket where she stocked shelves each evening. When Luke had asked for the phone numbers of her workplaces, she'd had to explain, embarrassed to the core, that she'd been fired from her job at a call center that morning. Her boss there had been unwilling to give her time off so she could attend the meeting at Judge Benson's chambers, claiming he'd cut her too much slack already over her son. Furthermore, her boss at the supermarket had told her that if she was late for work one more time, she'd be looking for another job.

This morning, she'd been frantic, worrying how she'd pay the rent if she lost not just one job, but two. She'd been mortified as she told Luke, watching his face crease—with disgust.

She'd thought the disgust was aimed at her until he'd pulled out his cell phone, dialed the number she gave him and told Jerry at the supermarket that his wife, Megan *O'Malley,* was moving to Colorado that day and therefore wouldn't be reporting for work that evening. She could hear Jerry sputtering on the other end of the phone. Luke had cut him off with a sharp, "You threatened to fire Megan if she got to work late this evening.

This is a courtesy call to let you know she won't be in tonight—or any night." Luke had then given him a post office box number to send her paycheck to and impressed on her ex-boss that he expected the check to arrive within the week; otherwise, he'd be taking action. After repeating virtually the same threat to Pat Reagan at the call center, Luke closed his phone and smiled at her. "I hope you don't mind, but I won't have you fired from two jobs in one day."

"Better for me to quit at least one of them?" she'd asked, still a little stunned by what Luke had done.

"Exactly. I have a feeling your self-esteem has taken quite a battering over the past months. I'm going to help change that."

At that promise, Megan started to fall a little in love with him all over again. Although she'd fought her own battles over the years, it was heaven to have someone in her corner for a change. And Luke was right about her self-esteem. It had never been particularly high, but having to work menial, minimum-wage jobs to make ends meet, while pursuing her studies, had caused her sense of worth to plummet. To further realize that all her sacrifices to provide a better life for her and her son were amounting to nothing made her feel as if she was on a nosedive to nowhere.

The flight attendant reappeared, handed the compress to Luke. He placed it on Megan's forehead. "This should help," he said. "Now, close your eyes and get some sleep."

She forced herself to breathe deeply and slowly, allowing each part of her body to relax. She succumbed to sleep, her last conscious thought: *What happens tonight?*

Luke watched Megan sleep, feeling a protectiveness toward her he'd never felt for Tory.

Even when Tory had supposedly miscarried months after they married, he hadn't felt anything for her. He should have ended the marriage then, when she'd claimed to lose the baby, but Tory had threatened suicide, so he'd stayed, feeling responsible for her.

It wasn't until many years later that he discovered Tory hadn't been pregnant. He'd been such a fool, allowing Tory to dupe him into marrying her.

Luke turned his attention to Megan, determined to purge any thoughts or regrets about Tory from his mind.

She sure was different from the girl he'd known nearly fifteen years ago. Back then, if the bubbles had gotten up Megan's nose, she would've giggled and asked for more. She wouldn't have apologized for anything. What had made her change? She seemed so unsure of herself. She'd been an economics undergrad back then. He'd been under the impression that she came from a wealthy family, since she was attending Wellesley College, wore a Rolex and her ski suit, boots and skis were top-of-the-line. She and her friends were staying at Spruce Lake's most expensive hotel, where the rooms went for more than a thousand dollars a night.

Luke sighed with disgust at himself. He'd chosen the Victorian Inn for the dinner where he'd intended to propose, because it was the most expensive in the county. He'd expected her to be impressed. Never mind that the bill would cost him at least two weeks' pay. Megan was worth it.

So, what had happened to all the wealth? he wondered. Had her parents lost everything in a stock market or property crash? He wanted to ask, but it seemed too intrusive a question.

The only thing that really mattered was that she was back in his life. Sure, he was angry, wanted answers as to why she'd kept Cody a secret, but there was time enough to deal with that. Luke was confident that once she'd settled in at the ranch, he and Megan could take up where they left off. Become lovers again. But first, they had to become friends.

"WE'RE HERE." LUKE'S DEEP voice broke into Megan's dreams.

Megan opened her eyes to find Luke leaning over her and thought she wouldn't mind waking up like that every day for the rest of her life.

"We're coming into Denver. You'll have to put your seat upright," he said, pressing the button on her armrest. "You've had a long sleep."

Megan was having trouble separating fantasy from reality. She felt drugged and shook her head to clear it. It couldn't be the champagne; she'd only taken a few sips.

The plane touched down and the pilot made his announcement about local time. Megan turned her watched back two hours, to just after 6:30 p.m. Then she looked across to check on Cody. It was the first time he'd been on a plane, but he hadn't displayed a second's concern about it. In fact, he was talking animatedly to Matt and pointing out the window at the huge airport terminal they were taxiing toward. He'd even removed his earplugs from his ears. Usually Cody wouldn't give an adult the time of day and would've ignored all attempts to engage in conversation, but Matt seemed to have the magic touch.

She smiled and said, "I can see an improvement in Cody already."

"Matt's got a way with kids." His mouth turned down in a slight grimace. "I wish I had his easy way of dealing with them. Especially my son."

Megan couldn't begin to imagine the regrets Luke must be having. He'd not only taken on a wife and a recalcitrant son but also a stepmother to his daughters and a half brother to them, as well. She wondered how the little girls would react to the changed family structure. Would they accept it? Or would they rebel? Megan shuddered. She knew exactly what her son's reaction would be in those circumstances.

"Relax. Everything'll be fine," Luke said, correctly guessing her thoughts.

Megan bit her lip. "I wish I had your confidence."

When the plane stopped at its gate, Luke removed their carry-on luggage from the overhead bins. An overnight bag for him and a couple of department-store shopping bags for Megan. He stood back to let her exit the plane ahead of him.

Since Cody had several department-store bags stuffed full of clothes Luke had bought him, they'd purchased an overnight bag at the airport, to save any problems with security. He watched as Cody drew out his bag and stuffed in the toiletry wet packs, usually reserved for overseas segments, that he'd talked the flight attendant into giving him.

Luke ignored the transgression. He figured he'd paid enough for the four seats to warrant a few souvenirs. He smiled down at Megan, warning her with a shake of his head not to protest. "At least we won't be held up at the baggage carousel," he said. Their cabin luggage was all they had to take with them.

TWENTY MINUTES LATER, they were all loaded into Luke's big SUV and headed toward Denver and the mountains beyond the Mile-High City. Megan sat up front with Luke, while Cody was in back with Matt.

"Oh! I'd forgotten how majestic they are," Megan remarked at the sight of the Rockies rising abruptly behind the city. She turned to Luke. "How long till we get home?"

Home. She couldn't believe she'd let that slip. A word so personal, so possessive, so intimate. Luke must think she was a gold digger for agreeing to marrying him so readily. For even agreeing to it at all! Luke's home wasn't her home. It was just where she and Cody would live for a while, until Cody was back on the straight and narrow.

"About two hours. Matt's wife, Beth, will have everything ready for us. She's been looking after Celeste today and doing the school run with Daisy and Sash."

Megan had overheard part of Luke's cell phone conversation in the jewelry store, and to her ears, it hadn't seemed to go so well. "How do you think the girls will react to two complete strangers suddenly becoming part of the family?"

Luke glanced over at her, frowning. "I know I probably made a mess of things in my phone call, but rest assured, Beth would've found the right way to tell them."

Megan twisted her hands in her lap. "Still… Maybe Cody and I should stay somewhere else for a while, until they can come to terms with everything. It must've been a big shock for them to be told they've got a new brother *and* a new mother."

"Relax. They're good kids. They'll accept you quickly. I'm sure of it."

Megan wasn't so sure, but she guessed Luke knew his daughters better than she did. She relaxed against the seat back and closed her eyes, unable to believe how tired she was.

"WE'RE HOME." LUKE'S VOICE woke Megan. Surprised that she'd dozed off again, she opened her eyes to find they'd pulled up outside a long, ranch-style house, its lights blazing brightly in the summer evening. The sound of dogs barking and children squealing filled her ears.

Luke had climbed out of the vehicle and was opening her door. A woman came out onto the veranda and stood silhouetted in the light spilling out of the house. She ran toward the car and then Matt's huge bulk was blocking the way as he picked her up and kissed her.

"Where is she? Where is she?" Megan heard a little girl demanding and looked down to see two big blue eyes staring up at her from between Luke's legs.

Megan climbed down from the SUV. Luke stepped back a little and the child squeezed between his legs and popped up between him and Megan.

"Are you my new mommy?" she asked.

Megan was touched by both the beauty of the little girl and the sweet innocence of her inquiry. The child reached out and stroked Megan's hand as though to check if she was for real. Megan squatted down so she could be at eye level with the child and smiled warmly. "Hi. You must be Celeste."

Celeste grinned broadly, then turned shy and twisted sideways as though seeking the protection of her father.

Megan held out her hand to Celeste and said, "I'm Megan and I'm very pleased to meet you, Celeste."

"Are you going to be my mommy?" Celeste asked again.

"Would you like that?" she asked cautiously, unsure how to approach the subject diplomatically.

"Oh, yes!" Celeste cried, and threw her arms around Megan's neck with such force it nearly knocked her backward.

Megan breathed in the sweet scent of the little girl, fresh from her bath, and felt a longing deep within her. She'd loved being a mother to Cody, but he'd stopped hugging her like that a long time ago. Megan laughed and lifted Celeste as she stood; she noticed Luke's grimace changing to a smile of relief.

"One down, two to go," he whispered to her.

She glanced around for Cody to introduce him to the girls. He was standing some distance from the group, studying another girl who was appraising him openly. She guessed that must be Sasha.

Megan took the initiative. "Celeste, I'd like you to meet my son, Cody. He's also your half brother."

"Does that mean he's only half a boy?" Celeste asked, wide-eyed.

Luke guffawed and everyone else joined in, but Megan saw the embarrassment on the little girl's face. After all, she'd drawn what was to her a logical conclusion. She held Celeste against her and nuzzled her soft cheek. "No, sweetie, although it does sound a bit like that, doesn't it?" She waited while Celeste nodded slowly. "It means that you and Cody have the same daddy, so Cody is half a brother to you."

"Who's his other half, brother to?"

Megan couldn't help smiling. Celeste's naiveté was delightfully refreshing. "You're just too gorgeous, did you know that? And smart, too."

"Am I?"

"Uh-huh."

Celeste hugged Megan. "I love you already."

Megan kissed Celeste's cheek. Maybe meeting Luke's daughters wasn't going to be so difficult. "I love you, too," she said.

When Megan felt Luke's hand at the small of her back, urging her toward the rest of the group, she stepped away from the SUV to where another child stood waiting and watching and occasionally telling one or other of the barking dogs to, "Shut up, you idiot!"

"This is Daisy, my little lady," Luke said with a touch of irony and a smile that melted Megan's heart. There was no doubting Luke's love and affection for his daughter.

Daisy looked up at Megan, then down at her feet and back up again as though sizing her up for a coffin. "Hello," she said. Turning to Luke, the girl added, "She's kinda skinny."

"Daisy!" The three other adults reprimanded her at once.

"It's fine." Megan hastened to appease them. She shifted Celeste to her left hip and held out her right hand. "I'm pleased to meet you, Daisy, and yes, I agree I'm too skinny. I'm hoping all this fresh country air will give me an appetite. What do you think?"

Daisy shook her hand vigorously, then nodded.

"Yeah, it will. But you gotta eat your veggies, or you don't get dessert."

"Absolutely," Megan said, straight-faced. She glanced toward Sasha, who'd finally dragged herself away from staring at Cody. "And you must be Sasha."

Sasha studied Megan's outstretched hand, then accepted it reluctantly, shook it once and let go. *Okay,* thought Megan. *This one's used to being the alpha female around here.* And that was fine with Megan. She had no intention of moving in on anyone's territory.

"Cody, come and say hello to your new sisters," Megan called, and he sauntered over.

"Did your hair growed like that?" Celeste asked Cody, and reached out to touch it.

Cody pulled away. "Get lost!" he yelled. "Don't you ever shut up?"

Luke had had enough of Cody's behavior. "That's it. You!" He pointed at Cody's chest. "In there. Now!" he commanded, hitching his thumb over his shoulder and gesturing toward the barn.

Megan was relieved to see that Cody was so shocked at the anger in Luke's voice, he didn't argue or disobey. He looked around the circle of people who were all frowning at him in anger, disgust or bewilderment. Celeste had turned her face into Megan's shoulder and was sobbing softly.

Megan rubbed Celeste's back and fixed her son with a look of utter contempt. How *could* he have used such language in front of the children and hurt such an innocent little girl? What had her son become? Tears burned the backs of her eyes.

She'd wanted to admonish Cody but he was with strangers and she didn't want to fracture his ego in public. On the other hand, it wasn't acceptable that he get away with such behavior. Thankfully, Luke had stepped in before she'd even had a chance to open her mouth. She watched Luke striding toward the barn, Cody behind him, dragging his heels. At least he'd gone with Luke; that was something. If she'd told Cody what to do, he would've ignored her completely.

She felt Matt's hand on her shoulder. "Don't worry, Megan. Luke's just going to talk to him, that's all."

Megan turned worried eyes to Matt. Had she really looked as though she thought Luke would hurt her son? Mortified, she turned back to the rest of the group. "I'm so sorry about that. I… His behavior was unforgivable." Celeste continued to sob quietly on her shoulder. "There, there, sweetie. It's all right," she cooed. "Cody didn't mean to be rude. He's just had a long day."

Celeste lifted her head. "He…he…he…*yelled* at me!" she sobbed, and dropped her head to Megan's shoulder again.

Megan didn't know how to placate the sobbing child. What a way to start your life with your new family!

Matt reached over and took Celeste from Megan's arms. She snuggled against him and stopped crying. Matt put his arm out and drew the other woman to his side. "Megan, this is my wife, Beth."

Beth extended her hand. "Welcome to our family, Megan," she said, shaking Megan's hand with considerably more warmth than Sasha had displayed.

Beth was tall, blond and elegant in spite of wearing faded jeans and a camisole under an unbuttoned chambray shirt. Her face glowed with health and contentment. Megan liked her immediately. "I'm not so sure we'll be welcome after that little outburst," Megan said as she glanced worriedly toward the barn. She half expected Luke to come out pulling Cody by the ear and tell them both to get in the vehicle and send them packing back to New York.

"Nonsense!" Beth said. She reached out with her other hand and caught both of Megan's in hers. "Luke will lay down the ground rules and then everything will be fine—you'll see. He's very much the boss around here and Cody needs to know that. Come on into the house. The girls have prepared a special surprise for you."

As they mounted the few steps to the porch, Celeste wriggled out of Matt's arms and raced to open the screen door, then stood back to allow Megan to enter first.

Megan's breath caught in her throat. Strung across the hall was a banner with the words *Welcome Home, Megan and Cody.*

Everyone piled into the house after her and Celeste looked up and said, "We made it ourselves. D'you like it?"

Delighted that Celeste had apparently recovered from Cody's outburst, she smiled down at the little girl and smoothed her fair hair. "It's the prettiest thing I've ever seen, and so thoughtful." She looked around at all three girls. "Thank you. I...I'm only sorry I haven't got a present for all of you." She cursed herself for not getting them something.

"I have."

Cody stood just inside the door, Luke behind him. He no longer looked grim, so Megan presumed their "talk" had gone well.

Celeste danced up to Cody, all unpleasantness forgiven. "What've you got for me?"

Megan was curious, too. Cody hadn't purchased anything apart from clothes for himself and the PSP Matt had bought him. He unzipped his bag and took out the airline wet packs and handed one to each girl.

"Wow!" Celeste tore the cellophane wrapping off and opened the zipper. "Look! It's got a little toothbrush 'n' paste 'n' a comb 'n' a face washer 'n' mouthwash 'n' socks…." She emptied the contents onto the floor and sat down to inspect them further, then seemed to remember her manners and stood and held up her arms to hug Cody.

His face red with embarrassment, Cody bent down toward Celeste.

"Thank you, Cody. I love it!" she said, and hugged him fiercely, then let him go.

Cody stood to his full height again. "You're welcome, kid, and about before…I'm sorry."

Celeste smiled up at him. "That's okay. You prob'ly missed your afternoon nap," she told him with absolute guilelessness.

Sasha and Daisy thanked him, too, but not so exuberantly. They looked more bewildered by their strange gifts than grateful. But Megan was thankful Cody had broken the ice with his peace offering.

"I'll show you your rooms," Beth said, "and then we can have supper." She led the way upstairs and opened a door off the wide hallway. "This is your room, Cody. I thought you might like it here. It was your father's room when he was a boy."

Megan noticed Cody didn't seem too pleased by that bit of news. He sauntered inside and looked around the room, which was about four times the size of his room back in New York.

"Is there another one?" he asked of Beth.

She looked taken aback. "Well, no. Except the nursery, and I'm sure you wouldn't want to sleep there."

Megan was beginning to feel a sense of foreboding. If there weren't any other bedrooms, where was she expected to sleep? Surely not with Luke? Hadn't he assured them there was plenty of room for everyone?

Cody threw his bag onto the bed and flopped down on it. Taking that as a yes, Beth started back downstairs to a hallway leading from the living room and then to another wing of the house. She opened a door. "And these are your quarters, Megan. I hope you'll be comfortable here."

Megan went into the room, the three girls following on her heels. "This is the sitting room," Beth explained, "and here's the bedroom."

Megan walked through the pleasantly decorated sitting room, the walls covered with framed photos of dark-haired boys and young men, presumably the O'Malley boys at various stages of growth. She resisted the urge to look closer, to find the similarities between Cody and his father and uncles. She stepped gingerly through the bedroom doorway, surprised to find how plainly furnished the room was. It was neat, but there was no sign that anyone else lived there. No clothes across the end of the bed or flung over the chair, no book opened facedown on the nightstand.

Luke came up behind her and Megan felt a chill down her spine. She was supposed to share this bed with Luke?

"This is my folks' quarters," he said. "They usually

live here at the ranch but they're on an Alaskan cruise at the moment. Beth thought you might be more comfortable in here...for now."

For now? Did he expect her to eventually move into his room? The thought had her heart racing and her face heating.

Beth opened another door off the bedroom. "The bathroom's through here and a closet, too. There's a kitchenette off the sitting room, so you can make your own tea or coffee if you like."

"We built this extension for my folks when I took over managing the ranch." Luke dropped Megan's bag on the bed. "But they've hardly used it. They're too busy seeing the world." As if sensing her discomfort, he said, "There's an apartment over the barn if you'd prefer. But it's not really habitable at the moment, since the plumbing's not connected."

"Oh," was all Megan could manage, immensely relieved that she didn't have to share the bed with Luke. *For now.* But what if his parents returned home unexpectedly?

"Do you want to freshen up or have supper?" Beth asked.

Megan observed the way Matt was looking down at his wife. *Oh, to have the love of a man like that!* she thought.

"I'll just wash my hands if that's okay. I'm sure the girls need to get to bed."

Celeste said, "We've had dinner, 'cause I have to be in bed at seven-thirty. But Aunt Beth said we can stay up a bit later, 'cause tonight's special."

Megan smiled at the little girl who was now her stepdaughter. She was adorable. The fact that this child had never really known a mother's love broke her heart.

Luke had explained during the drive that Tory had deserted the girls before Celeste's first birthday. She'd taken off with a rodeo star, leaving the girls with him. Having met them, Megan was even more bewildered as to why Tory would throw all this away for the itinerant life of a rodeo star's lover.

Megan vowed then and there that she'd more than make it up to Celeste, and Daisy and Sasha, too, if they'd let her.

"Come on, girls," Beth said. "I think I can hear my little Sarah waking up."

Forgetting completely about Megan, Celeste dashed out of the room and down the hallway, followed by her sisters.

SUPPER CONSISTED OF a beef casserole with mashed potatoes and peas. The girls, who'd already eaten dinner, had a dessert of ice cream and fresh fruit salad.

"I'm sorry it wasn't something a little more spectacular for your first night," Beth apologized. "But this is the girls' favorite meal and they felt you'd like it, too."

Megan smiled at them. "It's the most delicious beef casserole I've ever tasted. What's the secret?"

Daisy piped up. "Black Angus, the best beef in the world."

Megan was surprised by the pride in the girl's voice and by her knowledge. "You seem to know a lot about the cattle," she said, and ate another mouthful.

"Daisy's going to take over the ranch from Daddy one day," Sasha told her. It was the first time she'd addressed Megan directly since they'd sat down. And

Megan got the distinct impression she was warning Megan about *who* exactly was going to inherit the ranch!

"Oh, you don't have any interest in it?" Megan asked her.

"Hell, no!"

"Sasha! Penalty box," Luke snapped.

The girl's face fell. "Oh, come on! I haven't had any allowance for weeks because of that penalty box. Darn it."

"And you won't have any for the next few weeks if you keep that up, young lady," Luke said from the head of the table.

Sasha ignored her father and spoke to Megan. "I don't like dumb old cattle. I'm going to marry a man with a stud farm in Kentucky."

"In your dreams!" Daisy taunted from across the table.

Sasha narrowed her eyes. "Better than hearing silly old cows mooing all night and stepping in their poop all the time!"

"Sasha, penalty box!"

"Yeah, like horses don't poop," Daisy reminded her, completely ignoring the fact that her sister had just been fined for cussing. "What're you going to do? Get your husband to put diapers on them?"

Celeste giggled at that, then so did Cody. Soon the whole table was in uproar as Matt lifted a napkin in the air and pretended he was diapering a horse.

The rest of the meal passed companionably, but when Megan yawned, Beth took that as their cue to leave. "I'm sure you've all had a long day, so we'll get going," she said, standing. "Girls, could you help me clear the table and load the dishwasher, please?"

"Let me." Megan got up, but Matt laid a restraining hand on her arm as he stood to help his wife. "You'll be busy enough tomorrow with four children to look after instead of one. I imagine that's going to be quite a shock to your system. And a husband, too." He glanced at Luke, and Megan saw the look that passed between the two brothers.

Megan swallowed hard at that reminder of her new responsibilities. *A husband, too.* And *four* children. In one day, the size of her family had tripled, which would take some getting used to. Well, starting tomorrow she'd do just that—get used to it. For the moment, all she wanted to do was sleep.

"Will you read me a bedtime story?" Celeste stood beside Megan's chair and slipped her little hand into Megan's.

"Yes, of course." Megan stifled another yawn, not sure if she'd last to the end of the story. "But first, I'd better see everyone off."

"Don't worry about us," Matt said. "We'll be back tomorrow. The rest of the family's coming over for a barbecue and can't wait to meet you both." He walked to Cody's seat and held out his hand. "Nice to have you in the family, Cody."

Cody shook Matt's hand, surprising Megan. She mused that Matt sure had a way with kids. Normally, Cody would've ignored such a polite gesture and turned away.

Beth came from the kitchen. "All cleared up. Ready, darling?" she asked, and Matt went to collect their baby daughter from the nursery.

"I'll have to wait for my chance to hold her until tomorrow," Megan said wistfully as she gazed at the sleeping baby.

Beth laughed. "You'll have to stand in line. She's everyone's favorite toy around here."

"She has been for six months, darling." Matt gazed down at his wife and daughter with loving eyes.

Celeste tugged at Megan's hand and drew her toward the stairs, reminding her of the bedtime story. "Bye, everyone," Megan called. "It was so nice to meet you, Beth, Matt. See you tomo—" Her last words were cut off as she was dragged down the hallway by Celeste, impatient to get to her room.

Megan tried not to yawn too much while Celeste brushed her teeth. Then she sat on the side of the small bed and opened the book the child handed her. Celeste leaned over and gave Megan a big hug and kiss. "Just'n case I fall asleep before you finish," she said, then laid down and closed her eyes.

Megan began to read, making an effort not to yawn too often. She watched Celeste's chest rise and fall rhythmically and continued reading, yawning after every few words, not taking in one little bit of the familiar story.

Hans Christian Andersen's *The Little Mermaid* had been one of her favorites as a little girl. Night after night, she'd pester her nanny to read it to her.

But all she could comprehend right now was that it was a fish out of water story—in more ways than one. Exactly how Megan was feeling.

CHAPTER THREE

"D'YOU THINK SHE'S DEAD?"

"No, dummy. See? Her chest's goin' up 'n' down."

"She looks kinda dead." Megan opened an eye to find Celeste leaning over her. "Oh! You're alive. That's good. D'you wanna come and play with my dolls?"

Megan opened both eyes. Celeste and Daisy were right beside her bed. Sasha stood behind them, her arms crossed, wearing a stern expression. "Do you want coffee?" she demanded in a voice that said what she thought of people who slept half the day away.

Megan nodded. She rubbed her eyes and glanced at the bedside clock. Ten-thirty! Good heavens. Today was the first day of being a mom to four kids and she hadn't even been up in time to get their breakfast. The aroma of strong coffee filled the room. Sasha stood at the end of the bed, now with a tray in her hands. She placed it on Megan's nightstand.

"Daddy made you coffee early, but you weren't awake so he made you some more. You *still* weren't awake. I made this one," she said, and Megan could hear the exasperation in her voice.

Well, that's telling me, Megan thought. Luke had been in twice with coffee expecting her to be up and then Sasha had felt she needed to make some. Hoo, boy. What a way to start married life. She sat up and took a sip and tried not to sputter. It was strong enough to strip paint.

"I did it the way Daddy likes it," Sasha explained. "You like it black with no sugar, don't you?"

Actually, Megan liked it with cream and one sugar, but she wasn't going to upset Sasha any more than she apparently already had. She forced down another sip and shook her head when the caffeine kicked in, clearing the fog in her brain instantaneously. "Mmm, this is good," she managed to say around the cotton-wool feeling in her mouth, and looked down at herself. She was dressed only in her camisole and panties. She quickly pulled the covers up, wondering, *How did I end up here, undressed and without my bra?* She tried to remember how she gotten from Celeste's room to hers last night, but drew a blank.

She smiled at Celeste and Daisy, who were watching her intently. Sasha had left the room. "Did you sleep well, girls?"

Celeste climbed onto the bed. "Not as well as you. We been waitin' *ages* for you to wake up and be our mommy."

Megan smiled again. At least Celeste and Daisy seemed pleased she was here; she couldn't say the same for Sasha, though. The girl's disapproval was palpable.

I must've slept so long because of the country air, Megan told herself. She'd never slept till ten-thirty since her college days, and only if she'd pulled an all-nighter studying for exams. "Did I finish your story last night, Celeste?"

Daisy answered that one. "Nope, you fell asleep on her bed and Daddy had to carry you here. You were snoring."

Megan's face heated. Luke must've undressed her, too!

She ventured another sip of the extrastrong coffee and then Sasha returned bearing a second tray, this one loaded with crisp bacon and toasted bagels. The aroma had Megan's mouth watering. She'd barely eaten a thing at dinner, she'd been so tired. But now that the coffee had kicked in, along with the fresh country air, her appetite had, too.

Sasha set the tray on her lap and stood as though waiting for Megan's acknowledgment.

"Thank you, Sasha. This looks lovely, but you really didn't have to. I could've gotten up and fixed myself breakfast."

Celeste helped herself to a piece of bacon and crunched down on it. "Sasha does the cooking on the weekends, when Mrs. Robertson isn't here. That's what she gets her allowance for."

"Who's Mrs. Robertson?" Megan asked. Luke hadn't mentioned anyone else living here, too.

Daisy grabbed some bacon. "She's our housekeeper. When Grandma isn't here, she comes in and takes care of us during the week. She cleans the house and fixes our dinner 'cause Daddy doesn't have time. I get my allowance for helpin' with the animals," she added.

Megan looked at Celeste. "And do you get an allowance, sweetie?"

"Uh-huh, but not very much," she said with a heartfelt sigh.

Megan grinned. Celeste was so easy to love. "Well, now that I'm here, you don't have to do any more of those chores, Sasha." Megan addressed the older girl, who, unlike her sisters, hadn't taken up residence on the bed.

But instead of welcoming Megan's offer, Sasha's features became shuttered. "That's been my job since Mom left. I like doing it."

Megan didn't care for the idea of such a young girl being tied to the house, but on the other hand, realized she'd better tread carefully about taking over any responsibilities Sasha felt were hers. "All right," she said slowly. "Please let me know if you'd like any help."

"I don't need any help. I can cook and sew and clean." Sasha was sounding downright belligerent. The last thing Megan wanted was to get off on the wrong foot with her eldest "daughter." Getting along with Celeste was a breeze and Daisy seemed to be pretty easygoing, but breaking down the protective wall Sasha had erected was going to be a problem. Megan wished she'd paid more attention when Luke was talking about the girls. That might've given her greater insight into their characters—particularly Sasha's. The first chance she got, Megan was going to have a long talk with Luke and get a few things straight regarding her duties and the girls'.

"Will you do my hair?" Celeste asked.

Megan studied the little girl's attempts to braid her hair. It stuck out all over the place. She smiled. This was something she *could* do. "Sure, sweetie."

"Mine, too?" Daisy asked.

Megan looked at Daisy's wild mop of dark curls and didn't think there was much that could be done. "You've got beautiful curly hair, Daisy," she said. "What could you possibly want done with it?"

Daisy brushed it out of her eyes impatiently. "It gets in the way when I'm ridin' or tyin' calves. I wanna have it cut really short, but Daddy won't let me."

"I can see why. Most girls would kill to have hair

like yours." Megan reached out and combed her fingers through it. "It's so soft, too."

Daisy made a disgusted noise and left the room, saying, "I gotta go help one of the hands teach Cody to ride. He's already fallen off of Killer 'bout a dozen times."

"Killer!" Megan's body was drenched with fear. "You've got a horse called Killer and you let Cody on it!" she almost screeched.

Daisy crossed her arms and leaned against the doorjamb. "Relax. Killer's about as old as our uncle Adam, 'cept Uncle Adam's got more teeth," she said with a grin. "Cody's such a klutz he just can't stay on. Hasn't he ever been around a horse before?"

The only horses Cody had ever seen were the ones that drew carriages around Central Park. "Er, no, he hasn't," she confessed. "Do you think it's wise for him to learn to ride so soon?" She appealed to Daisy, who seemed to know everything there was to know on this topic.

"We live on a ranch. If he doesn't learn to ride, he's gonna to have to walk. We've got over five thousand acres." With that, Daisy turned and marched out the door.

Megan bit her lip. She'd assumed Cody was still in bed, too. Daisy didn't seem concerned about Cody's learning to ride on a horse called Killer, so maybe that was okay. Deciding she should get up and look around the place, get the lay of the land, Megan threw back the covers and put her feet on the floor. "If you'll excuse me, girls, I'll take a shower and then join you in a few minutes and we can see about your hair, Celeste." She looked at Sasha. "I could do something with your hair, too, if you like."

Sasha's expression became shuttered again. "I'm not a baby. I can do my own hair," she said curtly, and picked up the tray.

Oh, dear! I've done it again, thought Megan. "Thank you for the coffee and breakfast, Sasha. It was all delicious." Megan didn't think the odd white lie would go amiss if she was going to be practicing diplomacy.

THE SHOWER WAS GLORIOUS, with plenty of hot water and a strong spray—the total opposite of the often icy dribbles that emitted from the shower back at her tiny apartment in New York.

Megan made the most of it, shampooing her hair and then conditioning it. She thought again about how she'd gotten to bed last night and felt hot all over. Not only had Luke removed her cotton pants and matching jacket and top, he'd also removed her bra, leaving her to sleep in her camisole and panties. She rinsed the conditioner out of her hair.

Maybe Luke had carried her to her room and Beth had stayed to undress her? Yes, that sounded more plausible. More appropriate, anyway. She didn't know how to broach the subject with Luke to find out if that was the case.

When she stepped out of the shower, a foggy full-length image of herself stared back from the mirror. She wiped it with her towel, bent over and wrapped the towel around her head, turban fashion, then straightened and looked at herself. Daisy was right—she *was* too skinny. The worry of the past few months, since Cody had gotten mixed up with the wrong crowd, had taken its toll on her health.

Because she'd had to fill in the hours she'd missed at

work, either while trying to track down where he was or going to court with him, her appetite and eating patterns had been chaotic. Now her arms were too skinny, her hip bones stuck out and her legs looked twice as long as they usually did. She thought about Luke's hands on her breasts last night as he removed her bra—then picked up another towel and wrapped it around herself. She definitely had to find out who'd taken off her clothes, if only to stop her hormones kicking in at the thought of Luke—her *husband*—touching her in places she hadn't been touched, *he* hadn't touched, for many, many years.

Megan hurried to her bedroom and burrowed into the shopping bag, coming up with fresh underwear and a pair of jeans and chambray shirt. Luke had assured her the outfit was appropriate for the ranch. Until she saw what everyone else was wearing, and her clothes arrived from New York, it would have to do. In the meantime, she'd better get her only other set of clothes into the washing machine. Hadn't Beth said everyone was coming over for a barbecue tonight—or had she dreamed that?

"There you are!" Celeste said with relief in her voice when Megan stepped into the kitchen. "I thought you mighta gone back to sleep!"

Megan held up her brush, a mirror and some hairpins, clothes under one arm. "I was just seeing what I had to fix your hair," she explained, then looked at Sasha. "Do you mind if I do some laundry, Sasha? I'll need clean clothes for tonight."

Sasha looked her up and down. "What you've got on will be fine." She pointed at Megan's bare feet. "'Course you'll need some shoes. I got some riding boots that might fit you. What size do you take?"

Megan didn't see how a twelve-year-old could have size seven-and-a-half feet but she told her, anyway.

"I take an eight, so you can have an old pair of mine." She held out her arms for the laundry. "I'll go throw these in and then I'll get my boots."

Megan held on to the clothes when Sasha tried to take them from her and then relented. It wasn't worth wrestling with the kid over a load of wash. If that was the way she wanted to play it, then fine. For now... "That's very kind of you, Sasha," she said. "Thanks for both the boots and doing the wash. Is there anything I can help with in return?"

Sasha squared her shoulders and disappeared from the room without answering her. Megan stared after her, bewildered.

"Don't worry about *her*." Celeste gestured at her sister's back. "She's almost a *teenager!*" She climbed up on the table and sat cross-legged among a heap of glossy fashion magazines opened at various pages. "See these hairdos? Which one will work for me?"

Megan glanced at the sophisticated models with very complicated dos and didn't think any of them would suit her—at least, not for another twenty years. But she pretended to give the photos a great deal of consideration. "Hmm. Well, you know, of course, that all of these will need hot rollers and gallons of hair spray."

Celeste's face fell. "I don't have none of that stuff."

Megan lifted her brush to run it through Celeste's hair. "Will you trust me enough to do something special?"

Celeste gazed at her with excitement in her eyes. "Uh-huh." She nodded and lifted a mirror to admire herself. "Will I look as pretty as them?"

The little girl was as feminine as her older sister Daisy was a tomboy. "Oh, I guarantee you'll look a lot prettier than them," she assured her. She set to work brushing the tangles from Celeste's blond tresses. "You've got such pretty hair," she complimented the child. "It's like spun gold."

"Grampa says it's the same color as Grandma's when they were younger. 'Course, hers is kinda gray now, since she's so old."

They kept up a friendly chatter through the hair-dressing session, Megan curbing the urge to curse when the French braid she was trying to create didn't seem to be working out the way she wanted. Still, she hadn't tried to do one since college, so it was no wonder her fingers were a little rusty.

Celeste sat through the ministrations, constantly moving her head from side to side and asking, "Is it ready yet? I wanna see!"

"Not yet, sweetie." Megan chewed on her lip as she braided the strands of hair.

"That's okay," Celeste told her. "I like this."

LUKE STOOD JUST OUTSIDE the screen door to the back porch, watching Megan working on Celeste's hair. They were a picture of female contentment, although perhaps Megan—alternately chewing her lip or sticking out her tongue in concentration—didn't seem quite as contented as Celeste. If there'd been any doubts in his mind as to whether he'd done the right thing in marrying Megan so impulsively, they were dispelled as he stood there, battered Stetson in hand, watching his youngest child being mothered and fussed over.

He remembered carrying Megan to her room last

night, enjoying the feel of her in his arms, her soft sigh as he placed her on the bed. He'd removed her shoes and lifted her feet onto the bed, but since nights got cold in the mountains, even in midsummer, he couldn't leave her lying on top of the comforter. He eased it from under her and was about to cover her when he realized she probably wouldn't be comfortable sleeping in tight pants.

So he'd slipped them off her, swallowing at the feel of her bare skin beneath his fingers. He'd quickly covered her lower half. But then the jacket she wore might tangle around her during the night, waking her, so he sat her up and gently drew her arms from the sleeves.

She'd moaned slightly, stretching her neck. It probably wouldn't hurt to loosen her bra, as well.

He'd rested Megan against his shoulder and felt underneath the back of her camisole top. As he unfastened the clasp he told himself he was going to stop right there. But then she seemed tangled in the bra straps so he pulled them down her arms, then slid her bra out from under her top.

He'd swallowed again as he looked at the tiny scrap of fabric in his hands. This probably wasn't right, undressing a woman without her consent. But it was too late to undo what he'd done. And she *was* his wife. Not a stranger.

Gently, he lowered Megan to the bed, pulled up the covers and tiptoed out of the room.

As he watched his youngest daughter and his wife now, Luke knew that Celeste and Megan would be just fine. Daisy, too. Sasha was another matter. His eldest daughter had told him in no uncertain terms that she wasn't going to be calling Megan "Mom."

"I'm sure she doesn't expect you to, Sash," he'd said.

"As long as she knows I already have a mom and I don't need another one coming in here and taking over."

Luke had been baffled by her reaction. Since Tory had effectively stopped being a mother to Sash years ago—making only the occasional phone call, sometimes even forgetting her birthday—Luke wondered why she was vehement. Furthermore, he'd thought Sasha would welcome not having to shoulder so much of the responsibility she'd taken on when Tory had left.

On the plane journey back to Denver, he'd convinced himself that the timing of Megan's advent into their lives was perfect. Now Sasha would have a chance to be a carefree teenager. Maybe it'd take a little time, but he was sure she'd come around once she realized all the fun she'd be missing. Still, he'd better warn Megan before she started moving in on Sasha's "territory."

"THERE!" MEGAN SAID with relief as she finished the French braid.

Celeste turned her head this way and that. "I can't see!" she protested. Megan picked up the other mirror and held it behind Celeste's head.

"Ooh! That's so pretty," she cried, and moved her head from side to side again, admiring it from all angles. Then she spotted her father standing on the back porch. "Look, Daddy! Mommy's made me look so pretty!" She jumped down off the table and went to throw herself into her father's waiting arms.

Mommy! She called me "Mommy"! Megan thought, her heart soaring.

Luke lifted Celeste into his arms and settled her on his hip. "You sure are pretty." He turned and smiled at

Megan, filling her with a sense of unreasonable joy. She'd wanted to stay mad at this man, but it was impossible. All he had to do was smile and she was like a lump of putty in his hands, ready to be molded to his whim.

"You've got a fan here. But don't be surprised if she demands to have her hair done like this every day now," he said.

Megan raised one shoulder. "That's okay. I need the practice." She smiled shyly at Luke and wondered if she should ask him now about putting her to bed last night. Feeling her face warm with embarrassment, she decided to put the question aside for the moment. She cleared her throat. "Daisy tells me that Cody's learning to ride."

Luke put Celeste down and she ran out to find someone to show her hair to. He hung his hat on a peg near the door, walked to the refrigerator and grabbed a bottle of water. He turned back to her after taking a long swig. "Do you have a problem with that?"

Megan could read the challenge in his eyes. She had a problem with a lot of things, not least the fact that twenty-four hours ago she was a single mother living in New York City with her son. And today she was a married woman living in the middle of the Colorado Rockies with her son, three stepdaughters and a husband she barely knew.

Cody's learning to ride on a horse named Killer was a small matter by comparison. If Megan was honest with herself, she'd admit that she was secretly pleased he'd fallen off a few times and each time had gotten back up on the horse. It showed he hadn't quit. Cody's tendency to give up easily when the going got tough was something else that had worried her about his behavior this past year. He used to be so tenacious, so determined to finish anything he started, but lately, he'd found it easier just to shrug and claim things were "dumb."

Megan believed in taking risks, believed it was a way to personal growth and fulfillment. But she'd had to take so many in her thirty-five years that she would rather not have taken—like being a single mom. But despite her beliefs, despite Cody's supervision, she couldn't help worrying about his safety.

She leaned against the edge of the kitchen counter. "No, I don't have a problem with that. If you think he's safe, then I trust your judgment." Hard as that was to say, she meant it.

Luke gave a tiny nod, as though pleased with her reaction, then headed for the door.

"Luke…" He stopped and turned slowly toward her. "I…I think…that is…when you have some free time that…you and I need to talk."

He nodded. "After lunch we can take a ride over to the meadows by the creek. We'll have plenty of privacy there."

We'll have plenty of privacy there. Was that a threat—or a promise?

CHAPTER FOUR

"I'VE ARRANGED TO MEET my bank manager in town so we can get you a credit card," Luke said, and glanced at his watch. "We'd better get going. The bank closes at noon."

Megan shrugged, embarrassed at feeling like a kept woman. "Luke, I can't take your money."

"You're my wife. How do you think you're going to pay for groceries if you don't have a credit card?"

"Aren't the banks almost closed by now?" she said, trying to stall him. She didn't want to get into the financial side of their relationship yet.

Luke faced Megan and took her hands, forcing her to look at him. "He's staying late as a favor to me. I want to get this done today, Megan. It can't wait until next week. So stop making excuses to avoid it."

Feeling as if she'd been backed into a corner, she tried to make one more stand. "I have a debit card. I don't need a credit card. It's too easy to get into debt with one."

"If you want to keep your debit card, then that's fine. But we need to put money into your account. My bank manager can facilitate that."

"Okay," she conceded grudgingly. "I'll just freshen up." She turned to leave, hating to release Luke, but needing to get away from him. When he got up close like that, acting protective, it did things to her insides. Things she didn't want to examine. Not now.

"And while we're there, we'll get you a credit card."

Megan spun back, ready to deny she needed or wanted one, but Luke was already going out the screen door.

She hurried to her room, determined not to keep him waiting long.

As LUKE HELD the door open so Megan could precede him inside the bank, a man walked out.

"Gil," Luke said. "How are you?" They shook hands.

"Fine, Luke. And you?" His curious gaze encompassed Megan.

Luke drew her toward him and said, "You might not have heard the news, Gil, but I got married yesterday. This is my wife, Megan."

Gil smiled and offered his hand to Megan. "Congratulations and I'm pleased to meet you."

"Gil McIntyre is an old friend and the ranch accountant," Luke explained. "He keeps me on the straight and narrow. Doesn't let me get carried away with buying too much stock." He grinned. "I mean horses and cattle, not stocks and shares."

Megan smiled dutifully. She found it odd that an accountant would presume to tell a rancher how to run his business, but since she knew so little about ranching so far, she didn't inquire.

Several other people came out of the bank, and Luke and Gil moved aside to let them pass, continuing their conversation.

Luke checked his watch. "I think this stampede means they're about to close, so we should get moving. I want Megan to meet Joe Hickey and have him set up a credit card for her."

Gil frowned and looked at Megan. "You don't ha—"

"Like I said, we'd better go," Luke cut in. He pressed his hand against the small of Megan's back, indicating she should go ahead.

Megan turned to say goodbye to Gil.

"It was nice to meet you," she said.

"You, too," Gil said with a smile. "You must come over sometime and meet my wife, Betsy."

"Don't get too friendly with her, Gil," Luke said in a joking voice. "I might have to fire you soon. Megan's studying accounting and when she's qualified, I may just have her look after the ranch finances."

Gil's expression didn't change, but Megan sensed a wariness. *Was* he worried about losing this job?

"You know you can't fire me, Luke. Remember who found that error your previous CPA made in the accounts? And don't forget the huge refund you got from the IRS when I filed that amended return."

Megan felt that although Gil's words sounded teasing, there was a mild threat beneath the surface.

Luke didn't seem to notice anything awry. He laughed, clapped Gil on the back and said, "See you around, buddy. Say hi to Betsy for me."

Inside the bank, Megan couldn't shake her feeling abut Gil.

"Why did you cut him off earlier?" she asked.

"Because he was going to ask you why you don't have a credit card and that's none of his business."

"But he's your accountant!"

"And you're my wife, not part of the fiscal structure of the ranch. Our business as husband and wife is ours alone."

Although Luke's words were delivered a little harshly, Megan experienced an incredible feeling of being protected, safeguarded by Luke.

Against her own wishes, Megan was starting to fall in love with Luke all over again.

WHEN THEY ARRIVED back at the house, Luke nodded toward the corral. "Want to come and see how Cody's doing?"

"Okay, I'll just tidy up here and see if Sasha needs any help."

"About Sash. Can you go easy on her? She's used to making a lot of the decisions around the house, so I'd appreciate it if you'd give her some space."

Megan didn't like his suggestion that she'd given Sasha a hard time. That was the *last* thing she wanted to do. And for heaven's sake, the child was only twelve. Why did he allow a youngster to assume so much responsibility?

"I've worked that out already. Thank you," she said coolly and, after collecting her things, left the kitchen.

LUKE WATCHED HER GO, her back held straight. *Women!* First Sasha snapped at him and now Megan. *Hell.* He was only trying to help her get along with her new stepdaughter. He walked out, letting the door slam behind him. Who was he kidding? His son had barely exchanged three words with him this morning. Three words that weren't cussing of one kind or another.

Cody hadn't been happy about being dragged off to the barn last night, but there were a few ground rules around the ranch and Luke wasn't prepared to cut Cody any slack where they were concerned. He'd seen Megan plead with her son to behave, seen how fearful she was of his reaction. Well, that was going to stop. Cody was going to be *told* and expected to *obey*—starting with the number-one rule. No cussing around the children and no cussing in the house.

He'd told Cody that he could cuss all he liked out in the paddock or the barn, provided he'd checked to make sure there weren't any women or children around. He didn't really like the idea of Cody using bad language at all, but figured the kid had to have some outlet for his frustrations. If he came down too hard on him and forbade all swearing, the kid was likely to ignore him altogether.

The second thing he'd pointed out was that Cody was part of the family now. That meant he had sisters to consider, not just himself, and he wasn't to hurt them in any way.

Cody had looked puzzled. "I never hit anyone!" he protested.

Luke had put a hand on his shoulder. "I didn't say you did—or would. I mean that you hurt Celeste's feelings. She's a sweet kid who's never had a mom or a brother and she was very excited about meeting you. You didn't have to snap at her like that."

Cody had stuck out his bottom lip. "Yeah, well, I never had a sister before, either—or three of 'em—and I don't like how nosy girls are and how they talk all the time."

"Get used to it, son." He liked the way the word sounded, even if he wasn't too enamored of his son right now. "Other O'Malley men have managed to adapt to having women in their lives. They're not too bad—once you get used to 'em." He'd jerked his head toward the others. "Let's go back and get something to eat."

The mention of food had Cody's legs moving in long strides—typical of the O'Malley men.

Since last night, though, Cody had studiously ignored him in a battle of wills. At least the kid had gotten back up on Killer the first time he'd fallen off. Luke had been watching one of the ranch hands teach Cody to ride. The kid had been about to give up and storm back inside, but then he'd spotted Luke and climbed back on.

Luke had smiled to himself and stayed around to watch some more. Daisy and Brian, the ranch hand, were patient with Cody, encouraging him and coaching him on how to stay in the saddle. After he'd watched Cody nearly fall off a few more times, he walked away. By then Cody was more hooked on learning to ride than competing with his father.

LUNCH CONSISTED OF leftover casserole on toast. Sasha had insisted on setting the table and reheating the casserole herself. She'd allowed Megan to make the toast.

"This is Daddy's favorite Saturday lunch," she told Megan in a tone that implied she'd better not mess up the toast.

"Sounds like your dad likes home-style cooking. What do you like to cook, Sasha?"

"Anything Daddy likes to eat."

Megan thought that was a strange response. Didn't Sasha want to cook things *she* liked to eat?

"What are we supposed to prepare for the barbecue tonight?"

"I'm defrosting steaks. And Uncle Will is bringing ribs. You don't need to bother with anything."

Megan had had just about enough. It was clear the girl resented her being there. Well, tough! Because Megan wasn't going anywhere. Particularly after she'd seen the smile on Cody's face when he'd called to her across the yard to show her how he could sit on the horse and even stay on when it cantered around the corral. Megan had climbed onto the rail fence and watched him ride Killer, and then Daisy had mounted a huge horse and opened the gate to the yard. Killer had trotted out—with Cody on his back—into the open fields!

What if Cody panicked? What if the horse took off? Daisy had slapped Killer's rump and Killer took off at a slow canter. Cody held on, tossing his head back. His laughter came to her as they disappeared from sight.

"I'd *like* to bother, if you don't mind, Sasha," she said now. "I'd like to make some sort of contribution to this evening—to feel that Cody and I are part of your family."

"You don't have to. Everyone's bringing something so you don't need to do anything."

Sasha was determined to shut her out, her resentment palpable. Megan couldn't wait until she and Luke took that ride. She might suggest he have a long talk with Sasha—in the barn, if necessary!

She decided to change the subject. "How many people will be coming?"

Sasha picked up a knife and waved it in the air. Megan resisted the urge to duck. "Let's see," she said. "There's four of us and two of you and Uncle Matt, Aunt Beth and Sarah. Uncle Jack and Uncle Will and

Aunt Becky and their two kids. Uncle Adam *isn't* coming so that makes…"

"Fourteen," Megan said. "Counting the *six* of us."

Sasha shot her a glare.

Megan pretended she hadn't noticed. "Why won't your uncle Adam be coming?"

"He lives in Boulder. He keeps to himself."

"Sounds mysterious. What does he do for a living?" Megan was aware there were five brothers, but back when she'd known Luke, Adam had been in junior high.

Sasha was putting on a pan of water to boil and got out a packet of rice. Megan knew it couldn't be for lunch so assumed she was making it for tonight. "He's a firefighter."

"And he's not married?"

"No. Why? Are you interested?"

Megan was taken aback. "Interested in Adam?"

"Yeah." Sasha turned toward her challengingly.

"Sasha, I'm married to your father. Of course, I'm not *interested* in his brother."

"You could get it annulled. You haven't slept together yet—except to have Cody. Uncle Adam's awful good-look—"

"Sasha!"

Luke's raised voice from behind the screen door shocked Sasha so badly she dropped the knife. It landed point down in the linoleum between Megan's feet.

Luke practically tore the door off its hinges as he marched into the kitchen and stood over his daughter. "Apologize to Megan at once for that comment," he demanded.

"Why should I? You don't even know if he's your kid! I heard you telling Uncle Matt!" she cried.

Megan felt her blood chill. Luke didn't believe Cody was his? And he'd gone ahead and *married* her?

"That was before I went to New York, young lady!" he thundered. "Now, apologize to Megan!"

Megan held up her hands, trying to placate him. "Really, Luke, it doesn't matt—"

Luke cut her off. "It does to me." He turned on Sasha. "I won't stand for it, young lady. Do you hear me?" he roared. But Sasha, equally implacable, scowled at him, making no move to obey.

"There is no doubt in my mind that Cody *is* my son and consequently *your* brother, so get used to it. Fast! And Megan *is* my wife, whether *you* think this is a *real* marriage or not."

Megan wanted to cheer at his words. It felt so good to have someone standing up for her and her son. But on the other hand, Megan knew Sasha was hurting. She wanted to fold the girl in her arms, tell her everything would be all right.

"Then why aren't you sharing a bedroom?" Sasha was apparently unfazed by her father's rebuke. "People who are *really* married sleep together—or hadn't you noticed that?"

"And people who aren't married sleep together, too!" Luke ran his hand through his hair and got his voice under control. "The reason Megan and I don't share my bedroom is none of your business, Sash. And it's certainly none of your business to go suggesting she might want to run out on me—*us,*" he corrected, "and marry Uncle Adam."

"How do I know you're really married, then?" Sasha asked stubbornly. "Except for that dumb old ring you gave her, and that doesn't prove you're married. You should've asked if it was okay with us!" Tears filled Sasha's eyes.

Megan's heart went out to the girl, who believed her father had betrayed them by not asking their approval first. She placed a hand on Sasha's shoulder but the girl shrugged it off. "Do you really mind that much, Sasha?"

Sasha whirled to face her. "'Course I do! I don't want you coming in here and trying to be my mother, telling me what to do, taking over!" She turned back to her father. "You shouldn't have brought them here! It's going to ruin everything!"

Luke caught her heaving shoulders in his hands and pulled her against him. "It's okay, sweetie," he murmured. "I married Megan because it was the right thing to do. Cody needs a father. I wasn't trying to replace your mom with Megan."

Megan was aghast. What was he saying? That he wanted to be a father to Cody but didn't want her being a mom to his daughters? They'd *definitely* better have a long talk after lunch! She slipped out of the kitchen unnoticed and went to her room.

If she'd had anything to pack, she probably would've packed it right there, grabbed Cody and then gotten as far from the ranch as possible. She didn't need this. Didn't need the teenage tantrums and the rejection and bad attitude. The *hell* with Luke and his need to play daddy. The *hell* with Cody demanding they get married. The *hell* with all of it! First thing Monday morning, she was going to see about an annulment because she wanted out! "Dammit!" she cried, picked up a pillow and threw it across the room.

"You gotta pay the penalty box," a tiny voice said from behind her.

Megan spun around to find Celeste regarding her seriously, sweet little face puckered in a frown.

Her heart melted. If nothing else, this dear little girl needed her. Forget everything else. If she could make a success of being a mother to Celeste, then that would be enough for Megan. The rest of them would just have to live with it. She wasn't going anywhere or getting any annulment, because Celeste needed her—and she needed Celeste.

Megan opened her arms and Celeste ran into them. She picked her up and cuddled her, loving her little-girl smell mixed with horse and something sweet and sticky that she was smearing on Megan's cheeks as she kissed her.

"I love you," Celeste said, and hugged Megan tight.

"I love you, too, sweetie." Megan hugged her right back and wiped at her tears.

A polite cough from the door had Megan looking up to find Luke standing there. Sasha stood behind him.

He strode toward them. "She really does love you, you know."

"And I really love her, too," Megan said, then glanced at the door.

Sasha stood there trying to look belligerent, her arms crossed as she lounged against the jamb.

"Sasha's come to apologize," Luke said. "Come in, Sash."

"Luke, please, this isn't necessary." Megan could guess how humiliated Sasha felt being forced to apologize for her behavior. She knew Luke meant well but it would only serve to make things more difficult between the two of them.

Sasha sauntered into the room in much the same way

Megan had seen Cody walk when his pride had been shattered. "You can make some dessert if you want," she said.

Megan thought it was a strange apology but wasn't going to point that out.

Celeste clapped her hands. "Oh, goody, we can make trifle!" She squealed and wriggled out of Megan's arms. "Come on, Mommy, I'll help you," she said, grabbing Megan by the hand and trying to drag her out of the room.

"Sasha!" Luke's voice warned again.

Megan broke in before Luke had a chance to say anything else. "Thank you, Sasha. I'd like that very much." Ignoring Luke's warning growl, she let Celeste pull her out of the room.

"YOU GOTTA BOIL the water for the Jell-O first," Celeste was telling her as she got up on the table. "I'm not allowed to do that, so you'll have to. Then I can help you make the cake, but you'll have to open the cans of fruit." She got down off the table again and went to select some canned fruit from the pantry.

Megan laughed. "Okay, Miss Bossy, I'll boil the water. But I've never heard of Jell-O in a trifle before."

"It's *Irish* trifle," she explained patiently. "Handed down through generations of O'Malleys."

Megan smiled. "That sounds like something you've heard often."

Celeste rolled her eyes. "Uh-huh."

"Then I guess you'd better get me some Jell-O mix."

"Oh, yeah." Celeste got down and chose several different flavors from the pantry. "We can make lots of colors, 'cause there's lots of us."

Megan filled the kettle, and while they waited for it to boil, they opened several packets of Jell-O and placed the contents in bowls. "We'll let it cool while we're having lunch," Megan said. "Then we can make the sponge cake. How about putting those cans in the fridge so they can chill during the afternoon?"

Megan poured the boiling water into each of the bowls and stirred the Jell-O to dissolve, then moved them to a bench to cool before putting them in the refrigerator.

Luke lounged against the kitchen doorway, his arms crossed, watching them. "You two work well together," he observed, then walked to stir the Jell-O for something to do with his hands while he formulated what to say to Megan, "I'm sorry about Sasha," he said quietly. "It's going to take her a while to adapt."

Megan picked Celeste up. "Can we talk about this later?" She indicated over her shoulder that Daisy and Cody were coming up the steps of the back porch.

"Later," Luke said, and Megan wondered if his voice didn't hold a note of promise.

CHAPTER FIVE

"You sit a horse well," Luke said as they rode out into the meadows beyond the house.

They'd just given the horses their heads for a brisk half-mile canter and had reined them in to a walking pace.

Luke breathed in the air of the beautiful June day. His spirits always lifted on days like these and Luke hoped it would have the same effect on Megan.

"I had lessons when I was a child. Every Saturday morning at Miss Dustin's Riding School."

"Sounds upmarket."

Megan pulled a face. "It was. Can we talk about something else?"

Interesting. She didn't want to talk about her own childhood, yet she was a natural with kids. She'd sure wound her way into Celeste's heart. They'd made the sponge cake together and put it in the oven and Megan had left Celeste in charge of keeping an eye on the timer. Then, when the cake was done, Celeste was to get Sasha to take it out of the oven. Luke had warned Sasha that if there was the slightest hint the cake had been sabotaged, she was in big trouble.

"I'd prefer it if you let Sasha and me work things out between us." Megan's words broke into his thoughts and he pulled his horse, a huge bay gelding, up beside her mount, an old palomino mare called Sage.

"Whoa there, Rocket." He soothed the horse when it wanted to go racing toward the meadows near the creek where the sweetest grass grew. Megan turned in the saddle to face him. "I think your little outburst in the kitchen earlier today only made things more difficult. Sasha's been humiliated in front of the person she despises most. It's not going to be easy to reach out to her now."

"She has no right to despise you," he argued. "You haven't done anything wrong."

"In her eyes, I've hurt her by coming here, pretty much unannounced, and taking her place as head female in the house. Had I known what I was walking into or had time to think about it, I wouldn't have married you quite so readily."

Her forthright statement had him stopping his horse. "You didn't have any choice," he reminded her. "It was either get married or let Cody go to juvenile detention."

She turned Sage to draw level with him. "I'm not so sure he would've carried through on that threat."

"And *I* wasn't prepared to take that chance. He's my son and I'll do *anything* to save him from juvenile detention. We're married now, whether we like it or not."

Megan clicked at Sage and the two horses fell into step walking side by side again. "The circumstances are unpalatable to me, too, but seriously, have you thought about what happens next? How we're going to manage a marriage where the kids know we don't share the same room—let alone the same bed? That'll get around school awfully quick. People will start to talk."

Luke shrugged. "So let 'em. Our marriage is nobody's business but ours. We got married to give Cody the stable family life he needs. When we succeed at that, then we'll move on."

Needing to get away from Megan—being close to her made him want her too much—and to clear his head, Luke kicked Rocket into a gallop and took off across the paddock.

MEGAN WATCHED HIM GO, a chill invading her heart where love should have resided. *Then we'll move on.* Move on to what? Other partners, but stay married? She needed to keep reminding herself that theirs was nothing more than a marriage of convenience, created to save their son from juvenile detention. She shivered in spite of the warm June afternoon, then clicked her tongue at Sage, urging the mare to an easy canter, taking pleasure in the fresh air and solitude—two things in very short supply in her part of New York.

The meadow she rode through was rich with wild-flowers and the sky seemed to stretch on forever.

LUKE DISMOUNTED AND SLAPPED his horse's rump to indi-cate he could trot off and eat his fill, then helped Megan down, turning her to face him.

Resting his hands on her hips, he looked into her eyes as if trying to read what was there, then lowered his head to kiss her.

Startled, she pulled back. "Luke!"

He smiled slowly at her. "Just getting the wedding kiss I missed out on yesterday."

Megan flushed as she remembered how the judge had pronounced them husband and wife and told Luke he could kiss his bride. He'd bent to place a hurried kiss on Megan's cheek. It had missed and ended up somewhere near her ear, probably because she'd turned her head away. She cursed herself for being so angry with Luke that she'd fumbled the opportunity to feel his warm lips on hers.

Luke moved his hands farther around her back and pulled her closer, so they were touching from knee to waist. "We're married," he reminded her hoarsely. "Married people are allowed to kiss each other, you know."

Setting her hands on his chest, she left them there for just a moment, savoring the feel of his hard muscles beneath her fingertips, then gently, reluctantly, pushed him away.

"We need to talk, Luke. Isn't that why you brought me here?" she asked. She walked toward an outcropping of boulders by the creek and sat down. Picking a daisy, she examined it, then threw it in the water and wondered if Luke had brought his wife here. Had this been a special place for them? It was a beautiful spot; the wide, crystal-clear creek bubbled over submerged rocks and tiny wildflowers grew along its banks.

He hunkered down in front of her. "Okay, let's talk. Why didn't you tell me about Cody?"

Although Megan had been expecting the question, it didn't mean she was prepared for it. She lifted her shoulders. "It's a long story."

"I've got—" he glanced at his watch "—'bout four hours."

Megan forced a smile. "Let's just say I didn't think you'd be interested in hearing from some girl you'd had a short affair with during spring break, telling you she was pregnant with your child." At his look of disbelief, she said, "Remember, we hadn't even exchanged addresses or phone numbers. I was pretty sure that as far as you were concerned, our relationship ended the day I left Spruce Lake. I assumed you'd forgotten me by the end of the week."

"You didn't keep our date."

She bit her lip. When they should've been on their date, Megan was crying her eyes out at the airport as she waited for a standby flight back East. Away from Luke and his betrayal.

"I...I wasn't well."

"You could've called the restaurant. I was there for over two hours, looking like a fool, telling people they couldn't have my table because I was waiting for my date. My date who didn't show up."

I didn't show up because I'd learned the truth about you that afternoon, in the locker room at the rec center. You were engaged to Tory. I heard her talking to another girl, bragging about the big wedding you were going to have. About the baby you were having!

Megan wanted to scream the words at him. But saying them wouldn't change anything. She'd discovered it was better to leave the past in the past.

She sighed. "Let's drop it, okay? The reasons don't matter anymore."

"Don't tell me it doesn't matter!" He stood and paced. "I had a *right* to know I was going to be a father..." He halted and fixed her with a glare. "Unless you weren't sure who the father was."

That hurt. That *really* hurt. How dared he, of all people, accuse her of sleeping around when he'd already got another girl pregnant!

"I was sure," she said through icy lips. Angered, she

jumped to her feet and paced away from him, then spun around. "You knew I was a virgin!"

He didn't even have the grace to flinch. "Then why didn't you try to contact me?"

"I did!"

Silence descended on the glen. Even the creek seemed to have stopped its babbling.

Finally, Luke crossed his arms in a confrontational stance and said, "If I'd heard anything from you, I would've acted on it."

"I sent you a letter from the hospital, the day I gave birth to Cody," Megan said, trying not to let her voice waver. Even all these years later, the feelings of rejection, from both her parents and the father of her baby, hit her hard.

She didn't want to think about her parents right now. It brought up too many bad memories of how she'd always been made to feel second best. Both of Megan's parents had unabashedly favored her older brother. There was nothing Jordan could do wrong in their eyes. He was an A-student, a gifted sportsman, a golden boy. When Jordan had expressed an interest in following in his father's footsteps and studying law, he'd been given a brand-new imported sports car.

Megan hadn't particularly cared about that, but it was yet another example of how Jordan was always rewarded, while she was always criticized. Getting pregnant in her junior year of college had sealed her fate. Her feelings of rejection and being not quite good enough were brought into stark relief. She'd hoped that her brother would stand by her. But Jordan proved to be as fickle as she'd suspected and had cut her completely out of his life.

"I didn't get it," Luke said, waking Megan from her musings. He stood with arms crossed. Challenging her.

He didn't believe her, and Megan didn't believe him. She shook her head and turned away. Why, oh, why did she give in to Cody's demands and agree to marry Luke? Neither of them trusted the other and she didn't see how they ever would.

"Don't hide from me, Megan. And don't lie to me."

She spun back to him, more angry than she'd ever been in her life. She felt the fury in her stomach, her chest, her heart. She rushed at him and beat his chest with clenched fists.

"How dare you, you bastard! How dare you accuse me of lying! I wrote you a letter, and a month later I called the ranch! I did everything I could to contact you." The words and the anger spilled out of her as she hit him again and again as if it could purge fifteen years of wretchedness from her soul.

"Your *wife* answered the phone!" she screamed.

Luke had remained steadfast, taking her blows, but now he gripped her forearms, preventing her fists from striking him.

"*What* did you say?"

"You heard me!"

"I wasn't married when we were dating," he said in a slow, measured voice, as if it was important she understand that.

Megan wrenched her arms out of his grasp. "You were married when I called. The baby was *my* responsibility. There was no point in taking the matter any further."

She steeled herself against the knowledge that Luke had made love to her when he was already engaged to someone else. *Don't you know how cheap that made me feel?* she wanted to shout.

"It takes two people to make a baby, or at least it did the last time I checked. Your pregnancy was my responsibility, too."

"No, it was mine. Alone." At Luke's puzzled look, she explained. "Remember when you'd run out of condoms and I assured you it was a safe time of the month for me?"

Luke nodded. "I remember," he said hoarsely. He'd been so crazy for her, he hadn't wanted to delay, hadn't wanted to go out and buy more condoms.

"Turns out it wasn't a safe time, after all. It was my mistake and I paid for it."

Looking at Megan now, her shoulders slumped in defeat, her once-sparkling eyes filled with dull pain, he found it hard to reconcile her with the person he'd known back then.

He had to take some of the blame for the change in her. It couldn't have been easy raising a child on her own. She'd come from a wealthy, privileged family, been a junior at Wellesley when he'd met her, yet there was no sign of affluence in the outfit she'd worn yesterday. Gone were the designer labels she'd once sported. And her Rolex watch. Had she sold it to make ends meet? The guilt of realizing how bad things had been for her weighed heavily on him.

Wanting to keep Cody away from his old neighborhood, he'd been relieved when she consented not to return to her apartment to collect anything and instead agreed to have their possessions shipped to Colorado. They'd used the few hours before their flight to shop.

Megan had done so carefully, paying a frugal amount for her jeans and shirt in the department store.

He'd produced his credit card and insisted she buy whatever she wanted, but Megan had shaken her head in firm denial, paid for her clothes out of her well-worn wallet and gone off to buy a few toiletries. At least he'd managed to talk her into letting him pay for Cody's things—by pointing out she'd been supporting their son for fourteen years and now it was his turn. Cody hadn't had a problem with it, choosing name brands and stocking up on the latest gear for teens. Megan had stood back and let him go ahead, but she hadn't been happy about it—not one bit.

He'd wondered about that, too. Was she upset about the amount being spent? That she couldn't afford it and he could? Or was it something else? A fear that Cody would change his allegiance from her to him simply because he could buy their son the things she couldn't? That he would therefore buy Cody's love? Teens could be such fickle creatures and he could understand why Megan felt that way. Well, she could relax on that score, because Cody despised him as much today as he had yesterday.

"What about your folks?"

Her snort of derision said more than words.

"I take it they weren't pleased to learn you'd brought back a souvenir from spring break?"

She dragged her eyes up to his. "They weren't. And they were downright unpleasant when I refused to have an abortion or put the baby up for adoption. They washed their hands of me when I wouldn't tell them who the father was, so they could go after you with a shotgun."

He picked up a stone and rubbed it between his fingers, then let it fall. "Why didn't you tell them? Why didn't you chase me down as soon as you knew? I would've done the right thing by you."

The right thing? Megan wanted to lash out at him. *Oh, sure!* She wanted to cry. *As if you would've broken off your engagement to marry some lovesick idiot who happened to be pregnant with your child!*

Instead, she kept her emotions in check and said quietly, "We would've gotten married for all the wrong reasons. It wouldn't have lasted."

"I don't consider giving a child two parents and a family who loves him the wrong reasons for getting married. Tell me this. Why did you agree to marry me yesterday but you didn't want to marry me fifteen years ago?"

"You know why I agreed yesterday! I had no *choice.* It was either marry you—or lose Cody!"

"What made you think you could do it on your own?"

She shrugged. "Stupid arrogant pride, I guess. I was young. I thought anything was possible. And I was out to prove something to my parents."

"You took a chance on my son's life to *prove* something to your parents?"

She whirled around. "What are you implying? Cody's *life* was never in danger! Yes, I had to quit school, but fortunately I got a job working on the financial section of a Greenwich newspaper that provided on-site daycare."

"Since you dropped out of college by the time you had him, it couldn't have paid too well."

"It didn't. But it was the only job I could get where I could have a baby at work with me. I managed. I managed for twelve years until the newspaper closed down and then I had to take two jobs because Cody needed health care and it costs a lot to feed and clothe a teenager. And we had to keep finding new apartments because whenever I fell behind in the rent the landlord suggested there were other ways I could *pay the rent!*" She choked out the words, angry with Luke for pushing her so hard.

Curbing her anger, she said, "The same way some of the other desperate single moms 'paid the rent.' No way was I going to let *that* happen. I was trying to finish my degree one course at a time, but I'd lost interest in economics, so I switched to a more practical option. Everything I did, I did for Cody and I always worked around his schedule, his needs. Or...I tried to."

She hated the catch in her voice, but she was powerless to stop it. Luke was implying that she was a bad mother, that she'd taken unnecessary risks. Didn't he understand? She'd had no choice! "I couldn't do what my parents demanded." Her thinly held control broke and she covered her face with her hands and wept softly. "I couldn't kill our child," she whispered.

SHOCKED BY HER ADMISSION of how hard her life had been, Luke felt guilty that he couldn't have made her life and Cody's easier for them. Megan might not have wanted marriage, but he still could've supported them financially. He rubbed her back in soothing strokes. He was aware there were things she wasn't telling him, but for now, he'd let it go. She needed reassurance, not reprimands.

"You did a great job, Megan, in spite of everything. You should be proud. He's a good kid."

Megan looked up at him, her eyes brimming with pain. "A good kid who nearly ended up in juvenile detention."

"Thanks to you and a smart, caring judge, he didn't. And he never will," he said with conviction. He released her and moved away, feeling uncomfortable with their contact. At first it had been to comfort her, but now that Megan had recovered her composure, her closeness was doing other things to him—things Luke didn't want her noticing.

"Thank you," she murmured, and he turned back to her, surprised by her remark. "Thank you for believing the judge…for believing enough to take a chance on coming to New York."

Her voice was thready, and her lip trembled. Her emotions were naked, laid bare. Luke wanted to hold her, but resisted the urge. What Megan needed more than that, he thought again, was the reassurance that she'd done the best thing for Cody.

"No. I'm the one who should be thanking *you* for not succumbing to your parents' demands to get rid of him. That must've taken so much courage." He took her right hand in his, raised it and splayed their fingers, a symbol of togetherness.

"I'm not that noble. They convinced me to keep an appointment at the abortion clinic, but when I went there…" She took a heaving breath. "When I stood outside those doors and thought about what would happen to my baby in there—I couldn't cross that threshold." She released his hand, her shoulders slumped in defeat.

Luke placed two fingers beneath her chin, raising it so she had to look into his eyes. He needed her to know how he felt. Needed her to know she was no longer alone. "You *are* noble. And courageous and beautiful and the best mom Cody could have." He leaned forward and dropped a gentle kiss, on one cheek and then the other.

Her eyes held uncertainty mixed with wonder. "Do you *really* mean that?"

"Yes. And now that I've seen you with Celeste, I couldn't imagine anyone else being a mother to her, either."

Megan smiled, the first genuinely happy smile she'd given him. "She's just so sweet. I adore her already."

"And she adores you."

"I'm working on Daisy, but she's always on the go and doesn't seem to spend much time inside."

Luke couldn't help laughing. "She likes you a lot. She told me just after lunch."

Megan's eyes brightened. "I like her, too. She's completely fearless."

"She thinks you need fattening up," he said, and Megan laughed, too.

"I got off on the wrong foot with Sasha, though."

"Partly due to my interference and partly due to her pigheadedness. I won't interfere any more between you," he promised. "I figure you'll both have to shake things up and see how they settle. She's a good kid, generous to a fault."

"She is. She didn't hesitate to lend me a pair of boots and she likes to help out around the house."

Luke nodded. "I wish she wouldn't do so much, but it's something she's always done since Tory left, in spite of the housekeeper coming in during the week and Mom being here most of the time."

There was a silence. Then Megan asked, "You said she's only twelve?"

"Uh-huh."

"How long after I went home did you and…Tory get married?"

Luke frowned. "Why do you want to know?"

"I thought—since it produced three beautiful daughters—your marriage must have meant a lot to you."

Luke turned away and stared out at the stream. "Tory and I got married about a month after you left town."

Megan's heart contracted with pain at hearing that. "I see. So why would you have offered to marry me if you were already engaged to someone else at the time?" *Why did you sleep with me when you were practically a married man?*

Luke picked up a stone and tossed it into the creek, watching it skip across the water. Finally, he said, "Tory and I had been dating for a few months. I told you we'd split up a couple of weeks before I met you, and it was the truth. She was…too possessive."

Megan watched him, not commenting.

"When I finally got it through my thick head that you weren't interested in me," he went on, "I got roaring drunk one night, ended up sleeping with her and she got pregnant."

His explanation didn't match Tory's revelations to her friend in the locker room at the rec center. Something wasn't right. "If she got pregnant just a little later than me, then where's the child?"

Luke's face twisted bitterly. "She claimed she had a miscarriage. It happened a few weeks after we were married."

"I'm sorry," Megan said softly, and touched his arm.

Luke liked it when she touched him. It made him feel wanted. He'd honored his marriage vows, tried to love her, but Tory had thrown him aside, along with their daughters. It had taken him years to realize Tory was never pregnant, had faked the miscarriage. She'd taunted him with that during one of their many arguments.

"But you have three lovely daughters. I hope that's eased your pain."

Luke looked at her and managed a smile. How different would it have been for him if he hadn't been so stupid, hadn't let Tory trick him into marrying her? But he still wouldn't have known about Cody—and he wouldn't have had the girls. His marriage had been a living hell—parts of it—but his three daughters were the result. They'd made it worth suffering through the bad times.

"Luke, I can't pretend it's going to be easy making this marriage work, but I'm willing to give it my best shot—for the sake of the children. I…I'll understand if you need to seek the company of other women. All I ask is that you please not bring them home."

Luke stared at her, incredulous. "*What?* Just what are you saying?"

"I'm saying that I'll make the best of this marriage and that I'll look the other way if you need…female companionship outside of our marriage."

Luke shook his head to clear it. He couldn't be hearing her right. "Why would I want to do that?"

"Let's be honest, Luke. This is nothing more than a marriage of convenience between two people who barely know each other."

"But—"

"You made it pretty obvious last night that you don't want me sharing your bed. You put me in another room at the other end of the house."

Luke was dumbstruck. He'd put her at the other end of the house for three good reasons. He'd assumed she'd want nothing to do with him. She was exhausted. And she'd be out of temptation's way—although he'd spent tortured hours staring at the ceiling for most of the night.

He shook his head. "You've changed so much. You seem so unsure of yourself, Megan. Where has the carefree young woman of fifteen years ago gone?"

"I had to leave her behind a long time ago."

"Why? Because you had a child?"

"Not only that. To…survive."

They were both silent for a moment. Then she said, "I don't expect you to find me desirable anymore. That's why I won't stop you from looking elsewhere for… companionship."

He recalled Cody's implication that there'd been a variety of men in and out of his life. Was that why she believed it was okay? Was that why her expectations were so low and she seemed so defeated?

He wanted to yell at her, shake her, drag her into his arms to elicit some sort of response from her, try and dredge up some vestige of the person she'd been.

"You think I want another woman in my bed?" he demanded. "You think I'd break my vows? You think I'm that shallow?"

He hated the way she stood there, her silence confirming every word he spoke. Why would she think so little of him? Hadn't he tried to prove his commitment to her and Cody by marrying her? Yes, it might have been prompted by concern for his son, but he'd *never* treat her with such flagrant disrespect, such disregard.

At a loss to understand why they were so brittle, so distant with each other. "Touch me," he whispered. And waited. Hoping to find the bridge to her heart.

MEGAN SWALLOWED. THERE WAS nothing in the world she wanted more. So what held her back? For fifteen years, she'd longed to feel Luke's arms around her, know his kisses again, the way he made love so tenderly.

He was so close, she could lose herself in his masculine smell. She breathed in the scent of horse and hay and...Luke.

She lowered her eyes and let them rest on his mouth, then his strong neck, his wide shoulders, his broad chest. He was bigger than she remembered, more filled out, even more desirable now than he was all those years ago. She ached to have him wrap his arms around her, feel his lips on hers.

Megan dredged up every ounce of resistance she could muster to protect herself from Luke. She could never let him know she'd loved him all that time, wept with wanting to feel him hold her again. But she'd spent too many of those years suppressing that yearning; she couldn't allow it to crumble so easily, couldn't let down her defenses and confess the truth: that she'd loved him then and still loved him now.

"Touch me," he said again. But this time it sounded more like a plea than a command.

All she had to do was lift her hands to his chest....

She glanced back up into his eyes, saw the naked hunger in their depths

With a tiny intake of breath, she understood that his longing was as great as hers.

She raised her hands and placed them on his chest. He felt so good, so strong, beneath her fingers, she wanted to coil them into his skin, lay her face against his chest, breathe him in.

Warmth and sheer male strength emanated from him, emboldening her as she gazed into his eyes, daring him to take the next step. But he didn't. If anything, the hunger she saw there had deepened, become more raw.

It took all her willpower not to pull his head close to hers, to slip her arms around him and hold him so tightly the breath would be forced from their lungs. She wanted his lips at her throat, his mouth on her breasts, his tongue…

She molded her hands to his chest, wanting him, *needing* him, so much. But Luke was letting her lead this dance. If she wanted to, she could walk away. She knew by his stance that he was giving her that choice.

She ran her hands up his chest, to his throat and around to the back of his neck, clasping them behind his head. She was on sensory overload by now, powerless to resist him.

"Kiss me," he murmured, and she leaned into him, bringing her lips to his, needing the contact, longing for it, reveling in it.

"Kiss me the way you've wanted to be kissed all these years," he whispered.

And she did, realizing that Luke, too, must have dreamed of her kisses as she'd dreamed of his. He wrapped his arms around her so tightly, she gasped for air. He eased his hold a little, giving her space to breathe, and angled his mouth over hers. His kiss was at first demanding, then softened with tenderness.

His arousal pressed hotly against her belly.

With a tiny whimper of surrender, she gave him everything.

THEY LAY IN each other's arms, feeling satiated, complete.

Megan rolled away from Luke to stare up at the sky through the branches of the tree overhanging the creek. Tears of happiness ran from the corners of her eyes and she wiped them away, not wanting Luke to know how much their making love had affected her.

The word *profound* sprang to mind and she smiled secretly. No, it had been more than that, so much more intense. Had he hoped they'd make love when they headed out on their ride? He'd brought birth control. Surely that was a sign that he wanted them to share a bed, start living like a real husband and wife.

She rolled back toward Luke and placed a kiss on his chest.

We're going to make it! she wanted to call into the meadow. Wanted to let every living creature within earshot hear her rejoice.

Luke lifted her so she lay on top of him. He held her face in both hands and kissed her. "Thank you," he breathed against her mouth.

She smiled and said, "I was thinking of saying the same thing to you."

He kissed the tip of her nose and said, "Maybe now you'll realize you don't need a succession of men through your bed to keep you happy."

Megan froze. What was Luke saying? That he believed he hadn't been the only man she'd made love with these past fifteen years? She was too choked up, too shocked, to say anything that would dispel the notion. The unmitigated *nerve* that he could think that of her! She bit down hard on her lip and forced the tears not to flow, forced her breathing to slow. How *dared* he condemn her for something she hadn't done!

For fifteen years, she'd kept her feelings for Luke to herself. Kept the love in her heart a secret. Kept herself away from the potential hurt of another relationship. And here she was, in the middle of Colorado, right back where she'd started.

PUZZLED BY HER SILENCE and the sudden stiffness in her posture, Luke drew back to look into Megan's eyes. He saw nothing but loathing in her gaze. And unshed tears.

Megan leaped to her feet before he could grab her arms. She reached for her clothes and put them on, her hands fumbling with the buttons of her shirt. She gave up and tied the ends beneath her breasts. "How dare you treat me like a common whore," she whispered through clenched teeth, leaving Luke so stunned he didn't know how to react.

After pulling on her jeans, Megan caught Sage's bridle and swung up onto her horse. Without a backward glance, she turned the mare's head and rode out of the meadow.

CHAPTER SIX

LUKE CLAMBERED TO HIS feet and strode to where Rocket grazed. He rested his head against the horse's flanks, wondering why Megan had lit out of there so fast, said the things she had.

The only conclusion he could come up with was that she regretted their lovemaking.

She didn't want him. Not as her husband. Not as her lover. Theirs was a marriage of convenience. How could he have forgotten that so soon?

If Luke hadn't been expecting guests tonight—guests to celebrate his *marriage*—he would've gone down to Rusty's Bar. Instead, he had to get himself under control and ride back home and pretend he had a marriage that was going to work *for the sake of his children*. Certainly not for him.

He glanced up at the never-ending Colorado sky and tried to push away the memories at the edge of his subconscious—Tory turning up that night and relating to him what she'd overheard Megan saying in the change rooms at the rec center. "She was laughing at you, Luke. Saying she'd never laid a hayseed before, that the girls back at college would think it was hysterical that she'd seduced you and then kept you waiting. She wanted to see if she could fool you because you were just a lovesick country boy."

Dammit! He swung up into the saddle and grimaced

against the pain. Damn Tory! Damn Megan! Damn every blasted woman he'd ever met!

He'd believed Tory when she'd told him that. He'd known her since they were kids. Why *wouldn't* he believe her?

Tory had known about Megan, since she'd bumped into them at Rusty's one night. She'd been pleasant to Megan, leading Luke to assume she'd gotten over their breakup.

A couple of days after Megan had left, he'd run into Tory again, and she'd told him what she'd overheard. That had been such a low point, he'd drunk too much and let Tory take him home to bed. In the morning she'd informed him she was several weeks pregnant.

She said she didn't want an abortion, and Luke didn't feel right about it, anyway, so he'd done the only thing he could. He'd married her. He didn't love Tory, but when she'd miscarried, he'd been devastated. Over the next couple of years, doubts had started to surface, cracks had appeared in the marriage and he'd been on the point of asking for a divorce when Tory had gotten pregnant—this time for real. He'd stayed.

He'd stayed for three years and then when he couldn't stand it anymore and wanted out, she'd gotten pregnant again. The third time she'd been just as desperate to hang on to him, but as was Tory's nature, once Celeste was born, she'd lost interest in her marriage and children. She rarely spent a night at home, preferring to trawl every nightspot in the county.

They had blazing fights and, during one of them, Tory confessed that she'd never been pregnant and her miscarriage was a fake. Luke had already guessed, so he hadn't reacted and that had only enraged her more.

When she met a rodeo star at a local bar, Tory

claimed she needed more excitement in her life, so she'd packed her bags and left without even saying goodbye to her girls. Luke let her go.

He'd felt nothing for Tory by the end. Her obsession with him and other men had hurt too many people. He'd suspected Tory's crazy obsession with him had kept him and Megan apart all those years ago, but how could he prove it? She'd lied so convincingly it was hard to separate fact and fiction.

MEGAN MADE IT back to the ranch and her bedroom, barely maintaining her composure. It was only when she'd closed the door to her room and stepped under the shower spray that she allowed her pent-up emotions free rein. Humiliated by Luke's accusation and angry for succumbing yet again to his lovemaking, she wanted to rail against the world.

LUKE RODE BACK to the ranch cursing himself.

He'd thought he and Megan had a chance of making this work. He grimaced as he remembered the way she'd fumbled with the buttons and instead tied that scrap of fabric beneath her breasts and gotten up on Sage and galloped off as if she couldn't get away from him fast enough.

"What's bitin' your butt?" Daisy asked when he rode up to the corral fence. He leaped off Rocket's back, threw the reins over the railing and strode toward the house.

Luke turned. "Watch it, young lady," he warned, in no mood for smart remarks. "Or the penalty box is going to be overflowing this week."

Daisy liked hanging on to her money, so he knew she'd apologize.

"Sorry, Daddy. But Megan rode in here lookin' really bad a while ago and now you're comin' from the same direction."

Luke could see the hurt and confusion in Daisy's eyes. He walked back to her and ruffled her hair. "Sorry, squirt. It was wrong of me to take my temper out on you—or Rocket," he said, observing the gelding's heaving sides. He'd crossed over the creek and ridden the horse hard into the foothills behind the meadow to check on his brood mares and their foals. From there he could see the ranch house in the far distance. His haven, his home.

Apart from his family, it was the only solid thing he could rely on in his life.

"S'okay," she said, and shrugged out of his embrace.

"Can you give Rocket a brush-down, honey? I'll pay the penalty box for you."

Daisy brightened and said, "Sure."

Luke bent and gave her nose a peck. Of all his children, Daisy was by far the most independent and least demonstrative. Well, at least until Cody showed up.

"I've been thinking I should increase your allowance. You do more than your fair share around here."

Daisy's eyes widened. "Really?"

"Yep, really. And I might backdate it to the beginning of the year."

That promise got the desired response as Daisy threw her arms around his waist. "I love you, Daddy," she said.

"And I love you, squirt," he said, hugging her back.

He knew he wasn't demonstrative enough with his kids. He didn't mean to be so distant, never imagined he'd be such a hard taskmaster as a father. Life had sent him down a path he wasn't happy about traveling, but it wasn't fair of him to take it out on his daughters.

His throat closed as Daisy continued to hug him. He coughed to clear it, then gently pried her away.

"I've got to go talk to Megan," he said. "Can we discuss your raise a bit later?"

Smiling, Daisy shrugged. "Sure." She picked up a brush and started to groom Rocket.

He mounted the rear veranda steps, eased his boots off and opened the back door. Sasha and Celeste were in the kitchen cutting up cake.

Sasha looked up guiltily. "I was only trying to help Megan, Daddy. I'm not taking over," she explained. "She seemed upset, so I thought she wasn't well. Celeste and I are finishing the trifle for her."

Luke hadn't realized how stormy he must've looked himself until he'd seen the worry reflected in Sasha's eyes. "It's okay." He patted her shoulder reassuringly. "That was kind of you. I'll go talk to her."

"Me, too!" Celeste piped up, climbing down from her stool.

Luke scooped her up and put her back on it. "No, darlin', Sash needs your help here. I'll be back in a jiffy." He turned and strode out of the kitchen, through the living room and down the hallway. He paused outside Megan's door and rapped lightly. When there was no response, he turned the handle and stepped inside.

He could hear a shower running in the bathroom and walked to her bedroom. He paused outside the door and listened, then walked in.

Above the sound of running water he could hear Megan crying.

Unable to comfort her, fearing she'd lash out at him

for intruding, he made himself take a step backward.
And then another and another. Silently, he left her room.

Back in his own bathroom, he turned the faucet
on cold, and stepped under the punishing spray. *You
heartless bastard!* he cursed himself. *She's done nothing other than come here and try to help you to provide
a normal family life for our son. And now look what
you've done!* Luke had no idea exactly *what* he'd done
wrong, but he planned to find out, once Megan had regained her composure.

WHEN MEGAN HAD collected herself enough to face their
guests, she got out of the shower and dried off, then
splashed cold water on her face, hoping that would sub-
due the swelling around her eyes. The outfit she'd arrived
in yesterday, freshly laundered and pressed, hung on the
outside of her closet door. Her underwear, also freshly
laundered, was on the end of her bed, neatly folded.

There wasn't a hair dryer in evidence so Megan
brushed her hair and pulled it into a ponytail. Dressed
in her clean clothes, she took a deep breath and headed
to the kitchen. She'd been short with Sasha and Celeste,
who'd greeted her warmly when she'd come inside a half
hour ago and headed straight to her room. She needed
to make it up to them.

"I dunno," she heard Celeste saying, "I don't think
Mommy's going to be happy that we're makin' the trifle."

"Too bad," Sasha snapped. "It's gotta get chilled
enough for tonight."

Megan entered the kitchen and forced a bright
smile. Celeste sat on the kitchen counter looking so
serious, Megan's heart went out to her. She'd called

her "Mommy" again. How wonderful and *wanted* that word made her feel.

No longer needing to force her smile, she said, "Sasha's right, sweetie, the trifle does need to chill." She lifted Celeste off the counter and shifted her onto one hip, then turned to Sasha. "Thank you for thinking of that. I'm afraid I've been indulging myself in the shower too long."

Sasha merely nodded and continued pouring the custard over the trifle. "I made custard, too. You forgot to do that before you went riding. It had to chill, as well."

Megan couldn't understand this girl, who was so generous, yet wanted to push Megan away, usually with veiled accusations. "Thank you," she said, not wanting to inflame the situation. "I guess I just assumed there'd be some in the refrigerator."

"This isn't New York City. We live on a ranch. We don't rely on buying everything from the supermarket."

Duly chastised, Megan said, "You're right, of course. I'll have to get used to that, won't I?" she agreed, and moved Celeste to the other hip. She was a bit too old to be carried around, but Megan loved having her chubby little arms around her neck, squeezing perhaps a little too tightly.

"How about if I put you down here," she said. "We don't want my outfit too crushed before the guests arrive." She sat her on the kitchen table and started to unwind the French braid in Celeste's hair, which was coming out. "Thank you, Sasha, for ironing my outfit. How do you get the creases so neat and crisp?"

"Spray-on starch."

And lots of it, Megan thought, noting the stiffness of her collar rubbing against her neck. So there were clearly some things it was okay to get at the supermarket. She turned her attention back to Celeste. "Hold still, sweetie, and I'll redo your hair, so it's nice and pretty when everyone gets here."

"I need a bath first. You can wash my hair, too."

"Sure. Let's do that, but since I can hear Daisy running water upstairs, you can have your bath downstairs, okay?" She turned and let Celeste climb onto her back. "Will you be okay here, Sasha, or would you like me to help with anything?"

"I don't need your help," she said.

Have it your way, miss! And while you're at it, get that chip off your shoulder, Megan thought, then nearly bumped into Luke as she piggybacked Celeste out of the kitchen.

Luke caught her arm as she stepped back. The warmth of his touch sent desire licking through her body as she remembered the way he'd touched her as they made love in the meadow. She rejected that memory, determined this man would never get to her again.

"Can we talk?" he asked, his dark eyes pleading.

Surprised by the pain and intensity she saw in his expression, she said, "I'm going to give Celeste her bath."

"Now, please. It's important."

Megan bent to let Celeste slide off her back, saying, "Why don't you go get undressed and I'll start your bath?"

"Okay, Mommy." Celeste danced off toward the hallway. Moments later they could hear her clattering up the stairs to her room.

"Don't get in the bath until I'm there!" Megan called.

"Okay, Mommy!"

Megan smiled at Celeste's retreating back. She'd never get tired of hearing Celeste call her "Mommy."

She followed Luke to the downstairs bathroom. He put in the plug and set the bathwater running, then gripped Megan's hand and drew her down the hallway to her room.

Once inside, he locked the door and turned to her. "I want to apologize for my behavior this afternoon. I know you came here with the best intentions for our son's welfare. I appreciate that you're trying your hardest with my girls. I don't expect, and neither will I ask, anything more of you. I want to assure you that I won't be seeking the company of women outside our marriage and that…I won't trouble you for any more…marital favors, either." With that, he reached to unlock the door, but Megan stayed his hand.

"Just a minute," she said. "I've listened to you. Now you can listen to me."

Expressionless, he nodded.

"You took something very important away from me when you said those hurtful words about other men in my life." She drew in a deep breath. "That hurt so badly, Luke. You destroyed something in me that I've fought very hard for."

He stared at her blankly, then asked, "You mean you're not mad at me for making love to you?"

"No. I'm angry at myself for letting that happen so soon. I'm upset with you for that comment afterward."

"But—"

"I didn't have much self-esteem left after what I'd been through trying to raise our son on my own, but what little I had, I held very dear. I had *never*—would *never*—succumb to allowing a man to share my bed in order to get by. When you said that, it made me realize you neither respected me nor had any real understanding of how difficult it's been to raise our son on my own."

"But—"

"You should've known there was no one before you. And there's been no one since. Yet you were prepared to believe the worst of me, to humiliate me by insinuating those things."

Luke shook his head. "I'm sorry," he said. "I thought that was what Cody meant back in the judge's chambers. I thought it was the reason he wanted us to get married, so there'd be some stability in his life. Obviously, I misunderstood what he'd said."

"That sort of thing *did* go on in our neighborhood. But you misinterpreted what he said and applied it to me and that hurts so much."

Luke took both her hands in his. "I'm sorry from the bottom of my heart. I'd never intentionally hurt you, Megan."

He halted as though waiting for her to speak, and when she didn't he said, "We've let too many misunderstandings keep us apart for the past fifteen years. Can we try to put them aside and start fresh?"

"I'd like that," Megan managed to say. But deep down she wondered if the time to start fresh had expired too long ago.

"Mommy! The water's goin' over the sides!" Celeste's plaintive call brought them both back to the present.

Megan reached around Luke, unlocked the door and opened it. "Coming, sweetie," she called, then slipped past Luke and headed to the bathroom.

CHAPTER SEVEN

TWENTY MINUTES LATER, Megan felt almost as wet as Celeste. She lifted the child from the bath, set her on the mat, looked down at her damp clothes and thought glumly that Sasha wouldn't be happy to see how she'd treated her handiwork. They hung limply from her body. Her top and blouse hadn't fared much better, but as she didn't have anything else to wear, they'd have to air dry. At least she still had her jeans.

"Can you be a big girl and finish drying yourself while I go put on some dry pants?" she asked Celeste, then reached in to pull out the plug.

"Okay…but hurry, Mommy."

Megan placed a kiss on Celeste's forehead and slipped out of the bathroom. Sasha was waiting in the hallway with her arms crossed. She looked Megan up and down with disdain.

"I…I got wet," Megan stammered, wondering why she allowed this child to get her so flustered and feeling guilty.

"You can't wear them tonight even if I do get them dry," Sasha said, disapproval dripping from every word.

Megan kept her temper in check. "You said my jeans would be fine for this party, didn't you? And my top and blouse will dry quickly enough."

"Everyone'll be here any minute," Sasha told her. "You can borrow my hair dryer."

Touched again by Sasha's strange but basically generous ways, she followed the girl upstairs to her room. "This is a lovely room, Sasha," she remarked, admiring the professional finish. "I like the contrast of the orange and purple. It's very effective."

"It's mango and jacaranda," Sasha corrected her, and went to a chest of drawers for a hair dryer. "I painted it myself."

"I'm genuinely impressed. Do you hope to be an interior decorator when you grow up?"

Sasha handed over the hair dryer. "No, a doctor," she said, and walked out of the room.

Megan stood there for a full ten seconds, open-mouthed.

"Mommy! I'm *cold!*" Celeste called.

Megan glanced around the room once more, then returned to the downstairs bathroom.

Wrapped in a huge towel, Celeste bounced on Megan's bed while Megan changed into her jeans, then dried what she could of her clothes by holding the dryer over her chest and moving it from side to side. It only took a few minutes, then she sat on the bed and turned the dryer on Celeste's long tresses.

As she combed out Celeste's nearly dry hair, a knock sounded at the door. "Come in!" she called, then looked up, expecting it to be Sasha coming to admonish her again, perhaps for leaving the bathroom a mess, or Daisy to have a chat.

She was startled to see Luke. Based on what he'd said earlier, she'd assumed he'd never set foot in her room again.

"People are arriving," he said, "How long do you think you'll be?"

"I'm just finishing Celeste's hair and then I'll be right out."

"Mommy's makin' me pretty, Daddy," Celeste said. "Leave us girls 'lone, okay?" she added primly.

LUKE BLINKED. HE HADN'T realized how much his little girl was growing up. She'd taken charge of the situation, dismissing him in favor of doing "girl things" with her new mommy. Still…it was nice to see them together.

If only he and his son could share some "guy things…" Then maybe they could grow closer. A thought occurred to him, something that might help that wish come true.

"I'm leaving," he said, and bent to kiss Celeste's forehead. His face passed Megan's as he straightened. She didn't exactly pull back from his gaze, but she sure wasn't turning her face toward him for some of the same attention.

BY THE TIME Celeste pronounced that Megan had finished with her hair and gotten dressed, the house was full of children and adults.

"Megan, there you are!" Beth greeted her as they entered the living room. She planted a welcoming kiss on her cheek.

Megan relaxed almost immediately. She'd been dreading the moment she had to meet the rest of Luke's brothers and their wives, but Beth had effectively broken the ice.

Beth took her hand and drew her into the group.

"Everyone, this is Megan. Luke, maybe you should do the introductions."

Matt was holding Sarah. He kissed Megan and looked into her eyes, his expression one of concern. "I hope you're settling in?"

Megan nodded mutely. What had Matt's look meant? Had Luke told his brother they were already having problems? She pushed the thought away and turned to smile at the other occupants of the room.

"This is my brother, Jack," he said, indicating a tall, well built man with jet-black hair and brilliant blue eyes who came forward and shook her hand. Megan noticed that his hand was large and calloused, his grip firm. *Jack is a carpenter.* Luke's words rang in her head.

"Welcome to our family, Megan. I hope you and Cody will be happy here," he said, then stepped back.

"I'm happy to meet you, Jack," Megan said, glancing across at Cody, who stood scowling in the corner of the room. Apparently, he'd already met his new relatives and passed judgment on them. They were far too clean-cut and warmhearted for his liking, she guessed. "Have you met my son, Cody?" she asked, sending him a warning look. "Cody's learning to ride, thanks to Daisy's patience, aren't you?"

"Yeah," Cody said, lightly punching Daisy's shoulder. "Hey, kid. You wanna play catch?" he asked her.

Daisy gazed up at him; she obviously loved having someone around who didn't think doing your hair, playing with dolls or cooking and cleaning was the greatest thing on earth. "Yeah!" she said, and they disappeared outside.

Megan didn't realize she'd been holding her breath until the screen door slammed behind them. At least

Cody had made a firm friend in Daisy. They'd be good for each other. As long as Cody didn't swear around her.

Luke was saying, "And this is my brother, Will."

Another man, almost the same height and coloring as Matt, stepped forward and pulled her into a bear hug. Megan's breath left her in a *whoosh* and then a woman's voice said sternly, "Will O'Malley, leave that poor girl alone!"

He obeyed and moved back, grinning sheepishly to allow a woman with green eyes and an unruly tumble of dark auburn curls to come toward Megan. "Please forgive my husband, Megan. He has no idea how to be-have in company."

Megan looked at Will, who could barely wipe the smile off his face, and thought, *He knows exactly how to behave to get his wife's attention.* "It's fine. I just haven't been hugged quite so…enthusiastically in a long time." Megan laughed, breaking the tension.

"I'm Becky, by the way," the other woman said, then gave Megan a hug that wasn't quite as ferocious as her husband's. "I'm so glad Luke found you and Cody and brought you home." She looked around the room. "Now our family's almost complete."

At Megan's frown of confusion, Becky explained. "We think Jack and Adam need to find themselves wives, but as Adam barely talks to anyone, he's not going to manage it on his own. If we could only get him to move closer to home…"

Megan grinned at Becky's desire to matchmake for a reluctant but much-loved brother-in-law. "I take it he's the strong, silent type?" she said, and noticed Luke shifting uncomfortably beside her.

Becky nodded. "Oh, boy! Is he ever. Just like Luke.

Worse than Luke. Much worse than Luke. At least Luke can carry on a conversation. Sometimes." She dug Luke in the ribs.

Becky was right; Luke *was* the strong, silent type. He rarely wasted words. Rarely smiled, too, as though watching and waiting, gauging what was going on before committing himself. He hadn't been like that when she'd known him before. He was far more gregarious back then.

"And these are your children, Nick and Lily?" Megan asked Becky, gesturing toward the other two occupants of the room—a boy with his mother's red hair and vivid blue eyes and a baby, sleeping in her carrier—hoping she'd got their names correct. Becky beamed, clearly pleased that Megan had remembered her children's names.

"Nicolas, this is your aunt Megan," Becky said to the boy who was kidding around with Sasha.

It was probably the first time Megan had seen the girl smile. Obviously, she liked her cousin.

"Hi, Aunt Megan," he said, approaching her and shaking her hand.

Megan noted that he walked with a slight limp and wondered about it. "Hello, Nick," she said. "I'm pleased to meet you."

Cody and Daisy had rushed in the back door moments earlier, and she introduced Cody to everyone who hadn't met him yet, cringing at his sullen attitude but reluctant to call him on it in front of his new relatives.

Megan looked to her husband for guidance when the room fell silent. When Luke didn't respond, she cleared her throat and glanced back at the gathering. "Well, I suppose I should ask, 'Won't you all sit down?' so please—" she held her arms out, taking in the well-worn furniture of the living room. "Make yourselves comfortable. I think Sasha and Celeste have prepared some treats for you." She glanced at Sasha, who prodded Celeste and disappeared into the kitchen along with Nick.

Megan sat in a large, comfortable chair, and after Luke had finished serving drinks to everyone, he perched on the arm of it.

The children returned from the kitchen and passed some appetizers around. Sarah was standing unsteadily by her father, clinging to Matt's leg.

Becky reached into the duffel bag she'd brought with her. "I brought over some clothes of mine that don't fit me anymore. Beth said your own belongings won't get here for a few days. Although looking at you, I'm sure all my clothes will be too baggy. I don't think I've been as slim as you since I was about twelve." She laughed and said, "If ever!"

Megan observed Becky's generous curves and envied her. She knew Becky's comments were meant in jest, but they stung a little all the same. "Thank you, but I don't think I'll need them. My stuff should get here soon. Until then I can manage with what I have."

Beth dug into her bag, too, and produced a small pile of neatly folded clothes, saying, "But wait, as they say in the ads, there's more." She gave the pile to Megan with a smile. "I hope you can find something to fit you here, too, Megan."

Megan nodded and accepted the clothes, feeling like someone's poor relative. "I...I really don't think I'll need them," she said again.

"'Course you will," Sasha piped up. "You don't even

have a *nightgown.* Daddy had to put you to bed in your underwear last night."

Megan gasped. She'd never felt so totally mortified in her life. Her face was so hot it must be glowing beet red and her lips trembled at the accusatory tone of Sasha's voice. Why was Sasha doing this to her—and in front of everybody?

"E-excuse me," she finally managed to say, and got awkwardly to her feet. "I'll just put these in my room." She turned and fled down the hallway.

She threw the clothes on her bed. "Charity case!" she muttered angrily. "Little brat! And the rest of them think I'm a charity case!"

"Megan?"

Megan turned at the sound of Beth's voice. She'd walked into Megan's room and had obviously heard every word she'd said. Her face held pity.

Megan brushed at an errant tear. "Don't look at me like that!" she said. "I don't need to be treated like this!"

Beth closed the door, then urged Megan over to the bed and sat down beside her. "I'm sorry, that was all my fault. Becky and I didn't mean any harm by it. Matt told me you didn't have anything other than the clothes you wore to court and a pair of jeans and a shirt you bought on the way out of New York. He said the moving company could be a week, so I'm afraid I mentioned it to Becky this morning." She placed her hand on Megan's arm. "It's all my fault," she said again. "Please don't blame Becky. We meant it in the kindest way. We're sisters now," she said gently.

Megan reached over to grab a tissue to dab at her tears, angry at herself for letting her emotions surface like this. "I didn't need Sasha pointing out how incompetent I was. I guess that's what set me off," she murmured.

Beth placed her arm around Megan's shoulders. "I'm afraid Sasha's mother wasn't the kindest person on earth and Sash has inherited her sharp tongue. I apologize for her behavior, but you'll see—she'll come around. This is going to be a big adjustment for her, having another woman in the house full-time. She's really a very generous child underneath all her bluster."

Megan nodded. "I know. But she likes to stab me every now and then with her cattle prod."

Beth laughed. "That's better! Keep a sense of humor and you'll be fine. As for Becky, she was just treating you like one of us." She squeezed Megan's shoulder. "We're all so overjoyed to have you in our family and for Luke to have found his son. We'd never want you to feel uncomfortable about being here."

Nodding, Megan blew her nose. There was a knock at the door and then Sasha called, "Can I come in?"

Megan looked dubiously at Beth, who squeezed her shoulder again. "Give her time," she whispered.

Megan stiffened her shoulders and got up off the bed to open the door. Sasha stood there twisting her hands. Megan had never seen her nervous before.

"My daddy said I should apologize to you for what I said."

Megan let out a sigh. "If you want to apologize, that's fine, Sasha, but don't feel you should just because your father told you to."

Sasha seemed confused by that remark, glanced at Beth, and then back at Megan. "Yeah, well, I'm sorry. Okay?" she said with a touch of belligerence.

"I'm sorry, too, Sasha, for making a mess of the

clothes you'd taken so much time over. I should have changed into my jeans to bathe Celeste. I'd forgotten how much water a four-year-old can kick out of a tub."

Sasha nodded solemnly. "Well, are you going to come outside with everyone now?" she asked.

Megan turned to Beth, who smiled encouragingly. She turned back to Sasha. "Lead the way," she said.

EVERYONE HAD MOVED outside to the back lawn. The sun was setting in magnificent colors behind the mountains and the older children had a makeshift game of baseball going on. The adults either sat or stood around talking. When Luke noticed Megan standing on the bottom step of the porch, he came toward her and caught both her hands in his. "Are you okay?" he asked, his voice full of concern.

"I'm fine. A minor misunderstanding, that's all. I hope I didn't spoil the party by being so stupid."

Luke squeezed her hands gently between his. "I'm truly sorry about what Sash said. And my sisters-in-law just wanted you to feel welcome."

"I realize that now and I'll try not to be so sensitive in the future…."

Luke cupped her cheek and touched her lips with his. When she pulled back, startled, he said under his breath, "Work with me here, will you?" he said gruffly. "I don't need my wife treating me as though I'm repugnant to her."

Taken aback by his admission that he needed them to maintain an outward show of togetherness—and needing to feel Luke's touch—she looped her arms around his neck and pressed her lips to his.

She wasn't prepared for the explosion of sensation

and feeling that shot through her body as their mouths met again and Luke pulled her closer. Standing as she was on the bottom step, Megan wasn't that much shorter than Luke. Through the thickness of his jeans and hers, she could feel the hard evidence of his desire. It both shocked and surprised her. She'd thought Luke was indifferent to her after his declaration earlier and his plea to pretend to the rest of the family that they were happily married. She hadn't thought he could desire her.

She leaned close and Luke placed his arms around her, deepening the kiss. Megan closed her eyes and let the sensations assail her, allowing her fingers to comb through his hair.

The catcalls and whistles from the garden permeated the erotic haze surrounding her and when Luke ended the kiss, she was breathless and wishing they were alone. He might not love her, but God help her, she loved him, had never stopped loving him. She'd take every morsel of affection she could grasp.

"Talk about a cold shower," Luke muttered and took several deep breaths as if trying to control his reaction to her. "Maybe we'd better join the others?"

Megan nodded, hoping her blush of embarrassment wasn't visible in the evening light and let him lead her to where the others waited.

"We don't need to light the barbecue, we'll just sizzle the steaks on you two," Will declared, and laughed uproariously. The others joined in and soon Megan's self-consciousness was forgotten.

THE EVENING WENT WELL. The food was consumed with gusto, the children played happily together, and by the end of the night, Cody had come out of his shell and was talking to the other kids, especially Becky's son, Nicolas. Celeste had spent almost the entire evening sitting on Megan's lap, telling everyone that her new mommy had done her hair. The child's acceptance of her had eased the way for Megan and she was grateful for it.

The only sour note came when the dessert had been served and Becky had made a remark about giving Megan the recipe for ambrosia, saying, "Luke won't be able to keep his hands off you when you feed him that!"

Sasha, sitting with the children, had overheard it and announced, "That won't be a problem, since they don't even share the same room."

Megan had gasped with horror and looked around the gathering. There was pity on the faces of Beth and Matt, who knew they didn't share a room, but Will, Jack and Becky hadn't been aware of the fact until now and all eyes seemed to be boring into her, curious to know what was going on.

"Sasha, go to your room," Luke said quietly.

"But, Dad, it's true!" she protested.

"Go to your room."

She stood and threw her napkin on the table. "It's true! They don't sleep together!" she told the gathering. "I don't even believe they're married!"

"Go to your room, Sasha!" Luke's voice rose dangerously.

Megan put a restraining hand on his arm. "Luke, please. Don't make a scene. Leave her be," she pleaded softly. Megan hadn't missed the shocked look on Cody's face at Sasha's outburst, she was embarrassing him so much.

"Gosh!" Becky said, and laughed heartily. "Is that what you're worrying about, Sash? You think your daddy and Megan aren't properly married, so it isn't right for them to share a room?" She glanced around the rest of the adults at the table, as if trying to garner their agreement.

Megan was grateful that Becky was attempting to turn Sasha's reaction around to seem less offensive and downright rude. Even Cody seemed to have relaxed.

"Well, we'll just have to have another wedding," Becky declared. "A *real* one this time, with pretty bridesmaids and a ceremony and a big party afterward!"

That effectively diffused the situation and got the children involved, with each of them yelling excitedly about what they wanted to contribute and who was going to be wearing what. All except Sasha. Megan was staggered by their enthusiasm. Becky sure knew how to stir up a crowd.

"I can ask Mom and Pop to get back here by next weekend," Matt offered.

"And naturally I'll perform the honors, seeing as I'm a qualified judge," Becky said.

"I'll call everyone Luke's ever known and invite them." That was Jack. He turned to Megan, smiling. "And I'll make the calls for you, too."

Megan shook her head. Her family wouldn't be interested in coming and she had very few friends in New York, certainly none who could afford to travel all the way to Colorado. She felt Luke's hand reach for hers beneath the table and that small action heartened her. She stiffened her back and spoke up. "I appreciate that, Jack, but Cody and I are part of your family now, so I hope your friends will be ours."

When Luke brought her hand to his lips, Megan knew she'd said the right thing without having to reveal to his family the painful circumstances of her estrangement from her own.

"I can't help out much," Luke said. "I'll be up at the Cattlemen's Convention and sale in Wyoming until Saturday morning."

"Never fear!" Beth assured him. "The O'Malley women are here. When you get back on Saturday, all you'll have to do is scrub up, put on your tux and get out onto the back lawn in time for the ceremony."

Luke grinned. "Sounds good to me." He looked at Megan. "Is all this okay with you? They're not railroading you into anything you don't want, are they?"

Megan had lost her voice since Luke had lifted her hand to his lips. She shook her head, mutely. He was leaving her by herself on the ranch next week? And she was only finding out about it *now?*

Matt slapped his hands on the table. "I'm going to go call Mom and Pop while the kids clean up the table and load the dishwasher."

"Aw, Uncle Matt!" they cried in unison.

Matt held up his hands to stay their protests. "Come on, guys, your moms have worked hard to prepare this feast and your fathers have worked hard eating it, so it's your turn. I'll give a ride in my patrol car to the kid who works the hardest."

That had children flying all over, clearing tables, scraping plates, carrying things to the kitchen.

Becky watched them all disappear into the house, Matt bringing up the rear to go and phone his parents. "What a guy." She sighed. "Sometimes I wish I'd married that man."

Will guffawed and grabbed his wife around the

waist. "If you'd married him, then I wouldn't have a terrific sister-in-law like Beth."

Becky considered that for a moment, then nodded sagely. "You're right. Good thing I was prepared to put up with second best." Then she squealed when Will threw her up over his shoulder, fireman-style, and carried her into the house, Becky laughing and pummeling his back all the way.

Jack and Beth collected the remaining glasses and hurried after them, laughing as Will tickled Becky, making her squeal more.

Megan watched them go, longing for the happiness and love the other couples shared. She'd been alone for so many years, depending only on herself, she found it comforting to acknowledge that such closeness between families could exist. But now, having spent the evening with the O'Malleys, she wanted that camaraderie for herself.

"What are you thinking?" Luke asked beside her.

Megan turned to him, startled by the intense tone of his voice. Darkness had descended as they'd eaten dinner and now the garden was lit only by bamboo torches, placed at strategic points around the perimeter, and candles on the table. Luke leaned forward, cupping his hand around the nearest candle and blew it out, then moved closer to Megan.

Instinctively, she pulled back. She wasn't ready for this, despite what had happened earlier. Despite wanting to deepen their relationship. Her reaction had been unthinking—self-protective.

Luke gave a hiss of disgust, got up from the table and strode into the house.

CHAPTER EIGHT

MEGAN TOSSED AND TURNED most of the night. She'd handled things badly and upset Luke when she hadn't meant to. She'd seen the passion flare in his eyes. Did Luke have genuine feelings for her? Megan was afraid to ask. Afraid of the answer—either way!

When she stumbled tiredly into the kitchen the next morning, it was deserted. The house was silent. Apparently, everyone had already eaten breakfast and gone. A note from Luke was propped against the vase of flowers in the middle of the table. Megan opened it and read.

We've gone to help at Matt and Beth's house. Cody, too. Ben will give you directions. Keys are in the car.

Megan stared at the note. He must still have been angry when he wrote it, she thought. No greeting, no signature, just a curtly written note as if he didn't care whether she showed up or not. Well, she wouldn't, because she didn't have a driver's license. In fact, she hadn't driven since she'd dropped out of college. That was a legacy of living in New York—no need for a car and nowhere to park one, anyway.

She had toast and a cup of coffee for breakfast, then went in search of anything she could do around the house to fill in the time until everyone returned. The house was neat; the only thing that might need cleaning were the worn covers on the sofas. "Uh-uh!" she said. "Forget it. Little Miss Sourpuss's going to complain, no matter what I do."

Megan headed back into the laundry, seeking clothes to wash or iron. Everything was spotlessly clean, pressed clothes hanging, waiting to be taken to various rooms. Megan could work out by the sizes who owned what, so she took them to their respective rooms and hung them up. That done, she found some carrots and brought them to the stable, making friends with the various horses. Ben, the ranch hand, wasn't anywhere in sight.

"So much for getting directions from Ben," she muttered, and stroked Sage's nose. The horse nickered, pressing her muzzle to Megan's face. "What do you think of that husband of mine, Sage? I can't figure him out, that's for sure." The mare nodded as if agreeing.

The sound of a truck pulling up outside and a honking horn had Megan racing to the barn door, hoping it was Luke returning to say he'd forgiven her and that he wanted them to try and be friends...and maybe lovers.

Her face fell when she didn't recognize the vehicle. The door opened and Beth climbed down. "Hey, Megan!" she called toward the house.

"Over here." Megan waved.

Beth turned in her direction. "Is everything all right? Luke sent me over to get you. He got worried when you didn't turn up. You don't look too happy," Beth observed as Megan neared the truck.

Megan shrugged her shoulders. "I didn't know we were supposed to be visiting you today. Otherwise, I would've made sure Luke included me rather than let me sleep in."

Beth laughed. "I doubt you'd call it *visiting*. Our house isn't built yet. All the boys come over on weekends and work on it. We don't have a phone, and cell coverage isn't great over there, or one of us would've called you." She grinned. "You should see the guys. They're all so busy trying to show us women how macho they are. Anyway, when I asked Luke where you were, he suggested I come by. Hop in and I'll drive you."

Megan climbed into the truck, then got down again.

"Where are you going?" Beth called as she ran to the front door.

"To lock up." She stopped and bit her lip. She didn't even have a key to the house. Some wife!

"Don't worry about it," Beth said. "Luke never locks up."

Megan climbed back in. "I guess there are a lot of things I need to learn about living in the country," she said.

Beth reversed the truck and headed toward the gates. "You'll learn quickly enough. I came from L.A.—lived there all my life. I've been here less than two years and yet I feel so much a part of the place that L.A. seems like a distant memory."

"Did you meet Matt in L.A.?" Megan asked.

Beth turned out of the gate and gunned the truck down the gravel road. "No. I was pregnant with Sarah when I moved here. I met Matt the night I had her."

"You're kidding!" Megan faced her. "You mean to tell me he isn't Sarah's natural father? That's hard to believe."

Beth concentrated on the road as she took a left turn

and entered another valley. "I know. But I was actually widowed. I crashed my car into a snowbank on the way to the hospital. Matt rescued me, drove like a maniac to the hospital and stayed with me while Sarah was born."

"That's so romantic!"

Beth smiled at her. "Matt doesn't remember it quite that way!"

For the rest of the trip Beth told Megan about how she and Matt had ended up getting married. Megan was enchanted with her story. She could tell from the first moment how much Matt adored his beautiful wife and their daughter. *Oh, to have a love like that,* Megan thought, not for the first time.

"Give him a chance, will you?"

"What do you mean?"

Beth looked across at her, eyes full of compassion. "I know it's not going so well between you two. In spite of that hot kiss on the back porch last night."

Megan slumped in her seat. "Does *everyone* know that was just for show?"

Beth patted her thigh. "Relax. In spite of Sasha's little routine, everybody—except Matt and me—assumes that things are fine between you."

"In that case, the others will start picking up clues pretty soon, too." Why had she thought they could make this marriage work?

For Cody, she reminded herself.

Beth turned in at another gate, and as they made their way along the drive, Megan could see the frame of a substantial log home coming into view. Children were running through the fields chasing one another while the men worked. Becky was setting up lunch on long tables in the sun. "Oh, it's lovely," she breathed. "What a magnificent setting...and home!"

Beth pulled up beside the other vehicles. "Thank you. Will owned this ranch land. He carved it into ten-acre ranchettes and sold it off to save some old buildings in town. I'll have to take you down there to see what they've done. I'm sure you'll find it interesting. Will and Jack have really performed a miracle restoring the old buildings." She got out of the truck. "Matt decided to invest in one of the lots here."

Megan nodded approvingly. "Then he has exceptional taste in land—as well as wives." She smiled across at Beth. "I can imagine how it'll look, with lots of glass on this side to take in the views." She nudged Beth excitedly. "Walk me through it, okay? Tell me where everything's going to go. But who designed it?"

"Matt...with a bit of help from me. I'm an architect."

Megan realized she knew so little about her in-laws. If nothing else, she intended to make it her mission over the next couple of days to learn as much as she could. Maybe then she'd feel more like part of the family.

"Hey, there!"

Megan turned to see Luke approaching with his arms outstretched. He threw them around her and pulled her into a hug.

"I've missed you," he said, placing his hands on either side of her face and kissing her thoroughly.

Beth's words swirled in Megan's head. She and Matt knew it was just a performance. Well, she was going to make damn sure no one else did. Wanting to make up for rejecting his advances the previous night, she returned his kiss, her hands sliding up Luke's muscled back to hold him close. Only his T-shirt separated them and she wished it wasn't there. Wished her hands were gliding over his bare skin...

"Mom, stop it," Cody hissed from behind her, and Megan broke off the embrace.

"Cut it out," he muttered angrily. "You're embarrassing me!"

Feeling slightly unsteady on her feet, Megan held on to Luke as they both turned to face their son. Luke's hand rested possessively on her waist and Megan was pleased to note that he was as breathless as she was.

Luke found his voice first. "Cody. Your mom and I are newlyweds. No one else is embarrassed about this. Look around you." He raised his arm to encompass everyone who'd politely returned to their business.

"They were all staring before and I don't like it."

"Then get over it," Luke said harshly. His arm still around Megan, he led her toward the house.

Megan was surprised by Luke's tone. She halted and placed her hand on his chest. "It's not necessary to speak to him like that. He has a right to express his opinion."

Luke glared down at her. "He only talks to me when he wants to criticize or tell me not to do something that might offend him. I've had a gutful of it. It's about time he learned not to be such a spoiled mama's boy."

Megan's couldn't believe she'd just heard that. "*Spoiled mama's boy?* How *dare* you!" she said, and turned away so the others wouldn't see her stormy expression.

Luke caught her elbow and started walking with her down the driveway, away from everyone else. "Look," he said, and she could hear the exasperation in his voice. "I've had nothing but grief from that kid since he got here. He'll talk to my brothers, but whenever *I* try to talk to him, he clams up."

"Then maybe you'd be better off if I took my *mama's boy* and we got out of your li—"

Luke spun her around to face him. "Don't you even *think* about it," he said through clenched teeth. "You try to deny me access to my son like you have for the past fourteen years and I'll pursue you through the courts and get sole custody of him."

Fear tightened Megan's chest. "No!" she managed to gasp as tears spilled from her eyes. What hope would she have against Luke and his money? He could hire the best attorneys, who would immediately point to the fact that she was such a bad mother their son had almost ended up in juvenile detention.

Luke released her arm and ran a hand through his hair. "I'm sorry. I didn't mean that. I was letting off steam. Cody seems to be going out of his way to make my life hell and then rubbing it in by being nice to my brothers."

"And with your caveman tactics, who can blame him?"

"Megan, I'm trying here, okay? I *want* to be his dad, but it's damned hard when he keeps pushing me away."

"Just like Sasha keeps pushing *me* away," Megan said. She saw the deep frown lines across his forehead and ached to reach up and smooth them away. She believed Luke genuinely wanted to be a dad to Cody, but he was going about it all wrong.

Aware that they had an audience now that everyone was gathering around the tables for lunch, she stepped back, gesturing in her son's direction. "Don't try so hard, then. Let him come to you. You don't have to put up with him criticizing you, but don't bite back. Turn it around and maybe ask him how *he* feels something should be done." She smiled. "That'll shock him, because the truth is, he's in an environment that's so foreign to him, he's rebelling against it, by taking it out on you."

Luke caught her hand and brought it to his mouth, placing a gentle kiss on her palm. As warmth spread through her, she couldn't help thinking, *If only he meant that kiss, instead of playacting for the benefit of his family.*

"Okay," he said hoarsely, as though the kiss had affected him as much as her. "Just promise never to threaten me with leaving."

Megan studied him for a moment. She'd never seen Luke so vulnerable, never considered it possible that he'd fear her walking out.

She squeezed his hand in reassurance. "Don't call him a mama's boy, okay?"

Luke nodded. "I know. That was unfair." She could see in his eyes the love he had for their son. "It can't have been easy for you, being both mother and father to him, and it can't have been easy for him, either, and I'm sorry about that. But I think you've tended to indulge him rather than take a firmer stand."

She felt her anger flare, but before she could vent her feelings over that comment, Luke took her in his arms so it looked as though they were sharing lovers words rather than angry ones. "Let's not get into this now," he said, "but we need to talk when we get home, okay?"

Realizing that arguing would get them nowhere—other than into a potential full-scale argument in front of a dozen curious onlookers—Megan nodded and smiled, the kind of smile a woman would give her husband if they'd shared a secret. Luke smiled back and kissed her on the lips, then turned to walk her back to the rest of the group.

The children collected their lunches and went to sit on blankets spread beneath the trees on the other side of the house. The adults sat at the table Becky had set.

"Where were you, Megan?" Will asked. "Luke thought you must still be sleeping and sent Beth to get you."

Megan flushed. "I…I don't have a driver's license. In fact, I haven't driven a car for nearly fifteen years. I'm not sure I'd remember how."

Jack laughed heartily. "You'll remember! Or put it this way, you'd *better* remember. Those little princesses need transport to dancing lessons, swimming lessons—"

"Don't forget Daisy's tae kwon do," Becky threw in.

"And all those birthday parties and sleepovers they get invited to," Matt said, rolling his eyes. "You'll feel like you're running a taxi service," he warned.

Megan fretted. What if it took her ages to be good enough to take her driving test? "I didn't need a car in New York," she explained, "so I let my license lapse."

"I'll give you a lesson after lunch if you'd like," Beth offered. "The roads around here are deserted. You'll be fine."

The rest of the lunch passed pleasantly, and when the men went back to work, Beth walked Megan through the house, pointing out the various rooms and discussing decor.

They returned to the living room, where Jack and Luke were creating a rock fireplace. "It's absolutely enchanting," she said. "I can't wait to see it when it's finished."

"Neither can I!" Beth said with a laugh. "We're living in a tiny cabin up on Blue Spruce Drive, and although it was cozy at first, now that we're accumulating furniture for this house, it's getting a little *too* cozy!"

Matt appeared out of nowhere and grabbed Beth in a bear hug, complete with bearlike noises. "What's the matter, wife? Complaining about my need to nest?"

Beth turned, slipping her arms around his neck, and Megan moved away to give them privacy. As she did, she was confronted by the sight of Luke, who'd removed his T-shirt. His back muscles, sheened with sweat, rippled as he lifted the slabs of stone and his biceps bulged with the effort.

He didn't seem to be aware of her but Megan couldn't stop staring....

This wasn't good. She could no more control her body's reaction to Luke than change the tides.

Beth saved her from drooling by suggesting they take that driving lesson now.

BETH WAS A patient teacher, and by the time they drove back to the house two hours later, Megan felt her confidence returning.

"You should apply to take your test this week," Beth said as she climbed out of the vehicle. "I'll get the sheriff to set it up with the DMV if you like." She winked at Megan and they went to join the others. "If you'll excuse me, I think my little darling is hungry," Beth said as Matt met them, Sarah fussing in his arms.

After arranging with Matt to do her test later in the week, she went in search of Cody. He was behind the house digging a trench, working alongside his father. As if sensing her presence, Luke looked up and smiled.

"How'd it go?" he asked, jumping out of the trench.

"Matt's going to arrange for me to take my driving test. Beth says I'm ready and all I need to do is study the rules of the road. If all goes well, I should be driving the girls around in no time."

"That's great," he said, drawing her away. "Because we haven't had a chance to talk about the Cattlemen's Convention in Wyoming yet. I'll be leaving in the morning."

Megan folded her arms. "Leaving me stuck in the middle of nowhere with no way of getting around? What if something happens to the children?"

"Relax. One of the hands will be here to take care of you. He and Cody are switching places."

"What do you mean?"

"Cody's coming to Wyoming with me. He's looking forward to it."

Megan could feel her throat closing up with fear. "But he's never been anywhere without me before!"

Luke nodded. "In that case, isn't it time he did?"

"I…I need to think about this."

"What's to think about? We'll be back Saturday. It'll be a terrific opportunity for my son and me to get to know each other without you around."

"Excuse me?"

"Ah, let me rephrase that—"

"Don't bother!" Megan stormed over to where Cody was in the ditch. "Cody, you won't be going to Wyoming. I'll be enrolling you in school first thing in the morning."

"But I wanna go, Mom. School's dumb."

"School is *not* dumb, young man! You need to get your grades back up. You're going to school in the morning, whether you like it or not."

Megan was so enraged that Luke had taken over without talking to her first, she was trembling. And as for telling Cody he didn't have to go to school! Wasn't this one of the reasons for moving to Colorado? To make sure he *did* attend school? She felt Luke's hand on her shoulder and shrugged it off.

"Megan, if you'd let me finish… I was going to give you the good news that Cody's agreed to go to summer school to get his grades up. There's only a week of school left here in Colorado before summer vacation. He won't achieve anything much in a week, but he'd gain a wealth of experience from coming to the Cattlemen's Convention with me."

Megan's shoulders slumped. Luke was right, but she wasn't happy with the way he'd gone about it without consulting her first. At least no one else had witnessed the humiliating exchange between them. The rest of the O'Malleys had made themselves scarce.

She turned to face him. "If you're sure it will be of more benefit to him than school *and* that he'll really go to summer school, then I guess I can't object. But I don't like the sound of this arrangement of yours about the hand 'taking care of' the girls and me."

"Don't worry. Ben's been with our family for longer than I've been alive. He'll keep an eye on the ranch and your safety. Mrs. Robertson, our housekeeper, will be in every morning. She'll take the girls to school and pick them up, do any shopping, cook the evening meal and clean."

Megan felt completely redundant and couldn't help

her sarcastic retort. "And what am I supposed to do while Mrs. Robertson has all the fun? Play the lady of the manor?

Luke looked shocked for a moment, then threw back his head and laughed. He hugged her to him and murmured, "You know, I think we're gonna be all right."

Megan enjoyed being held in his arms.

"It'll help Cody and me bond, and I thought you could use the time to find out how to continue your studies. I'll support you fully, whatever you decide."

Once again, Megan felt the protective cloak of Luke surrounding her, shielding her from all the concerns she'd had to face alone just a few days ago. She placed a hand on his arm and said, "You make sure you bring my son back to me in one piece, okay?"

"No, I'll bring *our* son back in one piece. And furthermore—" he dropped a kiss on the end of her nose "—I plan to bring him back as a man."

CHAPTER NINE

LUKE AND CODY spent the evening packing for their trip.
Megan hadn't seen her son so animated in a very long
time, probably not since she'd taken him to Six Flags
Great Adventure in New Jersey years ago. They'd gone
by bus and stayed at a nearby B and B. The weekend
trip had cost her a week's pay and put her behind with
the rent, but had been worth every penny.

"You'll call to let me know you're there safely, won't
you?" she implored.

"Yes, Mom."

"And you'll call me every night, too?"

"Yes, Mom." Cody's voice held a touch of irritation
as he continued packing.

"And you'll call if you don't feel safe?"

"Mom!" Cody looked up and sighed. As if sensing
her fear, he came and placed his hands on her shoulders. The relief she felt at their warmth allowed her to
release her pent-up breath. "You gotta let go, okay? I'll
be fine. You know Luke won't let me out of his sight."

Megan was still trying to think of excuses to get
Cody to change his mind about going. "I know this is
a big adventure for you, honey. But I'm scared. We've
never been apart this long before."

Luke chose that moment to enter Cody's room and
ask, "All set, son?"

"I will be, once Mom leaves me alone to finish my packing." He gave her a pointed look.

Megan turned to make one last appeal to Luke, but he held up his hands. "Don't even think about trying to talk me out of this, Megan. Cody is coming with me. He *wants* to come with me. I could list about a hundred reasons this'll be good for him."

"Then I'll get a pen and paper and start *my* list of a hundred reasons it *won't* be," Megan said, about to leave the room, but Luke stopped her at the door. His grin made her anger rise. "This isn't funny," she protested. "I'm really upset about it."

Luke steered her out of the room and down the hallway. He opened a door at the end and gestured Megan through it.

As soon as she realized it was Luke's bedroom, she turned on her heel, intending to leave. Instead, she came up against his hard chest. He nudged the door closed with his foot and led her to the bed, where he sat her down.

Megan looked everywhere but at Luke. The room was furnished Western-style in masculine colors, lots of wood, leather, a hand-stitched quilt on the…bed. The enormous bed. The bed he'd no doubt shared with Tory.

She leaped off it and went to sit in the leather armchair by the window. Luke came over, knelt down in front of her and took her hands as she fidgeted with them in her lap.

"I wasn't laughing at *you*," he said. "I was smiling. In spite of your fussing over Cody, I know you're doing it because you love him. I only wish Tory had fussed over the girls even a fraction as much."

Megan's shoulders relaxed. "I'm worried," she admitted. "We've never been apart."

She swallowed painfully. "Except…except for the two times he ran away and spent the night out on the street. I guess that's really why I'm so scared."

"I know. I know." He paused. "Look at me," he said, obviously noticing she'd glanced out the window, afraid to hear what he had to say.

When she focused back on him, he told her, "I promise I won't let Cody come to any harm. I'll keep him with me at all times. I'll make sure he calls you every night, okay?"

Megan nodded slowly and he added, "But don't wait by the phone, because he won't have a moment to himself—other than maybe thirty minutes to call you at night."

"O…kay," she agreed.

"Honey." He leaned closer. "I'm not feeling any qualms about leaving you in charge of my three precious daughters. And the reason for that is, I trust you. You're a good mom."

Megan stared at him uncomprehending.

"That was a compliment."

Pleasure bloomed inside her. "I…I've never thought of myself that way. I…feel like I've been such a bad mother. A fail—"

He cut her off by touching his finger to her lips. "I've never believed that, and neither should you."

"My son nearly ended up in juvenile detention!" she said, leaping to her feet, needing to put space between them. Luke's bedroom felt far too intimate for her.

"But he didn't. And he never will. I know I said you were too indulgent, but I understand why. I—"

Luke was right. Angry with herself, but perversely needing to take it out on Luke, she said, "And don't you just love it that you rode in on your white charger and fixed everything?" she demanded. "Rescued the stupid heroine, too helpless to do anything for herself."

"Stop that!" He captured her flailing hands in his and held them firm. "I'm no fairy tale knight. And you're certainly not helpless! Where is this coming from?" he asked. "Why are you trying to make me feel like the bad guy here?"

Yes, why was she dumping on Luke? So she'd feel better about herself?

In her heart, she knew it was unfair to take it out on him, but he was such an easy target. "Because everything you do makes me feel like a failure," she confessed, hating the catch in her voice.

"Oh, honey!" He pulled her to him, wrapping his arms around her. "You're not a failure. I've never thought that, and I'm positive no one else has, either."

She shook her head, unable to find comfort in his embrace. "The look you gave me in Judge Benson's office said it all. You *loathed* me!"

LUKE DIDN'T REMEMBER thinking any such thing, but she seemed beyond convincing. All he could do was hold her and silently try to impart his strength, his respect for her and his gratitude for all she'd done for their son. The judge was right; beneath the bravado, Cody was a good kid. Lousy moms didn't raise good kids.

"I hate leaving while you're feeling like this," he murmured into her hair, enjoying the fresh-washed smell of it, the softness of her body against his. He drew back, knowing that in a moment he'd be reacting to her nearness. She was as skittish as a filly. Bringing her into his bedroom probably wasn't the best idea he'd had all day, but they needed privacy. Four active kids running around, a ranch to run and the fact that they weren't sharing a bed left them no time to talk in private. And now, while Megan was obviously feeling so insecure and he was heading to another state for most of the week, *definitely* wasn't the right time for taking their relationship to another level, emotionally more than physically. One that would convince her that he wanted this to be a real marriage.

And that reminded him…. "Are you okay about us getting married all over again on Saturday? I can put a stop to it, if you think it's too silly, or putting you under pressure."

She managed a smile. "Really? I can just see you telling Celeste it's off. Major tantrum, including some floor work, gallons of tears, screaming and slamming of doors."

Luke laughed and said, "I think you're right. Plus Daisy, in spite of pretending she's not interested in such girly events, would probably horsewhip me."

"Sasha would be overjoyed, however."

She would, but Luke had no intention of being pushed around by a twelve-year-old. "In the eyes of the law, we're already married, so that's irrelevant. But I'm not prepared to hurt Celeste or the rest of my family, especially my parents. They're cutting short their Alaskan trip to be here."

Megan chewed on her lip.

"What's wrong?"

"Let me get that pencil and paper. I need to list how

many things I'm unsure of. Number one being how your parents are going to feel about Cody."

Luke shrugged, unable to understand her concerns. "They'll love him on sight."

"Yeah…I'm sure they'll be impressed by their grandson's strange hairstyle, piercings and bad attitude." She shuddered. "I really want him to get rid of them and look…*normal* when he meets them."

"Let me see what I can do. What's your next problem?"

"You're trying to do the white knight thing again."

"Sorry, can't help it. I own horses. Gotta use them for something."

Megan smiled at that and Luke relaxed. He felt repeating the ceremony wasn't necessary. But what he felt didn't matter. It was too important to too many people not to go through with it. And although he'd exchanged the traditional wedding vows in front of friends and family before, it would be Megan's first time. Brides liked all that pomp and circumstance, didn't they? Which brought him to another thought, something he had to address before he left for Wyoming. "My family and friends know about the wedding and are coming, but in spite of what you told Jack, I really think we should let your folks know."

"They won't want to come."

"Of course they will. Granted, you've had your differences in the past, but this should be a time of healing for your family. How about if I call them up and invite them out here? Your friends, too—"

"No!" she said, slashing her hands through the air. "In fifteen years, my family hasn't once made contact with me. They knew where to find me. And none of my friends could afford to fly out here even if they wanted to come." She'd had friends once, girls who could afford to fly anywhere in the world first class, but they'd dropped off the radar soon after Cody's birth, if not before.

"Then I'll pay their fares."

She rounded on him, fire in her eyes. "Luke! Stop the white knight act. We're going through with this for the benefit of your family, nothing more! I don't *need* anyone else here."

Luke contemplated her words, particularly the ones about not needing anyone. He had the feeling that Megan had cut herself off from so many people, she truly believed she didn't need anyone in her life. Didn't need anyone's help. Or love.

"Okay, have it your way," he said. But he'd already decided to find Megan's parents and invite them to their only daughter's wedding. Because family was everything to him. *Family* was the way to happiness.

CHAPTER TEN

MEGAN CURSED HER ALARM when it woke her at five the next morning. She'd barely slept, worrying that Luke would go against her wishes and contact her parents to invite them to their wedding.

Although confident he'd never find them, she was still worried. Luke knew they'd lived in Boston while she was at school, but she doubted he'd have time to search the Boston phone book, calling every Montgomery there.

She'd heard from a distant cousin, who kept in sporadic contact, that her parents had retired to Florida several years ago. Her father had turned over his law firm to her brother. He'd also sold the family home for an undisclosed but reportedly exorbitant sum.

Megan hauled herself out of bed and into the shower, needing it to wake her so she could see Cody and Luke off. Feeling guilty for having overslept the past couple of mornings, she was going to make up for it by having breakfast waiting on the table by the time they came downstairs.

Twenty minutes later she headed for the kitchen, but Luke had beaten her to it. He was bent over, peering into the fridge, giving her a nice view of his butt. She was almost tempted to whistle. Maybe she would if they were on intimate enough terms to joke about anything sexual; instead, she cleared her throat.

He turned around and offered one of his rare smiles, warming her insides more than she felt comfortable with.

"Hi. You didn't need to get up," he said, closing the door with his foot as he took out milk and eggs.

"You were going to have breakfast and sneak off without saying goodbye?" she said.

"I was hoping to bring you breakfast in bed, wake you slowly and make love to you while you ate it."

Megan could feel the color leaving her face. She resisted the urge to clasp the back of a chair for support.

"Are you okay?" he asked, setting the eggs on the table and coming toward her. He pulled out a chair and pressed her shoulders until she sat.

"I…I'm fine, but please don't say things like that. One of the children could have walked in."

"The girls won't be up until at least six. And Cody was snoring his head off when I passed his room. He won't get up until I wake him."

"Then we're alone?" she asked, rising shakily and going to pour herself coffee, noticing that Luke had already brewed a pot and drunk half a cup himself.

"Probably not long enough for me to make love to you before breakfast," he teased, clearly enjoying himself.

"Luke."

"But one day soon, I hope we can."

She swallowed, facing him, the coffee cup held in front of her. "About…about our wedding night…"

He placed strips of bacon on the griddle. "Where

would you like to go?" he asked, obviously mistaking her intent.

She frowned. *Go?* "I thought we'd be staying here... at the ranch."

"We should have a honeymoon. I hoped we could escape for a few nights. My folks will be here, so they can take care of the kids. It'll give them a chance to get to know Cody. Without either of us around."

If Luke's parents weren't planning to continue their Alaskan holiday, that meant they'd be moving back into their quarters. And *that* meant the only place she could sleep was with Luke. For a fleeting moment, she thought about sharing Cody's room, but immediately discounted it. How would that look to everyone? Some marriage! Perhaps it would be better if they went away. Got separate rooms. Figured out how they were going to make this marriage work—or *appear* to work.

"All right."

"Do I detect a lack of enthusiasm for my plans?" He flipped the bacon and cracked eggs into another pan.

"I...don't know much about honeymoons. Can I leave the arrangements up to you?"

"My pleasure."

"But only for a couple of days," she hastened to say. "I don't want to be away from the children for too long."

He considered her carefully. "Okay. If that's all you want. I'll find something local. Sunny-side up or over easy?"

She handed him a plate and said, "Sunny-side up. Cody likes his scrambled."

"Done," he said, lifting two eggs onto her plate and passing her a toasted bagel. He placed the drained bacon onto her plate, too. "I already know how Cody likes his eggs since I made his breakfast the past two mornings."

"While I slept in," she said, feeling a lump in her throat.

He piled his own plate high with bacon, four eggs and two toasted bagels. Topped up both their coffees and joined her at the table. "You needed the sleep," he told her. "Don't feel bad about it."

Megan had read about people in emergency situations who found enormous physical strength or managed to carry on for hours rescuing people, and then once the emergency was over, they collapsed, as if the situation had completely drained their reserves. Although she couldn't compare her recent life with Cody to an emergency, her nerves had been on high alert for months. She'd barely slept, listening to see if Cody was sneaking out, getting into trouble. Worrying about him. And then, when Luke had taken over sharing the responsibility for Cody, it was as though her body had said, "Now you can rest," and she had.

They ate in silence, each thinking of the days ahead. A *thump* sounded from upstairs and Luke rolled his eyes. "Princess number two is awake. As you've probably noticed, Daisy never does anything quietly."

"I had noticed that," Megan said with a smile. "What would she like for breakfast?" she asked, standing and taking their plates to the sink.

"She'd like waffles, maple syrup and ice cream."

Megan looked at him, aghast. What a thing to feed a child for breakfast on a school morning! No wonder Daisy was so loud and hyperactive.

Luke got up and laid one hand on her shoulder. "Relax," he said. "She might *want* that for breakfast, but what she'll get is fruit juice, scrambled eggs and granola or a bagel."

Megan got eggs from the fridge and turned to Luke. "I take it these were laid by your own hens?"

"Yup."

"Um, when am I supposed to collect them? I've never been around chickens. Their beady eyes scare me. Will they attack me if I try to take their eggs?"

Luke roared with laughter, then sobered when he could see she was genuinely afraid. "Don't worry about them. That's one of Celeste's duties in the morning, but if you want, she'll teach you." He put out bowls for the granola, plus milk and honey, and started toasting more bagels.

Megan enjoyed watching him and wondered just how many meals Luke had prepared for his daughters over the years. From now on, she'd take over that duty, leaving him with one less burden on his busy mornings. She scrambled the eggs and added grated cheese—Cody's favorite way of having them. Plus, it sneaked in some extra protein. She also sliced tomatoes in half and set them on the griddle.

"I'll go and wake the others," Luke said, leaving her alone in the kitchen.

Megan poured the scrambled egg mixture into a pan and opened the back door to let in the freshness of the early morning. It was a little chilly, but the dryness of the mountain air made it seem bracing rather than cold. She gazed out at the dawn breaking over the distant mountains, then remembered the eggs and raced back to the stove to stir them before they burned.

"Here you go, pumpkin," she heard Luke say from behind her.

He was walking into the kitchen, a sleepy-looking Celeste on his hip, his arms protectively around her. Her heart seemed to expand at the sight and in that moment she knew with absolute certainty that her son would be safe with Luke. Sadness and guilt gnawed at her as she realized Luke had never been able to experience their son at that same age.

Luke might have claimed she was a good mother— something she still wasn't convinced of—but she was certain that he was a good father. A great father. He'd protect his children with his life. He'd protect her son from harm. Correction, *their* son.

He was about to place Celeste gently in her chair, but then she saw Megan and cried, "Mommy!" She thrust out her arms toward Megan, who took her from Luke with pleasure. Celeste snuggled her face against Megan's throat and sighed with a pleasure that sounded as if that was where she wanted to be more than anywhere in the world.

The rest of the children soon entered the kitchen. Daisy and Cody returned her greetings, but Sasha chose to ignore her and instead yanked out her chair, sat down and pulled the granola box toward her.

Megan was tempted to repeat her greeting, but decided against it. Perhaps Sasha wasn't a morning person. She could relate to that, since she used to love sleeping in. But that was a luxury she'd given up a long time ago.

Luke was about to open his mouth but Megan stopped him, saying, "I'm sorry, I cooked the eggs too soon. I'll make another batch." She'd forgotten about the granola, since Cody wasn't partial to it.

"I'll eat 'em," Cody said, reaching for the pan and dumping the entire contents onto his plate.

"Yuck! What's that stuff in the eggs?" Sasha demanded.

"It's called cheese, Sash," Luke explained patiently, rolling his eyes at Megan.

Since Celeste didn't want to let go of her, Luke took over making the new batch of scrambled eggs while the girls ate their granola.

"Well, I don't like it," Sasha sulked. "Don't put any in mine."

"Too late," Luke said, then dumped a handful of cheese into the mixture a good five seconds after Sasha had voiced her protest.

Cody wasted no time devouring his eggs, tomatoes and bagels, and was looking around for more to eat. Luke poured him some extra juice and asked if he'd like coffee. Cody seemed surprised, as if no one had ever asked him that. Which they hadn't. Megan didn't think it was a suitable drink for a fourteen-year-old.

"Okay?" Luke asked, holding the coffee carafe poised over a mug.

Megan appreciated his asking. "Okay, but make it weak," she said.

"Cool!" Cody said, and watched his father pour the coffee, then add some hot water. He sipped it and his nose wrinkled.

"Sugar might help," Luke suggested, pushing the bowl toward him.

Cody dumped in two spoonfuls, stirred and drank. A look of bliss crossed his face. "So *this* is what everyone raves about."

LUKE SMILED TO HIMSELF and decided that if his son hadn't tried something as relatively harmless as coffee, he probably hadn't been experimenting with street drugs, either, in spite of his tough-guy image. The knowledge filled him with hope that their trip wouldn't consist of him trying to keep Cody out of every back alley they passed in Cheyenne, searching for drugs. He hadn't seen a cigarette between his lips even once, although many of the hands smoked around the ranch during their breaks.

He had no doubt that Cody had probably tried cigarettes in his recent past, but at least he wasn't addicted to them.

Luke served the scrambled eggs to Daisy and Sash, completely ignoring his older daughter's protests. Daisy pronounced them delicious, finished hers and reached for Sash's plate. Sash smacked her hand, then picked up her fork and dug in.

Luke couldn't hide his smile as he looked across the table at Megan. They were going to make it as a family; he was more determined about that than anything else in his life.

He drank his coffee and glanced around the table, taking in the scene, storing it for later, when he was feeling lonely during his trip. Except this time he'd have one of his kids along for company. He'd always imagined Daisy would be the first of his children to accompany him to the Cattlemen's Convention. He wondered how she was feeling about that, not being first.

He watched her, eyeing Sash's eggs as she forked them into her mouth. Nothing seemed to faze his second—make that *third*—child. Strange how he'd have to get used to the new family dynamic. The birth order. He wondered how he would've felt if an older child had suddenly turned up in the midst of his own family. How would *he* have felt being relegated to second child when he'd been so used to being the oldest? He decided to allocate some special time to spend with Sash when he and Megan got back from their honeymoon. Perhaps Sash was jealous and that was part of the reason she was being so disagreeable. Maybe with Cody gone, she'd return to her usual sweet-natured self.

Then he saw Sash glaring at Megan and thought perhaps not.

Celeste, of course, had had no problem accepting not only a new mother, but also an older brother. In fact, his youngest child had been the glue that had held the family together over the past few stormy days. She loved and accepted Megan as her mother and, judging by the way Megan had slipped so easily into mothering Celeste, the feeling was mutual.

Cody had the look of the O'Malley men, but not quite the temperament. All the O'Malley brothers— apart from Will—had been conformists. Working at respected professions or trades, never giving their parents a moment's worry.

Although their mom maintained that Will was responsible for every gray hair on her head—of which there were few, since she was a blonde. It was their father who'd gone steel gray. Proof of Will's antics and itinerant lifestyle as a ski movie actor before he'd settled down to respectability with the town judge.

Luke wasn't sure Cody hadn't already added a few more gray hairs to his own head. These past few days he'd noticed that his temples seemed grayer. But that might also be a result of looking in the mirror more often—to make sure he appeared presentable enough for Megan.

The girls finished their breakfast and, amid noisy chatter and clattering dishes, cleared the table and started loading the dishwasher. "Leave that for me," Megan told them as she got up to help, Celeste still clinging to her neck.

Luke took a moment to drink in the sight of them together, then rose to take Celeste from her arms and put her in a chair at the table. His daughter whined but complied. He prepared her granola and sat with her while she ate. Slowly. He avoided glancing at his watch, knowing it upset Celeste when he counted down the minutes till he had to leave. But he and Cody needed to get on the road, and soon.

"Are you going to help Megan around the house this week, sweetie?" he asked, then cursed himself because Celeste dropped her spoon and began to answer him in long and breathless detail.

"We've got a few things planned," Megan said, as if she knew how to keep Celeste eating. "But you'll need to finish breakfast, Celeste, before we can start."

Luke glanced up at Megan, nodded and mouthed "thanks," then returned to watching Celeste eat. He kept up a one-sided monologue, careful not to ask any questions until she'd finished.

Luke was already missing his daughters. But if he was honest with himself, he was missing his wife, too.

He needed to get moving. Cody had come downstairs with his bag and loaded it into the truck. He was now out in the yard, reversing the Ford 350 up to the goose-neck trailer they'd be using to bring home a prize bull he'd arranged to buy from a friend in Wyoming. Orion, one of his old bulls, wasn't as virile as he used to be and needed to be replaced. Instead of using artificial insemination like many other ranchers, Luke preferred to breed the old-fashioned way.

He smiled at that, thinking about his upcoming honeymoon. He intended to make love to his wife—the old-fashioned way. Only this time he'd make sure he took plenty of condoms.

"What are you grinning about?" Megan asked, waking him from his musings.

"Trust me, wife," he said gruffly. "You don't want to know." He rose from his seat. "Time for us to hit the road. Will you see us off?"

"OF COURSE," MEGAN SAID, wiping her hands on a cloth and following him out the door, wondering exactly what Luke was smiling about and feeling a strangely uplifting sense of belonging when he'd called her *wife*. Her feminist sensibilities should have had her protesting his proprietorial remark, but instead, all she felt was pleasure. A sense of belonging in the nicest possible way.

The girls were outside watching Cody reverse the truck up to the trailer. Daisy yelled one set of instructions, while Sasha yelled the opposite. Cody was obviously learning how to handle his sisters, because he closed the window to block out their voices and expertly used the rear-vision mirrors to complete his mission.

Pleased that her son was already so accomplished at what she knew to be a difficult task, Megan turned to Luke with a smile and found him standing right behind her, his hands raised slightly as if he was about to put them around her. He lowered them and stepped back. "I...I'm amazed at how quickly he's picked up driving," she remarked.

"He's a natural. I'm sure he'll get his license the first time he tries."

"You won't let him drive to Wyoming on the highway, will you?"

It was back again, that fear she couldn't completely suppress. The fear that something bad might happen to Cody because she wasn't there to watch over him. "I'm sorry, that was a stupid question and totally uncalled for."

"Apology accepted. And for what it's worth, I'll only be allowing him to drive on private property while we're away. I've promised him that once he turns fifteen he can do driver's ed at school."

Startled, Megan said, "I'll bet that won him over. They didn't offer it at his school."

He touched the end of her nose. "Add that to your list of good reasons for moving to Colorado."

"I don't have a list for that," she said.

"Make one," Luke murmured, then kissed her.

Megan had expected a farewell peck on the cheek, but Luke covered her lips and moved his mouth over hers as he slid his arms around her. She tentatively lifted her hands to his hips, hoping the girls wouldn't choose this moment to look back at the house and see them making out. For making out they were. Luke was seeking entry to her mouth, his hands squeezing her back and roving lower. She needed to put a stop to it. But just a little longer wouldn't hurt....

The blast from the truck's horn had them jumping apart like teens caught in the act. Which was exactly what Megan felt like when she looked around to find four pairs of curious eyes observing them. Her heart still racing from Luke's kiss and the fright of the blast from the horn, she said, "I don't think we should subject the children to such, uh, public displays in future, since it seems to embarrass them so much."

"I think you're the only one who's embarrassed," he said. "They're just razzing us."

"Still…"

Luke held up his hands in a gesture of surrender. "All right, if it makes you feel uncomfortable, I won't do it," he said, and strode over to his vehicle.

Feeling foolish for making such a fuss, Megan barely had time to race down the steps to kiss her son goodbye as he changed seats with Luke. Moments later, the big truck roared out of the yard, leaving dust and a suddenly bereft Megan in its wake.

CHAPTER ELEVEN

CODY DECIDED IT wasn't so bad having a father. He still didn't feel comfortable calling him "Dad," but Luke seemed cool with it. In fact, Luke seemed cool with a lot of things. And pretty uptight about others. Like his cell phone.

He'd been mad as hell his first morning in Colorado when Luke had snatched it out of his hand while he was texting Goose, one of the guys from the 'hood. Luke had confiscated it, saying he didn't want him associating with anyone from his old life. Well, how dumb was that? These were his *friends*. He didn't have anyone near his own age to talk to in Colorado—except his sisters.

That had been a big adjustment. He'd never had siblings before, never had to share his mom with anyone. He didn't realize how much he depended on her until he'd had to wait in line for her attention.

He didn't want to whine about it, though. He wasn't a baby. Not like Celeste, who in Cody's opinion demanded too much of his mom's time.

His dad had given him back his phone just before they set off on their trip to Wyoming, saying, "I've replaced your SIM card *and* got you a new number."

Cody had been furious. How was he supposed to connect with the guys if he didn't have their numbers? And they couldn't contact him on his old number, since he had a completely new one. He'd clicked through his contacts list. It was full of O'Malley relatives' names. "In case you need to talk to anyone or you're stuck somewhere," Luke had explained with his usual abruptness.

There was no point in arguing about the fact that his father had taken away his SIM card. Cody knew he'd never get it back. He'd learned his father was really stubborn like that.

His dad had also given him a couple of driving lessons over the weekend. That had been the coolest part of moving to Colorado. He'd never imagined he'd learn how to drive. Some of the guys back in the 'hood had taught themselves to drive by stealing cars. Mostly they'd ended up smashing them—and themselves. And sometimes other guys in the car with them.

The one time Cody had accepted a ride, it had scared him so much, he'd made himself scarce whenever a heist was going down.

Anyhow, the truck his dad was teaching him on was far more powerful than any of the cars the guys had stolen in the 'hood.

Sure, his dad and he had words. But Luke never raised his voice at him. Not like the "fathers" back in the 'hood. They not only yelled at their kids, they often hit them, too.

Cody had been afraid that when he'd gotten mad at Luke over confiscating his cell phone, his dad might hit him. But he hadn't. Cody had really pushed him on that one. Called him names. The foulest names he could think of.

Luke hadn't shown any reaction. He'd just said, "That's at least a dozen contributions to the penalty box. I'll cut you some slack and call it an even ten. But next time, you'll pay the full price."

Since he'd exhausted his first week's allowance with that one infraction, Cody had been careful to mind his mouth after that.

And because he didn't have anyone he could call on his cell, Cody had rung his mom and his uncle Matt and even Daisy. Well, she'd called him. She'd wanted to know all about what he was doing, who he'd met that day, what he'd liked about the convention.

He didn't want to admit it but he really liked Daisy. She was gutsy. He thought she might be mad at him for being taken to the convention instead of her. But she was really excited for him. Cody had never had other kids get excited for him about anything.

And now they were in this fancy hotel. He'd never stayed in a hotel before. On the New Jersey trip, he and his mom had stayed in a B and B run by some old people and he'd had to keep quiet. He'd expected that he and Luke would be sharing a room. That would've been weird, though, sharing a room with someone he hardly knew. He was relieved when they'd walked up to the check-in desk and Luke had asked if they could have adjoining rooms. Luke had shown him how to unlock the doors between them. For a while there, Cody had thought Luke would insist on leaving the door between their rooms open, but he hadn't. His room was really cool. He had a king-size bed all to himself and the bathroom had free shampoo and stuff. The towels were super-soft, too. He also had a big-screen TV all to himself; he could watch pretty much whatever he wanted. Only problem was, the first night he was so tired after the long drive, he'd fallen asleep in front of an episode of *Dog the Bounty Hunter*. His mom had never let him watch it at home.

The next night they'd had dinner with a bunch of his dad's colleagues, other ranchers. He'd never eaten such amazing food. And so much of it. And to have waiters running around at his beck and call was awesome. He'd downed so much food and so many root-beer floats that he'd fallen asleep in front of the TV again.

By day three of the convention, he'd met just about everyone there was to know in the cattle industry in the West and learned a lot. He was amazed by how much his dad knew and kinda wondered why he even needed to come to the convention, but he guessed that was what they called networking.

His dad had bought a bull to replace Orion, who was getting on in years and not impregnating as many cows as he should've been. His dad preferred what he called natural insemination rather than artificial insemination. He'd felt a bit embarrassed when Luke was talking about cows having sex, but he'd been so matter-of-fact about it that Cody's embarrassment had evaporated. He'd also learned a lot about horse-breeding. Some of the ranchers had told him his dad was known for his horses and his training. They even said he'd been on the cover of a national magazine. Cody would ask him about it when he got the chance.

When they'd first left New York, Cody hadn't wanted to believe anything good about his dad. He preferred his uncle Matt. Matt was cool. He'd been stunned to learn his uncle was the county sheriff. But when Matt had taken him on a tour of his offices and the jail as a reward for cleaning up the dishes the other night, he'd decided he liked having a sheriff in the family. Matt had even let him talk to some of the prisoners. Trusties, Uncle Matt had called them. People doing weekend detention or short-terms. The really bad guys were in a sealed-off section of the jail. He got to go into the control center where he could see everyone, but they couldn't see him. Some of the guys in there looked really tough. They looked like older versions of some of the guys he used to hang out with in his old neighborhood. That realization had brought Cody up short. No wonder his dad had been in a hurry to get him out of New York.

THE WEEK FLEW BY for Megan. Looking after three active girls was more of a handful than she'd expected, but she loved every minute of it. Even Sasha seemed to have thawed a little, particularly when she let her sleep over at Nick's house for a couple of nights. She later learned that Luke forbade sleepovers on school nights, but Megan figured that if it helped to ease the tension in the house, then she didn't see any harm.

Becky and Beth had taken over planning the wedding, saying they wanted it to be a surprise for Megan. They'd issued invitations, arranged the catering, flowers and all the minute details involved with a wedding, albeit one that was less than a week in the planning.

Their organizational skills and generosity had allowed Megan the time to look into continuing her accounting course. She was now officially enrolled in a local college and was looking forward to getting back to her studies and completing her degree.

Her paychecks from her previous employers had arrived on Wednesday, surprising Megan with their promptness—and the fact that they'd been sent at all.

She smiled at the memory of Luke dealing with Jerry and Pat.

She'd taken care of her final rent and utility bills for her New York apartment. Their belongings had arrived by truck just yesterday. Now, with all the ties to her old life severed, Megan was looking forward to making a new life for Cody and herself in Colorado.

Cody called every evening to tell her about his day. He sounded as if he was having fun, meeting new people, making friends, feeling a part of the ranching community. It thrilled her to hear the enthusiasm in his voice. Her boy was back and she knew who she had to thank for it.

She'd been given driving lessons by Mrs. Robertson and Beth, been quizzed by Will on the rules of the road when he'd come to take her and the girls to his and Becky's place for dinner on two evenings.

Now, as she prepared dinner on Friday evening, waiting for Luke and Cody to get home—thankfully one day earlier than expected—Megan could see the tent erected on the lawns out back, the truck unloading chairs and tables for guests. In twenty-four hours she'd be married. Or rather, married again. Maybe the traditional ceremony would make her feel more married, more a part of Luke's life and family.

Luke's parents had arrived that morning from their cruise. Sarah and Mac O'Malley seemed excited to meet her and declared they couldn't wait to meet their grandson. Fortunately, they'd be staying with Will and Becky, meaning Megan didn't have to move out of their quarters and into Luke's bedroom. Not yet, anyway.

There was, of course, the tiny apartment over the horse barn, but it wasn't finished yet. Jack had told her he planned on finishing it, just as soon as Matt and Beth's new home was ready for them.

She liked the way the family meshed together, pulled together, helped one another out. They were good for Cody, exactly what her son needed.

The only sour note was that she and Luke had ended up arguing on the phone two nights earlier.

Before he'd left, Luke had told her to make herself at home, familiarize herself with the organization of the ranch. On Tuesday evening, she'd wandered into his study after returning from dinner at Becky and Will's, and seen the ranch books sitting on Luke's enormous desk.

Curious to learn more about the running of the ranch, she'd sat in his worn leather office chair, propped her feet on the desk and started going through the books, hoping to be able to help Luke with the accounting. She remembered Gil McIntyre's reaction when Luke told him she was studying accounting. His sudden change of demeanor, slight though it was, bothered her even now.

It didn't take Megan long to realize something was amiss. According to the checkbook and the printout of his bank records, Luke had made out large checks to a particular vendor, yet a quick search of the internet didn't bring up any reference to this vendor—All Western States Supply, Inc.

What sort of company could trade so heavily in ranch supplies, but not have a presence or a reference to it anywhere on the internet? It was too late to call Luke to see if he knew the vendor. One pervading fear filled her mind as she tried to sleep: How deeply was Luke involved in what appeared to be a dummy company?

Not until the following afternoon did Megan have

a chance to get back to the ranch books and do some cross-checking. She dreaded finding out that Luke was a cheat, but from everything she knew of him, it just didn't sit right.

Heart racing, she searched back through his bank records, until finally, eighteen months earlier, they reconciled perfectly. What had happened a year and a half ago?

And then she found it. The hair stood up on the back of her neck. Luke had changed accountants, from a firm that had handled the ranch's business for many years, to Gil McIntyre.

But why change to Gil? Simply because he was a friend? Because he'd found the anomaly that resulted in a tax refund? For all Megan knew, Gil could have been responsible for the anomaly in the first place.

Suspecting that Gil, based on his reaction to Luke's news that she was studying to be an accountant, was somehow involved in the dummy company, Megan called the companies that had previoulsy supplied the ranch. After asking their current prices on the goods he'd ordered, she did some quick calculations on the difference between their quoted prices and what Luke was paying All Western States Supply, Inc. He was paying at least ten percent over listed prices. But why? Just because All Western bundled the invoices into one, therefore saving a little time with checkwriting?

She then called the companies back and asked if they'd heard of or provided equipment and supplies to All Western. Many had, and they weren't happy about it. They'd received payments months after they'd sent out their goods. She asked if any supplied to Two Elk Ranch in Peaks County. They did, and none of them could understand why Luke and many of the other ranchers in the area had changed to this new billing system with All Western.

After thanking them and hanging up, Megan sat back and let out her breath. According to the checkbook, Luke had paid All Western immediately upon receipt of the goods, not months later.

If, as she suspected, Gil was skimming money off the top for supplying to the ranches now in his dummy company's network, it could amount to hundreds of thousands—possibly millions—of dollars.

Everything pointed to the fact that Luke was being embezzled by his so-called friend and he seemed to have no idea.

She checked and rechecked her figures and then, hands shaking, she'd called Luke.

After quickly explaining what she'd discovered, she waited for Luke's reaction. It was far from what she'd expected.

After a long moment, he said one word. "Megan."

In the way he said her name, she could hear the frustration and something that sounded like anger in his voice. "This is none of your business!"

Taken aback, Megan reminded him, "You told me to familiarize myself with the ranch organization. I assumed, perhaps foolishly, that you were referring to the *financial* organization."

When he didn't respond, Megan said, "Then you're aware of what's going on?" Surely Luke wasn't party to this fraud! Surely he wasn't cheating his parents and brothers out of their share of the ranch profits?

"It doesn't matter what I'm aware of. I didn't give

you permission to go snooping around and accusing an old friend of cheating me."

Megan could feel her own anger rising. "You made it my business!" she said. Feeling she needed to remind him, she repeated, "You told me to make myself at home, familiarize myself with how the business is run."

"You have no qualifications."

"Luke, I'm studying to be an accountant," she pointed out unnecessarily, needing to hammer the fact home.

"Like I said, you have no qualifications."

"I have more than you! And even a halfwit could tell that something fishy's going on here," she countered, furious at his patronizing remarks.

"Are you implying that I'm cheating on my taxes?"

Megan's pause before answering had him snapping at her. "Thanks! Nice to know my *wife* doesn't trust me."

"Oh, for heaven's sake, Luke, what was I supposed to think when I looked at the books?"

"I trust Gil McIntyre implicitly. He found an error our previous CPA made in filing the ranch's tax returns with the IRS. He's not only a friend, he was working at the firm at the time and offered to file an amended return for the previous year on our behalf, which resulted in a huge refund. Gil went into business for himself soon after and I followed him there."

Just as Megan suspected. How convenient for Gil to start up his own firm soon after finding the anomaly that had resulted in the tax refund. She was already wondering how many other clients of the original firm had also been contacted by Gil about a similar anomaly in their taxes and how many had followed him to his new business.

As she was about to suggest this to Luke, he said, "I

trust Gil. Do you understand that? This has nothing to do with you. So butt out!"

Megan felt as though she'd been slapped in the face, but she worked at keeping her voice calm. "Don't speak to me like that, Luke. Gil McIntyre is cheating you! But if you're okay with that, then fine."

Before he could say anything more, before she burst into tears at the harshness of Luke's tone, she hung up.

He called back immediately but she let it go to voice mail. Right now, she needed a long, hot soak in the tub. She was doing her driver's test the next morning and needed to put Luke out of her mind.

SHE'D SAILED THROUGH the test and that evening had told Cody the details. She took her test on Thursday at the Department of Motor Vehicles in Silver Springs. She'd been nervous but had passed without any trouble. Her son sounded so proud of her that her spirits lifted as he told her all about a bull they'd purchased to replace Orion.

"And Luke said to tell you we'll be home tomorrow night instead of Saturday."

As they said their goodbyes, Megan thought, *Luke couldn't find the time to tell me himself?*

She played back Luke's message from the night before, but all he'd said was he didn't appreciate her hanging up on him and that they'd talk about it when he got home.

Didn't appreciate? Well, she didn't appreciate him being so nasty when all she was doing was trying to help. Feeling perverse, she decided to work on the ranch books some more, make notes about the anomalies and get them in proper order. Maybe the physical proof of the figures being embezzled from the ranch accounts would prove to Luke what was going on. She was almost tempted to pay a visit to Gil McIntyre and ask him what he was up to, but decided against it. She'd noticed the accountant's name and his wife's on the wedding invitation list. The reception wasn't the time or place to confront him, either. Better for her to gather evidence of the dummy company's trading, lay everything out for Luke and for him to take whatever action he felt necessary.

THE SOUND OF the truck's horn had Megan racing to the front door and onto the veranda. She waited there, taking in the scene as they drove up, her son leaping from the truck and striding toward her. "Mom!" he cried, and caught her in a huge bear hug. "I've missed you," he said, and released her.

"I've missed you, too, honey," she said, stroking his hair. His newly shorn hair. And, to her relief, the piercings were gone. All that remained was a neat hole in his lip that she hoped would soon heal over. "I swear you've grown a foot in the past week," she said, stepping back but still holding his hands, unwilling to let go of him just yet.

What a difference a week had made.

He seemed to have filled out. As if he'd eaten well and gotten some exercise. And he was tanned. The resemblance between him and his father was uncanny.

"It's only been five days, Mom. I can't have grown during that time," he protested. He hugged her again and said, "I've gotta help Dad with getting the new bull settled. You should see him, Mom. He's magnificent. The ladies will be very happy to make his acquaintance, I'm sure!"

"Naughty boy!" she admonished, gently slapping his shoulder and watching him return to the truck. *Dad.* He'd called his father "Dad."

She watched Luke, surrounded by his daughters, all of them vying for his attention. He hugged each one close, kissed them. They obviously objected to his five-o'clock shadow as each one wiped her cheek with a disgusted expression.

They eventually dragged themselves away to welcome Cody home, leaving Luke alone by the truck.

Megan willed him to look at her. And he did. His gaze sent desire and want and need humming through her veins. Silently she begged him to open his arms, invite her in, tell her it was okay, that their fight didn't mean anything. But he didn't. Instead, he stood there staring at her, as if waiting for her to make the first move. Suddenly Megan didn't feel so sure of herself. What if she ran down the veranda and into his arms but he turned away? She'd feel like a fool. Totally rejected.

She tried to make her feet move, but they wouldn't. She willed Luke to come to her instead, take her in his arms and kiss her like he never wanted to stop. Say that everything was okay. Apologize for being a jerk. But he stayed where he was.

It was as though a wide, wild river divided them and they were each unable to leap into the treacherous waters....

Finally, Luke turned away and went to help Cody unload the bull. Megan pressed her lips together to prevent them from trembling as she returned to the kitchen. But the sight of the huge tent the caterers had set up made her stomach roil. What was she thinking? Luke didn't love her, didn't want her. He'd admitted he was only going through with this farce of a wedding ceremony for his family.

That implied he sure didn't want it. She fought the tears that threatened at the realization that she was so redundant around here. Luke had saved their son from street gangs and juvenile detention. Luke had a family who loved him, cared about him. She had no one but Cody and, judging by the way he was calling his father "Dad," she probably didn't really have him anymore, either. Her son's world had expanded, which she knew was a good thing, but it seemed to leave her without a role.

She made an effort to suppress her feelings of worthlessness, of being unwanted, but they overwhelmed her, welled up and threatened to suffocate her. She fled to her room, needing a sanctuary, somewhere she could cry long and loud, to rail against the injustice. She hated giving in to self-pity, but she felt so afraid. Afraid she was unworthy of being loved....

BY THE TIME she made it to her room, sanity had prevailed. The O'Malleys—the whole family, including Luke's parents—were coming for dinner in less than half an hour.

She couldn't greet her future in-laws looking as if she'd gone ten rounds in a boxing ring. So she splashed her face with cold water and went into the kitchen to make sure the Beef Stroganoff Becky had designated as Megan's contribution to the meal wasn't burning. Becky would be bringing salads and potatoes au gratin, Beth the dessert, Jack chocolates and the mysterious Adam had elected to bring appetizers. Becky had intimated to Megan that she didn't trust him to bring anything more substantial than a bowl of olives from the super-market deli, so she was fixing some crackers and dips.

Megan was looking forward to meeting Luke's youngest brother. All she knew of him was that he was a firefighter and lived in Boulder. He seemed to be a bit of a recluse.

"Hey, there!"

Megan spun around, startled out of her musings by Becky's enthusiastic greeting. Becky had her hands full, so she leaned toward Megan over the potato dish and kissed her cheek.

"That smells divine," Megan said, taking the dish from her and placing it beside the oven.

"One of Will's favorites. Mind you, he declares anything I make his favorite, so you can't count on him to be discerning."

Will arrived loaded down with a basket containing salads on one arm and his baby daughter, Lily, in the other.

She held out her hands to Megan, who gladly took her from Will. She and Lily had become friends over the past week, having spent several days together while Becky planned the wedding or they shopped together.

Soon the kitchen was full of O'Malleys and the noise level was rising in proportion to the number of people showing up, laden with food.

Thankfully, Sarah took over, directing her sons and grandchildren to set the outdoor tables and take the food outside.

Last to arrive was Adam. He was as dark-featured and well-muscled as Luke, perhaps a little shorter. He shook Megan's hand, his grip firm.

"We meet at last," were the first words to pop out of Megan's mouth.

Adam nodded but she sensed he was sizing her up. Searching for any flaws in her character. It was unsettling, since he hadn't actually returned her greeting.

"Neanderthal!" Will said, lightly clipping his brother on the back of the head. "Say hello to your new sister-in-law."

"Hello," he said obediently, and then he smiled and it lit up the room. "I'm pleased to meet you at last, too, Megan."

From then on, the evening went well. So well that Megan almost forgot how upset she still was with Luke. But she was soon reminded of it once everyone had left for home and the children had been put to bed.

She was coming downstairs from tucking Celeste in when Luke appeared out of the shadows, grabbed her hand and led her into the study.

He closed the door, dropped her hand and crossed his arms, demanding, "Just what are you accusing Gil of doing?"

So Megan repeated what she knew, showed him the anomalies she'd found, but felt as if she was talking to a brick wall. Luke's loyalties lay with Gil, because of their shared past and because of some stupid tax refund! For all they knew, Gil might have purposely made the mistake under someone else's name, then "discovered" it and wormed his way into Luke's confidence by refiling the return and gaining him the refund.

If she had time, she could probably trace it all the way back to when Gil worked for the other firm. See who'd really filled out the forms incorrectly in the first place. But she didn't have time; all she had was one angry husband who trusted some shyster more than he trusted her.

They had a terrible argument and, in the end, Megan

had said, "Check the books again, Luke. Check the notes I've made. I'm not wrong!" Then she yanked open the door, walked outside and pulled it shut with more force than necessary.

LUKE SMASHED HIS PILLOW, trying to get it into a more comfortable shape. But he knew it wasn't the pillow causing his restlessness. He'd been unfair to Megan. Downright patronizing, in fact. What if she was right about Gil? What if he had committed fraud?

Luke had been too stubborn to believe her and too dog-tired to check the books or read Megan's copious notes before turning in. He'd needed to get some sleep before their wedding.

Now he regretted it because the same thing kept playing in his mind—the fact that he'd handed over much of the bookkeeping to Gil once he'd appointed him as the ranch accountant. Luke had tried to keep his own accounts but it had never been one of his strong points and when Gil had found a company that would provide many of his supplies, Luke had been happy to write them checks, based on the monthly invoices that came via Gil.

Maybe he should've taken a closer look at that company a long time ago.

He kicked back the covers, determined to go and apologize to Megan—whether she was right or wrong. Then the time on the bedside clock caught his eye. Two-fifteen. Megan probably wouldn't appreciate having her sleep interrupted, no matter how contrite he was. It would have to wait until morning.

MEGAN'S TEARS WERE finally spent sometime after midnight. Coming to the ranch had caused so many of the old hurts of her childhood to resurface. She'd thought by cutting off all contact with her family that she could put those childhood demons to rest. And she had. For a long while.

But now those feelings of not being good enough, not being wanted, were back.

At one point during their discussion, Luke had gone ballistic. He'd repeated that he trusted Gil. Told her again that she wasn't qualified. She felt so completely alone. Where had the attentive husband of last weekend gone? The gentle lover who'd seduced her in a meadow on a carpet of wildflowers?

The past week she'd been on an emotional roller coaster and it didn't look as if the ride was going to end anytime soon.

She felt like death warmed over, emotionally and physically exhausted. She was going to look like hell in the morning. Not that it mattered. She wouldn't be walking up the aisle at precisely 11:00 a.m.

Megan wasn't really certain where she might be, but she wouldn't be saying her "I do's" to Luke. Not after the way he'd treated her. She'd been more contented before he came back into her life and tried to take it over, turned it upside down, causing bad memories to resurface....

LUKE ROSE EARLY and went to check on his horses. He was half hoping to find Megan in the kitchen, having an early-morning cup of coffee, but the house was silent. He strode out into the yard and headed for the barn. It was a beautiful day, not a cloud in the sky. A good day to get married.

He smiled to himself. He was looking forward to marrying Megan in front of his family and friends.

Their first ceremony had been too abrupt, forced on them by Cody. He probably should've put his foot down then and there, but he didn't know Cody well enough. All he saw was a defiant punk of a kid who swore he'd rather go to juvenile detention than Colorado if Luke didn't marry his mother on the spot.

They'd both been thoroughly manipulated by Cody, but Luke had to admit he was grateful for Cody's stand. Who knew where they might be today if they weren't married?

The only problem was, he and Megan hadn't been living like husband and wife. Would that change tonight? On their honeymoon?

He'd changed his mind about going somewhere local and had instead chosen somewhere special for them to spend the night on their way to the airport in Denver and their final destination in the Florida Keys. There was a spa hotel in Boulder that offered pampering for its guests. He'd booked a couple's massage for when they arrived later this afternoon, hoping that would help Megan relax, followed by a romantic dinner in their suite.

He'd pretty much scheduled everything—except his apology.

MEGAN SLEPT UNTIL after eight and was awakened by Sasha bringing her coffee and a bagel. Soon, her room was full of children, with Daisy lounging on the end of the bed, Celeste under the covers with her and Cody sprawled in the bedroom chair.

It was comforting being surrounded by her children. Only Luke was missing from the picture. Maybe he'd be missing forever if they couldn't resolve their differences before the wedding. Her heart had thawed a little toward him during the night. He was used to being in control of his ranch, but there was one aspect he'd handed over to someone else; maybe he'd realized by now that he'd made a mistake. It would be hard for him to admit he'd been embezzled and had failed to notice it until Megan's discovery. Luke was a proud man. Perhaps she hadn't approached him in the right way....

"Mommy?"

Celeste's questioning voice woke Megan from her musings. "What's up, pumpkin?"

"Are you mad at me?"

Megan smiled and hugged Celeste. "How could anyone be angry with a gorgeous little dumpling like you?" She kissed the top of Celeste's fair head.

"You look tired," Sasha said in her usual direct manner.

"I didn't sleep very well," Megan admitted, determined not to rise to Sasha's bait.

"Your eyes are all puffy," Daisy told her. "Have you been crying? My eyes always get puffy when I cry."

Daisy's admission surprised Megan. She, of all the girls, always seemed so composed, not prone to emotional outbursts. Maybe she didn't know Daisy as well as she thought she did. Maybe she should plan a mother-daughter day just for her and Daisy.

She threw back the covers and climbed out of bed. "I need to take a shower and you girls need to get ready for the hairstylist Aunt Becky booked to come and do your hair."

That was all the motivation Celeste needed. She bounded off the bed and dashed out the door. There was nothing that little girl liked more than having her hair done.

Cody unwound himself from the chair and muttered,

"Girl stuff, ugh," and left the room, followed by Daisy, who no doubt felt the same way.

Sasha seemed inclined to linger. Megan guessed she had something on her mind.

"What can I do for you, Sasha?"

The girl picked up the breakfast tray and held it in front of her. "Are you sure you want to marry my dad?"

"We're already married, Sasha," Megan reminded her in an even voice. "The ceremony today is for the benefit of your father's family and friends."

"Yes, but—"

Megan sank onto the edge of the bed and patted the spot beside her.

For a moment, she feared the girl would ignore her, but with a huff Sasha placed the tray on the nightstand and sat down.

Megan angled herself toward Sasha. If this was any other child, she'd have clasped her hands, but not Sasha. She was far too brittle, too prickly.

"Sasha, I know you don't like me very much. And whether you want to like someone or not is entirely your choice." She noticed the girl squirming. Obviously, she didn't like being called on her attitude. Well, tough. They needed to clear the air.

"I know you were upset to suddenly get a brother and stepmother dumped on you. Believe me, when I woke up last Friday I didn't expect that by the end of the day, I'd have a husband and three stepdaughters."

Apparently, Sasha had never thought of what a shock her changed family circumstances must've been for Megan, and a smile quivered on the edges of her mouth.

Megan smiled, too, trying to break the tension further. "So what I'm trying to say is this. If you have a problem with me, please don't sulk about it or make unkind remarks. Just talk to me about your feelings and we'll see if we can find some common ground."

Sasha didn't say anything for he longest time, and then finally she looked Megan directly in the eye and said, "Do you love my dad?"

Megan hadn't been prepared for that question but she answered it honestly. She shrugged. "I do have... feelings for him. But adult relationships are so...complicated."

"Tell me about it!" Sasha said with a sigh. "I heard you and Daddy fighting last night."

Oh, dear. Megan hadn't realized their voices were so loud. She'd remember that in future. "We weren't fighting. We were having a disagreement."

"There's a difference?"

"Like I said, adult relationships are complicated."

"What were you disagreeing about?"

Megan stood. "That's between your father and me for the moment. But I plan on getting it resolved as soon as possible. And I can't do that until I've had a shower and freshened up."

Sasha took that as her cue and picked up the tray again. She walked to the door, then stopped and looked at her. "Thanks for talking to me," she said.

Taken aback, Megan said, "You're welcome. I'm glad we talked too, Sasha."

MEGAN STEPPED UNDER the shower and let the cool water wash over her face. She'd glimpsed herself in the bathroom mirror and been shocked at how puffy her eyes were. All the more reason to do what she intended to do before walking down the aisle today. Because, yes, she'd decided she *was* going through with the ceremony.

Twenty minutes later, dressed in jeans and a T-shirt, she walked into Luke's study, left a note on his desk and collected the ranch books. She drove into town, found a store that did photocopying and, another twenty minutes later, she had triplicate copies of the accounts. After posting one copy to Matt with a note explaining the reason for sending them to him, she called Gil McIntyre's office and arranged to meet him there, telling him she'd be coming into money and needed some advice on investing it.

Gil had said he'd be more than happy to meet her. However, he wasn't quite so happy when he saw what she pulled out of her bag.

"What are you doing with those?" he demanded, his earlier affability evaporating.

"I just have a few things I want clarified, Gil, if you have the time."

Suddenly Gil seemed to realize that Megan was due to tie the knot in less than an hour. "I have the time, but you don't. Shouldn't you be getting all prettied up?" he said, indicating her casual outfit.

"I should be, Gil, but you see, there's a little matter of the argument my groom and I had last night regarding how you'd been 'taking care' of the ranch's financial matters."

"What do you mean?" he snarled.

Megan noted how quickly his manner changed. "I think you know exactly what I mean. As Luke mentioned when we met, I'm studying to become an accountant, so while he was away this past week, I went through the books. What I discovered is that you, posing as a dummy corporation, have been helping your-self to quite a lot of the ranch's profits."

"You can't prove that."

"Yes. I can," Megan said in as reasonable a voice as she could manage. She saw his hand slip beneath the desk as he opened a drawer. The way he kept his eyes on her was unsettling. Maybe she'd bitten off more than she could chew?

"Not if you're dead and the books are nowhere to be found," he said calmly, bringing a handgun out of the drawer and training it on her.

Megan felt her insides turn to water. This was the last thing she'd expected. She cursed her naiveté. *Then why did you make those copies and send one to Matt?* a little voice demanded.

"Put that away!" she said, desperate to keep the fear out of her voice. Gil McIntyre was a cheat and a bully, and she had to let him know who was in control. "I'm asking you to explain these anomalies. You don't need a gun to do that."

Gil raised the weapon, gesturing that she should stand. *So much for acting tough,* she thought, and rose slowly to her feet.

Gil rose, too, and came around the desk. He reminded her of some B-grade movie gangster, the way he held the weapon, standing far too close to her.

He angled the gun toward the door and said, "Move."

CHAPTER TWELVE

"WHAT THE HELL did you say to her?" Matt almost roared.

"Goodness! What *is* all this noise?" Sarah demanded as she bustled into the kitchen, followed by Will, Jack and Adam. All the brothers were dressed in tuxedos. Each looked as uncomfortable as the others.

"He scared Megan off," Matt said, his eyes never leaving Luke's face.

"What?" Sarah steered her two warring sons away from the kitchen—and the sudden interest the caterers were showing in their conversation.

They all ended up in the living room, where Becky and Beth were fussing over the girls' bridesmaid dresses.

Sarah turned and asked Matt, "What do you mean, he scared Megan off?"

"No one can find her anywhere. Luke thinks she took off like Tory did."

"On her *wedding* day?" Will said. "Don't be ridiculous! Even Tory needed longer than that to figure out what a grumpy pain in the a—"

"Will!" Becky snapped. She indicated the children. Celeste's lower lip was trembling.

"Where's my mommy? I want my mommy!" she cried.

"Well done, you two." Beth lifted Celeste onto her

hip. "Go take your squabbles somewhere else," she said, heading for the stairs, Celeste sobbing into her shoulder. She turned back, her face thunderous. "Go and find her and don't come back until you do!"

They all stared after her, surprised by Beth's outburst. She was usually the most unflappable of all of them.

Daisy crossed her arms and fixed her father with a glare. "So what have you done wrong *this* time?"

"Go to your room!"

"No!" Daisy defied her father's command. "I'm stayin' right here till you tell me what you and Uncle Matt were fightin' about."

Luke sighed. "We don't know where Megan is," he explained. "Any ideas?"

"Has this got anything to do with that fight you two had last night?"

Luke felt his face warm with embarrassment. He hadn't realized he'd raised his voice that much. Daisy wasn't one to be fobbed off with lies. "Probably," he admitted.

Daisy nodded.

"She wouldn't have gone anywhere without Cody," Sash pointed out.

"She's right," Will said. "And Cody's out back with Pop."

"No, I'm not. What's going on?" Cody asked as he joined them.

"Have you seen your mother?"

"Not since breakfast. Why? What's going on?" he repeated.

"We can't find your mom," Matt said.

Cody's eyes narrowed. "Does this have anything to

do with the fight I heard you two having last night?" he demanded of Luke.

"Yes!" everyone else answered for him.

"Have you checked your phone messages?" Cody suggested.

Luke hurried into the study to retrieve his cell phone. He'd left it in a drawer, not wanting to be disturbed by ranch business today. But the first thing he noticed was that the ranch books he'd left on the desk were missing and in their place was a note. Sure enough, it was from Megan. His heart chilled as he read it.

"Is it from Mom?"

"Yeah."

"Can I see?" Will asked.

Luke handed it over to Will, who read it, then looked up at Luke. "She sounds pretty pissed with you. Are you sure you want to go after her?"

"Of course I do, dammit!"

Matt snatched the note out of Will's hand, read it and returned it to Luke. "What exactly happened last night?"

"None of your business," Luke muttered.

Matt crossed his arms. "Okay, so you had a fight. At any point in the past week, did you tell Megan you loved her?"

Luke ceased pacing and frowned. "No. But I married her, didn't I?"

Matt's snort of derision had Luke's head coming up.

"You married Tory and you clearly weren't in love with her. What sort of message do you think that conveyed to Megan?" He paused and considered his words. "You *have* told her the truth about Tory, haven't you?"

Luke shook his head. "Not all of it. I didn't want to criticize the mother of my daughters."

Matt snorted again. "You idiot! Forget Tory. Megan is something else again. That woman didn't trick you into marrying her. Instead, she kept Cody's existence a secret because she believed you were married—which by then you were—and didn't want to cause any problems for you. She married you to keep her son out of juvenile detention and probably believes that's the only reason you married her—because you were *forced* to."

"She's the only honorable person in this whole mess and you're a fool!" Will burst out. "Quite frankly, I can't blame her for leaving. You don't deserve her."

"Where's my mom?" Cody tore the note from Luke's grasp. He read it aloud as everyone crowded around him. "'Gone to see Gil McIntyre. When I've proved I'm right, maybe you'll trust me. I'm not marrying you until you do. M.' Who's Gil McIntyre?" Cody demanded.

"The ranch accountant," Sarah answered, and crossed her arms. "What is going on, Luke?"

He quickly outlined the gist of his conversation with Megan the night before. "Her accusations were so outrageous, I told her to mind her own business."

Will crossed his arms, too. "Gee, the O'Malley charm gene sure missed you."

"Will!" his mother admonished. "This is serious." She turned to her eldest son. "Luke, could her concerns have any foundation?"

"I didn't think so at the time, but I looked at everything this morning and I suspect she might be right. I need someone independent, a qualified CPA, to take a look."

"But Megan's studying to be an accountant," Will put in. "She must have a grasp of these things."

"I didn't see how she could just come in here, read a few figures and deduce that we're being embezzled. She's not a qualified accountant yet and—"

"Neither are you!" Matt and Will roared together.

Sarah covered her ears. "Goodness! This is worse than when you were all in high school."

Jack, ever the peacemaker, put his arm around his mom. "Maybe you should take a seat. All this excitement isn't good for your heart."

"There's nothing wrong with my heart. But there's definitely something wrong with your blockhead of a brother!" Her blue eyes bored into Luke's. "No wonder she's gone off to prove herself. Go and find her and apologize for your incredible stupidity!" she roared.

Luke flinched at the harshness of his mother's words. And the volume. His mom rarely lost her temper, but right now she looked ready to explode.

He punched Megan's number into his cell phone, but it went straight to voice mail. He speed-dialed Gil's office number, but it merely rang.

He shrugged. "No answer. She's probably on her way back here."

"And if she isn't?" Matt said. "Think about it. If she's accused him of embezzling money from the ranch, and she's taken the books with her to prove it, she could be putting herself in a very dangerous position. Embezzlement is a serious crime, but if Gil disposed of Megan, and the books, then there wouldn't be any evidence."

"Disposed?" Cody's query had them all turning to him as if they'd forgotten he was there. "You mean he might *kill* my mom?"

"Daddy?" Sasha's eyes were filled with tears. "You've gotta go save her!"

Sarah ushered Daisy and Sasha from the room. Once that was done, she whirled on Luke.

"For heaven's sake, Megan's raised your son alone for over fourteen years. In spite of all her family's objections, she refused to have an abortion or give him away. She needs you, Luke. *Go and find her!*"

Becky strode out of the room, but when Luke's cell rang, she raced back in as he answered it, hitting the speaker button so everyone could listen in.

"Megan? Are you all right?" he asked, not caring how desperate he sounded. "Where are you, honey?"

He waited impatiently for her to answer, but it was Gil he heard. Luke barely recognized his voice. "I'm here, *honey,*" he teased.

"Where's Megan?" Luke demanded. "Put her on."

"Not so fast! I want you to know how it feels to have something you want taken away from you," Gil said.

"What are you talking about?" Luke demanded.

"Tory."

"*Tory?* What the hell do you mean?"

"I wanted her so badly—but she was only interested in you."

"And that's my fault?"

"You got her pregnant. After that, I never had a chance."

"Trust me, Gil. I did you a favor."

"Not the way I see it. Tory and I could've had a great life together. Instead I ended up with Betsy." Luke could hear the snarl in his voice.

"Betsy's a good woman, Gil," he said evenly. "You're a lucky man."

"I didn't want a good woman! I wanted one who knew her way around the bedroom."

Luke didn't know what to say to that. He seemed to be inflaming the situation by arguing. "Gil, I don't want to fight with you. Let me talk to Megan. Please."

"I guess I can allow you two lovebirds to have one final conversation," he said, and Luke could feel his contempt.

"Luke?"

Relief flooded him at hearing Megan's voice. But she sounded terrified.

Matt had called the sheriff's department to have someone drop by Gil's office and his home, and he'd just shaken his head to indicate they hadn't found him or Megan at either location.

"Where are you, Megan?"

"I...can't tell you. But I haven't been this scared since our first date. Lu—"

Megan's voice was cut off as Gil came back on. "I hope you enjoyed your final conversation with your wife, O'Malley." The phone went dead.

"Where is she?" everyone shouted as Luke looked up.

"Did she give you any sign of where she might be?" Matt asked.

Luke shook his head. "She only said she hadn't been this scared since our first date."

"Where did you take her?" Matt asked impatiently.

It was then that Luke realized Megan had been giving him a message. He started toward the front door. "For a picnic at Inspiration Point. I'll bet that's where he's got her!"

He was halfway to his car before Matt and the others caught up with him. "We'll take my vehicle," Matt said.

"No." Luke climbed into his big SUV. "You drive too slowly and I don't want to alert him with sirens." He started the car as Jack, Adam and Will climbed into the backseat.

Matt took the front passenger seat, pulled out his cell phone and dispatched vehicles to Inspiration Point, warning them not to use their sirens.

"Dad?"

Luke had been about to step on the gas, when his son's plea halted his foot. Cody had never called him "Dad" to his face before. It was a watershed moment in their relationship.

"Hop in, son," he said, his voice hoarse with emotion.

Will climbed over into the third row of seats, making room for Cody.

The SUV tore out of the gates of Two Elk, narrowly missing Frank and Edna Farquar in their enormous Caddy. Frank's pet pig, Louella, and Charles, their dog, had their heads stuck out either side of the Caddy's rear windows.

"Inspiration Point?" Matt echoed. "That makes sense when you think about it. One-thousand-foot cliffs straight to the valley floor."

"Do you mind?" Luke growled, jerking his head at Cody sitting behind them. His gut twisted at a terrifying vision of Megan falling over the cliff she feared so much. He stepped harder on the gas, the needle passing seventy as he took the turns in the road, crossing to the other side.

"Easy, Luke!" Matt warned.

"Get out if you don't like the way I drive," Luke told

him through clenched teeth. In his rearview mirror, he saw his brothers and Cody checking their seat belts.

"So, HERE WE ARE." Gil cut the connection and tossed Megan's cell over the cliff. She swallowed as she imagined him dispatching her as easily. "Just you and me."

Megan prayed that Luke would understand her cryptic remark about the location of their first date. But in case he didn't, she had some fast talking to do.

Raising her hands in a gesture of surrender, she said, "Look, how about if we forget this conversation ever happened? Luke said I should've minded my own business and that I wasn't qualified, that I didn't know what I was talking about. Maybe I made a mistake…."

"Too late. You've sown doubt in his mind. He'll come looking for me…and you. Only he won't find me because I'll be on the next plane to the Cayman Islands. But he *will* find you—or at least what's left of you—at the bottom of this cliff." He grabbed her arms and hauled her closer to the edge and glanced over.

Megan could feel her head spinning. Praying Luke would understand her cryptic clue, she stalled for time.

"Take me with you!" she said rashly. "Take me away from this hick town and that king of hicks, Luke O'Malley."

That got Gil's attention and he released his grip on her arm a little. "I thought you were looking forward to getting married today."

Megan gave an exaggerated snort. "Only for the benefit of his kids and his family. I'm just marrying him for his money, but since you've got a lot of it now, I might as well stick with you. We could have a good life together. Sun, surf…" She swallowed and added, "Sex."

Gil's eyes glittered with interest and she pressed on. "We could set up our own company down there, handling other people's finances, helping them avoid their tax burdens. We could make ourselves a nice little nest egg skimming off the top."

Gil's mouth lifted in what passed for a smile and Megan hoped she'd hooked him. "Come on. Let's get out of here," she urged, taking advantage of his momentary slip in concentration, leading him toward the car, away from the cliff edge.

They'd nearly reached his vehicle when Megan heard the sound of tires screeching on the curving road that climbed to the top of Inspiration Point. Someone was taking those bends awfully fast. Could it be Luke?

Gil must've realized it the same time she did. He dragged her toward the cliff once more. Megan fought with him, trying to gain a foothold on the gravelly surface.

"You bitch!" Gil screamed. "You tried to trick me!"

"No! Please don't do this," Megan begged as she was dragged ever closer to the precipice. She debated trying to turn the tables and shove him over, hoping to somehow escape his grasp. But she was no match for Gil's strength as he hauled her to the edge, then spun her around so that only the tips of her toes were in contact with the ground.

Megan squeezed her eyes shut, offering up a silent prayer that her death would be fast and merciful. And then her stomach rose to her throat as he shoved her backward over the cliff.

"No!" LUKE CRIED as his vehicle crested the last bend onto the top of the cliff.

Everything seemed to happen in slow motion as he

saw Gil shove Megan off Inspiration Point and then run to his car.

Luke spent a fraction of a second debating as to whether he should chase Gil or go after Megan—although he was sure there was nothing he could do to save her now.

"Leave him," Matt growled beside him. "There's only one way down and I have deputies coming up." He called them, telling them to apprehend Gil McIntyre, adding a description of his car.

Luke pulled up beside the cliff face and was out of his vehicle and peering over the edge before the dust had settled.

The dust stung his eyes and he wiped them impatiently. Heart pounding with fear, he tore off his tux jacket and sprawled on his stomach to get a better view, dreading what he'd see.

Thirty feet down he spotted a piece of blue fabric blowing in the breeze. He eased his body closer to the precipice.

"Whoa there!" Adam warned, holding his feet.

"I can see something!" Luke shouted. "Let me get closer."

"Better not to look," Adam said.

Luke ignored him, edging forward so he hung over the cliff, aware of other hands reaching out to steady him. And that was when he saw her.

He scrambled backward and turned to his brothers. "Get me some rope. She's about thirty feet down on a narrow ledge. I have to get to her."

Will started off to get rope from the back of the SUV, but Matt stayed him with a hand on his shoulder. "That's

too risky, Luke. Wait until mountain rescue gets here."
He put a call through to his office.

"That could take too long," Luke protested. "The
ledge is so narrow that if she moves even a couple of
inches, she'll go over the side." He took the rope from
Will, who'd ignored Matt and retrieved the coil that was
always kept in their ranch vehicles, and began to fasten
it around his waist.

Adam stayed his hand. "Let me go. I'm trained in
rescue."

Luke pulled out of his grasp. "No! It's too dangerous. I got her into this mess and I'm going to get her
out of it."

"Luke…" Matt warned.

"Look, you either help me or get the hell out of here!"
Luke exploded, in no mood for Matt's cautious ways.

Shaking his head, Matt took the end of the rope and
looped it onto the SUV's tow bar as Adam tied it around
himself to belay the rope out to Luke. "Be careful," he
warned as Luke stepped off the cliff edge. Within moments, he'd lost sight of his brother altogether.

Matt turned away and noticed Cody, white-faced
with fear, staring at the place he'd last seen his father.
He strode over to the boy and put an arm around his
shoulders. "Your mom will be fine," he said, not knowing if it was truth or lie, but needing to comfort his
nephew. No doubt Cody was thinking that if anything
happened to Luke, he could well lose both his parents
on the same day.

Jack, equally white-faced, set a hand on Cody's
shoulder and said, "I'll take care of Cody. You'll need
to help to coordinate the rescue effort and I have no experience with that."

Grateful to have Jack take over, Matt clapped him on the back and said, "Thanks," then returned to the cliff edge.

Will was lying flat on his stomach, calling directions to Adam about how much rope to let out. "Easy. Easy," he said. "He's almost there."

LUKE CONCENTRATED ON his footing, thankful that someone as powerful as Adam was on the other end of the rope, playing it out. He could hear Will clearly, giving directions as he was lowered to the narrow ledge Megan was lying on. He signaled to Will that he was stepping to the side to get around her. Once he was past, he stepped back and dropped down a little more so he was level with her head, his feet braced against the rock face. He indicated that Adam should stop playing out the rope.

There was no room on the shelf for him, but this position, however precarious, gave him some sense of safety, some reassurance that should Megan fall, he might be able to catch her.

She was lying on her stomach, her head facing toward him, her eyes closed. A small pool of blood was forming beneath her head.

"Megan," he whispered.

She didn't move.

"Sweetheart. I'm here. Can you open your eyes?"

Still nothing. Luke feared the worst. He was reluctant to feel for her pulse, knowing that if he found none, there would be no hope for her.

"Is she alive?" Matt shouted from above him, leaving Luke no choice but to reach out and place two fingers against Megan's throat. But his hands shook too fiercely, so he cupped a hand over her mouth and nose.

Relief filled him as he felt her breath against his palm.

Megan moaned and opened her eyes.

He could feel the biggest grin in the world splitting his face.

"Luke?"

She tried to lift her head and look around but Luke cautioned her. "Don't move, honey. We'll get you out of here as soon as we can."

"Out?"

"Rescue teams are on their way."

"Rescue? What? Where am I?"

She managed to lift her head this time, before Luke could stop her. Her eyes opened wide with fear.

And then she started to scream.

Nesting birds, disturbed by the noise, flew out of their aeries. The snapping of wings and the bird's screeching around his head caused Luke to lose his footing. He lost contact with the cliff face and dropped several feet below Megan before regaining his foothold.

"I take it she's alive," Will said with his usual irony.

Luke looked up at his brother and, for once in his life, he wasn't irritated by Will's easygoing manner. He smiled grimly and nodded his head, then alerted them to raise him a few feet.

That done, he took Megan's hand. "Honey, do you understand me when I say I don't want you to move? Not even an eyelash?"

Megan stared at him wide-eyed. "How? Where?" she asked.

"You don't remember?"

Megan shook her head, loosening several pebbles from her narrow shelf.

"Just. Don't. Move," Luke warned again. "Let me talk, okay?"

Unsure what to do to make her more comfortable, he said the first words that came into his mind. "I love you, Megan. I always have."

"Don't feel you have to say things you don't mean," she mumbled.

This was good; she was talking. "Everything's going to be fine," he told her. "Help is on the way."

"Cody?" she asked.

"He's fine. He's up there waiting for you."

"I'm sorry I didn't tell you about him all those years ago."

"Shh," Luke said, soothingly. The time for Megan to apologize for anything was long past.

"MEGAN..." LUKE'S VOICE, deep but unsure, penetrated the fog of pain.

She bit down hard on her lip. She couldn't bear to let him know how much she cared, how much she hurt inside. How little pride she had left.

Her head throbbed. But the pain that tore through her shoulder and legs was sharper. Excruciating. She closed her eyes to shut out the agony, trying to will it away.

She felt Luke's lips touch her forehead and again he whispered the words she'd wanted to hear for so long. "I love you. I always have."

Megan resisted the urge to shake herself. Instead, she opened her eyes and searched his face. Luke was an honorable man. He wouldn't lie to her about something so important, so sacred.

His voice husky with emotion, Luke asked, "Why did you leave town without saying anything all those years ago?"

She swallowed against the dryness in her throat and said, "I don't think you really want to know that."

"Of course I do."

Megan took a deep breath, then wished she hadn't as pain shot through her chest. He wanted the truth? Then he was welcome to it, in all its ugly reality. "I overheard Tory in the change room at the rec center, telling another girl about your marriage plans—"

"*What?* I wasn't going to marry Tory! We'd broken up two weeks before you came to Spruce Lake. I told you all that."

True. But when she'd overheard the conversation in the change rooms, she'd felt she had no choice except to believe what Tory was saying. "According to her, she was already pregnant when you met me, dated me…" Her voice broke. "*Slept* with me."

"She wasn't pregnant then. Nor, as it turned out, was she pregnant when I married her. Only I didn't find out the truth about that until a long time later." He sighed. "Sweetheart, we've both been victims of Tory's machinations. She told me you'd been bragging at the rec center how you'd laid a hayseed."

"You don't honestly believe I'd say something like that, do you?"

He shrugged. "At the time, yes, I'm sorry to say, I did. I was hurt and bewildered about why you'd left so suddenly. Left me in the restaurant, waiting with a huge bunch of flowers, a marriage proposal and a ring."

"*What?*" Megan was sure she must've been hearing things.

"I wanted to marry you, even though we'd just met. I knew you were the woman I wanted to spend the rest of my life with. Until you didn't turn up but Tory did and told me what she'd supposedly heard you say. That cut me so deeply, I can't even bear to think of it all these years later."

Megan closed her eyes and clenched her jaw, then looked back at Luke. "So what I overheard in the rec center was a setup?"

Luke nodded.

Tears filled Megan's eyes. How many years had they lost together because of the manipulations of one unhappy, obsessive woman?

"I love you." His breath whispered over her face. "I'm sorry I judged you as I judged her," he said, as if needing to convince Megan of his sincerity. "You're not Tory. You never were, you never could be. You kept Cody's existence a secret to protect me, but I didn't need protection from the truth, darlin'. I just needed you."

She swallowed the lump in her throat and said, "Don't let Tory come between us anymore."

"I won't," he vowed.

"RESCUE'S ARRIVED!" WILL YELLED down to them.

"We'll have you out of here in no time, sweetheart," Luke assured her. "Just stay calm and don't move."

He could hear commotion above him as rescue equipment was readied. Another head popped over the cliff face and Luke recognized the coordinator of mountain rescue for the county, Jasper Haynes.

"We'll be down in a minute. Tell her not to move."

Luke rolled his eyes and smiled at Megan.

"We need to get you up here first, Luke."

"I'm not leaving her," he called back, never breaking eye contact with Megan. "We haven't got much time right now," he said to her. "But I want you to know this. I'm sorry for being such a pigheaded fool. I'm sorry for not believing you and trusting your judgment about the ranch finances. And Gil's activities. But most of all I'm sorry I haven't allowed myself to love you the way you deserve to be loved."

She blinked away tears and he smiled. "I mean it, Megan. You're the best thing that happened to me fifteen years ago and you are now. I can't imagine my life without you and Cody in it. I hope you'll forgive me—"

He was silenced by Megan stretching out her arm and touching her finger to his bottom lip. Then her hand went limp, her eyes closed.

"Megan?"

She didn't respond. He couldn't help the fear in his voice as he called up to Jasper. "She's passed out! Get down here *now!*"

The words had barely left his mouth when a rescue litter appeared over the side, along with two rescue personnel in harnesses.

Bits of rocks rained down as the men made their way down the cliff face. Luke leaned over Megan to protect her, as much as he could, from the assault. Moments later, the rescuers reached them and Luke moved aside to allow them access to Megan.

They checked her vital signs, placed a cervical collar around her neck, bandaged her head wound, then gently slid her onto the litter and prepared her for transport up the cliff. Luke knew a little about mountain rescue techniques, having been involved in one years before when a hiker had fallen while climbing one of the Fourteeners surrounding the town. Some of the fourteen-thousand-foot peaks were a relatively easy hike, but others were more of a test. Every summer climbers got into difficulty trying to bag one. Thanks to the rescue squad's efforts, most survived. The titanium litter had a four-point webbing configuration with the main line attached to Megan and the belay line attached to the medic. Ever so slowly, they raised her up the face of the cliff.

Twelve tense minutes later, all of them were back on safe ground. One of the paramedics checked Megan over again before she was settled in the ambulance.

"Gil's been apprehended and will be charged with attempted murder," Matt told Luke as he waited impatiently while the medic examined Megan. "The rest of his crimes will be investigated fully and I've got a feeling we weren't the only victims of his embezzling. Gil won't be seeing the outside of a jail cell for many, many years to come."

Luke knew Matt's words were meant to comfort him, but Megan hadn't regained consciousness. He turned away from Matt, wanting to hide his distress from his brother, and saw Cody waiting by his SUV. He'd never seen anyone look so forlorn in his life. He strode over to his son and hugged him, trying to impart hope and strength.

"Will she…" Cody sobbed against his shoulder.

"She'll be fine, son. She's a fighter, remember that."

"She sure is," Cody told him, and Luke could hear the pride in his voice.

"I…love you, Cody," Luke told him, needing his son to know he truly did.

"I love you, too, Dad," Cody said, his voice breaking with emotion.

They held on to each other until the medic came over to see if Luke had any injuries, but he waved him away.

"Let's get going," he said. They climbed in beside Megan, and moments later, they were heading back down the mountain, toward the hospital in Silver Springs.

LUKE HELD MEGAN'S HAND on the ride to the hospital, praying her injuries weren't severe. She still hadn't regained consciousness and that bothered him. If only he'd driven faster, he might have gotten to Inspiration Point before Gill pushed her off the cliff.

He felt so impotent, he wanted to find Gil and punch his lights out. With any luck, maybe one of the other inmates down at the county jail would do it for him.

"Luke?"

He glanced down at Megan. "Hey," he whispered, unable to get more than a single word out of his dry throat.

"You looked so angry," she said softly.

He stroked her forehead. "Just thinking about what I'd like to do to Gil. None of it pretty."

She smiled and said, "My hero." Then she passed out again.

EPILOGUE

EIGHT WEEKS LATER, Megan and Luke finally got to repeat their wedding vows again, this time in front of their family and friends. That evening, after the guests had departed, Megan sat in the living room with the girls, remembering the past two months as Luke collected their bags.

The guest list had swelled considerably in the ensuing weeks and now included all the rescue and medical personnel involved in Megan's rescue and her hospital care. She'd been delighted to see them and thank them personally for everything they'd done for her.

She'd suffered from a subdural hematoma as a result of her fall and had been operated on that night. She'd also dislocated her shoulder, grabbing at the rock face as she fell. Had she not done so, she wouldn't have landed on the ledge—but *that* had resulted in two broken ankles. However, those injuries were a small price to pay to save her from certain death.

Luke hadn't left Megan's side during her hospital stay, but the most surprising visitor was Sasha, who'd insisted on helping with her recovery by reading to her from the newspaper and then, when Megan was up to it, doing crosswords together.

There was a surprise appearance—her parents and brother. Luke admitted, minutes before they were due to walk down the aisle, that he'd invited them. They'd been formal with her but their manner had thawed under the O'Malley charm, mostly Will's. He'd encouraged them to reconcile with her and get to know their grandson. It remained to be seen if they'd take any further interest in Cody's life…or Megan's. Right now, she was too happy to care.

There were still gaps in Megan's memory, mostly relating to when she'd first confronted Gil. In many ways, she was thankful she couldn't remember being pushed over the cliff. Whenever Megan thought of it, she felt sick to her stomach.

Apparently, she'd had the wherewithal to give Luke a clue as to where she was, but had no memory of their phone conversation.

She'd also lost a lot of blood from a gash on her temple sustained during her fall. Sasha had apparently been the first to offer her own blood for transfusion. She smiled at the thought and the probable frown on Sasha's face when she'd been turned down as too young to donate.

"Megan?"

She looked up into Sasha's eyes and smiled. "I was just thinking about you." She patted the sofa beside her.

Sasha took a seat and asked, "Are you okay? Today hasn't been too tiring, has it?"

Megan smiled again and stroked Sasha's blond hair. "No, honey, it's been a great day. Thank you for agreeing to be one of my bridesmaids."

Sasha grinned. "You gotta admit I look better in a dress than Daisy does."

"Well, as I've never seen your sister in a dress, I'll have to take your word for it. You looked so pretty. Like a princess—"

"Me, too, Mommy!" Celeste shouted. She bounced onto the sofa, earning a glance of reproach from her older sister.

Megan tickled her. "You, my little pumpkin, looked like a fairy princess!"

"Really?"

"Uh-huh."

"Too bad Daisy didn't want to look pretty."

"She did in her own way, standing up with her father and brother," Megan assured her.

"That's just plain weird, a girl wanting to be on the groom's side of the wedding," Sasha muttered.

Megan couldn't help laughing. "I think she looked just right in her new cowboy boots and jeans. She matched her father and her brother and uncles perfectly," she said. This time around, Luke had forsaken the tuxedos for clothing more suited for the ranch. Megan had already admired the digital photos taken of the wedding party, with the men—and Daisy—attired in cowboy boots, jeans, chambray shirts and cowboy hats, while the bride's party wore floral summery dresses that drifted in the breeze.

They'd said their vows beside the lake that stretched between the ranch house and the mountains that rose behind it. Megan couldn't imagine a more idyllic setting.

"You look happy."

She gazed up into Luke's warm brown eyes and moved over on the sofa to make room for him.

He squeezed into the space between Megan and Celeste and placed a noisy kiss on Megan's lips.

"Gross!" Daisy and Cody both said from the doorway into the living room.

Smiling, Luke repeated it. Megan giggled and Sasha

leaped off the sofa. "Old people sex!" she squealed and ran from the room with her hands over her eyes.

"What's old people sex?" Celeste asked as she watched them curiously.

"Nothing you need to worry about for a very long time," Luke said, then kissed her forehead.

Always curious, she asked, "How long? Next week?"

"Long after next week, darlin'," Luke told his youngest daughter as she climbed off the sofa and went to join her siblings.

"Speaking of old people sex," Luke murmured in Megan's ear. "Shall we head off on our honeymoon?"

Megan pushed at his chest. "I can't believe I agreed to go camping on horseback for our honeymoon. I must still be concussed."

"You're the one who didn't want to venture too far from the kids," he said.

"True. But—"

Luke silenced her protests with another kiss. When they both came up for air, he said, "Remind me what a bad idea it is when I make love to you tonight on a carpet of meadow grass sprinkled with wildflowers beneath a star-studded sky."

"I'm not sure which will take my breath away more, the scenery—or your lovemaking," she teased.

Luke stood and pulled her to her feet." The sooner we leave, the sooner you'll find out."

LATER THAT EVENING, satiated and happier than she could have ever dreamed, Megan lay in Luke's arms looking up at the starry sky.

Luke rolled toward her and nuzzled her ear. "Well?" he asked. "Which took your breath away more?"

Megan turned in his arms. "You know, I can't quite decide," she murmured. "I need some time to think about it."

"Take all the time you want, darlin'," Luke drawled. "We've got the rest of our lives."

* * * * *

We hope you enjoyed reading this
special collection from Harlequin®.

If you liked reading these stories,
then you will love
Harlequin® American Romance® books!

You love small towns and cowboys!
Harlequin American Romance stories are
heartwarming contemporary tales of everyday
women finding love, becoming part of a
family or community—or maybe starting a
family of their own.

Enjoy four new stories from
Harlequin American Romance
every month!

Available wherever books and
ebooks are sold.

American Romance®

Romance the all-American way!

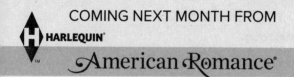

COMING NEXT MONTH FROM

HARLEQUIN
American Romance

Available May 5, 2015

#1545 THE COWBOY'S HOMECOMING
Crooked Valley Ranch • by Donna Alward

Rylan Duggan finds himself off the rodeo circuit and back at Crooked Valley Ranch—too close for comfort to Kailey Brandt. She's not about to forgive him for past wrongs, but their chemistry makes him impossible to ignore!

#1546 HER COWBOY GROOM
Blue Falls, Texas • by Trish Milburn

Linnea Holland doesn't trust men anymore. But cowboy Owen Brody shows he has a kind heart beneath his bad-boy exterior and makes her think she *can* trust him—and maybe even fall in love.

#1547 THE RANCHER'S LULLABY
Glades County Cowboys • by Leigh Duncan

Ranch manager and single father Garrett Judd still blames himself for his wife's death. But bluegrass singer Lisa Rose makes embracing life too hard to resist...at least for one stormy night.

#1548 BACK TO TEXAS
Welcome to Ramblewood • by Amanda Renee

Waitress Bridgett Jameson is done being the subject of small-town gossip. Falling for handsome, mysterious ranch hand Adam Steele seems like the perfect escape from Ramblewood...until she learns his secret!

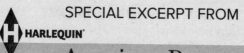
Despite still feeling shaky, Linnea descended the steps
and started walking. The day was quite warm, but she
didn't care. Though she spent most of her time indoors
working, there was something therapeutic about getting
out in the sunshine under a wide blue sky. It almost made
her believe things weren't so bad.

But they were.

She walked the length of the driveway and back.
When she approached the house, Roscoe and Cletus, the
Brodys' two lovable basset hounds, came ambling around
the corner of the porch.

"Hey, guys," she said as she sank onto the front steps
and proceeded to scratch them both under their chins.
"You're just as handsome as ever."

"Why, thank you."

She jumped at the sound of Owen's voice. The dogs
jumped, too, probably because she had. She glanced up to
where Owen stood at the corner of the porch. "You made
me scare the dogs."

"Sorry. But I was taught to thank someone when they
pay me a compliment."

She shook her head. "Nice to see your ego is still
intact."

"Ouch."

She laughed a little at his mock affront, something she wouldn't have thought possible that morning. She ought to thank him for that moment of reprieve, but she didn't want to focus on why she'd thought she might never laugh or even smile again.

He tapped the brim of his cowboy hat and headed toward the barn.

As he walked away, she noticed how nice he looked in those worn jeans. No wonder he didn't have trouble finding women.

Oh, hell! She was looking at Owen's butt. Owen, as in Chloe's little brother Owen. The kid who'd once waited on her and Chloe outside Chloe's room and doused them with a Super Soaker, the guy who had earned the nickname Horndog Brody.

She jerked her gaze away, suddenly wondering if she was mentally deficient. First she'd nearly married a guy who was already married. And now, little more than a day after she found out she'd nearly become an unwitting bigamist, she was ogling her best friend's brother's rear end.

HARLEQUIN®
A *Romance* FOR EVERY MOOD™

Love the Harlequin book you just read?

Your opinion matters.

Review this book on your favorite book site, review site, blog or your own social media properties and share your opinion with other readers!